LOVE & WAR

LOVE & WAR

The Alex & Eliza Trilogy

BOOK TWO

MELISSA DE LA CRUZ

PENGUIN BOOKS

For Mike and Mattie always

PENGUIN BOOKS
An imprint of Penguin Random House LLC, New York

First published in the United States of America by G. P. Putnam's Sons, 2018
Published by Penguin Books, an imprint of Penguin Random House LLC, 2020

"From Alexander Hamilton to Elizabeth Schuyler, [5 October 1780]," *Founders Online*,
National Archives, last modified November 26, 2017,
http://founders.archives.gov/documents/Hamilton/01-27-02-0001-0003.
[Original source: *The Papers of Alexander Hamilton*, vol. 27, *Additional Letters 1777–1802, Addenda and Errata, Cumulative Index Vols. I–XXVII*, ed. Harold C. Syrett. New York: Columbia University Press, 1987, pp. 6–7.]

Visit us online at penguinrandomhouse.com

THE LIBRARY OF CONGRESS HAS CATALOGED THE G. P. PUTNAM'S SONS EDITION AS FOLLOWS:
Names: De la Cruz, Melissa, 1971– author.
Title: Love & war : an Alex & Eliza story / Melissa de la Cruz.
Other titles: Love and war
Description: New York, NY : G. P. Putnam's Sons, [2018]
Summary: "As the end of the American Revolution nears, newlyweds Alex and Eliza are faced with new trials and temptations"—Provided by publisher.
Identifiers: LCCN 2017053081 | ISBN 9781524739652 (hardcover) | ISBN 9781524739669 (ebook)
Subjects: LCSH: Hamilton, Alexander, 1757–1804—Juvenile fiction. | Hamilton, Elizabeth Schuyler, 1757–1854—Juvenile fiction. | United States—History—Revolution, 1775–1783—Juvenile fiction. | CYAC: Hamilton, Alexander, 1757–1804—Fiction. | Hamilton, Elizabeth Schuyler, 1757–1854—Fiction. | United States—History—Revolution, 1775–1783—Fiction. | Marriage—Fiction.
Classification: LCC PZ7.D36967 Lov 2018 | DDC [Fic]—dc23
LC record available at https://lccn.loc.gov/2017053081

Penguin Books ISBN 9781524739676

Printed in the United States of America

Design by Theresa Evangelista
Text set in Electra LT Std, MrsEaves, and Andrade Pro

4th Printing

LOVE & WAR

I am more and more unhappy and impatient under the hard necessity that keeps me from you, and yet the prospect lengthens as I advance. . . .

Though the period of our reunion in reality approaches it seems further off. Among other causes of uneasiness, I dread lest you should imagine, I yield too easily to the barrs that keep us asunder; but if you have such an idea you ought to banish it and reproach yourself with injustice.

A spirit entering into bliss, heaven opening upon all its faculties, cannot long more ardently for the enjoyment, than I do my darling Betsey, to taste the heaven that awaits me in your bosom. Is my language too strong? It is a feeble picture of my feelings—no words can tell you how much I love and how much I long—you will only know it when wrapt in each other's arms we give and take those delicious caresses which love inspires and marriage sanctifies. . . .

—Letter from Alexander Hamilton to Elizabeth Schuyler,
October 1780

Part One

---•⊰◦⊱•---

Storming the Walls

1

Spring Harvest!

The Schuyler Mansion
Albany, New York
April 1781

Forget Paris. The French could keep their croissants and the Champs-Élysées. Who cares about London? Rome? Athens? From what she'd heard, they were just a bunch of ruins. And what of Williamsburg, Virginia? Charleston, South Carolina? New York City? As far as she was concerned, they could all fall off the map.

In all the world, Elizabeth Schuyler Hamilton thought there was no place more beautiful than Albany at springtime. Of course, the Pastures was dear to her as her childhood home, and even more so as the site of her wedding to Alexander Hamilton just last winter. Time had done little to dampen their affection, and she was more in love with her husband than ever. Perhaps it was this love that led to Eliza's delight at anything and everything around her.

But rose-colored glasses or no, it was hard to claim there was anywhere more glorious than late April in her hometown. The air was warm and the sun was mellow. Bare trees had covered themselves in soft green foliage and the sharp, tangy smell of fireplace smoke gave way to the softer aromas of hyacinths and crocuses, lilac and dogwood. Swallows darted through the air, snapping up flies and gnats, and newborn calves, foals, and shoats frolicked about the fields and sties. The mighty Hudson River was wreathed in mist at daybreak and teemed with fishermen's boats in the afternoon. Their nets hauled in plentiful catches of shad, whose roe had a delicate, almost nutty taste that paired perfectly with a salad of tender mustard greens.

But best of all was the bounty of blueberries and strawberries. All over the estate, hundreds of bushes sagged beneath the weight of thousands upon thousands of red, burgundy, and purple fruit. Every morning for a week, Eliza and her sisters, Angelica, Peggy, and five-year-old Cornelia— joined sometimes by their youngest brother, eight-year-old Rensselaer, known affectionately as Ren—traded in their sumptuous silks and bustles for simple, sturdy muslin skirts that they'd tie up high, showing ankles and calves in a bit of a risqué manner, and joined the housemaids in the fields to pick bucket after bucket of plump, sweet, juicy berries. (Well, not Ren. Ren hadn't worn a skirt since his christening.)

By noon, their lips were as stained as their fingertips (after all, picking involved a fair bit of "sampling," as Eliza put it), and the three oldest sisters repaired to the kitchen to do their work. Some of the fruit was packed in ice in the cellar, and some more was baked into pies, but most was simmered in rich syrupy jellies whose tart sweetness would liven up many a winter meal, slathered on fresh bread or griddle cakes or dabbed on turkey or mutton. A portion of the fruit was pickled, making for a delicious snack, salty at first, before exploding in your mouth in a burst of sweetness.

But as tempting as all these rich cooked treats were, Eliza's favorite way to eat them was also the simplest: fresh and chilled. Each plump fruit tasted like a thimble-size dollop of liquid happiness. That early spring afternoon, standing in the dappled light by the stone counter, Eliza alternated between a basket of strawberries and a basket of blueberries, savoring them one at a time.

"I can't decide which is more perfect!" she exclaimed to her sisters, who were gathered around the long rustic table that ran down the center of the kitchen, sorting fruit.

"Blech." Peggy Schuyler pouted with lips that were nearly as fruit-stained as Eliza's. "If I ever see another strawberry or blueberry again, it will be too soon!" she said as she reached for yet another blueberry and popped it in her mouth.

"Peg's right," Angelica agreed. "Sometimes nature's bounty is too much. A week ago I couldn't wait for the fruit to ripen. Now all I want are peanuts! What I wouldn't give for freshly roasted nuts right now!" But before the words had escaped her lips, she was already rolling a red strawberry between her fingers, letting it disappear into her mouth as well.

"With this war, we can't have peanuts till September anyway," said Eliza.

"Stephen says the war may be over before fall," said Peggy, referring to her fiancé, Stephen Van Rensselaer III. "The American coastline is simply too long for even an army or navy as powerful as England's to cover, and with French forces now fully committed to the cause of our independence, King George's men will find themselves both outnumbered and outmaneuvered."

"It is hard to imagine this war being over," Eliza said. "I feel as though we have grown up with it. But I do hope he's right! Alex and I have been married for half a year already, but we have yet to establish a household."

Indeed, as much as Eliza loved the Pastures, she was impatient to move out of her parents' house and into one with her husband. After their wedding, they'd only had a few blessed weeks together before he had to rush back to General Washington's headquarters. These days, Alex was chafing at their present living arrangements just as much as she was, and both were eager for more time on their own.

Though she loved her husband dearly, and knew he loved her, they had spent more time apart than together during the course of their brief romance and even briefer marriage. The flame that burned between them was bright, but they had yet to live alone as husband and wife. In many ways Alex was still a stranger to her. Their lives were mediated by family and servants and soldiers, and as such, their private lives were not as private as they would have preferred.

At least he'd been home now for a spell, although he was scheduled to leave again in a few days. Missing him was the lot of a soldier's wife, and instead of weeping and worrying, Eliza endeavored to be brave. Still, it was difficult, even in the midst of so much beauty, not to feel bereft. When Alex was gone, she felt his absence as a physical ache. She chided herself for being so selfish. While she was his wife, he was a man of the world, of the state, and she owed it to her country to share, didn't she?

Her own parents had endured many long separations during their marriage. Even so, General and Mrs. Schuyler had at least had a few years to establish themselves and start their family before their first parting.

Since Alex was leaving soon to report back to duty, festivities had been planned for later that evening. She didn't want to surmise how long he'd be gone, but hoped when he returned they would finally be able to settle down on their own. "I am ready to live under my own roof," Eliza declared.

"Hear, hear," Angelica seconded. "I have been married a year longer than you, and my husband and I see less of each other than when we were courting. Tell me: Do you know yet where he plans to make his residence?"

Eliza shook her head. "It will probably be New York City, which is most conducive to a career in law. But if he is lured into politics, we may well end up in Philadelphia or perhaps someplace farther south, if all this talk of creating a capital in the midpoint of the country comes to pass."

"*Uuuuuugh.*" The sisters' conversation was interrupted by a low moan from a corner of the kitchen, where Cornelia was sprawled across a stack of burlap bags filled with rice. Her face from nose to chin to plump cheeks was painted dark purple from greedily consumed berries. "Too—much—fruit."

"I told you, Cornelia," Eliza said, laughing in sympathy. "You must pace yourself or you'll give yourself a bellyache."

"Too—late," Cornelia moaned, rubbing her aproned stomach with fingers that were as dark as her mouth. But even as she did, she sat up and was soon shuffling toward the buckets brimming with fruit.

"Wait till tea, dear, and you can have scones with fresh jam and cream," Eliza said, catching her sister and turning her around. "Please head inside now and have Dot give you a good scrub. We can't have you looking like a harlequin at the party tonight."

Eliza expected Cornelia to protest being handed over to their ladies' maid. Instead, a piercing scream filled the sweet-scented kitchen. "Party!" the little girl screeched gleefully, running toward the door. "Dot! Dot!" she could be heard yelling as she disappeared into the courtyard. "Eliza says you must give me a bath RIGHT NOW!"

Eliza stared fondly after her youngest sister, then returned to Angelica and Peggy. Just two and a half years separated all three older girls. Though quite distinct in appearance, they were nevertheless so close that they were often referred to collectively as "the Schuyler sisters," as if they were triplets.

"Speaking of husbands: Will Mr. Church will be joining us this evening as well?" she asked Angelica.

"Oh, Eliza, don't be so stuffy! We have been married for ages, you can call him John!"

"Ha!" Peggy laughed. "I heard her talking to her husband the other day. Do you know she still calls him Colonel Hamilton in public?!"

"Peggy!" Eliza exclaimed. "You ought not to eavesdrop."

"It's not eavesdropping when all three of us are in the same parlor," Peggy said with a smirk. "Tell me, sister dear. Do you *always* address your husband so formally? I hope there are times when your discourse is more . . . intimate!"

Eliza felt a deep blush color her throat and cheeks. She did call him Alex when they were alone, but in public, she followed her mother's model and addressed him by his proper title. Fortunately, the hot kitchen was filled with steam from pots of stew and consommé for the party, and she hoped her sisters wouldn't notice. Still, she found herself helplessly tongue-tied.

"Oh, Peggy," Angelica said. "Always the provocateur!"

"Me?" Peggy laughed. "I am but an unmarried maiden, whereas you two are worldly wedded women. How could *I* possibly provoke *you*?"

Angelica couldn't help but grin. "I suspect that our polite Eliza will continue to address him as Colonel Hamilton among company even when they have been married as long as Mama and Papa."

"Unless he gets promoted like Papa," Eliza said, finally finding her voice. "In which case, I'll call him *General*

Hamilton. And you never answered my question. Will *John* be joining us this evening?"

"I believe so. He accompanied your colonel and Papa when they went into town this morning to attend to some work of his own, and told me he expects to finish by early evening. And Stephen?" Angelica continued, turning to Peggy. "Will your young man be there as well?"

"He said he is bringing half the Rensselaer cousins with him," Peggy replied with a nod, though she didn't sound happy about it.

"Is Mother Rensselaer still refusing to allow him to propose?" Eliza asked.

"I'm afraid so." Peggy sighed. "She says he is too young, but I don't believe it. When we first began courting, she was eager for us to marry immediately, but after what happened with Papa, she grew noticeably less enthusiastic. It's almost as if she thinks I am after him for his money!"

It was true that the Schuyler fortune wasn't what it once was. Four years ago, General Schuyler had been unceremoniously replaced by Horatio Gates as commander of the northern army, at about the same time that the Schuylers' Saratoga country estate was burned to the ground by British forces, destroying the better part of the Schuylers' income. Between the loss of funds and the cost of rebuilding, it had been a lean couple of years. But the family coffers had begun to recover at last, especially after Angelica's and Eliza's marriages. John Barker Church, Angelica's husband, had a booming business in trade, and Alexander Hamilton, though far from rich, was well provided for by the Continental army, and everyone said he had a bright, indeed limitless, future ahead of him.

Alas, that did not seem enough for the snooty Rensselaers.

"She is being absurd!" Eliza scoffed now. "It is *Stephen* who chased *you*. Why, that boy has been in love with you since he was in short pants!"

"Oh, has he started wearing trousers at last?" Angelica quipped, to a swat from Peggy.

Eliza laughed, then patted her younger sister's hand. "The Rensselaers wouldn't dare forever object to joining their family with ours. We are already cousins on Mama's side, and for all their money and land, they haven't nearly the prestige we do." She sighed. "Well, it sounds like dinner will be a full house. I look forward to seeing all three of our lads in the same room. It's so rare these days."

"I know!" Angelica said. "And soon enough the war will be over and you will be moving to New York City or Philadelphia or, heaven forbid, Virginia. John has been talking about returning to England, and I'm sure Stephen will want to build Peggy a house on some plantation-size corner of his vast holdings. This may be the last time we're all together for who knows how long!"

"Well then, let's make it the best party ever!" Eliza said. She stood up and grabbed a pie from the cooling rack, placing it in a basket. "And now if you'll excuse me, I'm going to take Mama a snack. Peggy, please don't wear the crimson silk Stephen gave you," she joked. "I cannot bear to be eclipsed by your radiance yet again."

"Ha!" Angelica laughed. "Telling Peggy not to dress up is like telling a goldfinch not to shine. Face it, Eliza, you're going to have to cinch tonight."

"And put on a wig!" Peggy added with a laugh. "Dot was teasing mine up for an hour last night, and it is *at least* three feet high!"

Eliza groaned, dreading the pinch of a corset and the itchiness of a wig, then reached for one last berry.

Springtime! In Albany! Not even the thought of all the painstaking effort that would go into looking presentable could ruin her day.

2

---◦⟨⊗⟩◦---

Allies and Conspirators

Schuylkill Tavern

Albany, New York

April 1781

*C*olonel Alexander Hamilton leaned against the nearby open window and drew in a few deep breaths. Both his father-in-law, General Philip Schuyler, and his brother-in-law, John Barker Church, were inveterate smokers, and after four hours, the small room in the back of Schuylkill Tavern was suffused with smoke. He desperately needed some fresh air. Yet the atmosphere outside was hardly more pleasant than that in the room. The tavern's back side (all puns intended) opened onto a narrow, muddy alley into which the local innkeepers regularly tossed their garbage and scraps, not to mention the contents of their guests' chamber pots. But as long as Alex inhaled through his mouth rather than his nose, he was all right. At any rate, he was at least not tempted to retch.

He scolded himself for complaining, for surely the price of inhaling a little smoke was nothing compared to now being part of Eliza's family—the Schuylers were one of the oldest and most prestigious clans in all of New York to be sure—but more important, Alex had been folded right into the middle of its loving arms. The family was even throwing him a good-bye party tonight before his imminent return to duty. Speaking of loving, the last six months had been the very definition of wedded bliss, as yearning for Eliza from afar did not hold a candle to the very happy reality of being her husband. Just the thought of his dear chestnut-tressed maid brought a warm smile to his face. He couldn't wait to see her later that evening.

The orphan in him also thrilled to think that he now had a father, a mother (although to think of the intimidating Catherine Schuyler as his mother was perhaps too large a leap, even if she seemed adequately fond of him, he did not want to overstep), sisters (how he loved to tease and spar with those girls) and now brothers as well. He spared a thought for his own lost brother, left behind in the Caribbean colonies, and turned his attention back to the matter at hand.

"We seem to have reached a deal then," General Schuyler said to his other son-in-law. "You shall provide five hundred rifles, twenty barrels of powder, and two tons of shot to General Washington at Newburgh, and the Continental army will pay you one thousand *pounds sterling*."

John Church smiled wryly. "I am aware of the irony of paying for arms to fight a war with currency from the very nation you are trying to defeat. But until the United States has a money of its own, British pounds remain far more fungible paper."

Alex listened to the men talk with one ear. The problem had come up countless times in the five long years of war: Thirteen colonies, each with its own currency, plus the bills issued by the Continental Congress. What it added up to was a mess, and the only thing that was going to fix it was a single currency issued by a central United States government. But if overthrowing British rule was a difficult task, getting the deeply independent-minded citizens of thirteen distinct polities stretching along a thousand miles of Atlantic Ocean coastline to agree on one currency was almost impossible to imagine, let alone achieve.

Still, one of Alex's great gifts was his ability to plan for the new nation to succeed and as well as to focus on immediate needs. Even so, these were problems for the future. The war for independence had to be won first.

He nodded to his brother-in-law. "Dear Mr. Church, I would like once again to convey General Washington's appreciation for all your efforts in support of the American cause. There are men in the far north who are still firing matchlocks, and I've even heard that some of the forces in the far southwest are armed with arquebuses that date back to the Spanish conquest."

John laughed. "I wish you were joking. Nevertheless, it is my honor and privilege to assist the Continental army. If only I could declare my support for the cause of independence more openly."

"It is a terrible burden, I am sure," General Schuyler assented. "A man wants to be judged based on his principles rather than rumors. But if your support for our side were more widely known, it would not be half as effective. The British would be seizing or sinking any ship that carried your 'linens' and 'teas' upon it, just as they do with those from our French allies."

"Yes, and they'd be seizing you, too," Alex said with a grim smile. "And I would simultaneously lose a brother-in-law *and* a contented wife. Angelica would be heartbroken without you, and if one of her sisters is sad, then my Eliza is equally miserable."

John smiled. "It is an honor for me to call both of you family as well as allies. Still, I *do* wish that I could tell my wife what it is that I actually do."

A chuckle from General Schuyler, accompanied by a cloud of smoke. "As Hamilton says, my daughters are inordinately close. It is excellent for family solidarity but not so good for state secrets. But never fear," Schuyler continued, clapping his eldest daughter's husband on the back, "one day you will be celebrated as a true supporter of our nascent country."

"It is only too bad that you will not be present to enjoy your acclaim," Alex said. "You remain determined to return to England once the war is over?"

"What can I say?" John shrugged. "I love this country and its people, not least my beautiful and brilliant wife, but I am an Englishman. I believe that a man should mind his own country and not meddle too long in the business of others. And Angelica is more European than she realizes. She will thrive in London society, as well as Paris and Berlin and Rome and all the capitals of Europe."

"It saddens me to imagine one of my daughters on the other side of the ocean. Yet it excites me to think of the Schuyler name and legacy extending even to European shores." General Schuyler turned to Alex. "Only don't you get any ideas about spiriting my Eliza off to the Indies. The Caribbean colonies may have better weather and more money than their North American counterparts, but my Eliza is as American as Mrs. Washington, and would not be at home anywhere else."

Alex laughed. "You shall not lose sleep over it, I guarantee. The Indies might have been where my body was born, but my mind did not fully awaken until I came to this country. This is my home as much as it is your lovely daughter's, and I cannot imagine living anywhere else."

The general nodded, but his expression seemed unsettled. "Aye," he said finally, the old-fashioned word harkening back to his Dutch roots. "You and my daughter are as well matched a couple as any parent could hope for."

Alex's brow knitted. "Your words are complimentary, yet your tone is clouded. Have I done something to offend you, sir?"

"What?" Schuyler started. "Oh no, no. I have two such fine sons-in-law of whom I am very proud."

"But?" Alex prompted.

Schuyler waved a hand at the munitions contract on the table. "These guns are destined for Yorktown, Virginia. General Cornwallis is gathering the bulk of his forces, and General Washington seems determined to cripple the British army and end the war in a single stroke. I take it that when you return in a few days you are still keen to accompany General Washington to the battlefield?"

Now it was Alex's turn to fall silent. He could feel his father- and brother-in-law's eyes boring into him. "Not exactly."

"Not exactly?" John repeated, taking a puff from his cigar. "That sounds rather ominous."

Alex summoned a breath. "I have decided to ask General Washington for my own unit to command."

It would not be accurate to say that General Schuyler goggled at him. The old Dutchman was too reserved in both life and command to ever betray his thoughts so openly. Still, there was a discernible straightening of the older man's spine. The thick wool of his uniform strained a bit, and his voice, when it came, was tight. "Patriotism and bravery are two of the finest qualities a man can possess. But there is a fine balance between zealousness and, dare I say, foolhardiness."

Alex opened his mouth to protest but his father-in-law— who was also his superior officer—spoke over him, so he held his tongue.

"You have been on the field of battle precisely once," said the general. "At Monmouth, where it is my understanding from General Washington himself that you acquitted your-self with valor, but also with what amounted to a reckless disregard for your own well-being. Washington said it was almost as if you wanted to die on the field of battle like some modern-day Norse warrior, as if only death by bullet or saber could assure you a place in Asgard."

"Sir, I can assure you," Alex began, compelled to explain. "There were no such thoughts in my head. Indeed, if there had been any thoughts at all, I do not remember them. I desired only to drive the enemy off the soil of my beloved country, and gave no regard to my safety whatsoever."

"This is exactly my point," General Schuyler said. "The difference between a commander and a soldier is that the com-mander fights in a cooler state of mind. He considers not just the individual skirmish or even the battle itself, but the course of the entire war, his own place in it, and that of all the men serving under him. If all our commanders fell to the bloody earth with their soldiers in each battle, we would have none left to lead the army. It would be a melee of undisciplined men mobbing about the field to be exterminated by the enemy."

Schuyler's words cut Alex to the core. Even General Washington had told him that his bravery at Monmouth was impressive, but his bloodlust to fight until he was struck down had made the general loath to send him back into battle. "You serve your country better intact," he had said. And in a rare show of personal attachment, he added, "I'd prefer you to live."

Alex had been flattered, in a way. He knew he was indispensable to Washington's office. But if the signs were reading true, the war was winding down. If the battle at Yorktown was successful, the British army would be decimated, and it was highly likely the overseas empire would at last concede that the American colonies were more trouble than they were worth, and surrender.

But Alex didn't care. He had come north as a teenager, brilliant but unworldly, and this country had embraced him and given him a chance to make a man of himself, and hopefully a fortune, too. How could he face his future children and tell them that he had spent the war in a paneled office with a pen in his hand and a warm fire at his back? When his future sons asked him how many battles he had won, how could he answer, "I did not fight. I was a secretary." His blood boiled at the thought.

"The counsel of very few men is of more value to me than yours, General Schuyler," Alex said. "And you may be assured that I will keep it in mind, just as I will keep my beloved and precious Eliza in my heart when I make my decision."

"She knows of your ambitions then?" General Schuyler asked pointedly.

Alex's words caught in his throat. He could not lie to his father-in-law. "We have not discussed it yet, but I know she will understand. She has your own bravery as a prior example, after all."

"Hamilton," John said sharply. "She will be crushed."

Again, Alex paused before speaking. He knew his brother-in-law spoke the truth. The reality of Eliza's tears—of her fear on his behalf—had kept him from sharing his plans with her until the last minute. He'd been determined to shield her from the news until it was inevitable, not wanting to break her heart just yet. After all, they had been discussing their own dreams for the establishment of their own home, and this would delay it indefinitely. Putting himself in the line of fire would also mean allowing for the possibility of a final separation between them, and the thought of his dear love as a grieving widow when their story had just begun was almost enough to dissuade him.

Yet—he had to put aside these fears for now. He would have a command; he would be part of this Revolution, if it was the last thing he accomplished.

Finally, he drew himself up straight. "Be that as it may," he said in the distant tone of a statesman or a commander rather than a husband, "I fight not just for myself now, nor even for my country, but for my wife and the family we will raise, and for the legacy of our name, which is yours as well. You must remember that I have studied war at the side of the man whose genius, bravery, and, dare I say, calculated patience has guided this country from bondage to freedom. If five years under General Washington has not prepared me to lead our brave boys into battle, nothing will."

General Schuyler said nothing for a long moment. Then he nodded. "I will speak on this matter no more. I do not wish to insult your honor or impugn your motives. And now, my dear boys, we have concluded our business and must rejoin our women. They do get upset when we are late for a party, especially one they are throwing in your honor, Hamilton."

3

Cousins and Confidences

The Schuyler Mansion

Albany, New York

April 1781

After supervising the cleaning of the kitchen and making sure everything was set for the party later that evening, Eliza traipsed up the stairs to her parents' bedroom, where she knocked on the door lightly. "Mama," she called through the closed portal. "It's Eliza. I've brought you a bit to eat."

A pause, and then her mother's strong voice came to her. "Enter."

Eliza eased the door open. The chamber on the far side was dimly lit, with muslin-backed silk curtains pulled entirely across all four windows. "Oh, Mama, were you sleeping? I'm so sorry, I'll come back later."

"No, no," Catherine Schuyler said, the bedsheets rustling as she sat up. "I was only drowsing out of boredom.

This forced indolence is far more taxing than my condition. Please, please, let a little light into my dreary cave."

Mrs. Schuyler's "condition" was revealed as soon as Eliza pulled open the curtains. Though her mother was covered by heavy cotton sheets with handmade lace borders and a light woolen blanket, not to mention her rather shapeless dowager's nightgown, it was still obvious that she was very, very pregnant.

"How *are* you feeling?" Eliza asked, carrying the tray of food to her mother's bedside.

"As I told Dr. Van Vrouten, I am absolutely fine. This is my twelfth time with child. I should think I'd have it rather figured out by now."

"Oh, Mama!" Eliza laughed. "Papa says that, despite your patrician pedigree, you are as hearty as a farm lass."

"Your father is a wise man. I only wish he were not in cahoots with that fool of a doctor."

Eliza smiled. The truth was that this pregnancy had been hard on her mother. Her ankles had swollen alarmingly with retained water, and her breath grew short when she walked up even a single flight of stairs—signs, according to Dr. Van Vrouten, that the large size of the baby was putting pressure on Mrs. Schuyler's internal organs, and inhibiting their full function. Two weeks ago, she had stood up from a settee, wavered a moment, then fallen back onto it in a faint. That was all General Schuyler needed to see: Since then he had insisted, following the doctor's instruction, that Mrs.

Schuyler keep to her bed until she had been delivered of her final child.

"Now, Mama," Eliza said as she cut an ample slice of blueberry pie and drizzled a bit of clotted cream over it. "You are indeed a strong woman, but you are six and for—"

"Ah-ah, my child," Catherine cut off her daughter. "I may be old enough to require bed rest, but I am not so ancient that I will tolerate having my age said aloud, even in the privacy of my own bedroom."

Eliza laughed again and handed her mother the dish of pie. "You are as handsome now as you were when I was a girl."

Though Mrs. Schuyler was generally rather reserved, she couldn't quite keep a smile off her face. A stout woman, the plumpness of her cheeks had staved off the wrinkles that marred the visages of others her age, and she did indeed look much younger than her unmentionable years.

"But not as handsome as my three grown girls," she said as she took a bite of the pie. "The berries cannot *still* be in season?" She laughed. "How I look forward to apples and pears."

"The grounds are almost picked clean. It was a bumper crop this year. We'll have preserves all through the winter, and won't run out in the middle of February like we did this year," said Eliza with a smile.

"I think that had less to do with the size of the crop than the number of people eating the harvest. I must say, we are an exceptionally full house these days." She took another bite before speaking. "Have you and Colonel Hamilton given any thought as to where you will settle down?"

Eliza sighed wistfully, half at the notion of leaving her childhood home once and for all, half in impatience at being fully ensconced in her own home with her own husband, beginning her own life.

"I was just discussing the matter with Angelica and Peggy. Colonel Hamilton wants to be officially relieved of his commission and witness the end of the war before he decides. There are those who are pressuring him to join the government when the war ends, but since we don't even know where the capital will be, we have no idea where we would have to live for him to do that. His own preference is for New York City, where he says a young man such as himself can most easily make a fortune. I prefer New York as well. It is too far from the Pastures for my liking, but not nearly so inaccessible as Philadelphia or something farther south."

Her mother nodded. "Schuylers and Van Rensselaers have lived in upper New York since Dutch times. I never imagined I would have a daughter live on the coast, but if there is one of us with the equanimity to survive the hustle and bustle of that teeming metropolis, it is you."

"Do you think?" Eliza said nervously. She looked out the window at the rolling green fields covered in ordered rows of fruit trees and grazing cows and sheep, sheltered over by a sky of liquid blue. "I do feel like such a country girl sometimes.

The idea of living in one of those, what do they call them, town houses? With all those stairs, and the rooms stacked one on top of each other? It sounds so . . . uncomfortable."

"All those stairs will be very good for the legs, my dear," Mrs. Schuyler said with a wry smile. "And New York is growing increasingly elegant. I hear they have even paved some of the streets now."

"And I hear the pigs run wild up and down them, rather than confining themselves to well-fenced sties like proper farm animals. But it doesn't matter!" she added brightly. "I'll be with Colonel Hamilton, and wherever we are will be home!"

She tried to picture it—the carpet, the wallpaper, the chandelier or sconces—but all she could see was Alex's face. *The decorations don't matter*, she said to herself. *Home is wherever we are together.*

"That's the spirit," Mrs. Schuyler said. "Speaking of domestic matters, I need to ask a favor from you."

"Of course, Mama, what is it?"

"I need you to serve as hostess at tonight's party."

Eliza understood immediately. Even if Dr. Van Vrouten had not ordered her mother confined to her bed, Mrs. Schuyler was far too advanced in her term to be seen socially. Even so, she was surprised by her mother's request.

"Me?" she said incredulously. "But Angelica is the eldest Schuyler lady. She should play substitute for you in your indisposition."

"Angelica is a Schuyler no more," her mother said quietly.

"But neither am I!" Eliza said, laughing.

"It is not the surname that matters," Mrs. Schuyler replied, "as much as the man who carries it."

Eliza sat back slightly. "I am afraid I don't understand, Mama," she said formally, though with a slight inkling that perhaps she did.

Her mother sighed and put her plate on the table beside her bed. "I will admit that I have softened toward Mr. Church in the years since he began courting your elder sister. He is a bit too British for my taste, but that cannot be helped. And while it seems the scandals that hounded him when he first showed up on our shores were base rumors and have been laid to rest, there persists an air of mystery about the man, and mystery translates to disrepute in our circle. It was a blow to our family's reputation when Angelica eloped with a nameless, fortuneless Brit who, though not a loyalist, remains a subject of Mad King George. But it would be an even bigger blow if your father and I appeared to countenance it by inviting his wife to play hostess to one of our events. Even if she does so happen to be our daughter."

Eliza sensed there was more to the story than her mother was letting on. "What do you mean, 'a blow to our reputation'?"

Her mother looked at her frankly. "You must promise me not to repeat a word of this to any of your sisters."

Eliza bit back a gasp. Her mother had never taken her into her confidence like this before. "Of course not, Mama."

"Stephen's mother has let it be known, and not so subtly I might add, that she disapproves of Angelica's choice of husband."

Now it all became clear. "You mean, that's why Stephen hasn't proposed to Peggy. Not because of our financial situation. But because of the whiff of scandal around Mr. Church?"

"The Schuylers are a proud family, and a wealthy one," her mother asserted, "but the Rensselaers are prouder and richer still. I should know. I am one." She laughed ruefully. "Stephen will be Patroon one day. It is largely a symbolic title, yet it still means much to my family. I believe their attitude will soften in time, especially if Angelica and Mr. Church move to England once the war is over. But until Peggy and Stephen are well and truly wed, I do not want to do anything that would spoil their chances. Peggy's happiness depends on it, not to mention the assured financial health of all the Schuyler and Rensselaer progeny for the foreseeable future."

Eliza was shocked, both by her mother's news and by her having to play hostess in a mere few hours to the elite of upper New York. She looked down at her hands, which were still faintly stained with blueberry juices. Then her mother's hand appeared in hers, clasping her fingers tightly.

"Don't fret, my daughter. You have reserves of strength that you yourself are not aware of." She smiled tenderly. "Think of it as a trial run for all those New York City parties you'll be throwing in just a few years."

"New York City!" Eliza said dreamily. "It's hard to believe it will ever happen!"

"It will," her mother said firmly, "and you will be the queen of Manhattan. By the way," she added lightly, as she helped herself to a second slice of pie. "We had a note from the governor's mansion this morning. Governor Clinton will be joining us this evening." If Eliza didn't know her mother better, she could have sworn she saw her smile turn wicked. "Try not to let him eat *all* the berries before he leaves."

4

---❦---

Lord and Lady

The Schuyler Mansion
Albany, New York
April 1781

The Pastures stood proudly on its low hill surveying the sprawling landscape. There were already a few carriages, both open and closed, parked in front of the house. As Alex and his father-in-law approached (John Church had gone ahead), they saw a covered two-wheeler advance toward the house, its cab tilted rather noticeably to one side. The driver stopped and a corpulent man dressed in a gaudy, ill-fitting gold coat emerged from the cab, which promptly sprung back to an (almost) even keel.

General Schuyler sighed heavily. "I can recognize that gold-plated rotten egg even from a distance. George Clinton is the only man I know who arrives *before* a party starts rather than fashionably late. It is to make sure the best of the victuals are still available."

Alex knew the name, of course, though he had yet to meet the governor of New York State. He thought the Schuylers were magnanimous to invite the man, seeing as he beat General Schuyler in 1777 for the governorship.

George Clinton had served in the French and Indian War two decades ago. He continued to fight for his country when independence was declared in 1776, simultaneously beginning a career in politics. Some people considered it a conflict of interest, since the idea of a political leader who was also an active army officer raised the specter of a military dictatorship—of a leader who held power by force of arms rather than votes. This was at odds with the very spirit of democracy this new country was attempting to foster.

None of this bothered Alex as much as Clinton's avowed position against any kind of central government or national authority. Clinton believed that every state should have absolute control over its own fate—to such a degree that he had even made noises about "invading" the neighboring state of Vermont after the war was over, and adding it to New York's territory. All the states should be equals, according to Clinton. Yet, as his threats made clear, he considered some states more "equal" than others.

"He's a dangerous one," General Schuyler added. "Claims to be a man of the people, but the only thing he has in common with the common folk is their pocketbooks, which he has emptied into his own. Not one tax dollar is raised without a penny ending up in Clinton's coffers."

"Greed is as old as civilization," Alex replied. "As lamentable as it is, it's the crassness of his mindset that really bothers me. No lie is too base for him to try to win people to his cause. He knows that by the time he is found out he will have invented ten more lies to cover the first, and if all else fails, he can always wrap himself in the flag and cry, 'To war!'"

"With Vermont?" General Schuyler chuckled ruefully. "Mrs. Ross may well regret that her name is associated with the Stars and Stripes when she sees to what use it is put."

"The flag has stood for many a noble cause as well. It remains for each individual American to decide what it means to him or to her," said Alex, nodding at the portly figure up the hill, who was being let into the house by a liveried servant. "Even that one."

"Indeed," the general agreed as they started up the long flight of steps that led toward the eastern, river-facing front of the house. "I can only wonder what brought him here tonight. Mrs. Schuyler did not lead me to believe that tonight's affair would host the crème de la crème of local society. Just a festive but quiet gathering of family and friends to wish you a safe and speedy journey back to General Washington's office."

"When all three Schuyler sisters are in residence, there is no such thing as a 'quiet' anything," Alex replied with a laugh.

And indeed, as the men drew closer to the house they heard the sound of music coming from the windows, opened wide to take advantage of the sweet, cool, early-evening breeze.

"What's this?" General Schuyler said half under his breath. "Surely Catherine did not engage the services of a band!" In his consternation, he used his wife's Christian name, and Alex caught him glance nervously around, as if someone other than his son-in-law might have heard him speak so familiarly of his most regal spouse.

Before Alex could hazard a guess, however, the door flew open, pulled inward not by Samson, the butler, or Hendricks, the chief footman, but by Eliza herself.

"Colonel Hamilton! Papa!" his wife said merrily, a sweet if somewhat nervous smile on her face. "I thought I glimpsed you riding up!"

Alex stared at his wife as she greeted her father. Her face bore only the lightest dusting of powder and the natural hue of her lips was enhanced with a paint only slightly darker—her beauty accented, rather than augmented, and framed by wisps of her chestnut hair that spiraled down her cheeks. He felt warm all over, but it was immediately damped by an icy chill on his spine, as he thought about telling her of his plans for Yorktown.

She accepted a kiss on the cheek from her father and turned to her husband with a flushed eagerness that went straight to his heart.

"Darling," he said, just as besotted as the day he'd first glimpsed her when he had come to this house as a mere messenger just three years ago. He pecked her on the cheek, for propriety's sake, though he lingered long enough to inhale her perfume, and his fingers paused lightly at her waist.

"Alex," she whispered, and sound of his name on her lips and her breath on his ear almost drove him mad with desire.

He forced himself to straighten up, even as his eyes caught hers meaningfully in the candlelight. From the way she held his gaze, it was clear that his ardor was returned, but her duties called. Eliza stood aside as her husband and father entered the vast entrance hall, some twenty feet wide and nearly twice as deep, stretching all the way to the rear of the house, where an ornate staircase led to a ballroom on the second floor.

Though the hour had just passed seven, the great hall was half filled already, and General Schuyler's eyes bulged as he peered into the side parlors and saw even more guests talking and eating and drinking.

"My goodness!" he said, chuckling even as one of the footmen hurried over to take his and Alex's tricorne hats. "Married less than six months and already the head of the household and the hostess of the evening! You have been studying at your mother's side, no doubt. But tell me, did she really contract for live music today?" He waved a hand toward the back of the hall, where two fiddlers and a flutist were plying a reel, though no one was yet dancing. "I did not realize we were throwing a ball and not a mere dinner."

Eliza stepped in a little closer. "The musicians are Peggy's touch, with a little help from Stephen. Apparently, they are the 'court musicians' at Rensselaerswyck, and he sent them over to make Peggy feel better about the contretemps occurring between his family and ours. I told her we hadn't even arranged for dance cards and all would be chaos, but you know Peggy. She just laughed and said, 'This is America, we can do what we want!' And so she has!"

Alex could tell from the lilt in Eliza's voice that his wife was pleased her sister had acted so rashly, but also a bit anxious, lest her father disapprove. And indeed General Schuyler seemed pensive. "I worry to think that Mrs. Schuyler is being kept awake by the festivities," he said.

"I checked with Mama immediately. I promised her that we would confine the evening's activities to the first floor, and she said that if she could not be present at the party she was glad to at least hear the merriment through the floorboards."

"Well then!" General Schuyler said warmly. "Let me find Samson and see if he can round up some cards and pencils, and let's have some dancing!" And with that, he headed off down the hall.

Alex used his father-in-law's exit as a chance to sweep his wife into a real embrace in a convenient alcove. "At last, we are alone. You smell utterly delectable," he whispered into her ear. "Is that . . . strawberries?"

"Maybe," she said, batting at him playfully with her fan. "It's probably just rose water, but we were eating berries this afternoon."

"Ah, that must explain the ruby color of your lips," he said, leaning in for a kiss.

"Colonel Hamilton!" Eliza laughed, pulling away before their lips could touch in public. "I have enough on my plate without having to keep you in line as well."

"Oh, do keep me in line, I can't wait," Alex couldn't help himself from teasing her, if only for the sparks it brought to her eyes. His arms went around her waist once more and pulled her toward him.

Eliza swatted at him again. "Darling! We have guests!"

"Hang them," Alex said, leaning closer. "Let's sneak off to the barn."

"We shall have to pitch hay later," murmured Eliza, as more guests wandered past them. She colored even more at her double entendre, which her husband found wildly irresistible. "But right now, society calls." She reluctantly pulled away from him, untangling herself from his embrace.

Alex took a moment to straighten his lapels. "Do tell, did your mother really make that comment about enjoying the music through the floorboards? Pardon my candor, but 'merriment' is not a word I associate with Mrs. Schuyler."

Eliza failed to suppress a wicked grin. "In fact, she said that if there had to be music, it would at least be muffled by floorboards and carpet, and should the din grow too loud she could always draw the curtains on her bedstead and drink a dram of brandy to speed her to sleep."

"That sounds more like the ebullient mother-in-law I know. But did she really cede her domestic authority to you? Angelica must feel slighted," said Alex, taking her arm as they strode through the parlor.

"Angelica and I spoke briefly. She understands that there are . . . reasons why she cannot act as female head of household for the foreseeable future."

Alex nodded. He knew—in ways that he could not inform even his wife—that she was referring to John Barker Church and the air of mystery—or rather disreputability—that clung to him. He longed to disabuse her of the notion that either John or Angelica had anything to be ashamed of, but there were certain responsibilities that stood outside the bonds of marriage, or even love. The safety of the Continental troops was one of them.

"One day," he said in a measured voice, lest she suspect something, "the rather tiny and, dare I say, inbred community of Albany society will realize that Mr. Church is as great a friend to America as any of her citizens who have been here for a century or more." He looked around the party. "Although I must say, it doesn't seem very tiny tonight. Who *are* all these people?"

"With Mama confined to her bed, no one was in charge of invitations, and so Angelica and Peggy and I all sent out cards—as did Mama, it turned out. It appears as if there are twice as many people here as our last great ball—do you remember? In the winter of '77?"

"You mean the night I met you and my future happiness was sealed forever? You impugn my honor, Mrs. Hamilton! If you weren't my wife, I would have to challenge you to a duel." His voice softened, and he risked a little kiss on the tip of Eliza's nose. "Though I confess you have already stolen my heart, so there is nothing left to shoot."

Eliza's resolve weakened and she leaned in against him, happily falling into his arms until a loud voice interrupted.

"I found them!" a female voice exclaimed. "So, here is where you two have been hiding!"

5

The Man Who Ate New York

The Schuyler Mansion
Albany, New York
April 1781

Eliza whirled to see Peggy and Angelica approaching with small plates of pastry in their gloved hands. Alex and Eliza separated from each other with sheepish smiles. But the Schuyler sisters weren't about to let them off that easily.

"'You have already stolen my heart, so there is nothing left to shoot'?" Peggy mocked. "And I thought this cherry jam was sweet! Lord preserve us. *Preserve* us," she repeated in a heavier voice. "D'you see what I did there?"

Angelica moaned. "Between Colonel Hamilton's purple prose and your purple puns, this party is off to a magnificent start!"

"Don't forget my purple tongue!" Peggy said, sticking hers out at Angelica, who couldn't help but giggle.

"Mama is going to banish us to the wilds of Ohio!" the oldest Schuyler girl said.

"Where we will obviously be the best-dressed girls for five hundred miles," Peggy replied. "Speaking of which, you have yet to compliment us on our gowns, Colonel Hamilton. We don't work this hard for no one to notice, I'll have you know. Be honest: If you had to do it all over again, which of the Schuyler sisters would you propose to, based on tonight's *ensembles*?"

Eliza laughed at her sister's brazenness and saw Alex's face go nearly as purple as Peggy's tongue. But he covered himself well. "This question may be more relevant than you realize. I understand that there is a proposed law for the new country that says a husband may trade in his wife in the first year of marriage, no questions asked."

Peggy gasped, but Eliza was not so easily shocked. "Just husbands? Are wives so easily contented with their men?" she said with an arched brow.

"To the contrary," Alex said. "Wives get five years to make up their minds, on the understanding that the fairer sex is far more patient than we brutes, and men are much better at concealing their faults."

"If only because they're hardly ever home," Eliza said with a sniff. "I feel as though I haven't seen you in three days. You sneak in after dark and are out before the sun is up. I'm not convinced you are who you say you are. Perhaps you are not even my true husband."

"Is that so?" said Alex with a grin. "What shall I do to make you remember?"

Eliza swatted the hand he tried to snake around her waist.

"She speaks the truth!" Angelica said. "I have quite forgotten what Mr. Church looks like. Is that him?" she said, pointing to a man who was at least sixty years old, as tall as a three-year-old maple sapling, and nearly as thin.

The girls laughed at Angelica's wickedness, then Alex interrupted. "I believe I was promised a fashion show."

Peggy beamed, and immediately stepped in front of Angelica. Eliza tried to slip away, but Angelica caught her wrist and pulled her back.

"Now, now, sister. Your marriage is on the line. No time to be modest."

"I am hardly modest," Eliza half grumbled, half teased. "I just have no desire to be exhibited like a prize pig."

"You should be so lucky as to take home the trophy," Angelica teased. "Now hush."

Peggy stepped forward. With another man, this display might have been unnecessary, since the sisters had already been conversing with Alex for ten minutes, giving him ample time to survey their outfits. But Eliza knew that her husband was the type of man who noticed the person rather than his or her garments. One time he spent an hour in conversation with General Lafayette, and when the latter had departed — and when they were safely alone — Eliza had asked him how he had managed to concentrate when the general's shirttail had been poking out of his trouser fly. Alex had merely looked at her blankly.

But now Alex summoned a breath and put on a serious

face, as though he were judging not pigs or even cattle, but something as valuable as a saddle horse.

Peggy was wearing a silk dress of the deepest, most shimmering reds, given a moiré effect by an overskirt of burgundy lace. Full panniers made it as wide as a love seat, making her already tiny waist seem that much smaller. Her corset was strapped tighter than a mummy's bandages, the bodice of her dress tightly laced and low cut, revealing an abundant serving of décolletage. Breasts, neck, and face were so heavily powdered as to be almost shimmering, which blended seamlessly into the silver pompadour wig she had lately taken to wearing. Amber dewdrops hung from her ears, matching the silver chain and pendant on her chest, which complemented her dark ruby lips and her flashing eyes.

"Very nice," Alex said. "I think the housekeeper said we were looking for a charwoman to clean the fireplaces. I'll let her know. Next!"

Peggy's jaw dropped open, and you could almost see her blush beneath her powder—*almost*. Fortunately, she was far too aware of her beauty to take him seriously. She raised an eyebrow, stepped aside, and allowed Angelica her turn.

Angelica had reversed Peggy's color combination. Her dress was gold and her jewels ruby. Her silhouette was less imposing, the skirts of her dress augmented by a small crinoline, though she had foregone a corset, and even lacing, giving her waist a daringly mobile mien. The powdering on her face and breasts was lighter, allowing the natural golden tones of her skin to be complemented by the richly gathered silks of her dress. She had taken the unusual step of selecting a dark wig to give the outfit a more solid cap, and Eliza saw Alex's eyes widen when he noticed it. Angelica had lovely brunette hair but her wig was as black as a raven's plumage, and the dark frame made her pale complexion seem almost pearlescent. Her lips were peach. Her hazel eyes seemed by turns green and gold depending on how they caught the light. Truly, her eldest sister was radiant tonight.

Alex pursed his lips. "Satisfactory. I would let you serve at table, if I were not afraid that you might distract my guests from their food."

"You flatter me," Angelica said archly.

"You haven't seen my dinners," Alex replied with equal color. "My food is not so pretty as all that. Next, please."

Angelica rolled her eyes and stepped to one side. And there was Eliza.

Or, rather, the back of her, for she was busily conferring with Hendricks, showing him how the small tartlets on his tray should be arranged so they didn't bunch up in a jumble "like leaves pooling behind a dam," as she could be heard saying.

"And tell Cook to slice the *bresaola* thinner," she said as the footman moved to rejoin the party. "It is not sausage. It is should melt in the mouth, not be chewed like jerky."

She started then, aware of eyes on her, and turned suddenly toward her husband. Her face was completely open, with the practical expression of a busy hostess rather than the tempting pout of a coquette. She had chosen a dress of American indigo, a rich blue that gave off purple tones when struck by candlelight. As was her custom (and despite her sister's teasing earlier), she had eschewed a corset, and the skirts of her dress were filled out by nothing more than a strategically draped underpaneling. She looked, in other words, not like a statue, but like a woman, and as Alex took in the sight of her, his eyes softened and his lips curled into a gentle, unconscious smile.

("Come, Sister," Angelica whispered to Peggy. "Our game is over.")

They eased back into the party as Alex stepped forward and took Eliza's hands in his. He did not bother to see if anyone was looking, but leaned in and kissed her softly, briefly, on the lips.

"Do you remember me now, Mrs. Hamilton?" he asked in a hushed voice, his blue eyes shining.

"It's coming back to me," Eliza said. "Kiss me again and perhaps I'll be able to place your—"

Her voice dissolved as Alex did her bidding and kissed her again, longer and more urgently this time. Eliza's breath caught in her chest as if her corset had been pulled too tight—but she wasn't wearing one.

"My darling," he whispered throatily.

"Oh," said Eliza, speechless and swooning at his touch, as he made his way dangerously close to her décolletage.

Alex looked around and pulled her deeper into the

shadows. He kissed his way back up to her lips, and for a moment, they both quite forgot where they were, until the coughing of a few disapproving guests brought them back to their senses. They quickly pulled away from each other.

"I have missed you, Colonel Hamilton," she said when she could speak again.

"And I you, Mrs. Hamilton," said Alex, helping her set her gown to rights as he straightened his lapels. "Fortunately, the war will be over soon, and it will be merely Mr. Hamilton again. General Washington is preparing—" His face clouded and his voice broke off.

Eliza peered at him nervously. "What is it?"

"Nothing," Alex said vaguely. "Just routine military matters. I will give you all the details later, after the guests have gone—if you can stay awake to hear them all," he added with forced levity.

"I sense that these are more than routine matters," Eliza said. "But you are right. This is a party, and you are its guest of honor. Everyone has come to say good-bye to you before you rejoin General Washington at Newburgh."

Eliza noticed another pained look from Alex but didn't inquire about it. Growing up with a military man for a father had taught her that he would tell her what he could, and pressing him would only cause them both distress.

"Come," she said then. "Let me present you to all these people who you will never see again—if you're lucky."

The next two hours were a blur of handshakes and hugs, colognes and perfumes, drinks sipped and sometimes swilled, foods nibbled and chewed. Eliza led Alex adroitly from one conversational group to the next, angling him in and making introductions, allowing her guests to pepper him with questions about General Washington or the war or what his plans were for Albany's favorite daughter.

General Washington was "the greatest of men," Alex replied every time; the war "would be over before you could say Yankee Doodle"; and as for Eliza, Alex said that he had every intention of making sure that the next twenty years of her life were as sumptuous as the first twenty.

"But how?" the widowed Mrs. Peter Rycken asked bluntly. "I hear you have no money and no profession. You can't be General Washington's errand boy forever."

Alex blushed and attempted to answer, but Eliza stepped in smoothly, with a cold smile at the nosy widow. "Alex was reading law before the war started," she said, "and his years at General Washington's desk have given him a unique opportunity to continue those studies, if he chooses to. But who knows? Perhaps he will seek out a career in public service. A new nation needs new leaders."

"Pah!" Mrs. Rycken exclaimed. "Government is not a career, it's a hobby for wealthy men. At least if they're honest. You strike me as an honest boy," she added, as if that were a character flaw.

"Indeed!" a male voice cut in. "The most ineffective leaders have always been the most scrupulous." A chuckle punctuated the still-faceless words. "That must be why I'm such a bad governor, ha-ha-ha!"

Eliza turned to see Governor George Clinton approaching them, preceded by his bloated stomach, plainly visible between the sagging folds of his unbuttoned coat, which was stained by the remnants of many meals and drinks. His lips were equally greasy and dark, and he held a whole pie in his right hand, from which he now took a large bite, exposing the dark creamy filling. Eliza did her best to keep her eyes fixed on the governor's as some of the blueberry compote spilled onto her father's exquisite Ottoman carpet.

Governor Clinton held out a blueberry-stained hand toward Alex. "George Clinton. But you can just call me Governor."

Eliza knew Governor Clinton well enough to understand that he was fully aware of who Alex was. He was far too cagy to ever approach a strange man at a party without finding out his name and particulars first.

She half hoped Alex would offer Governor Clinton a napkin instead of his hand.

Instead she watched, a little disappointed, as Alex allowed the governor to smear blueberry pie filling all over his fingers. "Hamilton. Alexander Hamilton."

"Colonel Hamilton, isn't it?" Governor Clinton said, omitting the obligatory "sir" that military protocol dictated. "Your *reputation* precedes you," he said, pointedly glancing at Eliza, not as though she was his wife, let alone the daughter of General Philip Schuyler, but one of the many young beauties Alex had been linked to before he met her.

He's gone too far! she thought. *Alex will not stand for this! Let him have it, Alex!*

But all her husband said was, "I-I believe you know my wife, Eliza Schuyler Hamilton."

"Know her?" Governor Clinton took another bite of pie. "Why, I bounced this young lassie on my knee when she was no taller than one of the lambs carved up on yonder table. My, my, Eliza Schuyler. I'd say that in the game of wife-hunting, Colonel Hamilton, you went out looking for a rabbit and bagged yourself a ten-pointed buck."

Eliza felt her cheeks burn. To be described thus, and in her father's house! This was too much. Surely Alex would recover his tongue now. She turned to him desperately, only to find him staring at his shoes as though they had come unbuckled.

"Oh, I'd say that she caught me, Governor," he said in a voice that could barely be heard, "but I wouldn't want to flatter myself."

Alex's words might have sounded sweet on any other occasion, but to Eliza's ears tonight they sounded hollow.

"It would be difficult for my husband to flatter himself," she said, "given all that he has accomplished at such a young age."

Governor Clinton swilled another huge bite of pie, although he hadn't quite finished swallowing before he answered.

"So I've heard," he said, spewing crumbs from his lips.

"Sailing into the colonies on William Livingston's purse, marrying into the Schuyler clan, with a link to the even wealthier Rensselaers, and attaching himself like a remora to the great shark that is George Washington himself. Amazing accomplishments for a man born on an island smaller than a good-size farm, and without facing a single musket ball on the field of battle."

From the tone of Governor Clinton's voice, it was clear he was baiting the younger man, though Eliza had no idea why. Not the she cared. Clinton had always been a boor, and intimidating people was his primary mode of intercourse. What she couldn't figure out was why Alex was acting so cowed. What did the man have on him?

"Well"—Governor Clinton shrugged—"I hear there may yet be chances for you to get yourself killed like a good American martyr."

Alex cleared his throat nervously. "Were I to die in the service of my country, I would not consider myself a martyr. Just a patriot."

"Have your wife tell the masons to carve that on your gravestone," Governor Clinton snickered.

"Colonel Hamilton seeks no glory on the battlefield," Eliza said, a defensive tone in her voice. "Only duty."

Governor Clinton snorted. "No doubt you know many things about your husband that I do not, but on this account, I can assure you that you are wrong. Colonel Hamilton has been begging General Washington for a battle command for the past two years, despite his utter lack of leadership experience. And now it seems he is making a play to lead a regiment at Yorktown, which has no more need of his 'expertise' than a lamb has need of its wool after its throat has been slit."

Eliza turned to Alex, who appeared to be even more fascinated by his shoes, one of which was doggedly tracing the pattern on the carpet beneath him. She felt her heart sink. Yorktown? A battle command? What was this? She was thankful that Peggy had made her put on a dusting of powder. She hoped it was enough to cover her flush.

"That is your second ovine analogy of the evening, Governor. It would seem you have mutton on your mind, rather than my husband's career," she said sharply.

"Your father does raise a tasty sheep," Clinton said, heedlessly rubbing his belly with his dirty fingers, "but I assure you I am quite correct as to my intelligence concerning Colonel Hamilton's military maneuvers, such as they are. He may outrank me in the army, but being governor does have its privileges." His tone softened in mock sympathy. "Oh, you didn't know?"

"Of course I knew," Eliza retorted quickly, her stomach in knots. At least now she recognized why Alex was so tongue-tied. Clearly, he was afraid his secret would come out, and now it had. "Nor am I surprised that you knew. Only that you would speak of our army's stratagems so casually. I thought secrecy was paramount in these matters."

"There are no secrets where Yorktown is concerned," Clinton replied. "I would say that you are throwing away your life, Colonel Hamilton, but your life is yours do with as you will, beautiful, wealthy wife or no. Yet the men who will be serving under you deserve a more qualified leader, and the chance to return to their families when the day is won.'"

Eliza glanced at Alex, who was struggling to meet her gaze, let alone Clinton's, or even stammer an answer to such discourtesy. It appeared she would have to be the one to rise to the occasion.

"I can assure you, Governor Clinton," she said coldly, "that my husband's love for me and his love for his country occupy very different spheres in his heart. I would not dream of asking him to choose between us. If he feels his country needs him at Yorktown, I fully support his decision, and I know that he will acquit himself with the highest level of bravery."

Clinton smirked, but admiration showed in his eyes at Eliza's defense of her husband. "If he has half your fighting spirit, you might just be right." And then, noticing his hands were empty, he turned toward the meat table. "And now I think I'm going to have some of that sweet, juicy lamb."

Eliza waited until the governor was out of earshot before turning to her husband.

"Darling—" Alex started. "I've been meaning to tell you—"

"How long have you known?" She spoke over him, her dark eyes flashing at his betrayal. "And you had no care to share the news with me? Your wife? Not even to discuss the ramifications of the choice you have made?" It was at times like these it was obvious that Alex was bound more to their fledging country than their fledging marriage.

Alex's eyes fell. "Nothing has been decided yet. I may not even—"

"How long, Alex?" Eliza demanded.

Alex looked up at her with guilty eyes. "I put in the request a few months ago. General Washington said he would give me an answer when I rejoin him at Newburgh."

"And you have reason to believe his answer will be yes." She choked back a sob.

Alex's eyes wavered. "I told him that if he did not give me a battle command, I would resign immediately."

"Resign!" she echoed, shocked.

"I am a soldier, Eliza, and a good one. Without a command, I would never rise in the ranks, never gain the respect and the honor I am due," he said. "Please, try to understand. I am no one, I am nothing. I did this for us."

She shook her head. "But if you resign, you forfeit your pay and your pension! We would be penniless for certain! You did all this without consulting me?"

"My darling, please," Alex said, grabbing her hands. "There are some decisions a man has to do on his own."

Eliza resisted the urge to pull her hands from Alex, lest she cause a scene. But her fury was so palpable that Alex dropped them of his own accord.

"A man maybe. But a husband—never," she said coldly. She stormed away from him, her head held high.

"Eliza, please!" he begged.

Eliza stopped in her tracks and turned back slowly to face him, her eyes boring into his. "You made your decision on your own. What do you care where I go?" she said, then whirled on her heel and plunged into the crowd.

6

———◦◦◦———

Separations and Reunions

Aboard the Pilgrim
Albany, New York, to Newburgh, New York
May 1781

*A*lex had a miserable journey to Newburgh. To speed his trip, John Church had arranged for him to catch a ride on the *Pilgrim*, a merchant vessel loaded with beaver furs. The beautiful weather had yielded to a summer squall, with sheets of rain whipping across the freighter's deck and rendering it uninhabitable to all but the most seasoned salts. Below decks was nearly as bad, though: unbearably muggy, and suffused with an odor of rotting meat from the uncured hides bundled in the hold. The captain was a grizzled mariner who claimed to be French but between his toothlessness and the pipe he kept clapped between his gums, Alex understood only about one out of five words that came from the man's mouth, despite his growing up speaking both English and French.

But that's not why Alex was miserable.

His parting from Eliza had been less than amicable, to put it lightly. Eliza had disappeared from the party after their argument, and did not resurface until the end of the evening, when she shook his hand in full view of the servants who were cleaning up the greasy platters and wine-stained glasses. "I hope you enjoyed your party, Colonel Hamilton," she said in a voice that could have frozen water. "No doubt you need your rest in preparation for your journey, so I will sleep in Angelica's old room tonight."

Two days later, his wife was still cold as a glacier with no hope of melting. Alex had tried to get her alone all the next day, but Eliza spent the entire morning and afternoon visiting friends. When she arrived home at dinnertime, she announced that she had "taken too much sun," and ate her dinner in Angelica's room, where she slept once again, refusing to return to their marital bed.

She only consented to speak to him the next morning, when she saw him off at the river pier. Her face was red and puffy. Clearly, she had not spent a pleasant night.

"My darling," he said, moving to take her in his arms. "Please hear me out. I am so sorry for having upset you. I should have told you earlier."

Eliza stepped back, and Alex was left clutching empty air. "It is not your apology I want Alex," she said. "I want you safe and whole."

Alex's eyes dropped.

"I understand you feel you have to do what you think is best," said Eliza as her eyes filled with tears. She batted them away angrily. "But why risk your life if you don't have to?"

"Because I love this country!" Alex replied immediately. "And because other men are risking their lives. What kind of man would I be if I was content to send others to the front lines while I took shelter in the general's tent?"

"You would be a man who came home to his wife!" Eliza cried. "You would be a man who could help his country in ways that others cannot. You have the mind of a philosopher, a political scientist, an economist! The United States will need men who possess all of these rare gifts if it wants to survive the transition from colony to country."

Alex reluctantly shook his head at his wife. "Though the Creator has blessed me with a reasoning greater than the average man, a sharp mind does not free one from corporal responsibilities—of putting his body on the line when the circumstances demand it. They say that the pen is mightier than the sword, but that is not true on the battlefield. For a few days, I will put down my quill and take up my blade like every other man, and on the other side of the battle I will be able to say that I risked my blood for my country like every other patriotic American."

"You see!" Eliza said. "It is not just that you feel a sense of responsibility. You want the glory of being a war hero, just like Clinton said!"

Alex's eyes went wide. "You would use that boor's words against me?"

"I would say anything if I thought it would get you home

to me safely!" she said passionately. "Anything at all," she said more softly now.

"But would you respect me when I returned?"

Eliza's eyes flashed angrily. "How much did *you* respect *me* when you sought a battlefield command and didn't bother to inform me? You think being called out by Governor Clinton is bad? Try learning from *him* in front of a roomful of family and friends that your husband thinks so little of you that he decides to risk his life without even telling you!"

Alex couldn't help but smile, though it was a sad, cha-grined expression. "So, we both have ulterior motives. I want a bit of glory, and you want a husband who treats you as a partner." He shrugged. "It appears war and marriage are both more complicated than we realized."

"And often hard to tell apart!" Eliza quipped.

"Listen to me, my dearest," Alex said then, catching Eliza's hand in his and placing it against his cheek. "I prom-ise that I will return to carry you across the threshold of your new home like a proper bride. To Philadelphia, perhaps, where you shall entertain the ambassadors of foreign nations, or New York City, where we will establish ourselves in one of the grand new town houses on Wall Street. You shall be the doyenne of society, and I shall be the most brilliant politi-cian and lawyer this young country has yet seen. And who knows, perhaps one day I'll run for governor, and chase that windbag out of office."

"Governor Clinton is harmless, you men just don't know how to handle him," Eliza said in a softer tone. "But you'd better come home," she continued. "If you don't, I will hunt you down and run you through myself."

They embraced then, for the first time in two days, and kissed each other—softly at first, and then urgently, so there was no question of the love between them. Alex buried his head in her neck, inhaling her sweet scent, wanting nothing more than to prolong the moment, but it was Eliza who pulled away first.

"Don't," she said when he stepped forward for one more kiss. "If I put my arms around you again, I do not think I will be able to let go, and I want to be brave for you."

And, blinking back tears, Eliza turned as quickly as she could so Alex wouldn't have to see her cry.

ALEX PASSED THE last hour of the journey penning a letter to Eliza—a thousand times "I'm sorry" and a thousand more "I love you"—hoping that she would forgive him, and only when he was done did he try to put his wife out of his mind and concentrate on the looming war.

The rain had ended by the time they reached Newburgh. Low hills crowded right to the river, with a small port built largely of reddish-brown bricks and, higher up, a bustling village of handsome brick and frame houses, with here and there an older building made of rough stone pieces joined by thick welts of mortar. A few cook fires burned, sending gray ribbons of smoke into the air, where they mixed with the wet blanket of mist that persisted after the rain. The mist was so heavy that Alex sweated uncomfortably in his heavy uniform.

Still, it was better than being trapped aboard the fur ship with its fetid cargo. Alex strode onto dry—well, solid—land purposefully, eager to get to General Washington's headquarters and find out whether his request for a command had been granted.

The first thing he saw was a chestnut stallion tied up at the edge of the broad wharf that abutted the pier. Its coat was the color of caramelized butter, its mane and tail so light they were almost golden. The animal was so fine that Alex was tempted to call it pretty, and yet it was no delicate creature. It must have been sixteen hands high and thickly muscled, and even as it waited, it had an air of martial readiness about it. This was no city horse or buggy puller, let alone a palfrey. This stallion looked like it could handle the stresses of the battlefield and finish off any enemy soldiers its rider failed to dispatch.

Alex couldn't take his eyes off it as he made his way onto the wharf. General Washington was famed for the white charger he rode into battle, and though the army had always supplied Alex with admirable steeds, he'd never been in possession of a horse of any great renown, as much as he was fond of his former mount Hector. But a horse like this would make any warrior more confident, and Alex found himself wondering who owned it, and how he might be persuaded to part with it. Never mind the price. But Alex's salary as an aide barely paid for his uniforms. This was merely a fantasy. Even so, it would be the kind of horse that would soothe some of

Eliza's fears about his chances in battle. It might even allay some of his own.

"If you leered at my horse any more openly, I would have to cite you for indecency," a rough voice called from the shadows.

Alex started, and peered beneath the overhang. He was only able to make out a tall man in Continental army blue.

"He is indeed a fine specimen," Alex agreed.

"Not nearly as fine as his owner," said the soldier, who stepped into the light, a sardonic grin splitting his wide, fair face, which was lightly dusted by whiskers nearly as light as his horse's hide.

"Laurens!" Alex exclaimed, dropping his satchel and rushing forward to throw his arms around his old friend. "You old dog! I did not recognize your voice at all!"

Laurens returned Alex's embrace warmly. "My old friend," he said. "I cannot tell you how good it is to see your face. There have been times in this past year when I despaired of ever seeing it again."

"Oh, come now," Alex said. "I know you were in France for much of that time, but surely it wasn't that bad."

"The climate is so damp in the plain, and those châteaux are so drafty. They may be larger than our plantation houses, but I will take the humbleness of Mepkin any day," Laurens said with another grin.

"Humble? Mepkin? Although I have yet to have the privilege of seeing your childhood home, I understand that it boasts four grand parlors, a ballroom, and more bedrooms than one can count on the fingers of one's hand."

Laurens smiled wryly. "Said the gentleman who has been living in General Schuyler's mansion for the past half year. What is the house called? The Pastures? It sounds positively rustic."

"If only!" Alex said. "At first Eliza and I attempted to establish a residence downriver in New Windsor, but I was reassigned and she was forced to return to the Pastures. I was able to rejoin her there only briefly, and then we decamped to De Peyster's Point just across the river from General Washington's headquarters"—he pointed at an invisible spot north and east of them, lost in the mists cloaking the river— "and then once again circumstances forced us to return to Albany. Eliza has told me she refuses to move again, until it is into a house of our own, and for good."

"My word!" Laurens laughed. "It seems you have traveled nearly as much as I have. I cannot tell you," he added in a more earnest tone, "how much it grieved me to miss your wedding to the fair Miss Schuyler. We are of an age when we could have many more bachelor adventures together, and I am almost jealous of her new hold over you. But you are such a well-met pair, I cannot help but be happy for you. Her sensibility will rein in your passionate nature, and her beauty will counteract your hideous visage."

Alex laughed at his friend's joke even as he grimaced inwardly, thinking how his passion and Eliza's sensibility had clashed so recently. He knew that Laurens was right, and that he needed someone to remind him that his responsibilities required more than enthusiasm. They required steadiness as well, and he knew that Eliza encouraged that quality in him. Nevertheless, he did not relish another clash of the kind they had before he left.

Aloud, though, all he said was, "I look forward to the day when I shall see you as happily married as I am, to a girl equally as sensible as Eliza, if not quite her equivalent in beauty."

"Let's hope not!" Laurens scoffed. "I cannot imagine the woman who could put up with such a selfish hedonist as I, nor can I imagine what I would do with a wife!"

Alex guffawed. "And what would a lady do with the likes of you!"

"But come now," Laurens continued. "Let us hurry to headquarters so you can present yourself to General Washington, and then we can get down to the serious business of drinking!"

"Indeed," said Alex. "Perhaps it is easiest for me to find you there. I have to take the coach, which does not seem to be in evidence."

"What? Do you not want to ride your horse?"

"My—" Alex looked up and down the wharf, but there was only one other horse visible, tied up farther down the rail. It was a well-built animal, though, it was no horse he'd ever ridden before.

When he turned back to Laurens, however, his friend's face was beaming, and he was nodding at the beautiful chestnut stallion nearer to hand. Still, Alex could not quite believe what seemed to be happening.

"I-is this not your horse?" he stuttered.

"It was until you stepped off that gangplank. I saw it two years ago when I was down at Mepkin. It was just a yearling then, but its russet tones reminded me a little of you. I told my father that if it fulfilled the potential it showed then, I should like to present it as a gift to you. When I arrived back home and saw how fine an animal it had become, I almost regretted my generosity. It is not the largest horse my father has ever bred, but it may well be the most beautiful."

Alex was shocked. "I do not know what to say. It is perhaps the finest gift anyone has ever given me since Governor Livingston brought me to North America."

"Well then. I know not who will prevail in the coming battle, but I do know who the handsomest pair of officers will be. And as my father said when he taught me to play cricket, it is not whether you win or lose, but how you look when you take the field."

"Do not jinx it," Alex said, unwilling to take his eyes from the gorgeous horse in front of him. "I have not received my commission yet."

IT WAS SOME three hours before Alex actually met with the commander in chief of the Continental forces. There had been the new horse to see to, for one thing—Alex could stable it with the army's other horses, but he had to make sure that the grooms knew this was a private animal, and it was not to be requisitioned by some scurrilous lieutenant who might fancy a finer ride than the war-weary mounts the army provided. Alex wanted to freshen up as well and change out of his damp shirt. Then, too, Laurens refused to let him out of his sight until he had shared at least one tankard of ale with him: "It will calm you," he said jovially, "and besides, General Washington will be in his office till late. There is no danger of missing him."

The sun was low on the hills to the west of Newburgh when Alex finally made his way to Hasbrouck House, a one-and-half-story Dutch stone farmhouse that had been provided to General Washington. An orderly waved Alex through to an inner vestibule, where a closed door made of heavy, plain maple planks separated him from his fate. He took a deep breath and knocked with a rap he hoped was not terribly intrusive, but still confident and decisive.

A pause, long enough that Alex considered knocking again. Then a gruff voice called: "Enter."

Alex pushed the door open carefully. He had not been in this office before, and he didn't know what lay on the other side. Heaven forbid he should slam the door into General Washington's desk and start the meeting off on the wrong foot.

The low-ceilinged room beyond was smaller than the general's office in Morristown, and much more rustic, but the desk was still some feet away, and after entering the room and closing the door behind him, Alex placed himself before the general, and waited for him to look up from his papers.

Washington was well-known to make his subordinates wait on him for sometimes twenty or thirty minutes while he finished a routine task, but he was apparently not in the mood for such theatrics today. He stowed his pen immediately and indicated a ladder-back chair opposite his desk. "Colonel Hamilton. Please, have a seat."

Alex resisted the urge to stick his fingers in his ears to see if they were stuffed with wax. In the five years Alex had worked for him, Washington had never said "please" to Alex, let alone invited him to "have a seat."

However, as the general continued to stare at him expectantly, Alex nervously made his way to the chair and eased himself into it, as if it might collapse beneath his weight. The rush caning was a little on the thin side and the back was uncomfortably straight, but nevertheless it held.

"I have reviewed the document you placed into my hands at our last meeting," Washington said. As always, his words sounded formal. But they also sounded so much like him, that to anyone familiar with the general, it was hard to take offense. Alex was not given to flights of fantasy where his commander in chief was concerned, but on the rare moments he had allowed himself to imagine Washington as a boy, or alone with his wife, Martha, he could not picture "George" choosing his words with anything less than meticulous care.

The document Washington referred to was a letter Alex had written, but in the general's voice rather than his own. Alex had written hundreds of such documents during the course of the war to which the general had affixed his signature. The only difference was that all those other letters—letters sending men into battle or pulling them away from it, to the gallows or giving them their freedom—had been written at Washington's direction, whereas this one was entirely of Alex's creation. Which is to say, after years of asking the general to give him command of his own battalion, he had simply written the promotion into existence.

It was an ultimatum of sorts, and Washington knew it. If he didn't sign, there would be no more business as usual. Alex had long since served his tour of duty and could resign at any moment. As Eliza had said, he would forfeit his salary and his pension, but there was no legal preventative to his departure.

Alex knew it was a bold move, which is why he'd delivered the paper right before he went away for leave. Washington did not like insubordination or cockiness, however he admired self-determination. He'd had a month to stew over it and cool whatever anger he might have felt when he'd first read it. Alex had taken the fact that he hadn't received a letter telling him that his services were no longer required as a good sign. Nevertheless, the general displayed a consummate poker face. He could be preparing to promote Alex to lieutenant general or throw him in the brig.

"You are aware that General Cornwallis has quartered nearly nine thousand British and German troops at Yorktown?" asked the general, leaning forward and placing his hands flat on the desk.

Alex wasn't sure what to say. He himself had passed on this intelligence to the general some time ago. He nodded, then stirred himself to speak. One did not merely nod at the commander in chief of the Continental army.

"Yes, Your Excellency," he said, employing the honorific he always used when he addressed Washington.

"After extensive discussions with General Lafayette and Count de Rochambeau, I have come to the conclusion that if we can pin Cornwallis's forces in the city, we can cut him off from escape. We will then be able to starve them into submission or bombard them to oblivion. Either way, Cornwallis will have to surrender. The British forces will be decimated, and the war—in effect—over," said Washington proudly. The general relaxed his shoulders a bit, as if the war had already been won.

Alex held his neck unnaturally stiff to keep himself from nodding again. Having written most of the general's correspondence on these matters himself, he was intimately acquainted with the deliberations. "Indeed, Your Excellency. I couldn't agree more."

Washington nodded, and a rare smile crossed his face. "Lafayette has seven thousand French and American troops in position outside the town to keep Cornwallis's men from escaping farther inland."

Alex grunted in agreement.

The general continued. "Additionally, Admiral de Grasse has agreed to provide three thousand troops from the West Indies. This would give us a numerical advantage but not an overwhelming one, especially since de Grasse's men will be at great risk when they disembark from his ships. It is therefore imperative that our own forces join the fray, though it would be a difficult march of some four hundred and fifty miles. We have two thousand men of our own, and Rochambeau has agreed to put his seven thousand troops under my command. Obviously, we cannot make nine thousand men invisible, but the count and I have devised a maneuver that we think will disguise our true intentions from the British."

Washington kept a placid expression, so it took Alex a moment to realize the general was making a joke. He allowed himself a smile. "May I inquire as to the nature of the maneuver, Your Excellency?"

"We will split the men into multiple units and march them in parallel tracks some tens of miles apart. If British spies do catch wind of us, they are more likely to conclude that the troops are being deployed to multiple locations rather than heading toward a single target." Washington tapped the battlefield maps that were laid out on the desk.

Alex immediately saw the beauty of the plan, but he also had reservations. "Isn't it risky splitting our forces up, sir? Won't they be more vulnerable to attack?"

Washington frowned, and crease lines deepened across his weathered cheek. "They would be, if the British had a large army within striking position. But they have no forces that can reach us before we will have accomplished our mission."

Alex had to admit that the plan was a stroke of genius. Though he had never said so to anyone other than Laurens, he had often had concerns about Washington's military savvy. There was no doubt about the man's leadership capabilities—not to mention his ability to inspire both his troops and the general populace. George Washington was a fine specimen of a man, tall, strapping, with a commander's profile and confidence. He would make an excellent head of state one day—governor of Virginia, perhaps, or maybe, if the thirteen colonies could work out their differences and consent to a centralized government, a prime minister, or if things should work out another way (God forbid!), a king.

However, while unquestionably brave, Washington's military strategies had always struck Alex as unnecessarily blunt. This maneuver, however, was inspirational. Alex could feel himself salivating to be a part of it. The British were no cowards, but they would be fools to put up a protracted fight— which would only result in hundreds, perhaps thousands, of casualties—and they would still lose.

Was the general telling Alex all this in order to make him that much more grateful for his promotion, or to make a denial of his field command that much more painful? Alex didn't think Washington was quite so base, but he was well aware that the man despised violations of protocol and could hold a grudge.

"When do you anticipate the movement will begin?" he said now, in a cautious voice.

"The troops should be ready by August. We need to wait for Mr. Church's shipment to arrive before we depart." He gave Alex a curt nod.

It was typical of General Washington not to confirm with Alex that the arms deal had been successfully negotiated. It was possible that he had received word by some other channel—perhaps General Schuyler had dispatched a courier—but more likely he had simply assumed that Alex had completed his assigned task. It was not that Washington had unquestioned faith in Alex or General Schuyler, although he certainly believed in their abilities. It was more a case of belief in himself. He had ordered something be done, and would assume that it had been accomplished unless otherwise informed.

"Well then," General Washington said. "I believe you are fully versed in the plans. I will dismiss you so can prepare for departure."

Alex was so used to standing when Washington said he was dismissed that he immediately rose from his chair and turned for the door. Still, he couldn't believe it. The general had turned down his request for a command of his own! And still expected Alex to accompany as an aide-de-camp! It was not to be borne! He had to say something, but what? Before he could protest, however, the general had more to say.

"Colonel Hamilton?" General Washington called after him. "Aren't you forgetting something?"

Alex turned to see the general holding out a sheet of paper. He could have sworn he saw the tiniest smile playing around the corners of the older man's mouth. "Your Excellency?"

General Washington merely shook the page at him. Alex crossed to the desk and took it. To his surprise, it was the very letter he had written in the general's name, promoting him to field commander. And there, at the bottom, was Washington's signature. Alex had signed the name himself so many times that he knew it better than his own. He stared at it as if it might be a forgery, but it was indisputably real.

"Your Excellency," he said again. "I don't know what to say. Thank you."

"You can thank me by driving the redcoats off American soil in three months' time. For now, I suggest you get acquainted with your men. Those New York regiments have something of the frontier spirit about them. You will have to inspire them to follow you, or risk losing their respect and loyalty."

There was undeniable pride in General Washington's voice, and Alex had to take a moment before he could answer. It was a long time coming, and Alex soaked it up.

"I have your example to guide me," he said finally, then bowed and walked from the room, holding the piece of paper tightly in hand.

A battle command at last! Glory and bloodshed would be in his future! He could hardly wait.

7

———⧫———

The Home Front

The Schuyler Mansion
Albany, New York
July 1781

Spring was over (and so were the berries, to the relief of everyone's waistlines). High summer was always slow to come to upstate New York, but when it did arrive, the heat could be as oppressive as a Maryland or Virginia bayou. The advent of summer also brought a slew of letters from the front lines, letters that Eliza read and reread again and again, lingering on the effusive declarations of love from her absent husband. She wrote back with the profusions of forgiveness he desperately asked for, as well as admonishments that he take good care of himself so he could return to her before long. She told him she was proud of him for having secured his long-desired command. He wrote back that he was grateful for her strength at the news, and that he could not wait to fly back to her arms as soon as the war was ended.

But the war was not over, not yet, and since Albany was a riot of mists and odors raised by the heat, Eliza and her sisters avoided town as much as possible. Despite its name, the Pastures was perched on a hill above the fields, and its wide entrance hall caught the easterly breezes and kept the main body of the house relatively cool.

The front parlors and front bedrooms also stayed cool, and though Mrs. Schuyler's old Dutch soul felt that it was "gauche" for a lady to sleep in a bedroom facing the road, practically "risqué," even she consented to move to an east-facing room after three sweltering nights when the mercury refused to dip below eighty degrees, and nipped at one hundred during the day. This being Mrs. Schuyler, she insisted on taking her bedstead with her, despite the presence of a perfectly comfortable bed in what was, after all, the Schuylers' finest guest room, which had slept many a general and governor. (Perhaps that was the issue. Though Mrs. Schuyler would never say so out loud, Angelica speculated to Eliza and Peggy that their mother could not abide the idea of laying her body where a man who wasn't her husband had slept.)

By now the house had become a women's abode. General Schuyler had gone to the Schuylers' summer residence near Saratoga, both to oversee its ongoing reconstruction after its burning by General Burgoyne in 1775, and to attend to the replanting of the estate's orchards and fields, from which much of the family's income derived. He had initially refused to go, saying that he needed to be close to his wife during her lying-in, but Mrs. Schuyler had shooed him away, saying that he had done nothing but fret during her eleven previous childbirths. She did not expect that to change for her twelfth. "Nature will take its course as it always does," she said, "and Providence shall see to the child's well-being or call her home as God wills."

"Her?" General Schuyler had asked softy. "How can you know?"

"I have been with child enough to know. Your sons were feisty, even irksome, during their time with me. But your daughters are demure even before they are born."

"Demure?" General Schuyler said with a laugh. "Are we talking about the same daughters?"

Mrs. Schuyler patted his knee, pretending to be annoyed. "Like kittens," she said. "And this one has been the easiest of all. Were she not so big, and were I yet a younger woman, I imagine that I would still be up and about supervising the servants and children."

"Put any such thought out of your head at once!" General Schuyler commanded, but in a soft, even worried voice. "If anyone has earned her rest, it is you."

Mrs. Schuyler patted his knee again, gently this time, and sent him off to husband his crops. Alex was also gone by then, and John Church had traveled to Boston to see to his mysterious importing business, accompanied by Stephen Van Rensselaer, who was attending classes at Harvard University. Aside from the servants, the oldest male in the house was sixteen-year-old Johnny. In another house, he might have strutted his stuff a bit, but in the absence of General Schuyler he knew his place, and deferred to his sisters and mother in all matters of household organization. He and thirteen-year-old Philip Jr., who seemed immune to the sweltering heat, spent most of their time playing soldier, "patrolling the perimeter" of the Schuyler lands, as Philip put it, armed with a pair of matchlocks and trailed by eight-year-old Ren (whose request for a rifle of his own had been roundly refused). Though they never caught wind of any redcoats, they often returned home with a brace of hares or grouse to liven up the dinner table.

In the absence of their menfolk, the sisters fell back into girlhood routines, albeit with a more mature bent. Angelica had once been wont to read racy French novels and regale her sisters with titillating stories of how "Continental women" comported themselves. Now she perused French broadsheets to educate herself about America's strongest ally, and went so far as to declare that she believed that one day soon the French would follow the American example and throw off the yoke of monarchy.

Peggy glanced at the same papers. Her French was abysmal but it didn't matter, since she was largely concerned with the illustrations of the latest fashion trends. A few years earlier she would have harangued her mother or father with requests for this or that brocade or jacquard or watered silk, but even if their father hadn't been absent and their mother abed, it was unlikely she would have asked for anything so profligate. Even she knew the end of the war was in sight, and every last cent of the young nation's resources had to be channeled into the victory effort (though she did direct her maid to alter the fit of several of last year's dresses to reflect the changes in hemlines and necklines).

Eliza, ever the practical middle sister, continued the fund-raising and fabric drives that had made her simultaneously the most admired and most dreaded girl in the capital region (Elizabeth Ten Broeck, a Van Rensselaer by birth, and aunt to Stephen—which is to say, as filthy rich as filthy rich can get—declared that thanks to Eliza's constant "alms-gathering" she and her daughters were dressing in "cotton and rags"). Eliza threw herself into the work, not least to distract herself from thoughts of Alex and his looming battle. By now, though, most of what could be gathered had been gathered, and it was unlikely that anything Eliza procured (besides money, that is) would make it to the front before the fighting was over.

She felt a bit at a loss as to how to contribute until one day, as she was preparing to leave Mrs. Anne Bleecker's house with the latter's monthly pledge, she heard a small, bright voice singing in one of the parlors. She peered in, where she beheld a girl of nine or ten sitting upright on a tufted chair, singing to an otherwise empty room. Her voice was sweet and pure and sad, and Eliza remained hidden at the edge of the door, lest she interrupt the girl's recital. At length, a hand on her arm drew her attention. It was Mrs. Bleecker, who guided her to an adjacent parlor.

"I can see you are curious about the latest member of

our household. Her name is Anne. She is the daughter of our neighbors that were, the Carringtons."

"That were?" Eliza said in confusion. "Did they move away? And if so, why did they leave such a sweet girl behind?"

"For the only reason parents would leave their children behind—six of them in total. Corporal Carrington perished in service of his country at Kings Mountain in South Carolina, and poor sweet Josephine—her parents were French, the dear thing—succumbed to fever near the end of last winter."

"An orphan!" Eliza said, immediately thinking of Alex.

Mrs. Bleecker nodded. "Such kin as they have were unable to take in any but the two youngest. Mr. Bleecker and I could not sit idly by while the rest disappeared into the streets or the sticks, and took in Anne early this spring. God help her older siblings, for we know not what happened to them. Even in her sadness it has been a joy to have a young child in the house again, with our sons and daughters grown or . . ."

Mrs. Bleecker's voice broke off, and Eliza took her hand. Her host had lost her only two sons in the war as well.

"You are doing the Lord's work," Eliza said sympathetically. "Colonel Hamilton was fostered in a similar fashion after his mother's death, and no doubt saved from a life of penury. I wonder, though, are there many such children in poor Anne's condition here in Albany?"

"More than you realize. Thousands of men have died in service to the great cause of independence, many leaving behind wives and children made that much more vulnerable without a man to provide for or protect them. I do not know the total number of children in the Albany area who have been orphaned by the war, but I would imagine that there are some scores of them. And Albany without even a foundlings home to take them in! It is incumbent upon those of us with the means to make sure that these children, whose parents gave their all for America, do not meet the same sad end."

Once again Eliza reached out and took Mrs. Bleecker's hand. "You are an inspiration to us all. I only wish there was one of you for every Anne out there."

"She is a blessing, as I've said." She was silent for a moment, then continued in a more delicate tone. "And what of you? Do you and Colonel Hamilton plan to start a family sometime soon?"

Eliza felt the color rush to her face. Thankfully, it was a warm day and the parlor stuffy; she hoped her cheeks were already a bit pink.

"Oh, we are both so young, and Alex is so busy with the war. He hasn't even decided what he'll do after it is completed, and thus where we will live. I would not want to cart a child like a piece of luggage as I have done in the past several months. When we are settled . . ."

This time Mrs. Bleecker put her hand on Eliza's.

"My dear, if age has taught me one thing, it's that, in the matter of children, one is never 'settled.' They will always find a way to upset the most well-managed domestic routine. And yet, even in the most chaotic of times, one always finds a way of making do."

"Speaking of which," Eliza said, standing, "I should be getting home. Mrs. Schuyler is very close to her own time, and she grows unsettled when she does not know where all seven of her children are."

She took her leave hastily, but as she passed through the front hall, she peeked into the opposite parlor again. Anne had finished singing and now sat with a book in her hand, turning pages with the idleness of one who is not reading but merely glancing at old familiar words, as if to remind herself of a favorite world but not sink too deeply in it.

"She wants for playmates her own age," Mrs. Bleecker said. "When hostilities cease and regular schooling resumes, we will arrange for her to study with some of her peers. But until then I'm afraid she has to make do with two middle-aged companions."

Eliza stared at the girl a moment longer, thinking in part of her orphaned husband and in part of the family she hoped they would have together, then took her leave and began the long walk back to the Pastures. It was not too far a distance—perhaps four miles—but she did not want to overtax herself in the heat. As she leisurely made her way along the well-packed soil, her mind began to race ahead, faster than her feet. How odd that her mother's pregnancy had not made her think of children of her own, whereas a single comment from a family acquaintance awakened slumbering feelings she had not realized she possessed.

The truth was, she and Alex had hardly spoken of starting a family, even as they enthusiastically did all they could to start one (ahem). But they had not yet been blessed, and perhaps that was a blessing in itself for now. Eliza knew Alex's own childhood had not been happy. He had never said as much, but Eliza suspected that he doubted if he was temperamentally suited for fatherhood. He was an exacting man and a perfectionist, a trait that endeared him to an authoritarian like General Washington (when it wasn't annoying him), but did not exactly inspire love from one's children. Respect maybe, but not love. And Eliza knew Alex wanted to be loved by his children, not because he was their father, but because he was lovable.

And she? What did she want? Her primary experience of motherhood had been through Mrs. Schuyler. Her mother had been pregnant an astonishing twelve times, and seen no fewer than four of her children, including a set of triplets, die before they could even be baptized. Perhaps even more sadly, she lost three others before their first birthdays. True, seven lived and provided their parents with all the joys that children can impart, but one death for every life? It seemed almost too high a price to pay. She wondered how her mother had endured such loss without succumbing to despair or morbidity. Eliza didn't know if she had that strength.

And if her children-to-be lived? What then? To be responsible for another life, from its food to its clothing to the shaping of its mind. It was an awesome responsibility, and here Eliza was, barely a woman herself. How could she expect to rear and mold a brood of her own, when she was still trying to decide not only who she was, but how she would be in the world? She recognized that motherhood was indeed an awesome profession, but just as fatherhood was not the whole of man's life, she didn't think that raising children should be all a woman concerned herself with either.

She couldn't "take a job" in the conventional sense, but still, there were fulfilling endeavors to which a respectable woman could devote her energies. There were charities—hospitals, schools, orphanages—that were bigger and more complex than many businesses, and did arguably more good in the world. But if she were to saddle herself with children, it might be twenty years or more before she could begin to do any real work of that nature.

And as their less-than-smooth parting indicated, she and Alex still had a lot to learn about who they were—as individuals and as a couple—before introducing children into the recipe. Plus, now that he had his own command on the battlefield, who even knew if she would still have a husband at the end of this war.

"No!" she said out loud, horrified at the very thought, just as she rounded the last hill and the Pastures came into view on its promenade. "Alex will come home to me. He *must* and he will. And children can wait for now."

Even as she spoke, however, she saw a boy running toward her. She recognized him as Lew, who worked in the barn with his father, Llewellyn, a Welshman who served as the estate's ostler.

"Miss Eliza! Miss Eliza! Come quick!"

"Whatever is the matter, Lew?" Eliza said, catching up the panting boy.

"Miss Dot sent me! She said to fetch you as soon as I saw you!"

Dot was calling, and it could only mean one thing. For Dot was not only a ladies' maid but a handy midwife, who had brought all fourteen of Catherine Schuyler's children to the world.

The baby was coming.

8

War at Last

On the March
White Plains, New York, to Yorktown, Virginia
September 1781

The 1st and 2nd New York Regiments, along with a pair of patchwork Connecticut divisions, set off for Yorktown, Virginia, on September 7, under the command of Lieutenant Colonel Alexander Hamilton. The three-week march was grueling, even for the mounted officers. Ten-hour days in scorching heat, the sun beating down on their tricorne hats and turning them into little furnaces atop the soldiers' heads, dense wool coats draped around shoulders and arms growing heavier and heavier with each step. The occasional cloudburst brought rain and brief respite from the heat, but any relief was offset by the burden of marching in sodden clothing through muddy roads churned to slurry by hundreds of booted feet.

Some of the men tried to ease their load, doffing their caps or removing their coats and tying them to their packs, but Alex ordered them to don them again. As a self-made man, he knew the importance of appearances. He kept the brass buttons of his coat secured from waist to neck and his hat firmly screwed in place. If you looked the part, most people would assume you *were* the part, and he wanted any news of advancing Continental troops to be tinged with awe rather than derision. Whether the stories reached the ear of either General Washington or General Cornwallis was immaterial, the accounts had to be glowing. He wasn't just marching to battle, after all. He was marching into history, into glory.

I am so proud of you, Eliza had written in her latest missive, when she heard the news of his command. His brave Betsey, whose only resentment was that he had kept his ambition from her instead of allowing her to share in his dreams for glory. *I will come back to you, my love. I promise,* he had written in return.

Alex was mounted on his brilliant new chestnut stallion, christened Mepkin in homage to the friend who had gifted it. While as an officer he didn't have to carry a pack, ten hours in the saddle, even with breaks for water or food, can leave the legs feeling like jelly, and he was developing tender spots in parts of his body that he didn't like to think about. But when the army made camp each evening, he eschewed whatever cabin or house had been requisitioned for the night, giving his place to one of the many soldiers who had developed fever or some other ailment during the day's march. Instead, he slept under the open sky like the enlisted men.

In the morning, he washed himself with a bucket of frigid well water, shaved with a dry razor, and donned his uniform, smoothing the wrinkles as much as possible. He made the rounds of his men as they ate their breakfast, inquiring after their blisters and sunburns and passing along whatever news he might have received overnight about the soldier's hometown. He himself ate only a few pieces of jerked beef or venison with hardtack, and only on horseback, after the march was underway.

No one had told him to do this, and certainly it was not the kind of thing he had ever seen General Washington do. Washington inspired by his regality, his air of unapproachable greatness. He was well over six feet tall and nearly fifty years of age, and a wealthy country squire to boot: He could get away with such a performance. Alex was just in his twenties, and a nameless orphan from the West Indies. If he was going to win his men's respect and loyalty, he was going to have to do it by caring about them as individuals as well as soldiers. That he would not give any order that might put them in harm's way without first considering the very real lives that would be affected by his decision.

Seventeen days into the march, one of his men, a Private Baxter, caught his foot in a wagon rut and turned his ankle quite severely. It was impossible to tell if it was broken or simply badly sprained, but in either case Baxter was unable to walk. After more than two weeks on the road, it would have been onerous for Alex to demand his exhausted men carry Baxter in a stretcher. It was not yet noon, and there were still six hours of hard marching ahead. Without hesitating, Alex ordered that Baxter be put on Mepkin, and he marched the rest of the day on foot with his enlisted men.

Alex remained at the head of the column, and though he replied jocularly to the occasional familiar comment from one of his soldiers, he also maintained military jargon, reminding them that he was still their commander. It was exactly the right balance. If his men had been guardedly respectful in their regard to him before, open affection was in their eyes when he made his usual rounds. When they addressed him as "Sir" or "Colonel," it wasn't begrudgingly, but with genuine respect.

Two days later, exhausted but feeling more prepared for the coming battle than he had at the start, Alex and his men reached Williamsburg, where Washington and Rochambeau would make the final preparations for the siege at Yorktown. Alex saw his soldiers to their temporary barracks, then cleaned himself up and reported to headquarters.

It was early in the afternoon, and he'd only marched two hours that day, so he felt comparatively fresh. Still, he was extremely grateful to accept his first cup of coffee in three weeks, as well as several thick slices of bread that didn't taste of ash or mold. He had just finished a second slice when he was summoned into Washington's office.

General Washington sat at his desk with two other men. Alex recognized the first as the Count de Rochambeau, a distinguished man in his middle fifties in the dark wool jacket of the French army. The third man was similarly attired, but it wasn't until he turned his head toward the door that Alex realized it was his old friend, the Marquis de Lafayette.

"My dear Colonel Hamilton," Lafayette said genially but respectfully. Though the two had spent many an evening making their way through a bottle or three of fine French wine, Lafayette was greeting him in the presence of Washington and Rochambeau with the deference due his rank. Still, his handshake was warm, and the look in his eye promised a more rousing welcome at some more convenient moment. Alex greeted General Rochambeau next, and then General Washington, who once again bid him to take a seat. Only then did he notice a large map spread out on a low table placed between the chairs.

I could get used to this, Alex thought. *But I probably shouldn't.*

There was some brief talk about Alex's march and Washington's opinions on Admiral Grasses's *Ville de Paris*, a 120-gun French warship. Then without preamble, Washington said, "We have been discussing final plans for the assault of Yorktown."

Alex sat up straighter. It was unseemly to be excited by the prospect of battle, yet he couldn't help it. He felt his heart beat as if someone had just dealt him a hand of poker, and a peek discovered he held a brace of aces.

"General Cornwallis sought to evacuate his troops by sea, but the French have managed to thwart the attempt. Some seven thousand British troops are for all intents trapped behind their battlements."

Alex wanted to yell in triumph, "We have them!" but he contented himself with turning to General Rochambeau and saying, "The American people will learn of the great contributions the French made to their liberation."

Rochambeau made a funny face at this rather formal pronouncement. "Any enemy of the British navy is a friend of the French," he said drily.

Alex allowed himself to crack a smile at the count's witticism.

"We have concluded," Washington continued, "that the only way to complete a second trench that will allow us a cannon within range of the British position is to take redoubts numbers nine and ten, which protect the main body of their troops in Yorktown." He indicated the forts' positions on the map. "The British have fortified them with earthen walls and a timber palisade. Our engineers tell me we could blast through the walls fairly easily, but moving the cannon into position would alert Cornwallis to our intentions. We must prevent his troops from falling back into Yorktown proper, protracting the siege. Therefore, we have concluded that the redoubts will have to be stormed on foot, and the palisades toppled with axes. The forts are not heavily manned. We will suffer casualties, undoubtedly, but we should be able to take them with minimum loss of life. Once the positions have been secured, we will dig our second parallel here, place our cannon within range of Yorktown—"

"And then we will blast the British to hell," Rochambeau interjected. "Forgive me for interrupting, General," he said to

Washington. "The thought of a British defeat gets my pulse racing."

Mine too, Alex thought, though that wasn't quite correct. He had no great animus against the British. He just didn't think they had any business ruling a country three thousand miles away from their own, a group of colonies that was, moreover, ten times larger than the mother country. It was the thought of battle itself that excited him.

"It has been decided," Lafayette said now, "that the assault on redoubt nine will be a French column under the able command of our German ally, Lieutenant Colonel Wilhelm von Zweibrücken. The assault on redoubt ten will be by the First and Second New York infantry units, and the Fifteenth Connecticut."

Alex kept his face neutral. "My men have arrived in fine form, General. They are ready for the challenge."

"Ah yes," Lafayette said, squirming slightly in his chair. "About that."

Alex peered at his old friend. "Yes, General?" he said in as formal a voice as he could muster.

"It has been decided that in order to foster a greater spirit of camaraderie between the French and American forces, the First and Second New York and the Fifteenth Connecticut will be commanded by my aide, Major Jean-Joseph Sourbader de Gimat."

Alex stared at his friend, unable to believe this turn of events. Lafayette knew how important the opportunity to command a battlefield assault was to him. Alex also knew that Lafayette had not awarded command of the assault to Major Gimat in an effort to build "camaraderie" between American and French forces. He had done it for the same reason that Washington had given the command to Alex: because his longtime aide had insisted that he, too, be given a chance for glory before the war was over. On one level, Alex appreciated the loyalty Lafayette was showing to his officer. But as a friend, he felt utterly betrayed.

"I was under the impression," Alex said tightly to Washington, fighting to keep his voice calm, "that when you asked me to lead the First and Second New York and the Fifteenth Connecticut, it was not just on a march from New York to Virginia."

Washington's face showed no reaction to the bitterness in Alex's words. "General Lafayette makes the case that even after we take the redoubt, the ensuing siege could last some weeks. During that time, American and French forces will be quartering together and often skirmishing with the enemy. It is important that every single soldier fighting for the American cause feels that he is a member of one army and not two, as it were. That there be no unnecessary divisions between people fighting for the cause of freedom and mercenaries fighting merely for a salary."

"There is not a single American soldier," Alex said, turning back to Lafayette, "who is unaware that the French grievance against the British is many generations older than our own, and compounded by the two countries being separated by the few miles of the English Channel rather than by the vastness of the Atlantic Ocean. We welcome the French here with unqualified affection and, as you so aptly put it, 'camaraderie.'"

"That may be," Lafayette said. "But whether the war is won or lost, after it is over the Americans know that our French troops will go back to the far side of the Atlantic, while they will stay here. We need to erase that thought from their minds."

"And you think that putting four hundred patriotic Americans under the command of an officer whom they have never met and whose motives and, dare I say, abilities are unknown to them is the best way of doing that?" he asked, his voice rising.

"I assure you," Lafayette said, an edge coming into his voice for the first time, "that Major Gimat is entirely qualified to lead this assault, else I would not have entrusted the command to him."

Alex checked himself. He knew he had come close to going too far. Whatever Lafayette's reasoning behind promoting Gimat, Alex knew his friend would not risk one of his officer's lives merely for the sake of giving him a shot at glory, let alone the lives of hundreds of soldiers and the chance to end the war.

"I apologize if I seemed to suggest otherwise," he said in a tense voice. "Nevertheless, you must know that it is what my men will be thinking." He summoned a deep breath and spoke before Lafayette or one of the other two generals could answer. "I have spent the past three weeks on the road with these soldiers," he said passionately, turning to General Washington. "I have marched with them, eaten with them, bunked with them. I have gotten to know their wives' and children's names, their brothers and sisters and mothers and fathers. They have learned how this country took me in and gave me the chance to better my lot in life in spite of the fact that I had neither name nor fortune.

"These men know that I go to battle because *I believe in the United States of America*. In what it offers both to its natural-born citizens and to the downtrodden across the globe, who see the New World as a place where they can make a fresh start and improve themselves, regardless of rank. And that, Generals, is why these men fight. Not just for their freedom, but for their country, and for what it offers them and their children and their children's children. They will not share that bond with a French interloper, let alone one they have never met, but they share it with me. And that sense of kinship may well be what makes the difference on the day of the assault."

General Washington listened to Alex's impassioned speech with his usual stony, unreadable face. There was a long moment of silence. Then, "I have heard each of your arguments and see merit in both of them," he said. "I will consider them overnight and give you an answer in the morning."

Alex knew that Washington was merely stalling. He was not a rash man, but there was no real considering to be done. He had only to choose if he was going to reward a fellow patrician in Lafayette, or a faithful subordinate in himself.

"With all due respect, General, I need an answer now," Alex pressed, as courteously as he could.

Washington blinked. From such a reserved man, it was the equivalent of a gasp. Then Alex could have sworn he saw a bit of a smile flicker over the man's lips. "Well then, Colonel. You may lead the assault."

Alex was stunned to silence. Though he believed every word he just said, he hadn't thought they would have any effect. Washington was a man of his class, and his generosity rarely extended itself to the plebeians. He recognized talent and ability, but only to the degree that their possessor was useful to him. All other things being equal—and Alex had no doubt that Gimat had studied as faithfully at Lafayette's side as Alex had studied at Washington's—he would always side with gentry against the common people.

"You have earned this, Colonel Hamilton," Washington said now. "With me, and with your men. I trust that you will lead them, and the Continental army, to victory." He paused and continued with a hint of a smile. "That you are capable of eliciting this kind of quick, resolute decision-making from me helped you win your case."

"Thank you, Your Excellency," Alex said, when he found his voice. He turned to Lafayette. "My condolences to Major Gimat."

Lafayette shrugged, an amused twinkle in his eye. "Ah well. There will always be another war."

9

Hot Towels!

The Schuyler Mansion
Albany, New York
September 1781

"Eliza!" Peggy gasped as her older sister burst into the house. "Thank God you're here! Mama's time is upon her!"

Peggy's face was simultaneously ashen and splotched with color, and her hair hung loose around her face. Eliza didn't think she had seen her sister look so bedraggled since she had first discovered powder. Somehow the sight of Peggy so distressed immediately made her calmer, and she took her younger sister's hand and patted it soothingly. "Lew tells me Dot has been fetched."

"Yes, yes. She says Mama has been very naughty and bore her early pains without telling anyone. She is very close now," said Peggy, wiping her forehead.

"And what does Dot say we should do?" asked Eliza. "Should we call Dr. Van Vrouten?"

Peggy made a face. "Dot says no, she has it handled."

Eliza did not quite understand. She felt a stab of panic. "So what does Dot need from us?"

"Dot says she would like a pot of chocolate."

Eliza blinked in confusion. "Chocolate? For Mother?"

Peggy shook her head. "No. For her. For Dot." When Eliza still looked at her blankly, she continued. "She said if I wanted to be 'useful' I could fetch her a nice pot of chocolate and a bowl of sugar."

Eliza smiled inwardly but kept her face passive. If Dot was ordering the mistress's daughter to make her chocolate, there couldn't be anything too amiss. "Yes, well, why don't you see if you can find Mary or Rosie and get them to help you with that? And some clean towels and hot water. I seem to recall that these are often needed during births."

Peggy still looked frazzled, and the truth was, while their mother had given birth quite a number of times already, the three older girls were still shielded from the messy reality of the endeavor. It was only now that they were allowed to be by their mother's side. The rigors of childbirth, Mrs. Schuyler and Dot believed, were best kept away from the girls' "delicate" constitutions while they were growing up.

Eliza sent Peggy on her way, then hurried upstairs to her mother's room. At first, she panicked because the bed was not just empty but missing, but then she remembered they'd moved Mrs. Schuyler to the front chamber when the hot weather set in. She hurried forward and knocked once before letting herself in.

Since Catherine had never allowed her daughters to assist in one of her deliveries before, Eliza wasn't sure what she expected. But she certainly didn't anticipate peals of laughter coming from the bed.

"Oh, I know!" Catherine Schuyler said merrily. "Philip Jr. really was incorrigible. I tell you I could feel him holding on with his little fists, just refusing to come out. Boys really are the worst! Eliza!" she added in a gay voice. "Do please close the door! This isn't a barn stall."

Eliza paled, but then her mother giggled again. She eased the door closed, then slipped to the side of the room.

"That was such a long lying-in," Dot said, cackling. "I'm not sure who it was harder on—you or General Schuyler. He must have lost half a stone in perspiration!"

"I'll tell you who it was harder on: my beautiful hallway carpet. The general paced so long he practically wore away the flowers in the weave. And that carpet imported all the way from Persia!"

Her mother laughed once more, a relaxed belly chortle the likes of which Eliza had never heard pass her mother's lips. Only then did she notice the brandy decanter and glass on the bedside table. Eliza had filled it herself last night. Now at least a third of the bottle was gone—a feat all the more impressive given the tiny size of the cordial glass beside the table.

"Uh-oh!" her mother said now. "Eliza has spied the evidence of our mischief! Oh well, might as well have another."

Dot refilled the small cordial eagerly.

"Dot," Eliza said as the midwife handed the glass to Mrs. Schuyler. "Do you really think my mother ought to be indulging in spirits at this exact moment?"

In answer, Dot only looked at Mrs. Schuyler, who made a pouting face. A moment later, both women giggled wickedly. Eliza realized it wasn't just her mother who had been indulging. She didn't know if it made her feel better that her mother had drunk less than she'd thought, or that the woman who was to deliver her of her child was somewhat intoxicated as well.

"Now, now, Miss Eliza, don't you fret," Dot said. "The brandy relaxes your mother, which eases the experience. And she and I have done this more times than I can count."

"*I* can count," Mrs. Schuyler said. "We have done this eleven times before. Eleven! And I can promise you that THIS IS THE LAST!"

"At any rate," Dot said, "we have done this so often that we could play a game of skat at this point, and still get the job done."

"Oh!" Mrs. Schuyler said, handing her (empty) glass back to Dot. "One moment, please." Her face twisted into a grimace of pain then. Not agonizing pain, but as if she had stubbed her toe or was experiencing a heavy bout of indigestion.

Eliza had of course heard about the pains of childbirth and knew they could be quite severe, but the whole concept of labor still remained a little vague to her. So, it alarmed her to see her mother in such a state. "Dot, what's happening? Do something!"

By the time she'd asked the question, however, her mother's face had relaxed, and she was nodding at Dot to refill her glass.

"What, Miss Eliza, have you no idea how this works? There's nothing wrong, it's just a contraction."

"A contraction?" Eliza parroted, having no idea what the word meant. All she could think of was the linguistic meaning of the term.

Just then there was a knock at the door, and Angelica slipped in. She looked noticeably flushed and, despite the heat, wore a long, light blue shawl around her shoulders. She carried a tray on which sat a pot of chocolate and a pair of glasses, which she handed to a grateful Dot.

"I am so sorry I wasn't here sooner, Mama. I was visiting at the Van Alens, and Cary"—Lew's brother—"came to fetch me. If you can believe it, I have just ridden three miles in a man's saddle! I galloped right past old Mrs. Vandermeer, who looked as if she might faint!"

Eliza had a flash, then, to a year and a half ago, when she too had ridden in a man's saddle—with Alex sitting behind her. He had rescued her from a coach with a broken axle and, in order to fit her astride his horse, had had to rip her skirt and petticoats so they didn't drown them both in fabric. She told her mother all about it. It had been one of the most romantic moments of their courtship, although, as with almost everything else that happened to them as they were falling in love, it had ended in a fiasco based on a silly misunderstanding.

Oh well, she thought, remembering the feel of Alex's body behind her own. *All's well that ends well.*

She wondered where he was at the moment, and if he was thinking of her, then braced herself for her mother's inevitable scolding at the anecdote she had just shared. Mrs. Schuyler was inflexibly strict when it came to her daughters' decorum in public.

But her mother just shrugged her shoulders. "No matter. You have a husband now, you have no need to worry about your reputation, let alone the condition of your maidenhood! Why, Mrs. Vandermeer's first child was born six months after she married, and he was ten pounds if he was an ounce!"

Eliza almost clapped her hands to her ears. Had her mother actually implied that Mrs. Vandermeer had engaged in the most private marriage ritual before she was actually married?

"M-mama's," she stuttered to Angelica. "Mama has been drinking."

"I *see* that," Angelica said in voice half amused, half stunned.

"Apparently, it relaxes Mama, which, how did you put it, Dot? 'Eases the experience.'"

"Indeed," said Angelica.

Eliza was not at all sure what to say next. "Um, Dot was just explaining to me what a contraction is."

Angelica scowled. "You mean, 'don't' for 'do not'?"

Peals of laughter from Mrs. Schuyler and Dot.

Even Eliza had to smile. "Not exactly. Apparently, it has something do with, um, delivering the child from Mama's womb."

"Exactly!" Dot said. "When the child decides it's time to be born, it knocks very gently at the door of the world. This tells the muscles that surround the mother's womb to constrict in a very specific manner. It's a bit like wringing the water from a towel. You start at one end and squeeze toward the other. So does the womb. Lightly at first, to position the child properly, then more strongly as it pushes toward daylight."

"Now, this is the one area on which Dot and I disagree," Catherine Schuyler chimed in. "I do not think it is the child that tells the mother it is time to be born. I think it is the mother that tells the child it is time to GET OUT!" Mrs. Schuyler directed the last words directly at her abdomen in a voice that, though loud, was suffused with both humor and love.

As if in answer, her face twisted into another grimace.

"What is this?" Angelica asked in alarm, grabbing Eliza's hand.

"It is one of the contractions," Eliza said. "It is, uh, quite normal, and as you can see they do not last long."

"Oh, they'll last much longer soon," Dot said. "They're coming closer together now."

"Yes, she's quite eager now," Mrs. Schuyler said, patting her stomach. "Girls, may I suggest you have one of the footmen—on second thought, make that one of the maids—bring in a pair of chairs and sit yourself rather out of the line of sight. There are a few mysteries that should persist to the end between mother and daughters."

"I'll just get them myself," Eliza said.

"Bring a glass, too," Angelica said. "I think I might join Mother and, uh, Dot in a tipple."

Eliza darted from the room. There were a pair of lightweight cane chairs flanking a walnut sideboard in the hallway, and she carried them back in quickly, then ran back out and grabbed a water glass from the same sideboard. It was a rather large glass for a cordial, but Eliza didn't think anyone was standing on ceremony today. And she was pretty sure she was going to join Angelica in that "tipple."

She hurried back into the room just as her mother was grimacing again. What struck her now was the disconnect between her mother's downturned lips and her calm, if slightly impatient, eyes. She seemed less bothered by the pain than by the protracted nature of the experience, as if she were eager to get back to her regular routine. With another woman, one might have said she was eager to hold her newborn in her arms, but Mrs. Schuyler had not started out particularly affectionate—her husband was "softhearted enough for two," as she often said—and a dozen childbirths had rather sapped what little energy she had for that kind of thing.

The spasm passed as Eliza poured some brandy into the glass and took a seat beside her sister. Dot had moved to the foot of the bed and was washing her hands and forearms in a bucket of steaming water.

Angelica took the glass gratefully. She shifted uncomfortably in her chair, arranging and rearranging her shawl around her bare arms, as if, despite the heat, she were chilly. Despite her fussing, however, the light fabric mostly bunched in the middle of her dress—a high-waisted garment in pale yellow muslin, and daringly loose around the waist. An unusual style for Angelica, who, like Peggy, enjoyed showing off her tiny frame (or at least enjoyed the attention it got her), but Eliza supposed it was too hot for even someone as style conscious as her oldest sister to cinch. Indeed, now that she thought of it, Angelica had been favoring this particular style since the weather had first turned summery six weeks ago.

She nodded toward the bed, where their mother had closed her eyes as if to compose herself. A few beads of sweat had appeared on her forehead, but otherwise she seemed completely tranquil.

"Is this the fate that awaits us now we are married?" Eliza couldn't help but whisper to her sister.

"Only if you are blessed, my dears," said Mrs. Schuyler without opening her eyes. "Only if you are blessed," she repeated, but this time Eliza noticed that her hands were squeezing the bedclothes with whitened knuckles.

Angelica sipped again, then handed the glass to Eliza.

"Have you had any word from Colonel Hamilton?"

Eliza, surprised at this obvious change of subject, took a sip of brandy, then immediately wished she hadn't. The liquor was far too warming for a day like today. She should have asked for some chilled water instead. And the mention of Alex's name made her blood run hot, although it was with fear now, and not anger.

"He wrote me several days ago. He was on the march to Williamsburg, where they will stage the invasion of Yorktown. He should be there by now." She was glad for the letters—as long as they arrived, it meant he was still alive.

Angelica plucked idly at the fabric bunched in her lap. "Do not worry, nothing will happen," she said soothingly to her sister.

Of course, Eliza was worried, but she didn't want to say it out loud and give voice to the fear. "I am rather more worried about what is going on right here," she said, nodding at the bed. Their mother was in the throes of another contraction, which was lasting longer than the previous ones.

"Dot says that childbirth has a way of taking care of itself."

"Not that. I meant the idea of Mama . . . intoxicated. It rather changes my whole picture of her."

Angelica let out a little laugh. "Oh, I like her this way. I think we should conspire to get Mama to drink more often."

If their mother heard them, she didn't answer. Eliza noticed that not only were the contractions lasting longer, they were also occurring more frequently. Dot's hands were busy beneath the sheets, working in trancelike precision. Though neither she nor Mrs. Schuyler spoke, it was clear the two women were in harmony with each other, working to bring another Schuyler sibling into the world.

"But tell me," Eliza said. "Why were you visiting the Van Alens? You have never seemed overly fond of them previously. And why on earth are you wearing that shawl on such a hot day?" she added as her sister fussed yet again with the long wrap of cloth.

Angelica's hands froze as if she had been caught doing something improper. Eliza turned and saw that her sister's face had gone ashen, yet with bright spots of color in the cheeks. She looked back at Angelica's hands again, and thought that they seemed to float slightly above her lap. But it was not that, exactly. No, it was as if Angelica's lap were somehow . . . thicker. Now that she thought about it, she realized Angelica had been eating rather more than usual lately, extra servings of bacon at breakfast (well, who could blame her?) and, more oddly, extra portions of fiddlehead ferns for dinner. Angelica had always hated fiddleheads — said they tasted as bitter as poorly made vinegar. But now she ate them ravenously. It was almost as if she had a . . . craving.

A strange realization came over Eliza. She looked again at Angelica's hands dancing over her thickened lap. Still, she couldn't bring herself to articulate the word, even mentally. Angelica was her sister, after all. Even if she was married now, she still couldn't be . . . Could she?

A heavy sigh came from the bed. "Oh, Eliza, my sweet, sweet, naïve girl. Don't you realize you are going to be an aunt?"

Eliza laughed nervously. "Don't you mean sister, Mama?"

"I am in labor, my dear. I am not ill, nor have I lost my wits, nor my words. I mean aunt."

"Aunt?" Eliza repeated dumbly.

"Oh, for heaven's sake!" Dot said from the opposite end of the bed. "Open your eyes, girl. Your sister is pregnant!"

Eliza turned to Angelica, who was looking at her with wide eyes, her face a mixture of exultation tinged with fear. She nodded to Eliza's unvoiced question, and then the sisters threw their arms around each other in glee, the sound of their merriment filling the already overcrowded bedroom. And as she held her sister's body and felt the soft mound of Angelica's stomach press against hers, all the arguments that she had conjured against children during her walk home evaporated. She realized she, too, longed to be a mother. To raise a family of Hamiltons with her Alex. She hoped that she, too, would soon be similarly blessed.

Dot looked up and found Mrs. Schuyler's eyes. "I must say, I've been in some rather peculiar birthing rooms. But this takes the cake."

Mrs. Schuyler smiled wryly down at her midwife. "You know the Schuyler sisters," she said. "There is no situation so august that they cannot find a way to have a laugh. Why, I bet this new one will be born with a smile!"

10

Into the Fray

The Trenches
Yorktown, Virginia
September 1781

*A*lex made his way slowly up the ranks of men, nodding at this one, shaking hands with that. The setting sun was behind him, bathing his men's faces in golden tones, but every time he stepped close to one of them his shadow would cast the man into darkness. Alex did his best not to think of that as an omen.

"You wanted stories to tell your sons, Enright," he said to one. "We'll give him a good story tonight, I promise!"

"Private Carson! Are you really eating soup at a time like this? Let's hope it's not leaking out a bullet hole a few hours hence!"

"No, Corporal Fromm, we will *not* be taking British scalps as trophies of war. Feel free to pilfer a new pair of boots, though. Those look about as solid as cheesecloth!"

The men—his men—looked at him with sardonic yet resolute expressions, the forced jocularity of soldiers pretending they weren't frightened of the death that might very well be awaiting them in the next hour or two. Their faces were streaked with mud, which Alex had jokingly told them not to wash off. "A paler bunch of boys I never saw! Two weeks in the sun and you still have cheeks like fish bellies! A little mud'll help to hide you from British eyes once the moon is up!"

Like his soldiers, Alex struck a carefree, even comical tone. Unlike them, however, there was no pretense in his façade. Though he knew the action he was about to undertake was extremely dangerous, and that some of his men, and quite possibly himself, would be killed, he felt no fear. He had promised Eliza he would return to her side, and he meant to keep his promise. As far away as he was from her, she was ever in his thoughts and in his heart.

True, he had sought a command because it would help his reputation and further his career, especially if he chose to pursue politics as more than hobby or a purely intellectual pastime. What he hadn't been able to admit, even to himself, was that he *craved* the battlefield, the chance to put his life on the line for something he believed in, and, yes, to take the lives of people who opposed those values.

When he had served under General Washington at Monmouth, he plunged into the fray like an enlisted infantryman rather than take advantage of an officer's prerogative to give orders from afar. In this, he followed Washington's example, but he continued to fight even after the enemy had been routed, risking death time and again as he hunted down fleeing soldiers, until, at last, his horse was shot from him and he narrowly avoided being crushed by the collapsing animal.

He could feel that same battle-lust growing in him now. A few hours ago, he and his soldiers had completed digging the forward trench of the American position — a backbreaking task that took four hundred–plus soldiers the entire day. Alex's unit was comprised of men who understood the engineering needed to fight a battle: sappers who could cut a path through forest and brush with speed, and miners who knew the craft needed to dig a well-made trench.

It was impossible to know what the British troops were up to behind the twenty-foot walls of their palisade, but no cannon balls had come flying over the spiked timber poles of their fort walls as yet. Alex had grabbed a shovel and worked with the rest of his men, in part to inspire camaraderie (he could not use the word without grimacing at the memory of Lafayette's attempt to wrest his command from him), in part because he could not bear the idleness of waiting.

The work was exhausting but his mind had continued to race about chaotically, and as soon as the trench was completed, he led his men in a macabre dance just outside the range of British rifle fire to taunt the enemy with their accomplishment. Drummers beat their skins and pipers blew shrill scales through their reeds, as bone-weary soldiers danced their way into fatigue and out the other side.

He needed to get their minds off the coming action, and off death itself. For ten minutes, they cavorted as though at a barn dance, laughing, jigging, and whooping like, yes, lunatics escaped from an asylum, and though they may well have then looked like the most undisciplined bunch of soldiers ever to don a uniform, now were they calm where before they had been jittery. They sat in little groups of threes and fours, chewing on jerky or hardtack and sharing flasks with brotherly solidarity, their eyes alert even as their limbs were relaxed. They looked ready to charge forward at a moment's notice.

Afterward, when Alex had jumped back into the ditch, he found a scowling Laurens waiting for him. Laurens's presence wasn't a surprise. Alex had requested that his friend be assigned to his unit as one of his three battalion leaders. Laurens had been delayed in his arrival, though, and this was the first Alex had seen him all day.

"Laurens!" he exclaimed. He extended his hand, but his friend ignored it.

"Have you taken leave of your senses?" Laurens demanded.

Alex pulled up short. He stood up straight and squared his unbuttoned jacket on his shoulders as best he could. "Excuse me, Colonel Laurens?" he said in the most imperious voice he could summon in his breathless state. "Have you something to ask me?"

"Have you taken leave of your senses?" Laurens repeated, before throwing in a sneering "*Sir.*"

Laurens's eyes flickered to the men who were jumping down from their dancing into the trench, and Alex knew just what he meant. "You refer to the current bacchanal?"

"Assuredly so. Dancing like coyotes whose fur is on fire in full view of the enemy."

"I assure you that my men were well out of reach of the British, and should they have fired their cannon we would have—"

"Hang the British!" Laurens interrupted him. "Do you want to be stripped of your command before you've even taken the field?"

Alex's eyes went wide. For the first time, he realized just how foolish his actions must have looked to an outsider. Yet he knew, too, that it had been the right thing to do. His men were tired and, though they would never admit it, frightened as well. To storm a twenty-foot palisade with nothing but bayonets, axes, and ladders was as risky a venture as war provided, and some of his men would surely die.

Laurens leaned in close now. His face had softened, as if he had read the thoughts that had raced through Alex's head. "Listen to me, sir," he said. "I have served in the infantry, and I have led it as well. I know the emotions that are coursing through your men right now. This is a momentous night. If we are victorious here, we may well establish unequivocally the freedom and independence of these thirteen states—not colonies but states—and the nation they comprise. But to accomplish that, your men need the brilliant and composed Lieutenant Colonel Alexander Hamilton, not the fierce, fearless, but, dare I say, sometimes foolhardy boy who has made his own way in the world since he was barely into his teens."

Part of Alex heard the wisdom in his friend's words, but part of him was still angry at being called out—and for doing the right thing, no less, regardless of the optics. "I can't help but note that that boy has done rather well for himself," Alex said now, but in a softer tone.

"Indeed, he has: by channeling his anger and energy into mature pursuits, and putting childish fancies behind him." Laurens lowered his voice, but it only increased in intensity. "It is not just these men who need you, Colonel, nor even your country. You have a wife now. You have a future."

Alex allowed an image of Eliza to fill his mind. Eliza in all her beauty and strength and intelligence, shaking her head at his over-exuberance, and he knew Laurens was right. He stood silently for a long moment, letting his friend's sage words sink in. At length, Laurens stepped back and snapped a smart salute.

"Colonel Laurens, sir!" he barked in a grade-A military voice. "Reporting for duty, sir!"

Alex saluted back, yet still couldn't help himself. He grabbed a nearby shovel and tossed it to his friend. "I believe the latrines have yet to be completed, Colonel. See to that, will you?"

A wry grin split Laurens's face. "And to think I gave you a *horse*," he said, then slung the shovel over his shoulder and marched away.

Now, some three hours after Laurens had reined him in, Alex's manic energy was gone, and in its place was a calmer resolve. He was still eager to engage with the enemy, but he knew he would not rush in foolishly or make any rash decisions. War required blood, yes, but cold blood, not hot. He shook his hands and joked with his men, and knew that when the signal came he would organize them into serried ranks and lead them decisively into hellfire. They would fight as soldiers, not barbarians, and if they secured victory they would do so as men, not animals.

As American citizens, he said to himself, *not subjects of a distant crown.*

He came at last to the end of the ranks and ducked into the small command tent that had been established there. Inside waited Laurens and Major Nicholas Fish, with whom Alex had served many times under Washington's command, and a third man whom he never formally met, though he had seen him in the company of Lafayette.

"Major Gimat," he said, extending his hand before the Frenchman could greet him.

"Colonel Hamilton!" Gimat barked, jumping to his feet. "Major Gimat, reporting for duty!" His English was as impeccable as his uniform, though both were tinted French.

He saluted Alex and then, seeing that Alex's hand remained extended, shook it firmly.

"I trust there are no hard feelings about yesterday's shake-up," Alex said in a quieter tone, so that only the Frenchman could hear him.

Gimat allowed himself a smile. "What shake-up, sir? I didn't hear of any shake-up."

"Good man," Alex said. "Now then," he said, turning to include Laurens and Fish. "I want to make sure we're versed on tonight's plan of action. General Rochambeau's sentries are observing the British position. When they see the guard being relieved, they will dispatch runners to alert us. We will have approximately five minutes to prepare the men for the charge, at which point our cannon will unleash a fusillade into the sky. The bombs are for illumination rather than attack. The sappers and miners will dig the last yards forward and then clear two breaches into the enemy pikes. The remaining soldiers will give them exactly four minutes to accomplish their task, then follow after. Once we clear the pikes, we will proceed directly to the palisade. Four ladder teams will scale the wall and lay down protective fire for two advance teams, who will cut through the palisade with axes. And then, well"—he brandished his bayonet-tipped rifle— "we fight."

He turned to Major Fish. He was three years younger than Alex, a rangy, powerful man with a thin, sharp nose and lively eyes. He had fought for the revolutionary cause since his teenage years in the Sons of Liberty, an organization that dated back to before the Declaration of Independence, and whose daring raids helped spur a cowed populace to throw off their overseas oppressor. As pure a patriot couldn't be found in the all the soldiers on this side of the British line.

"Major Fish," Alex said, "it falls to your sappers to lead us onto the field. Are they ready?"

Fish nodded curtly. "Their saws are as sharp as razors and their chains coiled tighter than an angry viper. You have provided us four minutes to take down the enemy's pikes, but I predict we will have them shredded in two. Their axes will knock the enemy's timber walls to the ground like a nor'easter snapping the masts off a hapless whaler."

"I have no doubt that they will. Colonel Laurens, Major Gimat, your men know this is to be a battle fought primarily with blades, not bullets. There will be no time for reloading in such close quarters."

"Nearly all my men have been equipped with bayonets, sir," Laurens replied in a military tone that betrayed no hint of the friends' intimacy. "Those who haven't are well armed with sabers."

"My men are similarly equipped, sir," Gimat followed. "They are aware that we outnumber the enemy and that we can swarm them into submission. I have told them to fight as fiercely as if this were French soil they were defending. If the British have any sense, they will surrender once we take the palisade down, and most of their boys will live to book journeys back to British soil, where they can return to their potato farming."

"I believe it is the Irish who grow the potatoes, Major," Laurens said with a bit of a laugh.

"You say potato, I say *pomme de terre*," Gimat said. "In either case, I am sure it will be only a few years before the British come traipsing on our side of the Channel, and I will once again have the honor of planting redcoats in the ground. Like potatoes," he couldn't help adding.

"One war at a time, Major," Alex said wryly. "Well then. It seems we are ready. Now all we do is wait."

Gimat produced a small silver flask from his jacket. "Perhaps a drink to seal our union. I have grown rather fond of your American whiskey. It tastes like sin and burns like pepper, but it 'gets the job done,' as they say, with remarkable alacrity."

"I can think of no more fitting occasion," Alex said, taking the flask and pulling a slug of fiery liquid into his mouth, then handing it back to Gimat. Gimat passed it to Laurens, and then to Fish, before drinking himself.

Gimat had just finished screwing the lid back on the flask and stowing it when heavy footsteps were heard outside the tent flap. The sentry asked for the password, and a breathless voice answered, "Rochambeau!" A moment later the flap was pulled aside and a young soldier entered.

"The redcoats are pulling their guards off the wall," he panted, not even bothering to locate the commanding officer. "The cannon will be fired momentarily."

Alex nodded at him. "Gentlemen," he said. "To war."

He shook Fish's and Gimat's hands as they headed out of the tent. Laurens grabbed his friend in a bear hug, kissed both of Alex's cheeks, then departed into the night.

Alone in the tent, Alex pulled the latest letter from Eliza from his pocket, one he had committed to memory so that reading it was redundant.

My dearest,

On July 5, Catherine Van Rensselaer Schuyler II entered this world in the presence of myself and Angelica. She is a bright-eyed, strong girl whom we have already christened Kitty, which was the name by which Mama says she was known in her youth. (Tho' I have a hard time imagining anyone having the temerity to refer to Catherine Van Rensselaer Schuyler I as "Kitty"!) To compound the day's joys, Angelica informed me that she and Mr. Church are expecting a child of their own! Oh, Alex, it is happening! The war is ending and a new generation is being born! The first generation to grow up as Americans! It is a privilege almost too great to contemplate. Oh, my darling, I cannot wait till you are here again—till we make our home wherever we make it, in Albany or Boston or New York or Philadelphia! Hurry back to me, and let us lead this nation into the future!

Your loving wife,
Eliza

And *they say I am the eloquent one,* Alex thought as he wiped at his eyes, which had grown curiously moist.

"Must be the dust," he said wryly, though no one was there to hear him. He folded the letter quickly and put it away in his pocket; the words within it had stirred his soul and spurred him forward—he grabbed his bayoneted rifle and an axe leaning against a tent pole and ran outside, ready for battle.

A quick glance showed him that Laurens, Gimat, and Fish had taken their positions at the heads of their respective battalions. Their men were arranged in line on one knee, like so many sprinters at their marks.

"On my command!" he called out.

No one answered him, yet there was a palpable sense of attention—of leather creaking and sabers rattling in their sheaths.

A moment later, the first cannon barked its explosive *BOOM!* and a whistling tore through the night.

BOOM! BOOM! BOOM! BOOM!

One after another, the cannons fired. By the time the fifth went off, the first shell was exploding high in the sky. A flash, as of long, slow, branched lightning, turned night to day, exposing four hundred grim, determined faces.

"Sappers forward!" Alex yelled.

Fish's faint voice answered him, even as the flash flickered out. "Sappers forward!"

Twenty men sprang up as the second shell exploded, puncturing the darkness with another brilliant flash of light. The next several minutes were an eerie spectacle, as darkness fell only to be ripped away again and again. With each flash of light, the sappers seemed to have surged ahead like hungry swarming locusts, breaking into two groups and advancing toward the long line of angled pikes, or abatis, that formed the first line of British defense. *Hop, hop, hop, hop*: Every flash brought the two mobs five feet closer to the thicket of sharply pointed trunks and limbs. Then, as the last shell exploded, Fish's men were upon them, their axes and saws glinting in the final flickering light.

Ribbons of smoke drifted down from the sky, lighter than the renewed darkness, and a smell of burned gunpowder wafted through the air. From across the wide no-man's-land could be heard a bugle on the far side of the palisade.

"We are under attack!" Alex was just able to hear a British voice call. "The rebels are coming!"

We are rebels no longer, Alex thought. *We are Americans.*

He pulled his watch from its pocket and glanced at it in the glow of a shaded lantern. Some two minutes had elapsed since Fish's men had charged forward. He thought of the major's boast that his team would have breached the pikes in that time, and almost considered ordering the charge ahead of schedule. Each minute saved would give the British that much less time to prepare their defenses.

Calm yourself, Colonel, he told himself in his best approximation of Laurens's voice.

The subsequent two minutes were the longest of his life. As the clock ticked its final seconds, he raised his axe high above his head. Again, the sense of tensing bodies and focused attention rippled across the arrayed men. His watch ticked past the 120-second mark.

"Charge!" he screamed, then turned and ran toward the enemy's walls.

The next minutes were a blur. Alex had a vision of himself as from the British palisade, racing forward with his hatchet held above him. Behind him he heard a great roar as nearly four hundred soldiers let out a blood-curdling cry and surged after him. The thud of their boots—even Corporal Fromm's worn-out ones—shook the ground beneath his feet. Rather than throw him off balance, though, they propelled him forward like a swimmer on a wave being hurtled toward shore.

In the ghostly light of the partial moon, a shadowy wall appeared in front of him. In three more steps, he could see it clearly enough to tell that it was the British abatis. The enemy soldiers had cut thousands of branches and slim trunks from nearby forests and orchards, leaving the twigs and leaves attached at one end but sharpening the thicker part into evil-looking points. The branches were netted together and weighed down with rocks so that a spike-fronted wall nearly five feet tall faced the advancing soldiers. Anyone who ran headlong into them would be impaled in a dozen different places. Anyone who stopped to pull the wall apart faced being picked off by enemy rifles.

But Major Fish's sappers had done their work. A pale void opened up in the prickly wall, no more than five feet wide, but large enough so that three men could run through abreast. The confluence was still dangerous, but safer than attempting to try to scale the timber wall piecemeal.

The enemy will concentrate their fire on the breaches, Alex thought.

As if an answer, Alex heard the familiar *pop* of a rifle from about a hundred feet away, and one of the sappers fell to the ground. Alex didn't pause to see if the man were dead or capable of being saved. Helping one man risked losing a dozen, a hundred others. He leapt the body of his fallen compatriot and continued to race forward, joined now by the sappers, who had dropped their saws and pulled out axes. Together with the horde of soldiers behind them, they ran toward the next obstacle, the twenty-foot-tall wall of the palisade itself. The palisade was made of the tree trunks from which the pikes had been sheared. Some were a foot thick and more, tightly bound together with hempen rope and smeared with pitch besides, to make them all but unclimbable.

This was the most dangerous part of the mission. The only way into the British fort was through the palisade. Literally. With axes. It would take at least ten minutes to cut through the walls, during which every American soldier would be a sitting target for British soldiers firing down from the walls. Men *would* die. There was no getting around it. But there was no other way.

Alex reached the wall first, his axe still shaking over his head. He glanced up the wall and saw a pale face looking down at him over the long snout of a rifle. He threw himself to the side as a cloud of smoke burst from the rifle and heard the *whizz* of a musket ball fly past his ear even before he heard the report of the weapon. He rolled on the ground but was up immediately, shaking his axe at the face above him, knowing it would be half a minute and more before the man could reload his gun. He drove the axe into the timber wall of the fort, biting a chunk of wood from it and leaving a pale cut behind, then waved the axe at the soldier above him.

"The next cut is in your skull, you British blackguard!"

It was all theater, of course, both to frighten the enemy and rouse his own men. Having struck the symbolic first blow, he handed off his axe to the first Continental soldier who came within reach.

"Sappers, get those ladders in place!" he called to four teams of men, each of whom carried a twenty-five-foot ladder. The purpose of the ladders wasn't to get the men into the fort, just to apply extra pressure on the British defenders, and draw their fire. The sappers leaned the ladders against the walls and fearlessly began scaling them. As expected, the British concentrated their guns on the ladders, lest the sappers take the upper tier of the wall and all but assure that the Continental forces would break through.

"Rear line, fall in!" Alex called. "Take out those defenders! Protect our boys on the wall!"

A predetermined group of twenty men fell to a knee behind the advancing soldiers and trained their rifles on the top of the palisade. They fired in rounds, five men shooting, then reloading while the next five fired and the next and the next, keeping a steady round of bullets flying at the wall. It was unlikely that they would hit the British soldiers, who were protected behind the spike top of the palisade, but their fire kept the enemy jumping about, making it harder for them to take aim at the sappers scaling the ladders.

At the same time, nearly fifty Continental soldiers armed with axes began hacking at the base of the walls. There were so many blades flashing in the moonlight that it seemed as if a swarm of fireflies had appeared out of thin air. The rain of repetitive blows against the timber walls sounded like a flock of maniacal woodpeckers. Wood chips flew through the air like sawdust. It seemed like the trunks would collapse in seconds. But wood is wood, and not even bloodlust can make it disappear. The blades continued to flash, but the wood held. There was nothing to do but wait until the wall fell.

On the near ladder, the first sapper reached the top of the wall. His rifle was at his shoulder in an instant, and he fired. Then, with the agility of a monkey, he swung about to the underside of the ladder and swung himself to the ground, allowing the next soldier to charge for the top.

At the next ladder over, however, things didn't go so smoothly. The sapper reached the top of the wall, but before he could bring his weapon to bear, a shot ran out and he fell backward off the rungs. One of his feet caught the soldier behind him, nearly knocking him from the ladder. Only when he saw the tattered sole of the falling soldier's boot did Alex recognize him. Corporal Fromm.

But there wasn't time to mourn. Alex dropped to one knee and aimed his rifle at the top of the wall. He found the

sniper who had taken out Corporal Fromm, who was franti-
cally reloading his weapon. He took aim and squeezed the
trigger. The soldier twitched, not like he'd been hit by a bullet, but as though a bee had stung his shoulder. Then his rifle
fell from his hands and he slumped forward over the spiked
top of the fence.

There was no more time to gloat than to mourn. Alex
reloaded as quickly as he could, emptying his rifle, pouring
in more powder, packing it, then dropping a ball in place. He
didn't really expect to get another chance to fire his weapon,
though.

He checked the axemen's progress. They'd concentrated
their effort on three different areas. As their tools struck the
wood, the tree trunks rattled. Gaps were opening up between
them, exposing the light of the enemy's fire behind.

He heard a voice in his ear.

"Won't be long now."

He turned to see a familiar face beside him.

"Laurens!" he said with warmth. "I am so happy you
made it through."

"The British are scared," Laurens answered. "They're
barely trying to defend the line."

"Do you think they'll try to run when we break through?"

"I think there's a good chance."

"That is unacceptable," Alex said, as though he were
sending back a burned slice of pie at an inn. "General
Washington wants them defeated but captured, not

regrouped farther inland." He paused to consider. "Our best intelligence suggests there are no more than one hundred twenty men holding the redoubt. I want you take your battalion and circle around the rear of the fort. If the British soldiers try to run, let them know there is no escape. Exercise prudence. We want prisoners, not a slaughter. I will lead the charge here with Fish's and Gimat's battalions."

"You will have no more than two hundred men. That's a numerical advantage, but not a guaranteed victory. Are you sure?"

"The enemy will not have time to count our numbers. They have seen what's on the field, and will expect all of us coming through the breaches here. Fear will do the work for us."

In the dim light, he could see pride in his friend's eyes. Laurens stepped back and saluted. "I won't let you down, sir," he said, and disappeared into the crowd.

As soon as he was gone, Alex headed toward the closest breach. He found Major Gimat there and ordered him to assemble his men for the assault. He ran to the next breach, dodging the bodies of fallen Continental soldiers—and the occasional redcoat shot from the wall—in a macabre game of hopscotch. The sappers on the ladders had secured their positions at the top of the wall, however, making it all but impossible for the British soldiers to take potshots, so at least the carnage had stopped.

He made it to the next breach and found Major Fish, gave him the same order. Even as he spoke, there was a splintering sound and a voice called mockingly, "Timber!"

Alex looked up to see one of the trunks twist and fall to the ground as his sappers ran out of the way. The gap weakened the whole line. Within seconds, two more trunks had fallen, then a fourth and a fifth. A six-foot gap stood in the wall now.

Gimat reappeared. "The men are ready, sir."

"Very good, Major. I will lead the charge myself."

Gimat blinked, but that was the only reaction he showed. "As you wish, sir."

He moved back, and Alex stepped to the front of the line.

He turned to the sea of pale faces. "Gentlemen," he said. "We do this not for glory but for America." He held his bayoneted rifle above his head. "Charge!"

11

---◦◦◦◦◦---

Home Invasion

The Schuyler Mansion
Albany, New York
October 1781

*A*ll summer and into the fall, Eliza's thoughts continually drifted to her husband, off on his command, off at battle, and she had learned to live with the constant worry. The few letters she received from the front had done much to assuage her concerns, but it was hard to find comfort in the pastoral peacefulness of home when she knew Alex was far from safety. Even months later, she still chided herself for their less-than-ideal parting, and kept the letters that did make their way to her tucked safely in her pocket at all times, so that she might remind herself of the reality of his existence and his love.

"He is all right," said Angelica, as if reading her thoughts. Her sister linked arms with her as the remaining womenfolk walked the heavy steps between the rows of flowers that lined the garden path that morning.

Eliza squeezed her sister's elbow in gratefulness.

"Tell me something, Mama," said Angelica, attempting to keep Eliza occupied with more trivial matters. "Why is it that the Pastures lacks a porch?"

"A 'porch'?" Mrs. Schuyler repeated, as if the word were a Native American term she had never heard, like *squash* or *moose*. She preceded her daughter into the octagonal gazebo at the center of the ornamental garden south of the mansion and took her seat in a low-angled chair fashioned from round sawn logs whose bark had been abraded to polished smoothness over the years.

"Yes, a *porch*, Mama," Angelica repeated, laughing slightly as she took a seat beside the older woman. Her pregnancy had grown noticeably more pronounced in the three months since she had revealed it to the family. She pulled a little at the waistband of her dress, which, even though it had been let out, was still tight around her midsection.

"Baby Kitty wants to know, too," Eliza agreed, looking down at the moon-faced bundle in her arms as she followed her sister and mother into the gazebo. Her youngest sister had just been fed and changed and was swaddled in the lightest bit of lace because of the unseasonable October heat, which, while not oppressive, was still warm enough to make Eliza wish that she could go without a petticoat like little Kitty.

As she seated herself, Mary, a housemaid, began efficiently unpacking foodstuffs from a large wicker basket, preparing a picnic with the assistance of Lew, who carried a second basket filled with china and silver.

"Gently, Lew," Mary chided. "Just because it's called bone china don't mean it's hard as your bones—which the mistress will have me crack if you break any of her mother's Spode."

"A porch?" Mrs. Schuyler repeated for the second time. Eliza, glancing at her mother, couldn't tell if she was teasing Angelica, or really was that obtuse.

"A porch, Mama," Angelica said with theatrical exasperation. "You are familiar with the concept, yes? A covered but open-air addition to a house whereupon the residents of said house can enjoy a nice spot of mint tea without having to walk a quarter mile up and downhill."

"Don't forget the scones!" Lew threw in, his wide eyes staring at a mound of sugar-dusted pastries that Mary was unwrapping from a brightly flowered kitchen towel.

"Mary, do give that young boy a scone and send him off before he upsets that entire basket of dishes," Catherine Schuyler said. After Lew had accepted his treat, she continued. "Why on earth would I want to take my mint tea on a *porch* when I can have it in such a bucolic setting as this, with the smell of flowers in the air, and the most lovely views in every direction, and birdsong, too?"

In fact, the only thing that could be heard were Johnny, Philip, and Ren engaging in some kind of brotherly activity somewhere out of sight. Judging from the amount of screaming, they were either having a great time, or one of them was going to show up at dinner with a blackened eye. Probably both.

"I believe the trek Angelica mentioned has something to do with it," Eliza said. "It is seventy-eight steps down the hill from our house. And while this is indeed a lovely setting, there are nearly as many flowers to smell right next to the house, including those roses Papa planted when Cornelia was born, and the birds sing at the top of the hill just as sweetly as they do down here, and I daresay the view is actually a bit better, what with the higher vantage point, and no shrubbery in the way."

"Ah well, there you're wrong, little missy." Catherine Schuyler gloated with the air of someone who has caught out her interlocutor in a grievous error. "On a *porch*"—she still said the word as if it were a foreign concept, although it was clear now she was having a bit of fun—"you could only see in one direction, whereas down here you can see in all four."

"There's one thing you *can't* see from here, though," a breathless voice added. It was Peggy, trotting down the steps with a clutch of fans in her hand. "The road," she finished as she distributed the fans among the three women already seated.

Eliza glanced over and realized that it was true. A line of lilac trees, out of bloom now, but still thickly covered in green heart-shaped leaves, blocked any view of the road.

"And if we can't see the road," Peggy continued as she took her own seat and snapped her fan open and began immediately waving it at her face, "it only follows that anyone passing on the road can't see *us*, which is of course the point. Mama is a fine modest member of the Reformed Dutch

Church. She sleeps in a rear bedroom and has her dayroom on the sunset side of the house rather than the sunrise side like everyone else. She doesn't believe in a family displaying its activities for all to see. She finds it unseemly."

"Oh, I wouldn't say 'unseemly,'" Mrs. Schuyler protested. "Unseemly is the way you are fanning your face like Cook trying to save a custard. A porch is merely . . . common."

Peggy blushed and immediately slowed her hand. Eliza, who had been fanning herself and Kitty nearly as vigorously, also slowed, but still laughed at her mother's teasing.

In the three months since Kitty's birth, the family dynamic had changed in tone. Mrs. Schuyler, who seemed to know that this was her last child, had relaxed into a benevolent, almost grandmotherly playfulness, treating her eighth child as a pet to be indulged at every occasion, and softening in her attitude toward her adult children. The stern mother of yore was still there, as witnessed by her chiding about Peggy's fan, but it was delivered in a tenderer tone, sometimes even teasingly. Mrs. Schuyler no longer acted as if the slightest breach of etiquette—serving oyster forks with the fish, say, or wearing any color brighter than midnight blue on a Sunday—were a disaster from which the family's reputation would never recover.

Eliza thought fondly of how Alex would enjoy this change in his mother-in-law. Her husband was still a bit awed and cowed by her mother.

"The truth is your father didn't want a porch," Catherine said now. "I amend that. Your father wanted a grand Palladian affair, with Corinthian columns and a pediment decorated with a frieze, if you can believe it. I told him it was scandalous enough that we had natural figures"—*natural* was Mrs. Schuyler's code word for *nude*—"inside the house, on that wallpaper everyone loves to ooh and aah over, but I absolutely was not going to have . . . exposed . . . *cherubs* leering at my guests every time they entered or exited my home. As your father is never one to compromise, we ended up without said porch."

"Well, I for one love having picnics down here," Peggy said. "It makes an occasion of it. It might be less work up at the house, but it wouldn't be nearly so special."

"That's because you're not the one carrying a child," Eliza said. "I believe Kitty has gotten bigger every day she's been alive."

"That is the preferred direction, is it not?" Angelica teased. "Imagine if she were to get smaller? It would be most peculiar. And might I add, *you* are not carrying a child, you are merely holding one and can put it in the arms of a nurse at any time. *I* am carrying a child, and may I say that with each passing day, I grow more and more in awe of Mama, who did this more times than I can count and never let on how truly uncomfortable it is. It feels like Dot has cinched me into the tightest corset and is now trying squeeze a melon in between the whalebone and my ribs."

"In my day," Mrs. Schuyler said, "a woman didn't talk about her condition. It was—"

"Unseemly?" Peggy teased. "Or merely common?"

"Vulgar, I should say," Catherine said in a serious voice — so serious that Eliza thought her mother was putting on a show. "But what do I know? I am just an old woman of six-and-forty years."

"Well, if you say 'six-and-forty' like a member of Queen Elizabeth's court, people *will* think you an old woman."

"Well, what should I say? 'Forty-six'?" Mrs. Schuyler shuddered. "What next? Shall I go about town without a bonnet?" She lifted up the hem of her dress until it was higher than the cuff of her summer boot, revealing a few inches of pale pantaloon. "Expose my ankle? Or, I know, why don't I just *adopt a profession*? Perhaps I will study law, like Eliza's Colonel Hamilton, or be a merchant, like Angelica's Mr. Church, or, hold on, why don't I just name myself Patroon like Peggy's Mr. Van Rensselaer!" Mrs. Schuyler chortled wickedly. "You girls with your modern ideas! Always thinking things can be improved upon when the old order has worked century upon century."

"But has it?" Eliza said. "I mean, if the old order worked so well, then why are we fighting this war? Why don't we continue to let some king on the other side of the ocean impose unjust taxes on us, and take the better part of our income simply because he happens to be the son of someone who happened to be the son of someone who happened to be the son of someone who—"

"Yes, I think we see where you are going with this," Mrs. Schuyler interjected. "But these are the sorts of questions men ask, and men answer. It is a woman's place to maintain a steady keel, so that our menfolk always have a safe haven to turn to in an ever-changing world."

"Why, Catherine Van Rensselaer Schuyler!" Angelica said. "I never thought I would hear you adopt such a—such a *meek* position, not just for all women but for yourself! You are one of the most strong-willed, independent, and capable women I have ever known. During the five long years of this war, there have been more months than not when Papa was away and you ran this house singlehandedly, assuming all of his duties in addition to yours. And, I might add, turning more of a profit off the farm than Papa ever did!"

"For shame!" Mrs. Schuyler said, but Eliza thought she detected a submerged pride in her mother's voice. "I only stepped up as was my duty. What I did was nothing special."

"Perhaps it *was* 'nothing special,'" Eliza chimed in. "But if that's the case, doesn't it prove that the female sex is capable of doing anything that males can do? I say they are the ones who are nothing special!"

"Anything?" Mrs. Schuyler scoffed. "Would you stand behind a plow and furrow the fields? Would you shoulder a rifle and march to war?"

"It seems to me that it's the horse that does the work in the first instance, and the bullet in the second. Neither requires any great feat of manly strength."

The women fell silent after this exchange, their thoughts all filled with the ongoing siege five hundred miles south, in Yorktown, Virginia. It had been more than a week since Eliza had heard from Alex, and the silence was close to driving her mad. By now, her anger had completely faded, and even her fear had subsided to a dull ache. But that didn't mean he wasn't on her mind a hundred times a day. The glimpse of a ribbon that he had worn in his hair could bring him to mind, or one of his old jackets lurking at the back of a wardrobe, or even just his empty seat at table.

But she always tried to steer her thoughts away from him, lest she begin conjuring fantasies about what was happening to him at that moment. Did his silence, for example, mean that the siege had escalated to actual battle, or that the battle was over? Was it possible that Alex had fallen —

No! she said to herself, cutting short this train of thought.

She looked down at the sleeping face of her newest sister. Kitty had been sickly for the first few weeks of her life, and Eliza had been terrified that she would meet the same fate as Cortland, her mother's last child, who had only survived a few weeks before succumbing to one of those unnamable maladies that so often steal young babes away. She had fretted over Kitty's bed as if she were the girl's mother, and though Dr. Van Vrouten declared that none of her symptoms were life-threatening, Eliza's ministrations had helped ensure that they did not become more alarming. But as Kitty's health improved, Eliza had been plagued by a new fear: that somehow Kitty's life had been bought at the expense of her husband's. She knew it was folly. That neither illness nor God worked in such a way, but the eleven days since she had heard from Alex had been excruciating for her, and she longed to receive word that he had survived the command he had demanded, and not succumbed to the perils of battle as Governor Clinton had so mockingly predicted.

"Speaking of boys," Peggy cut into Eliza's reverie in a bored voice. "Have you noticed Philip and John and Ren have fallen suddenly silent? I do hope they haven't slipped into a hole somewhere."

Eliza strained her ears, and indeed heard nothing but her mother's singing birds.

"They're probably hunting something. I expect we shall hear a gunshot at any—"

She was cut off by exactly the sound she prognosticated, not once but two, three, four, five times, in rapid succession.

"Did I count five shots?" Mrs. Schuyler said. "I don't understand. The boys only have the two old muzzle-loaders, and they could not have reloaded that quickly."

Eliza wondered at her mother's expert knowledge of munitions—well, she was a soldier's wife, after all—but before she could ask, she heard the light tread of multiple running feet. A moment later, her three brothers appeared at the base of the garden path and tore toward the feminine quintet in the gazebo. The two older boys each held one of eight-year-old Ren's hands in one of theirs, and were all but carrying the smaller boy as they charged up. Their guns flapped loosely in their other hands.

"Mama! Mama!" John called. "Redcoats!"

"Redcoats!" Philip and Ren echoed.

"Mama!" John cut them off. "A party of redcoats and Indians is advancing upon the house from the northwest! There are at least fifteen of them, maybe more!"

"What?" Eliza said, standing so suddenly that little Kitty roused from her nap and let out a thin mew. Eliza peered toward the northwest but could see nothing over the well-grown trees of the cherry orchard. "Are you absolutely sure?"

"They fired at us! The white men are dressed as civilians, but there can be no mistake! We must get to the house and prepare to defend it!"

Eliza turned to her mother for direction. Catherine Schuyler was pushing herself to her feet with an inscrutable expression on her face. Before the shocked gaze of her three oldest children, she strode purposefully to John and snatched the rifle from his hand, then turned to Philip and grabbed his, and then, to the gape-jawed astonishment of her audience, threw both weapons deep into the flowerbeds.

"There will be absolutely no defending or firing of any kind!" she said with more passion in her voice than Eliza had ever heard. "Are you mad? If you fire on a British war party, they will cut you down as though you were soldiers on the line. I will not watch my sons shot down in my own house!"

"Mama!" Philip began, but Catherine whirled on him.

"Not another word, or as our Lord and Savior is watching, I will turn you over my knee! To the house, all three of you. And you girls, what are you waiting for? Get up the hill now! Are you going to greet a party of gentlemen in the garden like a group of lolling milkmaids? Up! Up!"

The stunned group began a straggling march up the stone steps that led from the garden to the house. Eliza was still carrying Kitty and found herself clutching the infant so closely to her chest that her sister was beginning to fuss. She willed her arms to relax, yet it was impossible. It seemed unbelievable that even as Alex was risking his life to challenge the British in Virginia half a thousand miles away, she and her mother and sisters and brothers were under fire right here in Albany.

It is a sign of British desperation, she said to herself. But that didn't make her feel any safer. Or less outraged. *Cowards!* she thought. *Going after women and children!* Her heart raced as she thought of her family's safety, and of Alex's distraught if anything were to happen to her.

Halfway up the slope, she turned back. To her horror, she saw a swarm of dark-coated figures down at the bottom of the hill. They were pale skinned and dressed in European attire, no redcoats visible, but they didn't need uniforms to identify themselves as the enemy, anyone could see the hostile expressions on their faces.

"Eliza, please!" Peggy said, taking her arm. "Do not gawk! Get inside!"

She hurried up the hill, but she couldn't help but feel she was running into a trap. Why had her mother had thrown the boys' rifles away—the only weapons they had to defend themselves! Rationally, she knew Mrs. Schuyler was correct. If the boys were foolish enough to fire at their attackers, they would be executed in a hail of answering bullets. But to be corralled in the house, with no weapons and no route to escape! It shook her to the core. Yet what else could they do but trust that the men chasing them up the hill were not so dishonorable that they would fire upon civilians?

The last thirty seconds as they ran up the hill were the longest of Eliza's life. She hunched her shoulders, as if they would somehow provide more protection if the men behind her did choose to fire. But no shots rang out, and at last the Schuyler clan was at the top of the hill and running around the corner of the house to the back door. One by one, they ran inside into the rear hall, where several of the maids were already gathered at the foot of the stairs with Mary and Samson the butler.

"Should I barricade the door, madam?" he asked as soon as John, who insisted on being last through the portal, was inside.

"Leave it open," Mrs. Schuyler commanded. "We do not want to inflame the passions of our besiegers by forcing them to hack their way in. Please take the maids and my children upstairs and wait in the hall. Do not hide, and if the men do come upstairs, speak to them as briefly but respectfully as possible."

"Mama, you must come, too!" Peggy said.

"Nonsense," Mrs. Schuyler replied. "This is my home, and I will greet any and all visitors as is proper for a mistress when her husband is not as home."

"Mama, I must insist," said Peggy. "Papa would never allow anything to happen to you. We can take care of these men."

"Yes, Peggy and I will greet them," said Eliza determinedly. "Mama, go upstairs."

For a moment, Mrs. Schuyler seemed ready to argue, but seeing the fierce look of determination on both her daughters' faces, she nodded instead.

"Upstairs. All of you," said Eliza. "Peggy and I will deal with this matter. Angelica, you cannot remain downstairs in your condition."

Angelica held her sisters' gazes gravely and then, taking Ren's hand, led him upstairs. John and Philip followed.

"Are you certain we can do this?" asked Peggy when they had gone.

"We have no choice," said Eliza, who turned to the door when she realized something. "Mary? Is Cornelia upstairs already?"

Mary gasped. "It was time for her nap, and it was just so hot upstairs!"

"Mary!" Eliza said sharply. "Where is Cornelia?"

"She must be sleeping in the east parlor!" cried Peggy.

Eliza turned and, all but dumping Kitty in her mother's arms, pushed past Mrs. Schuyler and dashed down the hall toward the front of the house. She ran into the east parlor, where her five-year-old sister lay stretched out on a sofa.

"Cornelia," she said in as gentle a voice as she could muster, though it sounded quite shrill to her ears.

Cornelia's eyes fluttered open. "Lizzy? Is it tea time?"

"Not exactly, dear. But come along now, and I'll have Mary fetch you a nice bowl of fresh cream and baked apples."

Cornelia sat up slowly, and Eliza had to hurry her along.

"Schleepy!" she called as Eliza dragged her into the hall—just as the front door burst open, only a few feet behind them, and a horde of men began streaming into the house.

Eliza grabbed Cornelia and pushed her into Peggy's arms. Peggy drew back, trembling as she held their youngest sister.

"Gentlemen!" Eliza said in her brightest voice even as she backed toward the staircase, which was a good thirty feet behind her. "Forgive me for not opening the door myself. I did not hear you knock."

"Quiet, girl!" one of the ruffians spat. "We have no interest in you or your fellow brats. Where is Philip Schuyler?"

"Gone to alert the Albany militia," said Eliza, thinking quickly. "If you know what's good for you, you will hie back to whatever cave from which you crept before he returns."

"Yes!" said Peggy stoutly. "Papa will be here in any moment!"

In fact, General Schuyler had left yesterday for the estate in Saratoga, preparing for the harvest, and no help was on the way. Eliza doubted their improvisation would fool their attackers. But maybe—the men seemed to think General Schuyler was still in residence, after all.

"Oh, is he? And how do we know he is not hiding upstairs like a frightened child?" sneered the Brit.

Eliza placed herself in front of Peggy and Cornelia, to shield them from the men, and drawing herself to her full height, scoffed at the notion that her father would be so cowardly. "The answer to that question is implicit in your presence here. You have come for our father because you know him to be a military man of great renown and fortitude. If he wasn't, he wouldn't be worth your while. Do you think such a man would cower from a ragtag bunch of irregulars who themselves don't have the courage to wear the uniform of their allegiance?"

The front of the hall had completely filled up with armed men now. Their expressions were leering and contemptuous, yet they held themselves in check, though one Brit was eyeing a silver ewer with a gleam in his eye.

If that is the only thing they take, Eliza thought, *we will be getting off easy.*

"You have a saucy mouth," the apparent leader said. "Especially for a genteel, unarmed woman."

"I am armed with my God-given womanhood, which is more than enough to protect me from the likes of you. And soon enough our father will be back with twenty men, and then I wonder what will protect *you*," said Eliza angrily.

The men looked nervously at one another, some doubtfully, but others with palpable alarm.

Eliza took the moment to push Peggy and Cornelia farther back, and soon Peggy was climbing the stairs two at the time, Cornelia giving off a little cry.

"Bah!" another soldier said now, stepping forward. "Let's see your womanhood protect you from this." And so saying, he grabbed an axe and hurled it right at Eliza.

"Eliza!" screamed her mother from the shadows of the stairs as the axe flew through the air.

But Eliza stood calmly in the doorway, the weapon quivering in the doorframe beside her.

"Is that all?" she said coldly. Before anyone could answer, she continued. "I would suggest that you leave while you can. Our father loves this house almost as much as he loves the people who live in it, and he will not take this nick in his walnut paneling in good humor."

She held her chin high and hoped they wouldn't notice how much she was shaking. To her relief, their ire seemed to be spent.

"It is a lovely house," the first man said finally, the fight drained out of him. "And one way or another, I'm sure the general will be returning to it soon. Suffice to say I look forward to making his acquaintance."

"I am sorry to say that I cannot affirm General Schuyler would feel the same way. Nevertheless, you may be sure that if you do return, he will have an appropriate reception prepared for you."

A smile flickered over the man's face.

"You are a formidable woman, Miss Schuyler. I thank God you were not born a man."

"As do I," Eliza agreed. "Every day. And it is not Miss Schuyler to whom you speak. It is Mrs. Hamilton."

THE GARRISON AT Albany dispatched four soldiers to the Pastures in case the enemy raiders returned. They arrived the following morning and came with more than guns. "The siege at Yorktown was victorious!" one of them exclaimed, sweeping Mrs. Schuyler up into a hug as though she were his own mother. "Cornwallis has surrendered! The British are done for!"

The family—even Mrs. Schuyler—burst into cheers. Everyone but Eliza, who felt a sinking feeling in her stomach. This was partly to do with the appearance of the officer who had made the proclamation. He was roughly of the same age and height as Alex, though his hair was darker (and thinning noticeably on top) and his complexion more sallow. He had the same sharp nose as her husband's, and piercing, lively eyes. His chin was rakishly pointed, giving his mouth a pouting appearance. Eliza could not help but feel she was looking at her husband's apparition, perhaps even his shade, if not quite as handsome.

"Pardon me, Colonel—"

"Burr, Mrs. Hamilton. Lieutenant Colonel Aaron Burr," said the soldier.

Eliza had heard the name, though she could not remember the context. Perhaps from Alex, perhaps from her father.

"I wonder, Colonel Burr, if you have received any letters from Yorktown intended for—"

The soldier cut her off when he reached into a pocket and pulled out a letter. "There was chaos for some days, as you can imagine, but we received quite the cache of mail in yesterday's post coach. Wives and mothers all over Albany will be breathing easier today."

Eliza took the letter with a trembling hand. She recognized her own name on the outside, written in Alex's hand, but it was entirely possible that the missive had been penned before the battle, and constituted the last words of a man who no longer walked this earth.

She unfolded it anxiously, surprised at how few words were written inside. Alex's letters were rarely shorter than two or three pages, but there were barely that many lines scrawled here.

My darling Betsey—

Does Wall Street mean anything to you? No? Well, my dearest, I beg you to familiarize yourself with it, for it is the most fashionable street in all of New York City, and as a defeated General Cornwallis is my witness, it is the street where we shall raise our family and conquer New York society. Pack your bags, my dearest. We are moving to the city!

A.

Eliza's heart pounded in her chest harder than it had yesterday, when she faced a dozen enemy soldiers. Alex was alive! Her dearest, most-beloved husband had survived! She couldn't contain her glee.

Dropping the letter to the floor, she threw her arms around the officer's shoulders and pressed a kiss to his startled cheek. "Oh! Colonel Burr! Thank you! Thank you! You are nothing but a lifesaver!"

The In-Between Years

1781–1783

*E*ven before General Cornwallis handed the white flag to General Washington, Alex had already written Eliza from the battlefield, letting her know that he survived the assault unscathed and that he was on his way home.

Now, at last, their life together in New York City was going to start.

But war refuses to accommodate anyone's schedule, even America's (future) first Secretary of the Treasury, and the woman who founded New York's first private orphanage . . .

After the Battle of Yorktown, Cornwallis was so humiliated by his defeat that he refused to attend the formal ceremony of surrender, claiming to be ill with malaria. Ever conscious of decorum and rank, General Washington had in turn refused to accept the sword proffered by General Charles O'Hara, a Cornwallis subordinate, and instead directed him to hand it to Major General Benjamin Lincoln, his second in command at the battle. Alex was equal parts impressed by Washington's majesty and appalled by his rigidity. This, indeed, was a man who could be king, if that's what he desired. He only hoped America could resist the temptation to call on him in that capacity.

Afterward, Alex submitted another letter to General Washington: his resignation from the army. Washington commended him for his bravery and leadership on that fateful evening, telling Alex that he could add "war hero" to his list of accomplishments, and happily (or at any rate sanguinely) accepted Alex's resignation, which capped five years of service to the cause of independence in general, and to Washington in particular. He alluded that he, too, was eager to shrug off the mantle of leadership and return to Mount Vernon, his great estate on the Potomac River in Virginia. He didn't ask what Alex planned to do with the next phase of his life; though, he did say that he hoped Alex would not "turn his back" on the country he had, with his "bravery and brilliance," helped create. Alex assured him he would not, saluted him one final time, and took his leave.

Alex immediately set off for Albany to retrieve Eliza and spirit her away to their new home in New York City, which for a variety of reasons held promise as a future capital of the country, and thus was the only place worthy of a family as ambitious as the Hamiltons.

But although Cornwallis had surrendered and British forces on the continent were decimated, King George's army remained firmly in control of Manhattan and its surrounding islands and, against all predictions, refused to surrender or *retreat. The redcoats were too numerous to chase out without great loss of life—not only to the attacking forces, but also to the nearly ten thousand Continental soldiers being held in British prison ships off the coast of Red Hook, Long Island.*

The American brass feared that a preemptive move on Manhattan might spur the British to sink the ships, or burn them. Only later would they learn that such a fate would have been a small mercy for those thousands of prisoners of war, who died of illness, exposure, and starvation.

Right up to the end, the British held on to the notion that New York State might even cede Manhattan, Staten Island, and Long Island to the crown, which the empire could use as a way station between the Canadian colonies and its numerous territories in the West Indies. This was a pipe dream, of course—neither General Washington nor Governor Clinton would tolerate any British holdings between the Straits of Florida and the St. Lawrence River. Still, the transfer of authority took nearly two years to complete to the satisfaction of both parties.

The Hamiltons would have to remain in Albany for a little while longer. Their reunion at the Pastures was as joyful as their parting had been filled with sorrow and recrimination.

Alex galloped up the hill, so eager to see his beloved that he practically flew off the horse upon arriving, and Eliza felt her heart burst with relief and joy to see her brave lad home at last.

There were many tears shed on both sides that fine day, and Alex vowed he would never again leave her side. Eliza, as happy as she was, allowed him his promises, even as she understood that if they were to have a long and happy marriage, she would have to understand and forgive the promises that were broken even under the best intentions.

Alex told the story of the battle once and once only, after which he never spoke of it in Eliza's presence again. He completed his law studies at a breakneck pace and passed the bar exam in July 1782. New York State normally required new lawyers to serve a three-year clerkship with a judge before they could appear in court, but this requirement was waived for veterans returning from the war, who were deemed to have given more than enough time to their country. He did, however, have to sign an oath of loyalty, renouncing any ties to the king of Great Britain and pledging allegiance not just to the United States of America, but to the "free and independent state" of New York.

With the city of New York still in British hands, Alex hung out his shingle for the time being in Albany, where he quickly found himself in great demand: partly because his connections to the Schuyler clan served as an entrée to wealthy society; partly because his status as a war hero and confidant to General Washington drew curiosity seekers to his door by the dozens. His services were also needed for a reason Alex and others found unfair and distasteful: The state of New York, under Governor Clinton's direction, had passed a law barring all loyalists (citizens who had remained loyal to the British crown instead of declaring for the American rebels) from practicing in New York courts.

Loyalists made up a full third of the population, and though many living near the coast chose to return to the mother country, or emigrate to Canada, most of those farther inland identified as Americans, regardless of where their government was located. Alex disagreed with Clinton's law, as well as other provisions penalizing Colonial Americans who had sided with Britain in the war. They had lost, and that was punishment enough; anything else was punitive, and the country would need them if it was to succeed.

Alex was one of five from New York elected to the Congress of the Confederation, a position he accepted with great trepidation. Certainly, a part of his hesitation was based on the fact that Congress met—for the moment at least—in Philadelphia, which meant he would again have to separate from Eliza (breaking the promise he had made). But the main reason was his belief that the Congress of the Confederation was a useless, bureaucratic organization, having no authority except over itself and the Continental army (and even that was only nominal, since the army hadn't been paid in years—soldiers were starting to mutiny, and some even marched on the Congress's headquarters).

Any laws this Congress passed had no jurisdiction over the thirteen newly minted states, each of which was its own ultimate authority. It had no license to collect revenues by tax or duty or any other measure, which is to say, it could pass such laws but couldn't compel their enforcement. Alex's contempt for Congress was more than offset by the despair he felt for his new country. If a strong central government wasn't established, he felt, uniting the thirteen states into a single nation, then the so-called confederation was bound to crumble as the various states began competing against one another for resources and wealth rather than working for the common good. After six months, he resigned his seat in Congress and returned once again to Albany.

For her part, Eliza was kept busy as well. Her performance as her mother's surrogate during Mrs. Schuyler's lying-in had so impressed the matriarch that she came to rely on Eliza more and more, particularly where Kitty was concerned. Additionally, Eliza was indispensable to Angelica when her time came, and was there to welcome her nephew, Philip Church, into the world. The family progeny weren't the only children she served. The plight of Anne Carrington—Mrs. Bleecker's hapless charge—had so moved her that she devoted much of her energy to finding homes for other Albany children left orphaned by the war or other hardships. It seemed the least she could do until she and Alex were finally able to start a family of their own.

Both the Dutch Reformed Church and Church of England had established small foundling homes for orphaned children. Eliza raised money and resources for each one, even though the Schuylers had been Dutch Reform all the way back to the Reformation, and the Anglicans—later Episcopalians—counted many loyalists among their parishioners. Some of the women whom she had been canvassing for the past seven years looked a little askance at her nonpartisan activities, but Eliza took an even firmer stance on this line than Alex. In the first place, many of the loyalists were family friends, including men *who had served with General Schuyler when he was in the British army, before an American army ever existed. But it was more than that.*

"It is not a child's fault," Eliza insisted, "if her father fought for King George any more than it is to her credit if he served in the Continental army. Children do not have a political affiliation. They are all God's innocents, and deserve our compassion and our aid." Not only did she gather funds, food, and clothing for the parentless children, she frequently insisted that her friends accompany her on visits to the orphanages in hopes they might adopt a child there. "Now, Kate, you have already an eleven-year-old and a six-year-old at home. I don't see why you cannot take nine-year-old Louisa back with you. She will be able to wear Henrietta's outgrown clothes and look after Natalia while Henrietta is at her studies. Why, she will practically save you money!"

And so two years passed, an interim period bookended by two events in the lives of the young married couple, one tragic, the other joyous. In the late summer of 1782, Alex's cherished friend, John Laurens, perished in the Battle of the Combahee River. As with New York, the ravaged British forces had managed to hold on to several other cities, including Charleston in Laurens's home state of South Carolina. Laurens had returned to his native state to help free it from the pestilence of British occupation. Under the command of General Nathanael Greene, he led numerous raids against the besieged but still numerous redcoats, until, on the 27th of August, he was "shot from the saddle" during one such encounter.

Some witnesses said that Laurens's party had been ambushed, while others maintained that the heir of Mepkin had recklessly led a charge against an enemy brigade that outnumbered his troops three to one, which General Washington seemed to allude to in his remembrance of the fallen soldier: "He had not a fault that I ever could discover, unless intrepidity bordering upon rashness could come under that denomination."

Alex, as was his wont, kept his grief largely to himself, but in a letter to General Greene he wrote: "How strangely are human affairs conducted, that so many excellent qualities could not ensure a more happy fate! The world will feel the loss of a man who has left few like him behind; and America, of a citizen whose heart realized that patriotism of which others only talk. I feel the loss of a friend whom I truly and most tenderly loved."

The pall of Laurens's death hung over the Pastures for many months, until June 1783, when Margarita Schuyler—Peggy to her family and friends—at long last married Stephen Van Rensselaer III, who had been courting her for the past five years. It was an occasion so long delayed that Peggy joked to Eliza and Angelica that she feared the principal emotion at her wedding would be "not joy but relief." For her parents' part, General Schuyler congratulated his daughter on a "game well played," while Mrs. Schuyler commended her nephew/cousin/son-in-law for "staying the course."

The young couple was married at Rensselaerswyck, in the so-called New Manor House north of Albany, which Stephen's *father had built when Stephen was still a child. As grand as the Pastures was, the Van Rensselaers' home was grander still, with stone quoins of New York State brownstone and rich chocolate stucco troweled over the bricks to give it a stately, if somber, appearance, complemented by a wide porch with elegant torus-shaped balusters and Corinthian capitals on the stone columns.*

Inside, however, in the first-floor great hall, was the same Ruins of Rome wallpaper that graced the Schuylers' home (General Schuyler pointed out, not so very sotto voce, that he had commissioned his set more than five years before Stephen II ordered his, ahem). At the wedding, Peggy was resplendent in a burgundy dress with a brilliantly embroidered mint-green underskirt and a wig that threatened to brush against the chandeliers hanging from the twelve-foot ceiling, while Stephen looked stately in a midnight-blue velvet frock coat that recalled the uniform he had been too young to wear during the war. When bride and groom had at last said their "I dos" and kissed each other on the lips, a hundred Schuylers, Van Rensselaers, Ten Broecks, Jansens, Vromans, Quackenbushes, Van Valkenburgs, and Van Sickelens, along with a handful of Livingstons, stood up and cheered this (re) uniting of two of the state's dynastic families.

For if Angelica had married "the Englishman" and Eliza had married "the genius," Peggy had married "gentry" through and through, and between the Schuylers' military and political connections and the Van Rensselaers' vast fortune, the new couple's future as the first family of New York was assured.

And so, two years passed even more quickly than Alex or Eliza realized, Alex busily laying the groundwork for a career that would enable him to support a family and Eliza accumulating the skills that would enable her to raise one. If only her husband would slow down a little, as the two years were such a whirlwind, there was little time to focus on starting the family she began to crave more and more. For while she supported his efforts in the founding of the nation, she wished he would put in a little more effort in the founding of their own little establishment.

It was a heady time of chaos and change. Both young spouses contributed to the political and moral character of this new nation that had, against all odds, torn itself off from the most powerful empire on earth, and found itself in the unexpected position of having to decide what kind of nation it would be. Would it be a monarchy or a republic? A loose confederacy of thirteen competing states, or a unified polity whose far-flung and disparate regions each contributed their unique strengths to make up for the deficiencies and weaknesses of the others?

And above all, how would it conduct itself? Though the colonies had won their liberation from England, they had never been a purely English society. There were Irish, Welsh, and Scottish strains, for one thing—Alex's father was born in Scotland, and though Alex knew little about him, he knew his father would raise his fists against any man who dared accuse him of being English. The Dutch legacy persevered in New York as well (both General and Mrs. Schuyler had been raised speaking Dutch as well as English, and still used the former language when *they wanted to keep secrets from their children). The French influence was strong in the northeast, along the border with Canada, and west of the Mississippi, in the Louisiana Territory. The Spanish presence was strong in the deep south in Florida, where they supported the British cause during the Revolution, and along the coast of the Gulf of Mexico. There were German and Swedish enclaves, and of course the large African population, consisting of 40 percent of the thirteen colonies' people. The vast majority—but not all—had been brought to the New World as enslaved people. Regardless of their station, they made profound contributions to the new country through their labor, art, music, and tenacity, even though slavery would not be eradicated for nearly a century more—a profound injustice in the history of the new nation that just fought for its own freedom.*

Then there were the Native populations that had been here when the Europeans arrived, hundreds of different tribes and confederacies and nations, some numbered only a few thousand, others had hundreds of thousands of members and commanded great swathes of land that dwarfed most of their European counterparts. As the annual Thanksgiving celebration reminded them, without Native American instruction and aid, most of the early European settlements would have perished. New World foodstuffs had made significant changes to the European diet, from potatoes to squash to tomatoes to corn, and of course tobacco—and chocolate!—and had changed the way Europeans conceived of creature comforts. Hundreds of words now peppered the language, from chili *to* chipmunk, *from* hurricane *to* hammock, *from* piranha *to* poncho *to* peyote, *and with those words came ideas about how to relate to this land that Europeans had forcibly taken as their own, and christened "America." Liberty and justice for all?*

And so the myth of American exceptionalism was born, even as it managed to skirt the troubling history of its founding, that a nation dedicated to the ideals of freedom and justice was also established by the twin foundations of slavery and theft.

In any case, all these different cultures had unique strengths of character and industry, and no doubt many people would have been content to separate themselves according to culture and language and replicate Old World divisions in the New, state lines replacing national borders and people pushing ever westward when their neighbors grew too close. But more and more people realized that if the United States of America were to be truly united, they were going to have to forge a common national identity.

Chief among these visionaries was Alexander Hamilton, whose accomplishments during the Revolutionary War would soon be overshadowed by the work he did for the budding republic. Alex knew that the differences between people and points of view couldn't be eliminated or ignored. Those differences had to be celebrated, and put to work for the good of the nation. As with most political ideals, such lofty sentiments were easier said than done. Fortunately, it had two tireless champions in Alexander and Elizabeth Hamilton—assuming, that is, they could harness their unique gifts to a single yoke, and finally learn to work as a team.

Part Two

Tearing Up Wall Street

12

⸻ ❧ ⸻

American Honeymoon

The Hamilton Town House
New York, New York
December 1783

*A*t last, after three years of marriage, winning the war for Independence, surviving the Battle of Yorktown, and finally leaving the comforts of the Pastures, Alexander and Elizabeth Hamilton stood in front of a handsome three-story brick-and-brownstone town house located at 57 Wall Street, in New York City. With a little help from Eliza's dowry, well-informed family connections whispering about a fantastic deal on a pretty little piece of well-located property, and Alex's quick decision-making to snap it up before someone else did, it was theirs. The young husband's hands shook as he unlocked the front door with the key. His wife stood behind him, eager and impatient to see their new abode. With a flourish, he opened both doors and turned to his bride with a smile. "Voilà!"

Eliza clasped her hands in delight, and Alex's eyes softened to see how sweet she looked in the late afternoon sunlight, the golden rays shining on the chestnut tendrils of her hair. This was home now, their home, his home. After years of living as a student and a soldier, and a guest at his in-laws' sumptuous residence, he finally had a place to call his own. "Hold on," he said, before Eliza could take another step.

With a huge grin, Alex literally swept her off her feet and carried her over the threshold. Eliza giggled in his arms, giddy to think that they were all alone at last—with no servants, sisters, little brothers, or parents in sight. So what if the house was practically empty! The lack of tables and chairs, china and silver, candles and ale and compote and even such banal necessities as salt and pepper were more than made up for by the blessed privacy she and Alex finally shared, not to mention that the *one* piece of furniture they did own was an enormous, overstuffed feather bed.

It was on this bed that he laid her down now, and Eliza felt almost coquettish, gazing up at Alex from her dark lashes as she slowly divested herself of all her layers, enjoying the ragged breathing coming from him as he quickly stripped down and joined her under the covers. His blue eyes glittered in the dim twilight, as he held his body above hers.

"Two years ago, when you were in Virginia, I was so worried," she whispered, craning her neck upward to kiss him on his. "Part of me wondered if you would ever come back. I don't think I ever told you that."

"My dearest, bravest girl," he murmured, bending down to kiss her on the soft spot near her ear. "I am home now. You are my home."

"Yes," she said, closing her eyes as he covered her mouth with his.

And then there was no more time or desire for conversation, as even the most articulate statesman in America found words paled in comparison to the sublime experience of being with his beloved.

THE MARRIED COUPLE spent the first two days strolling the frigid streets of New York, hand in hand, oblivious to the cold and marveling as the abandoned storefronts and town houses filled overnight with newly-minted Americans, some of them returning to a city they had thought lost forever, others taking advantage of the hundreds of empty houses and shops to establish a toehold in a major metropolitan area at prices that would never come around again.

By night they dined at the beautiful walnut table that had at last arrived from Albany, covered with a gorgeous muslin tablecloth whose delicate blue-and-gold tracery Eliza's great-grandmother Rensselaer had embroidered more than half a century ago, set with the Crown Derby china dinnerware they had found at a local shop, along with a lovely set of silver that Stephen Van Rensselaer had given them as a wedding present, and that had slept in its velvet-lined case for the past three years.

For the first few days they drank from a pair of mis-matched, battered pewter steins Alex had brought home with him from Yorktown ("That dent was caused by a bullet aimed at my heart," he said with a twinkle in his eye), but on their third day of New York residence, he returned home with a pair of truly exquisite crystal goblets. The taller one was etched with a brilliantly lifelike depiction of Zeus visit-ing Danaë in the form of a shower of gold, while the shorter showed the hapless nymph Echo spying on Narcissus, who was too busy staring at his own reflection in a pool of water to notice her. They were the finest glasses Eliza had ever seen, let alone held in her hands—and she had taken many a meal in the Van Rensselaers' magnificent manor house— and, though Alex could tell she didn't want to seem ungrate-ful, she was unable to prevent herself from asking how much they had cost. Alex blushed, then pulled a potato out of his pocket and said, "Let's just say we'll be eating a lot of these for the next few weeks." Fortunately, he had had a bottle of wine in another pocket, and Eliza's momentary start of alarm was quickly ameliorated.

In fact, the goblets, like everything else they bought for the house, had been a steal. But when you had six large rooms to furnish, and food to be purchased at black market prices, plus rent on top of that—and no income coming in!—the debts were starting to pile up. Alex's valise was stuffed with bills of sale and IOUs and promissory notes for dozens of dif-ferent vendors. Fortunately, conditions were tough all over the island, so that pretty much everyone was living on credit and willing to be generous in their terms. Even so, Alex knew he needed to find clients soon, or their first stab at independence would be over before it had ever really begun.

Eliza decided not to chide Alex for his expenses. He would set up his law practice soon enough, and soon everyone would want him as their counselor. She had great faith in her husband, and her frugal nature would serve them well until he was established.

As their habit, in the morning of the second week of their residence, they headed out for their daily walk, arm in arm. The air was cold but crisp, and pleasantly tinged with the smell of wood smoke and, faintly, the salt of the sea. Just a few doors up from their new house they came to a much larger building, a handsome Palladian edifice with a four-columned portico jutting out from the second floor. The street was relatively quiet, and what traffic there was centered around the building, where official-looking men marched determinedly in and out, trailed by retinues of assistants and clerks. A simple plaque affixed to the building's white stone front told the reason for so much activity:

CITY HALL

Eliza stared across the street at the building, which was on a par with the Van Rensselaers' manor house in size and grandeur. Yet, unlike the country mansion on its wide lawns and manicured gardens, this was surrounded by other buildings, from the two-hundred-foot-tall spire of Trinity Church up the street, to the upright elegance of town houses like the one she now occupied with her husband.

"It is strange to me, who grew up surrounded by acres and acres of garden and field," she said, "to live in a house that is located not just on the same street but the same block as a municipal building, let alone City Hall."

Their talk was interrupted by the squeal of a pig dashing down the street. "That is municipal life," Alex said, laughing. "It has everything the country has, only it's all smaller, and on top of each other."

Indeed, after a lifetime spent on the outskirts of a modest enclave like Albany, Eliza had been nervous about moving to a city as large and cosmopolitan as New York. She had been surprised to find a landscape that reminded her a lot of her native village. The southern tip of Manhattan was criss-crossed with a few dozen streets of three- and four-story brick town houses, not unlike the streets that crowded Albany's riverfront. Their dense, truncated perspectives felt a little mazelike to someone raised with the vistas from the top of a hill in a mansion surrounded by gardens and orchards. But the houses themselves were handsome and generously pro-portioned, and within a few blocks gave way to more familiar, shingled houses with Dutch gables enclosed by white pickets or rustic zigzagged logs containing well-tended kitchen gar-dens and chicken coops and rabbit hutches (and, it must be admitted, the occasional pigsty).

About a mile north of the Battery, these close-knit plots surrendered to open farmland. Here, Bayard's Hill, with its small fort atop it, overlooked the sprawling calm waters of the meandering bays and inlets of Collect Pond, which, she was told, would be covered with ice skaters as soon as its forty-six acres of becalmed water had frozen fully through. To the west was the same Hudson River that bordered Albany 150 miles north. It was wider here, and choppier, thanks to the Atlantic tides. Mirrored on the opposite side of Manhattan was the so-called East River (which Alex had explained to her was not a river at all, but rather something called an estuary, a channel connecting two bodies of salt water, in this case Long Island Sound and New York Harbor). But whatever it actually was, it looked just like a river to her.

And then, of course, there was the ocean itself. Eliza had been as far south as Morristown, New Jersey (where Alex proposed to her), but had not made the trek to the coast because marauding British troops had made the area too dangerous. (She still shuddered to recall how close Alex had come to death when he rode north to persuade her parents to let her marry him rather than the odious Henry Livingston.)

And now they were walking down Pearl Street—so-named for the nacreous shells of the oysters that thrived in the waters surrounding Manhattan. Eliza had seen no sign of their shells, let alone pearls (though a slight odor of fish was discernible in the stiff breeze that blew off the water). In truth, she had turned her gaze out to the vast gray horizon, dotted here and there by anchored ships, a combination of trading vessels waiting for normal commerce to renew so they could fill up their holds before heading back across the Atlantic to the new nation's trading partners. And, here and there, an American military frigate kept watch for British ships whose captains might not have learned of the peace during the four weeks it had taken them to cross the Atlantic.

Eliza found the endless expanse of water both soothing and alarming. It was the first time she had ever contemplated just how large the world was. It was difficult to conceive that there was land on the other side of all this water—not one continent but *three*—Europe, Asia, and Africa, whose vastness, she had seen on maps, was far greater than both North and South Americas. Her whole life had been spent in a single town of a few thousand souls, with just a couple of journeys of a few hundred miles to broaden her knowledge of the world. One of those trips—the journey to Morristown in 1777—had resulted in her marriage to Alex, which only underscored that the strangeness of the world wasn't to be avoided, let alone feared, but to be sought out for the treasures it could bring. She stared out at the white-frothed swells for several minutes, contemplating the journeys that were ahead of her, some physical, some emotional, and then she took Alex's arm in hers and said, "Come. We have work to do."

Their path today led away from the water, but they were still close enough that Eliza could feel its wind at her back, the dampness, the omnipresent smell of salt that she was coming to associate with her new home. A coastal winter could be harsher than one farther inland, but Mrs. Schuyler had seen that Eliza went off with two quilted petticoats and a new wool coat with a sable collar, so she was more than warm enough.

As she and Alex strolled farther up the street, she nodded at another town house, nearly identical to theirs (though she couldn't help noticing that its parlor windows were already adorned by lovely curtains in a rich blue brocade).

"Have I told you about our new neighbors?" she asked her husband.

"You have not," Alex answered. "How is it that you have made their acquaintance already? We have only been in the city for a week, and all that time was spent interviewing servants and buying necessaries. How have you possibly managed to meet anyone?"

Eliza petted his arm in hers. "Never discount a lady's network for efficiency of communication."

"So who *are* our new neighbors?"

"I suppose it is proper to say that *we* are *their* new neighbors, since they have been here for some months, as the sumptuousness of their draperies suggest. It is Mr. Aaron Burr that was colonel, and his new wife, Theodosia, the former Mrs. Prevost."

She felt Alex start. "You do not mean the wife of General Augustine Prevost, the British officer?" he asked, astonished. Prevost was well-known to Alex as the man who had led British forces during the Siege of Savannah in 1779, when American forces had been decimated when they tried—and failed—to retake the great Georgia city. "I did not realize he had died, or divorced."

"No, not Augustine, but his brother, Jacques Marcus, who was a colonel, and died in the Indies. You met her, you know," Eliza continued. "You told me that you dined at her estate, the Hermitage, in New Jersey."

Alex's face lit up with the memory. "So I did! With them both, in fact. Colonel—I mean, Mr. Burr was quite flirtatious, as I recall. And she married at the time! And a decade older! And a passel of children besides!"

Eliza didn't know if her husband was scandalized or amused. On the one hand, Alex had been so ardent about putting aside the differences between patriots and loyalists. On the other, Burr had been, like Alex, a colonel in the Continental army, and was, if anything, even more keen to assume a leadership role in the new government than Alex was. Women may not have been allowed to vote or serve in government, but everyone knew that a society wife controlled her husband's social calendar, and thus his social circle. A somewhat disgraced loyalist wife did not seem like the kind of choice that played well for an ambitious patriot like Burr.

But then, she told herself, *since there were no more Schuyler daughters for Mr. Burr to marry, I guess he had to make do.*

"Five," Eliza said out loud, "to which they added a daughter of their own this spring, also called Theodosia."

"Well, who would have guessed! The great patriot Aaron Burr, marrying a loyalist!"

"Are you shocked?" Eliza asked. She didn't bother to keep her voice down. By now they were well past the house, and she had no fears of being overheard, if Mr. and Mrs. Burr were, in fact, at home.

"No, not at all," Alex said. "The divisions between patriot and loyalist are not nearly as great as war would make them seem. You mark my words, once the United States has established itself, it will renew cordial relations with England. We have far more in common than we do in opposition. But Mr. Burr was always rather . . . stiff in his views. I wonder that he overcame them."

"Perhaps it was simply love," Eliza said.

Alex took a moment to lift her gloved fingers to his lips and kiss them. "Well, perhaps it was," he said in a musing tone. "In which case, there is hope for us as a species. Still, I don't suppose we'll be having them over for dinner any time soon."

"What, you do not approve of the union?" she asked.

"Oh, not at all. I approve. I approve heartily."

"I take it you do not care for Mr. Burr?"

"Not particularly," Alex shrugged. "The few times I met him he struck me as being rather too impressed with himself, when his success seems to me to have more to do with family connections than any great ability on his part."

Eliza passed over this in silence. As the daughter of a Schuyler and a Van Rensselaer, she would have a hard time blaming someone for exploiting their pedigree, especially if they put it to good use. And it was important that she and Alex begin to build a network of friends, acquaintances, and others who would prove useful as they climbed the social ladder.

"Mr. Burr was quite helpful to my family during the war," she confessed finally. "I never told you what happened at the Pastures while you were at Yorktown."

He turned to her in surprise. "You have kept something from me?"

Eliza turned pink. "I did not want you to worry, and when we were reunited I was so happy it slipped my mind."

She told Alex the story of the redcoat invasion and Mr. Burr's role in their rescue. He listened intently, holding her even closer as if afraid to lose her to the enemy even as she was safe in his arms.

"I am so thankful, my angel," he whispered, not caring who could see him nuzzle her hair with his nose as he kissed her forehead. "But alas, we cannot have the Burrs to dinner."

"Why not?"

Alex laughed. "Have you forgotten? We only have a chair each and no servants to serve at table!"

"Oh, you!" Eliza said, swatting him with a gloved hand. "You mustn't tease me!"

WHEN THEY RETURNED home, they worked in one room or another—shelving Alex's law books in his study, moving a portrait of Catherine Schuyler from the front parlor to the dining room to shield it from the strong light that came in the south-facing windows, since they had no curtains yet ("Mama does like to be close to food," Eliza couldn't help quipping as Alex centered the picture over the fireplace), or rearranging the small but growing number of silver serving dishes in the glass-fronted hutch as new pieces came in.

But at a certain point the serious business of decorating would always give way to more playful rearranging, as Eliza stood all the forks and knives on the mantel like couples dancing a reel, or Alex took the squashes from the larder and laid them on the dining table draped in Ipswich lace like so many sleeping infants. One or the other of them would pretend to be upset by the other's mischief, and then the perpetrator would be forced to make it up with kisses and sweet-nothings, until finally the misbehaver would grab a candle and say, "Let me make it up to you upstairs."

13

Hamilton by Her Side

After six years of British occupation, the great city of New York was a shell of its former self. Before the war, it had been the third-largest city in the northern colonies, with more than twenty-five thousand residents. It trailed only Philadelphia and Boston in size, and was on course to overtake both. But after the British conquered Manhattan in 1777, that number dropped by half as thousands of patriots fled the invaders. During the six years of British rule, the city's population gradually recovered as loyalists from all over the colonies left the island for safe haven. Their numbers were swelled by thousands of redcoats shipped over from England, who used the city as their base of operations for the war. The once-vibrant metropolis was transformed into a massive army base, replete with all the vices one expects when large numbers of pent-up young men cluster together for months at a time. It seemed that every other storefront had been transformed into a drinking house—or a house of ill repute.

After Cornwallis's defeat, however, both the British troops and the loyalists who depended on them for protection departed in huge numbers, some for England, others for Canada or the Caribbean. When General Washington officially entered the city on November 25, 1783, he found a ghost town of just over ten thousand people. Washington entered Manhattan this time at its northern tip, crossing over the Harlem River into Harlem Heights, reversing his journey of seven years earlier, when he had been chased from New York City all the way up Manhattan by the British commander, William Howe, and narrowly escaped onto the mainland. It was important to General Washington to ride the entire length of Manhattan to show that the whole island—all twelve miles of it, and not just the city clustered on its southern tip—was once again an American province.

For the first ten miles or so, Washington encountered nothing but forest and farmland. The farms were fallow for the winter, but even so, one could see the desolation. The sheaves still stood in many fields from last fall's harvest, half rotted from rain and freeze and thaw, while herds of cows clustered forlornly before the closed doors of abandoned barns, waiting in vain for someone to drain their swollen udders, and brown chickens scratched for stray grains in the frozen soil, with nothing hunting their eggs besides foxes and skunks. After mile after mile of this, the neat white-and-brown farmhouses slowly grew more numerous, but only occasionally did one see smoke coming from a chimney or a sturdy farm wife retrieving a basket of apples or squash from the fruit cellar.

Finally, about two miles from New York Harbor, the city itself came into view. From a distance, it looked as Washington remembered it, and at the sight he must have breathed a sigh of relief that the British hadn't burned it like modern-day Vandals or Huns desecrating the new Rome. As he got closer, he could see that some buildings had indeed been burned, but these were so scarce and randomly placed that he suspected they were simple house fires, unquenched due to the lack of a fire brigade. Hundreds more buildings stood empty, though, with many others only nominally inhabited and often in terrible disrepair. Shutters sagged on hinges and broken glass had been replaced with wood or oilcloth. Holes gaped in gabled roofs where shingles had not been replaced for nearly a decade.

Even more haunting, though, were the dozen or so derelict ships that stood a half mile off the island, and the smells of disease and death that wafted across empty streets from the salty chop of the East River. The British had anchored a chain of some of their oldest (and least seaworthy) frigates off Manhattan to house their prisoners of war. Even now, hundreds of American soldiers, starving, ill, and freezing, were still desperately awaiting release. By some accounts, eleven thousand patriots had died in these ships, nearly three times the number who perished on the field of battle. Bones would wash up on shore for years to come.

Yet the city still stood at the mouth of the Hudson River, from which the furs and grains and timber of the Northeast flowed to European markets, poised to become a great mercantile center and quite possibly the capital of the new nation. Its climate was milder than Boston's and its island status rendered it easier to defend than Philadelphia or Williamsburg. The Congress of the Confederation was so convinced of the city's bright future that they chose it as the new nation's temporary capital, after stints in Philadelphia and Trenton. Washington shared Congress's high estimation of the city's symbolic value.

Still resisting all calls to take a position in the government, Washington chose Samuel Fraunces's Queen's Head Tavern as the place to resign his commission and bid his faithful troops farewell on December 4, 1783, before returning to Mount Vernon, his beloved plantation in Virginia. One era was closing, while another was beginning, and though the past was cloaked in victory, the future was shrouded in uncertainty. Was this the end of the beginning for the emerging nation, or was it in fact the beginning of the end?

NOT FAR FROM Fraunces Tavern, Eliza Hamilton stood in the middle of her new front parlor staring forlornly at her husband, who was balanced atop one of the room's few chairs measuring the windows with a long spool of tailor's tape.

"I don't understand why you don't just walk over to Pearl Street and bid adieu to General Washington," she said cautiously, to her husband's white-shirted back.

Alex waited until he had measured the height of the window and recorded the figure in his notebook before answering. "If General Washington had wanted to bid *me* adieu, he would have invited me," he said curtly, before climbing down off the chair and carrying it to the room's second window.

"Oh, Alex, you're just being stubborn."

Alex didn't meet her gaze. "I served at the man's side for four years."

"I mean about the window," Eliza said with some exasperation. "They are very clearly the same size. There is no reason to measure them both."

For a moment, it seemed as though Alex was going to ignore her. He remounted the chair and reached his tape to the corner of the window. Then a chuckle erupted from him, and he hopped from the chair to the floor. "I suppose you're right, my darling."

Eliza pulled her chair closer to the fire. Though it was barely noon, she had been on her feet for some six hours, having awakened at six to a cold fireplace and even colder bed—Alex had already risen, and must have secreted himself in the study so as not to disturb her. She had dozed in bed for a few minutes, waiting for the maid to come in to tend to the fire, but then she snapped awake when she remembered that there weren't three chambermaids and an equal complement of footmen to attend to such mundane duties. If she didn't light the fire herself, no one was going to.

Alex heard her going up and down the stairs and emerged from his study to join her, and though Eliza thought to go back to bed once the fire was going, there were ash buckets to be emptied first, coal and wood to be brought in and distributed among the house's three floors, and then the measuring tape had appeared in Alex's hand, and here they were.

She fixed him in the eye and smiled wanly. "You're also being stubborn about General Washington."

Alex opened his mouth to argue, then thought better of it. He looked about for somewhere to sit, but there was only the faded floorboards, bare of any rug or carpet.

"You shouldn't take this personally," Eliza continued. "I have heard from at least three different people that General Washington invited no one to see him off. The only reason he came to the city was to sign the documents that formally transferred governing power from General Carlton back to the state of New York. By all accounts, his goal was to slip out with as little fanfare as possible."

"A ludicrous idea," Alex dismissed.

"Don't be disrespectful," Eliza said curtly. "And yes, maybe it was unrealistic of General Washington to think he could escape to Virginia without some kind of ceremonial before his men. But can you blame him? By your own description, he was never a public personality and accepted his role as commander in chief only because of his love for his country.

But the bonds he built with his men—including you!—were real, and he deserves a final embrace from them before he resumes life as a country squire."

Alex sighed. He had been up since four in the morning answering letters, and was as weary as his wife. The bare window made the room rather cold on this late fall day, and so he walked toward Eliza and sat at her feet in front of the fire, his back leaning against the draped fullness of her woolen skirts. "Mark my words, Eliza, he shall not remain a country squire for long. This country is not yet willing to accept a unifying central government, but it will rally behind its heroes—"

"As the gathering at the Queen's Head demonstrates," Eliza put in.

"Indeed. And when General Washington realizes that the independent nation he fought on behalf of for seven years is in jeopardy, he will return to public service. As I said, the American people are not yet ready to accept a single government. But they *would* accept a single leader—if that leader were General Washington. Although I suppose his title wouldn't be general then. It would be prime minister or perhaps president or, heaven forbid, king."

"Oh, Alex, no! You don't think the American people would ever again consent to become subjects of a monarchy, do you?"

"Stranger things have happened. The problem with kings and queens is that when a worthy figure appears—a Solomon, say, or a Charlemagne—their grateful subjects make the mistake of thinking that their descendants will be every bit as wise and just as they are. But the ability to lead a nation is not a heritable trait like hair color or skin tone. It is a rare skill, indeed, and manifests itself only in persons whose unique combination of temperament, training, and experience have made them capable of seeing past the benefits that they can derive from their country, to the benefits that they can bestow *upon* that country."

Eliza smiled to herself, glad that Alex's gaze was fixed elsewhere—she didn't want to make him self-conscious, or think she was mocking him. Even after four years, she was still moved by her husband's articulateness and vision, and she found tears had come to her eyes. He had the ability to sound as though he were reading from the pages of a well-edited book, even when he was speaking off the top of his head.

She stroked a lock of his strawberry-blond hair. "It sounds as though you are declaring your own qualifications for the role," she said, curling the strand around her index finger and giving it a teasing tug.

"Me? To be sure, I hope to serve my country. But if I am honest about my own capabilities, I am less executive than administrator. I am, perhaps, too selfish to be a great leader. So selfish," he added, turning to her with a smile and catching her hand in his, "that I would rather measure rooms for curtains and carpets with my beautiful wife than abase myself one last time before a man who was willing to make use of my services but not reward them until he was threatened with losing me. Well, let him have his turtle soup with his admirers. He has earned their veneration. But

I have earned his, and if he cannot see that, then I see no reason to leave the far more amiable company in which I find myself." And, pulling her hand to his lips, he bestowed upon it a dozen quick kisses.

Eliza listened to her husband with mixed emotions. On the one hand, she understood his frustration. So much of their marriage had been consumed by the war, by Alex's service to his country, and by General Washington's needs. But she also knew how much General Washington had meant to Alex, and how much his country meant to him, too. Still, she also adored it when he kissed her hand like this, and it was another moment before she was able to speak again. Duty could be an annoyingly inconvenient thing, but that was the blessing of marriage: There would always be time for more kissing later.

"Turtle soup?" she said at last, making a face. "The general eats that? Really?"

"I am told it is quite delicious."

"And I am told that opossum has a gamy flavor not unlike rabbit, but I'm still not going to eat anything that sports a hairless tail like a rodent. Well then," she continued, "far be it from me to ask you to leave my—what was the word you used—"

"Amiable."

"Yes, my amiable company." She patted him on the head and he lolled under her touch like a spaniel puppy. "But perhaps you would care to accompany me to the Broadway, where I saw a charming dry goods merchant."

Alex chuckled. "I think it's just called Broadway. No 'the' needed."

"I like the way 'the Broadway' sounds," Eliza retorted, to further laughter from Alex. "At any rate, I found this shop quite charming, and thought that we might find some fabric for the curtains, and perhaps also something to cover the sofas and chairs that Mama is sending from Albany."

THEIR LACK OF china was solved not a half hour later, in the mercer's shop that Eliza led Alex to on Broadway. In the middle of a relatively scant, though not unattractive, assortment of brocades and jacquards sat an entire service of the finest bone china Eliza had ever seen, painted with an intricate yet delicate pattern of brightly colored birds and flowers: cups and saucers, plates and chargers, salad bowls, dessert plates, and a full complement of serving dishes as well, including a four-legged covered fish plate that could have held a thirty-pound lobster.

It was an odd display to see in a fabric store, and Eliza was half afraid it was for show only, to set off the embroidered tablecloth beneath. She was delighted, then, when she made inquiries of the proprietor, to learn that the dishes had been left behind in one of the many empty houses the British abandoned when they fled the city. They could be had, she was told, "for a song," though the price she was quoted, fifty shillings, seemed more like an opera than a ditty. In comparison, they were only going to pay their servants two pounds a month, for instance, in addition to room and board.

"A song?" Alex echoed, overhearing. "Well, turn up the lights, Broadway, because I'm about to start singing!" And, in fact, he crooned over the dishes as if they were a nursery full of newborn infants. Like Eliza, he savored the finer things in life, but unlike his wife, he had not grown up surrounded by them. On the one hand, this ensured that he never took his newfound privilege for granted, but it also made him a bit covetous, and sometimes a spendthrift as well. An impoverished childhood never fully leaves you, and Eliza was learning that her husband needed to surround himself with expensive items to remind himself that he was no longer poor—even if he wasn't exactly rich either.

Eliza agreed that they were exquisite, but she had never thought of eating off dishes that did not originate with her family, or the family of friends. Still, they were as fine as anything that had ever graced her mother's table, and clearly had belonged to gentlefolk. And she knew the price, however dear, was indeed a bargain. Her mother had paid as much for a single soup tureen. Admittedly the tureen was as large as a Russian samovar, but still. This was a steal, and she knew it, and before the offer could be rescinded, Alex was making out a promissory note and signing it with more flourish than John Hancock inscribing his name on the Declaration of Independence.

The Hamiltons were so astounded at their find they almost forgot to pick out material for curtains. But soon enough the dishes were purchased, along with the fabric, and Eliza made arrangements with the proprietor to return with Rowena to retrieve them. They had finally hired a few servants: Rowena, a middle-aged lady and her young son, Simon, who were starting the next day. Normally, Eliza would have sent her maid alone, but the proprietor told her that he expected to receive a wide assortment of pewter, crystal, and plate in the coming days, as more abandoned houses were claimed by Americans, and their booty entered the market.

"The spoils of war!" Alex said cheerfully as they left the shop. "At this rate, we shall have a home to rival the Pastures in a few months' time!"

Eliza nodded, though she couldn't help but feel a twinge of guilt as she imagined all those families fleeing and leaving behind their heirlooms and memories. It could have easily been the treasures of the Pastures in the store, if the war had gone the other way.

"Don't let Papa hear your ambitions for our home," she admonished. "He'll be moved to outdo you, and Mama is already at wits' end with his extravagances." As she tucked the four pounds' worth of promissory notes in her string purse, she couldn't help but wonder if she, too, would soon be attempting to rein in a profligate husband. Well, her father had always made good on his debts and then some, and he had not half the mind Alex had.

We'll be fine, she told herself.

They walked for a few minutes, discussing this or that detail of the household, when their conversation was cut short by the staccato of a single drum beating out a military cadence.

"What on earth?" Alex said, involuntarily snapping to attention.

Before Eliza could hazard a guess, the drummer came into view around the corner of Broad Street, followed by a great throng of men in Continental military uniform. The men wore sabers but were otherwise unarmed, and there was nothing urgent in their demeanor. Indeed, they seemed slightly somber. Still, Alex asked incredulously: "Have the British returned?"

"I think not," Eliza said softly. She nodded at the rear of the column.

A large gray horse came into view, and on it sat the imposing figure of General George Washington. His cheeks were florid, as if he had just come from a warm room and had not yet accommodated himself to the chill December day. A sheepish but proud smile was on his sealed lips, and when Alex turned to Eliza, he saw a similar expression on her face.

"What is this?" he demanded.

Eliza shrugged. "It would seem that General Washington's troops are seeing him off to his boat," she said in a light tone.

Alex scoffed, and Eliza couldn't tell if he was amused or annoyed, or both.

"It would seem that you knew he would be passing down 'the Broadway.'"

"How on earth would I know something like that?" Eliza said, meeting Alex's gaze with a flat expression, though her eyes were merry. "I am merely a lawyer's wife, after all."

"Didn't you say something about a ladies' spy network?"

"I'm sure I said nothing about spies," Eliza protested. "Still, someone might have mentioned something about a formal farewell . . ." She shrugged. "I do not recall."

By now, the procession was upon them. Eliza recognized at least half a dozen faces from Alex's time in General Washington's office, but her husband's attention remained focused on the great man himself. Washington did not wave at the people who came out of houses and shops to see him, but his face turned back and forth, and he acknowledged his admirers with regal nods.

Only when his eyes met Alex's did a ripple of recognition overtake his expression. He remained impassive, but Eliza could have sworn she saw an eyebrow twitch. Then, finally, one more nod, just a little bigger than the ones he had offered to his anonymous fans.

Eliza turned to Alex. His face was as stony as General Washington's, but two spots of color had come up on his cheeks, and she didn't think it was the sea breeze. He neither moved nor spoke until the small procession—twenty men, perhaps thirty—had passed, and then he took Eliza's arm and they turned for home, still without speaking.

The silence stretched until they were on their own steps, when Eliza could bear it no longer.

"You are not angry with me?" she implored. "I thought it important for you to see each other. If your time with General Washington has shaped everything that is to come for us, it is equally true that General Washington's fate was immeasurably enriched by his association with you, and I wanted him to see that."

Alex took a deep breath before answering. "I am not angry," he said finally, and then, as if he heard the cold formality of his tone, he leaned forward and kissed Eliza on the tip of her nose. "I could never be angry with you, my love. But that part of my life is over. I am your man now, not General Washington's."

14

Paperwork

The Hamilton Town House
New York, New York
January 1784

It wasn't until Eliza had to run a household on her own that she realized how much she took for granted at the Pastures. As it was, Rowena was serving as cook, charwoman, and lady's maid until they were in a position to hire a full staff. Meanwhile, young Simon tried to fill in for the rest. The delay was partly based on a shortage of available servants in the recently liberated city, partly on a shortage of funds. Alex's law practice in Albany had been busy but not exactly lucrative, with many of his clients paying him in kind—smoked hams, canned fruit, and even the occasional live poultry—rather than in cash. Most of what they had to hand had been spent in securing a fine house in the "right" part of town, which both agreed was necessary if they were going to make a good impression in their new city. Everything else was happening on credit, which the Schuyler name, and Alex's wartime fame, helped secure.

"By the by, how is Rowena working out?" Alex asked on their second Monday in the city as they made their way to the hallway together after breakfast. He was headed out to the office, paper-stuffed satchel in hand.

His voice was careful. While they were both sympathetic to the loyalists' circumstances, it was quite another thing to have one in such close proximity as a servant in their home. Eliza had been wary of hiring the woman, a widow in her early forties whose husband had perished in the war—fighting for the British. Unlike many other loyalists, however—including her former employers—Rowena had not abandoned New York after the British surrender. She openly admitted that she preferred being part of the world's mightiest empire, but England itself was a country she had never visited and had no desire to live in.

Rowena had been born in New York, she said, and intended to die here—to be buried next to her husband in Trinity Cemetery. But her loyalist past had not endeared her to the newly minted Americans who were either returning to New York or taking advantage of (relatively) inexpensive real estate to move here, which was the only way Alex and Eliza had been able to afford her. It had taken all the courage of their convictions, however, to take on someone who had, until a few weeks ago, been an enemy of the state, for all intents and purposes. Still, Eliza said finally, if a privileged couple like the Hamiltons could not practice what they preached, how on earth could they expect less fortunate Americans to do the same?

"I must say," Eliza said, helping Alex with his coat, "she is quite pleasant. Aside from brief trips away from home, this is the first time I have ever been waited on by anyone other than the family servants, many of whom have been with us since before my birth. But Rowena has such an easy manner about her that it has been quite comfortable. I know she is a cook by training, but she is such a gifted lady's maid that I am tempted to offer her that position when we are able to hire more servants."

"I don't know," Alex said as he opened the front door and buttoned his jacket against the bright, cold December day. "The brisket she served yesterday was amazingly succulent, and those dumplings she made for breakfast? I could eat them thrice a day."

"Mmmm," Eliza said in agreement. "I asked her where she managed to find nutmeg and allspice in a city that hasn't seen regular cargo ships in more than half a decade. She told me she had a network of spies that would have won General Carlton the war if he'd had access to them. I thought that was a bit cheeky of her, but if it will keep her pantry well stocked, I am more than willing to overlook a little impertinence."

"Hear, hear," Alex said with an arched eyebrow. "As long as she's not sending spy messages, keep the dumplings coming." Then he kissed his pretty wife on the nose and headed off to the office.

ALEX HAD NO clients that first day at work—he had not expected any—but there were dozens of letters that he'd been neglecting for the past fortnight, including several from the Continental Congress and the state legislature in Albany, and though the replies were largely automatic, they were still time-consuming to answer, especially in the absence of a secretary or amanuensis. Although he had always known his value to General Washington as an assistant, he had attributed his worth to his mind—his fluency in French, his skill with bills of lading picked up on the docks of St. Croix, his ability to master currency exchanges and interest rates and, well, math.

Now he was realizing that the mere act of writing General Washington's letters was what actually ate up the bulk of his time. But there was simply no way he could employ an assistant now. You could pay a mercer or carpenter on credit, you could compensate a servant with housing and food, but an employee required money in order to pay his own bills, and money—*cold, hard cash*—as opposed to the nearly bottomless credit that came with Eliza's patrician lineage and Alex's vaunted service to General Washington. Cash was the one thing the Hamiltons did not have.

In point of fact, no one in the newly created country had much money. Or, rather, they had too much money, but nearly all of it was worthless. Despite the United States and England being officially distinct entities, the British shilling remained in active circulation, as England's economy was far more stable than America's. The Continental Congress had issued its own dollars—"Continentals"—but these were nearly valueless, owing to Congress's inability to collect taxes or duties, and were far less common than the currency issued by all thirteen of the new states, some in dollars, others in shillings. But despite the similarity in names, a Georgia shilling was worth three times a Delaware shilling, and a New Hampshire dollar could buy ten issued by the Congress. It was a vexing situation, but exactly the kind of problem that Alex's mathematical mind liked to work on. If only there were time!

And while he did not want to admit it to himself, he was keen on securing the sort of lifestyle for his wife that she had been accustomed to all her life. He had warned her against her future as a poor man's wife, but he did not want that future to be true. Alex remembered the look on her face when he had chosen the best glasses and china for their domicile. *She will never want for anything,* he promised himself. *Even if I have to work myself to the bone.*

His hours were consumed by letter writing, and whatever time left over was given to the review of countless new laws. For the past seven years, the thirteen states had been too busy fighting the British to worry much about the humdrum details of government. Now that the peace had been secured, however, they were making up for lost time. In the absence of a strong central government, each state was adopting its own legal systems just as it did its own currency, or perhaps *adapting* is the more apt word, since most of them were borrowed in large chunks from various Old World law codes. This was the new system's only saving grace, since legislatures across the country were literally passing hundreds of laws in a single motion, and it would have been impossible to keep up with them otherwise.

Alex had studied the old codes both at King's College before the war and during his apprenticeship in Albany the last two years, but there were hundreds of minor changes to apprise himself of, as well as the many wholly original laws that had been added to them. It was dull work, but it had to be done if he was to make an appearance in court, let alone make a living to pay all those invoices that had made their way from his satchel to his new desk (also bought on credit). Being a regimented lover of order, he might even have enjoyed sifting through the minutiae of the changes, if all the while he was poring over the pages he had not been aware that he had someone beautiful waiting for him at home. Somehow, "paperwork" had been left out of their wedding vows, but Alex was realizing just how much a part it really was . . .

Most of the new laws were fairly routine and, if scatter-shot, unobjectionable. However, there were a sizable number that concerned the new country's relationship with the substantial portion of its population—by some accounts as much as a quarter of the country—that had remained faithful to King George during the war. Perhaps the only place the loyalists weren't represented was in the victorious American legislatures, who had purged them from their ranks, and now wanted to punish their defeated co-citizens

for their misplaced allegiances. A few were executed as trai-
tors and a few more were imprisoned for collusion, but
most were simply fined or else had their property seized,
and still more were denied the right to work in their chosen
professions.

Alex wasn't surprised by the vindictiveness—war was a
vicious thing, and it had brought out the worst in the British,
as their prison boats testified—but he was still dismayed by
it. The United States and its territories was a vast country,
larger than any of the nations of the Old World, save Russia,
but its population was relatively tiny. Nearly all of its people
clustered along the eastern seaboard, leaving large swaths of
territory virtually uninhabited and thus undefended. There
was no way such a nation could survive if three-quarters of its
population was in conflict with the other quarter. They would
have to find common cause and recognize that, for better or
worse, they were all Americans now. As Benjamin Franklin
had said at the signing of the Declaration of Independence:
"We must, indeed, all hang together, or we will most assuredly all hang separately."

And so, one day's work stretched into two, three, then
the whole week. Meanwhile the office remained devoid of
clients. Though Alex had written letters to several dozen
friends, acquaintances, friends of friends, and a few total
strangers announcing his presence in New York, his door
remained silent and his mailbox empty save correspondence
related to the formation of the new government.

And because he didn't yet have a secretary, he was forced to deliver most of his notes himself. Having left the horse Laurens had given him at the Pastures (the cost of stabling it in the city was nearly equal to the rent on his house!), he had to rely on the city's hansom cabs or simply hoof it.

The weather, though quite cold, was not unbearable, and it wouldn't have been unpleasant work if it hadn't been so time-consuming, and if the bills had not continued to pile up, and if any of it had borne pay dirt.

Alex was adamant that they would not resort to Eliza's suggestion that they write her father for a loan or two. But after two weeks, Alex began to fear that he was going to have to start haunting the courts like that breed of dishonorable attorney who preys on hapless individuals who have inadvertently run afoul of the law, or fallen victim to unscrupulous merchants or landowners, only to forfeit still more of their possessions as payment to attorneys defending them from charges that never should have brought in the first place.

Sometime during the third week, however, just after the noon hour (Alex knew because he had only a moment ago pulled his watch from his pocket, wondering if it was too early to pop down to the tavern on the corner of Stone and Broad streets), there came the sound of a knock at the door of his outer office.

Lacking an assistant, Alex rose from behind his desk to answer it himself. If he was surprised that someone had knocked at his door, he was still more shocked to find that the person on the far side of the portal was a woman, not much older than his Eliza. Both the woman's coat and bonnet, Alex noted, were of fine wool, but well-worn, and told a story of a prosperous person fallen on hard times. When Alex saw the black satin mourning ribbon affixed to the sleeve of the woman's coat, he instantly understood. The young woman was a widow, her husband no doubt a casualty of the recent war.

"Good afternoon," he said, extending his hand. "May I help you?"

"Good afternoon," the woman said in a formal, though not unfriendly, tone. Her handshake was similarly peremptory. "I was told these are the law offices of Mr. Alexander Hamilton?"

Alex felt a proud smile flicker across his face. It was the first time he had heard the words said out loud. "Indeed, they are, Mrs. —"

"Childress," the woman said. "If he is not too busy, I wonder if I might meet with him."

Alex laughed. "He's not too busy at all. Please, do come in," he continued, stepping aside and gesturing her into the office. "May I take your coat?"

"Thank you," Mrs. Childress said, removing her coat. Alex hung it up on a peg, then led the woman into his office, where he was mortified to realize that there was no second chair. How had this not occurred to him in more than two weeks of occupancy? He scurried behind the desk and pulled his own chair out and offered it to Mrs. Childress.

If his new client—he hoped she was a client, and not a woman looking for work—noticed the irregularity, it didn't show on her composed, though somewhat tense, face. She sat down and stared straight ahead, while Alex, after weighing his options, decided to half lean, half sit on the corner of his desk, so that he would not be standing right next to her, forcing her to crane her neck up at him.

After several seconds of silence, Mrs. Childress said, "Could I have a glass of water?" She didn't look at him when she spoke.

"Ah, of course," Alex said, somewhat nervously. At least there was an ewer in the room, which he had topped off from the street well when he arrived that morning. Only one cup, though. He discreetly wiped it clean, filled it, and handed it to her. She took it in one of her black-gloved hands, but didn't drink from it, instead placing it on the corner of his desk.

After several more seconds of silence, Alex cleared his throat. "If I may ask, what brings you here today?"

"Oh, if you don't mind," Mrs. Childress said in somewhat confused voice—as if she were embarrassed almost—"I would prefer to speak to Mr. Hamilton directly."

Alex felt his cheeks color, and the woman's did in turn.

"Unless there is another Mr. Hamilton who occupies these offices when I am out, then I am he."

"Oh!" she said, immediately realizing her error. "When you opened the door, I thought you were the servant!"

Alex smiled sardonically. "Please think of me as *your* servant, Mrs. Childress. One who has yet to procure a secretary to open his doors and fill his glass."

"It's not that," Childress said. "It's just, well—you are so young!"

Alex felt his cheeks go redder. "Revolution has a way of foreshortening life," he said, but even as the words left his mouth, his eyes alit on the dark attire shrouding her frame and he realized his comment must have sounded glib to her.

But she seemed to take it sympathetically. Her eyes followed his, and one of her gloved hands reached up to touch the ribbon.

"I do know that," she said in a distant voice. "I have worn this ribbon so long now that I almost forget it's there. Not a day goes by when I don't think of my beloved Jonathan."

Alex's mouth opened to murmur a condolence even before she finished speaking, but at the name "Jonathan—" His voice caught in his throat. *Ah, Laurens!* he thought. He wished he could say that he thought of him every day, but the truth is he had pushed his dearest friend from his mind almost as soon as he heard of his death, lest he be overcome with grief. *Whoever said war is glorious is a lying fool.*

"I am so sorry for your loss," Alex said when he had recovered himself. "Is the legal matter that brought you here perhaps related to your husband's passing?"

"Legal?" Childress said in a bemused voice. "Well, I suppose it is a legal question, though to me it seems an act of straightforward perfidy." She summoned a deep breath. "My husband that was, Mr. Jonathan Childress, arrived in this country from Liverpool as a teenager. He was indentured to Mr. Philip Ruston, who operated a prosperous alehouse on Water Street, and after completing his seven-years term of service had formed such a bond with his master that he stayed on as brew master and, eventually, partner. When, in 1769, Mr. Ruston prepared to depart this world without any natural-born heirs, he named my husband the beneficiary of his estate, and so he became owner of the enterprise. My husband was known to be a gifted brewer, so much so that in addition to brewing all the lagers, ales, and stouts for his own establishment, which he continued to call Ruston's in honor of his benefactor, he also supplied the needs of eight other inns in the city. He was on his way to becoming a rich man indeed when independence was declared, and—"

Childress paused, less for breath than to calm herself. Alex indicated the cup on his desk, and she took a small sip.

"My husband loved this city and this country. He considered them his home. He married me, who was born right here in Westport, Connecticut, and bore our son and daughter with the expectation that, like a more modest version of the Livingstons of New York State and the Carters of Virginia, the Childress name would become synonymous with the American upper classes. Yet to Jonathan, America was always an extension of England, which had made him and, he felt, made also this country. When his king called on him to defend the union of the mother country with its far-flung colonies, he did so willingly, and when he was taken home on the field of battle, I do not believe he regretted his choice. Though I have no doubt he thought sadly of the family from which he was being taken.

"I confess that my loyalty to one side or the other was never as pronounced as was my husband's. I wanted peace far more than I wanted to be a British subject, or an American one. While all this was happening, I oversaw the business my husband built with, if I may say so myself, a fair degree of skill. Despite the imposition of the British occupation and the grudging assistance of male employees who did not at first enjoy being subordinate to an employer of the female persuasion, I expanded the number of establishments to which we sold, raising it from eight to twelve over the past seven years.

"Of course, our clientele were much diminished as many patriots had fled the city, but so thirsty were they and their British occupiers that I was compelled to purchase a building on Baxter Street and transform it into a brewery. I outfitted it with the newest vats and stills so that I could meet demand and maintain the quality of our product, a task at which I was so successful that Ruston's Ale became well-known as one of the very finest in the city, and indeed in the colony."

"You mean state, don't you," Alex prodded gently.

Mrs. Childress smiled ruefully, and though tinged by sadness, the smile still lit up her face. "I suppose I do."

He cleared his throat.

"It would seem that you survived the war with less privation than did many," he said, yet even as he spoke his eyes were taking in once again the frayed edges of the once-fine mourning gown, echoed in the worry lines that framed her mouth and eyes. From her story she was a wealthy, even unctuous, woman, but her dress and face were at odds with her words.

Mrs. Childress stared at Alex blankly. "Money cannot buy a husband or father," she said finally.

Alex struggled to keep his face impassive. "It cannot," he concurred. "So, tell me: Is the issue something to do with your late husband's estate?"

A short laugh erupted from Mrs. Childress's mouth. "Issue? Yes, that's what it is, all right." She sighed as if she could not believe what she was about to say. "Though it has almost nothing to do with my husband's affairs, and everything to do with mine. It would seem that the Baxter Street building I purchased had been owned by a patriot of the name Le Beau, who was away at war when General Howe drove General Washington from Manhattan Island in 1777, though I only learned his name much later. Fearing retribution, the remaining Le Beaus fled the city. They had been gone for some three years when I purchased the property, and, as I said, I knew none of this. The transaction was handled by a British colonel by the name of Lewiston, and the sale and deeds were reviewed and approved by a military tribunal. I had no reason to believe that this was in any way unusual, let alone illegal.

"Nevertheless, when the British left the city and the Americans entered, my building was seized from me by the

Continental army, who promptly ransacked it, draining and destroying every last cask on the premises, and removing every piece of distillery equipment to who knows where. The building itself was returned to the heirs of Mr. Le Beau, who, like my husband, met his end in the war. I say 'returned,' though that is not quite accurate, for Mr. Le Beau's family had relocated to a small village in Pennsylvania called Harrisburg and have shown no desire to return to New York.

"I sank all of my family's fortunes in the purchase and outfitting of the property, Mr. Hamilton, and now find myself deprived not only of my investment but of the means to make my living. Even the original inn on Water Street that my husband received from his employer threatens to be taken from me, as it was collateral on the loan with which I purchased the Baxter Street property. Unless some redress is done to me, my children and I are ruined. My creditors shall turn us out of our house, and likely throw me into debtors' prison to boot. In short," she said, turning to Alex with the first trace of emotion in her voice, "I am penniless, unless you can save me."

As she'd spoken, Alex's mind had turned over all the new laws he'd reviewed in the past weeks. As he understood them, the sale of Le Beaus' building to Mrs. Childress fell into a gray area. If it had been directly seized from them by the British, any subsequent sale would have been invalidated. But since the Le Beaus appeared to have voluntarily abandoned their property, the British, as the government of good standing, had simply disposed of the building as they saw fit. No doubt George Clinton's courts would take a skeptical view of such an interpretation, however, and Alex knew there was very little chance he would be able to recover the property for Mrs. Childress.

But if the court ruled the sale invalid, then by their own logic, Mrs. Childress's loan would also be rendered null and void, which would at least clear her of her debts. And if he could recover the costs of the stolen ale and distillery equipment, he might be able to put a little cash into her pocket, which might enable her to keep her business solvent—and out of prison. But getting the Continental army to pay a loyalist what amounted to war reparations was a tall order indeed, and one that seemed likely to lose Alex more friends than it would gain him. It was not exactly the ideal first case for a young lawyer.

He peered down at Mrs. Childress, who was looking up at him with anxious eyes. He opened his mouth to respond, but she spoke over him.

"I know that you fought on the opposite side of the war from my husband," she said. "I know that you served with General Washington himself, and that you distinguished yourself at the Battle at Monmouth, where my Jonathan fell, and at Yorktown as well. But I've also heard that you have argued eloquently and passionately for reconciliation, and even gone so far as to challenge some of the laws that penalize those of us who supported the losing side. I am not wise in the ways of the world, but I know that only a man like you—a known patriot and hero—has any hope of convincing an American jury that a wrong has been done to me. But honesty compels me to tell you that I cannot pay unless you are victorious in your suit." Another small smile cracked her sad face, offering a glimpse of the vibrant woman she must have been before war ripped her life asunder. "I can, however, give you all the beer you can drink."

Alex wondered if he were making a mistake even as he replied. "As it happens," he said with a grin, "I have quite a taste for beer."

15

Bonds of Sisterhood, Part One

The Hamilton Town House
New York, New York
January 1784

Meanwhile, a week or two after Alex got his first client, one afternoon, Eliza found herself in the middle of her dining room, pensively studying the silver serving dishes displayed on the walnut cabinet. The four-legged covered platter with its intricate repoussé lid—large enough to hold four chickens, two geese, or a whole turkey—occupied center stage on the eye-level shelf, flanked by a pair of four-pronged candelabra that had been made by Paul Revere himself. On the next shelf down was a large oval salver stood upright on a carved ivory stand to better show off the illustration intricately etched into its base, which showed the Pastures in all its glory and remarkable detail, right down to the panes of the windows and the mortar between each brick.

To one side of the salver was a pedestaled cake plate, while the other side was occupied by a medium-size soup tureen, which, while round like the cake plate, had four legs and thus did not create the most symmetrical of arrangements. There were a pair of large porcelain serving platters from the famous Bow porcelain factory, but Eliza was skeptical about mixing silver and china, and, as well, the pattern on the platters was a dark burgundy and made little statement except in the brightest daylight—not exactly ideal ambiance for a dinner party. Not that she had any plans to throw a dinner party, of course.

Alex spent so much time in the office in the past month it was hard to plan a social gathering, let alone a dinner à deux, since he was often home long past mealtimes. She was alone rather often, hence the ten minutes she had just spent staring at a motley collection of china and silver. When they lived at the Pastures and Alex was busy at work or war, she had her family to spend time with. But here in New York, she was all by herself, and there were only so many different ways one could arrange one's dishes.

Eliza had been under the presumption that once they had a home of their own, they would have more time for each other, but with Alex consumed with his work, it appeared the opposite was true. For the first time in her life, she was truly lonely. Without her sisters around her to tease her, the young ones running around, and her mother fussing, she found her life very empty indeed. She understood that Alex was working hard for them—for their future—but she wished he would come home earlier once in a while. He had already given the early years of their marriage to the war, and now it seemed, he would give these years to his work.

She perked up at the thought that while she didn't have family around, they could make new friends in New York. Alex had expressed a fondness for the idea of a dinner party, recalling the intimate yet lively gatherings he had experienced at the home of William Livingston when he first came to the United States, not to mention any number of occasions at the Pastures—"Although your mother does seem to prefer a ball to a seated affair," he had joked.

At any rate, if and when they began entertaining, Eliza wanted the house to look its best, and as she studied the cabinet, she contemplated the radical step of removing *all* the silver and replacing it entirely with patterned china. Her parents had gifted them a mismatched if numerous assortment of pieces, but each was fine in its own way. Plus, she and Alex acquired quite a few nice specimens since their arrival in New York, including the prized set of Crown Derby they purchased on the day of General Washington's farewell. None quite matched the others, but this might give the effect of a curated collection accrued over time rather than an assortment of hand-me-downs, which is what, for the most part, it actually was. It would be a little bohemian, and quite possibly outré, but she and Alex were young, after all, and did not need to decorate like a pair of sixty-year-olds.

"It cannot hurt to try," she said out loud, though there was no one else around to hear her speak. Indeed, the house had been empty a lot lately, despite Rowena's and Simon's cheerful presence as they were often out on some errand or another. Alex's work with Mrs. Childress had brought in a dozen more clients, all former loyalists whose property had been seized. He had taken them all on, but the bulk of his attention was devoted to the Childress case, which he thought stood the best chance of securing some kind of compensation for the plaintiff, and would thus serve as a precedent for subsequent cases. Eliza was not fully versed on the legal intricacies of the case, but she had met Mrs. Childress once in Alex's office, and immediately saw how such a woman could appeal to a jury. She was refined, independent, articulate, and attractive as well, even in her shabby widow's weeds.

A *little* too *attractive*, Eliza couldn't help thinking, but tried to suppress the jealous instinct. She had married a brilliant, ambitious, and charismatic man, and she did not want to hold him back. She trusted him with her heart, and she knew that his heart was hers alone, in that she was fully confident.

She had just finished removing all the silver dishes from the cabinet and pulling the china from its various shelves and cubbies in the kitchen and crowding the dining table with them when the front door knocker thudded hollowly from the hall. Rowena had gone to market, which, given the still-erratic state of food supply in the city, could take the entire day. Simon was hiding in whatever nook or cranny he secreted himself in when his mother was out, so Eliza hurried to answer the door herself, assuming it was another maid of some lady or other who wanted to leave her card to arrange for a social date. Wives of the men who'd served with her husband, as well as friends of her parents.

There was no reason to be lonely when she could answer these social calls and fill her days making new acquaintances, and Eliza decided she would do just that starting tomorrow.

She pulled the door open and, as she expected, a woman's form greeted her. Eliza immediately noted the luxurious fur of the hat and stole protecting its owner against the January cold. But her head was turned to the southeast, looking down toward the water, so at first Eliza couldn't see who her visitor was. *One of those women who doesn't send her maid to do her calling,* Eliza thought.

But not even she was prepared for the face that greeted her when her caller turned toward the opened door.

"Peggy!" Eliza threw her arms around her sister without thinking. "Oh my darling, you cannot imagine how wonderful it is to see you!"

"Eliza!" Peggy returned the hug with as much enthusiasm as her sister. "How are you, darling?"

"Good, now that you are here!" Eliza felt a rush of joy at seeing her beautiful sister once more, and so unexpectedly. She ushered Peggy in and closed the door against the frigid air. "It's so nice to have company after being alone in the house for weeks and weeks."

"What? Weeks? Where's Alex?" Peggy asked, frowning from underneath her rather fantastic hat with a profusion of ostrich feathers.

"Oh, you know. Seeking out clients and trying to understand all the new statutes Governor Clinton keeps passing has Alex quite busy." An image of Mrs. Childress's pretty blond-ringed face flashed in her mind, but she banished it immediately. "What with the vagaries of establishing a law practice in a city and state that is daily rewriting its laws, he is practically there day and night."

Peggy peered into the house, as if she might see Alex hard at it. "But surely you can just pop in to see him for coffee now and then to make sure he pays attention to you?"

Eliza looked where Peggy was looking. "Oh, you think Alex's office is located in this house? My dear, have you never been in a city home before? Only the wealthiest of the wealthy can afford that kind of capacious residence. Here the rooms are stacked on top of each other like dovecotes, with the kitchen in the basement and the bedchambers on the top floor, and all the receiving rooms sandwiched between. He maintains a study here, but it would be inappropriate for seeing clients, as they would have to tramp through the front parlor."

"You mean this is . . . *all* . . . of the house?" Peggy seemed to think Eliza was putting her on.

"Peggy! This is considered a very fine home in New York City! It's not large, but we have three floors. And come summer, the garden in back will be lovely. We can't all marry Rensselaers, after all. Speaking of which—where is Stephen? And, forgive me for being abrupt, but, what are you doing here?"

Peggy looked simultaneously confused and coquettish, as if she had scored some kind of secret victory. "Didn't you get my note? I wrote nearly two weeks ago to say that we were coming down." As she spoke, she unbuttoned her cloak and held it out absently for a footman who never materialized. Eliza took it herself, hanging it in the small wardrobe they'd acquired, and led her sister into the living room. She took Peggy's amazing headgear as well, and marveled at the towering creation.

Eliza shook her head. "I know that New York is supposed to be a cosmopolitan city, and we live but one block from City Hall, but I'm afraid it is only half domesticated. The British left it in such a state of disrepair as boggles the mind, and it is still very early in the redevelopment process."

Peggy followed all this with a frown of confusion. "I take it you mean that my letter didn't arrive," she said when Eliza was finished.

Eliza laughed. "Only messenger-delivered mail has arrived for the past three weeks." She indicated a sofa, which Peggy ignored, taking in the whole of the room with a few sweeping glances that made Eliza acutely conscious of the smallness of the room as compared with the great salons of the Pastures and the Van Rensselaer manor house. "But the city has other charms."

"Like fine china, I see," Peggy said, walking from the drawing room into the dining room. "This piece is lovely," she said, holding up a fluted gravy dish covered in lilacs so lifelike you could almost smell them. She glanced at the empty china cabinet. "Rearranging?"

"It's tricky," Eliza said. "We have not quite enough pieces to fill the cabinet the way Mama does, but we still want things to look nice."

"Well, I think they look nice on the table. You should leave them there."

"On the table? But how would we eat?"

"Why, with them, of course."

Eliza shook her head. "I know you are the unconventional sister, but this is a little . . . *je ne sais quoi*, even for you."

"And you're the smart sister, but you are not following my meaning. Leave them on the table because we're having a dinner party!" said Peggy.

"A dinner par—you mean, tonight?"

"Why not? Stephen and I have no other plans. We're staying with Helena and John Rutherfurd. Do you know them? Helena is the daughter of Lewis Morris of Morrisania, just north of Manhattan. I guess they used to own New Jersey or something? They sold much of it to the Rutherfurds, so I guess Helena is bringing it back into the family. And Helena's uncle Gouverneur Morris is visiting. I say 'uncle' but he's her father's half brother and is not even thirty. He's *quite* handsome. If I were still single, or you were . . ."

"Peggy! You scandalize me." Eliza was looking around the dining room with its dishes scattered everywhere, wondering how it could possibly be readied for dinner. "But Rowena has already gone to market," she protested weakly. "She will not have shopped for such a large party, if there is even that much food to be found."

"Not to worry. I'm a Van Rensselaer now. Stephen knew about the shipping interruptions in New York, and brought along, oh, I don't know, a *lot* of food. Like a whole cow and a whole pig and chickens and turkeys and ducks, and, well, pretty much anything an invading army might need. Oh, that was a bit crass of me. Too soon?"

Eliza just grimaced at her sister's humor. "But how will we get it here? Rowena cannot possibly—"

"You *must* have some kind of help, don't you?"

"Rowena's son, Simon . . ."

"We'll send him over with a note. The Rutherfurds have a houseful of servants. They can easily bring over what we need."

"But Alex will not know about tonight—"

"The boy—Simon?—can tell him. Is Alex's office far from here?"

"It is just off Hanover Square on Stone Street."

"Which could be in Philadelphia for all I know, but I'll assume it is close by." When Eliza still hesitated, Peggy grabbed her hand. "Come now, sister. You've have been in this city for well over a month. It seems like an easy place to disappear into. Let's make sure that doesn't happen."

Eliza hung fire for one more moment. The thought of a party excited her to no end, but to plan it without Alex seemed a bit of a betrayal. What if he was too tired when he got home to enjoy it? But she knew that it was more likely he was as frustrated by their routine as she was, and the surprise would delight him to no end. And who knows what sort of contacts or clients he might pick up?

At last she nodded her head eagerly. She rang the bell, and a (long) moment later, Simon's footsteps could be heard on the stairs. The towheaded boy, not yet ten years old, appeared in a wrinkled blue velvet jacket that had been hastily buttoned over much rougher homespun garments. Rowena had recently started training him for eventual service as a footman, a career that Eliza didn't think suited him at all. He was athletic and outdoorsy and had a sure hand with animals. At the very least, he should work in a stable, but Alex had said he was the type to run off at sixteen like a modern-day Daniel Boone. From the state of Simon's hands, it was clear he had been working with what he called his "kit"—a motley assortment of leather and metal that he used to repair tackle for the local stable.

"Yes, Miss Eliza—I mean, Mrs. Hamilton?"

While Peggy wrote a note to Stephen explaining what was needed, Eliza told Simon of his errands. Then, while Peggy told Simon where the Rutherfurds lived, Eliza penned her own missive to Alex.

Darling Husband—

A remarkable surprise has occurred! Peggy and Mr. Van Rensselaer have arrived in town, apparently in advance of a note from them alerting us to their appearance. They are staying at the nearby home of Mr. and Mrs. John Rutherfurd, and I have invited them over for dinner tonight (by which I mean, as you can probably guess, that Peggy invited herself for dinner, and I could not talk her out of it). They will be bringing their other houseguest, a Mr. Gouverneur Morris, who I believe worked with General Washington, and it should be quite a festive evening! Stephen has brought plenty of victuals, and Peggy says that she has brought her new maid as well, who can wait at table so poor Rowena isn't overwhelmed.

Our first dinner party! And in New York City! I do hope you'll be able to leave the office a little earlier this evening! A home never truly becomes a home until you share it with other people!

Your loving,
Eliza

Simon looked thrilled by the prospect of an errand out of doors, not to mention out of the kitchen, and hastily donned his overcoat and dashed off.

Eliza and Peggy passed the rest of the afternoon catching up over a pot of mint tea. "So how are you, truly?" asked Peggy. "We have missed you."

Eliza choked back a half sob and tried to cover it up with a laugh.

"Why, Eliza! Is it as hard as all that?"

Eliza shook her head. "No, no. I have missed you so much, that is all—it feels as if we are so far away from each other now. I wanted to live on my own so much, but now that we do, I miss our family."

Peggy nodded in sympathy. "But Stephen and I will come into town often, so we shall see each other more than we wish," she said with a naughty smile. But she kept Eliza's hands in hers, as if to reassure her sister that while she might be alone in New York, she was not alone in the world.

"How is life in Rensselaerswyck Manor?" she asked Peggy, who had been living there now for half a year.

The house was only half as large as the Pastures, Peggy said, but practically empty by Schuyler standards. Stephen's father, Stephen II, had died at the age of twenty-seven, when Stephen was just a boy, leaving two other children besides his namesake eldest son: Philip, who was two years younger, and Elizabeth, which prompted Eliza to quip that in all of upper New York State there seemed to be only half a dozen names: John, Stephen, Philip, Catherine (Stephen's mother's name as well as their own), Elizabeth, and Margaret, with a couple of Corneliuses and Gertrudes thrown in for good measure.

Elizabeth Van Rensselaer was ten years younger than Peggy and "a jolly fun girl," though not "half as bright as *my* Eliza," but what Peggy really missed was the sound of little children playing. At her words, Eliza found herself blinking back tears. She too missed the sound of children's voices playing games and making plans . . .

Mrs. Stephen Van Rensselaer II was not yet fifty, yet she had the air of a woman "twice her age," and while she had remarried a Reverend Eilardus Westerlo, she was still referred to in Albany society as "Mrs. Stephen II."

"When I mentioned that Papa was the first man in the United States to bring the *Ruins of Rome* wallpaper back from Europe," Peggy said, laughing, "I thought Mrs. Stephen II—she insists that I refer to her as such—was going to crack her teacup, so white did her knuckles grow! You are so lucky, Eliza!" she continued. "The house I share with my husband will not be ours until Stephen comes of age, so we have two more years in the smaller cottage on the property before we can move to the Patroon's manor house."

While they talked, Peggy began idly returning the silver to the display cabinet. To Eliza's delight, her sister put everything back exactly as it had been, the four-legged serving dish flanked by the candelabra, the illustrated salver bookended by the cake plate and soup tureen. "Such lovely pieces, and so nice to have things that mean something to you rather than to some relative long gone from this world!" Eliza blushed and didn't say anything, happy that she hadn't had time to replace all the silver with china as she'd planned.

About a half hour after Simon had gone, Rowena returned. The housekeeper's face went ashen when Eliza told her of the dinner plans, but then she steeled herself and muttered, "Just leave it to me, Mrs. Hamilton," before disappearing into the kitchen.

About an hour after that, a stout woman dressed in the drabbest of drab browns appeared. Improbably, her name was Violetta. She was Peggy's new lady's maid, a fixture from Stephen's youth, who looked as though she'd be more comfortable gelding calves than adjusting a corset. ("But you'd be amazed at what she can do to a wig with a teasing comb and lard," Peggy enthused. "Her creations are positively sculptural!") Violetta brought two boys from the Rutherfurds with her, and after a brief consultation with Eliza ("I will make do with what I have to work with, Mrs. Hamilton"), had the lads shifting furniture about like a general rearranging wooden soldiers on a painted map, banishing Eliza and Peggy to the second floor.

It wasn't until they mounted the second-floor landing and Eliza caught a glimpse of herself in one of the two-year-old dresses that were her usual outfit around the house that she realized she still had to come up with something to wear. Peggy, of course, looked exquisite. You'd never know she'd just spent three days on the road. She was wearing a spring-green gown, with delicate pale yellow embroidery and tiny but detailed pink and periwinkle flowers. She wasn't wearing a wig, but it didn't matter with Peggy. Her raven tresses seemed only to have grown more lustrous, and her coiled braids, though probably meant to be practical for travel, still managed to give her the regality of a Greek statue.

Eliza, on the other hand, had been living without a lady's maid for the first time in her life, and had been doing her hair by herself for nearly a month. She had wound it up in the simplest bun, with but a few spiraled wisps to frame her face. Alex, who never shied away from pomp and circumstance in public, said he much preferred this look for day-to-day life and endearingly called Eliza his "sweet peasant girl." But she knew that such a look would not do to entertain guests like the Rutherfurds and Morrises, who, if not quite as wealthy as Schuylers and Van Rensselaers, were nevertheless important local gentry.

But before she could wonder how to rectify this alarming situation, Peggy was pushing her down on the simple cane-bottomed stool Eliza used as a tuffet in front of her vanity. She grabbed a brush and comb from the Spartan surface of the table, pulled the pins that held Eliza's hair, and met her older sister's eyes in the mirror before them.

"You cannot imagine how long I've waited to do this."

Eliza couldn't help but blanch. "You've never styled your own hair in your life!"

"Silly, I'm not going to do this alone," Peggy said, as Violetta entered the room with crimping irons and powder.

16

———⚬❦⚬———

Dinner Is Served

The Hamilton Town House
New York, New York
January 1784

A little over an hour later, Eliza could hardly recognize herself. Violetta had teased her mane into a dramatic halo with a spiraled fall that hung down to her shoulders and accentuated the taut, slender column of her neck. In front were the same wisps of hair that had been there before, but they were somehow longer and more elegant, and the whole mass had been dusted with powder, giving it an adamantine sheen.

Eliza's face and décolletage had also been powdered, so that her exposed skin blended almost seamlessly into the silver dress Peggy had picked out for her. Eliza protested at first, saying the silver silk with its metallic bronze piping was too severe for her. But as she glanced in the mirror, she saw that Peggy's eye had been unfailing and that Alex's "sweet peasant girl" had been revealed to be in possession of a refinement and power that she hadn't suspected was in her. She didn't know whether to be pleased or frightened.

Violetta, however, was less confused. "My dear," she breathed, returning to the room after assessing the situation downstairs. "You clean up *quite* well." Then, hearing the impertinence in her tone, she quickly assumed her professional demeanor. "Mr. Van Rensselaer has arrived, along with Mr. and Mrs. Rutherfurd and Mr. Gouverneur Morris. I have taken the liberty of impressing Simon as footman. He is serving them a cordial."

"A cordial?" Eliza knew that she and Alex had nothing so fancy in the house. Indeed, all they had were casks of Mrs. Childress's hearty but humble ale. She turned to Peggy. "More of your stores?"

Peggy nodded. "One of Stephen's tenants brews a remarkable honey wine. Sweet yet surprisingly delicate. Very potent, though—sip slowly."

Eliza laughed and turned back to Violetta. "Thank you, Violetta. Please tell my guests I'll be right down. Has there been any word from Mr. Hamilton?"

Violetta shook her head. "Simon said a clerk in an adjacent office let him into Mr. Hamilton's reception room, where he left his note. Mr. Hamilton himself was not on the premises."

An image of Ruston's Ale House flashed in Eliza's mind, and the row of third-floor windows that Alex had once pointed out to her as Mrs. Childress's apartment. When Eliza asked how Alex knew this, he told her that he had often had to call on her to get her to sign some document or other. "It is a quite charming apartment, spread out almost like a country house, and Mrs. Childress is a very amiable hostess indeed."

Eliza banished the thought of Mrs. Childress's face and house, and her face in her house, and Alex's face—

She shook her head to clear it.

"Well, he will have finished his errands by now, I'm sure, and returned to his office, and from there it is only a short walk home. I'm sure he'll be here soon." But in her heart, she wasn't so sure. What if he was detained at the home of a potential client? If Eliza knew anything about the rich men Alex was courting for business, it was that they loved to hear themselves talk, and Alex was not in a position to cut them off. He could be held prisoner for who knows how long. Really, she wished her husband would recognize that there was more to life than work sometimes. She was trying not to be too frustrated with him, as she knew he was simply doing his best to establish his practice and secure their future.

But what was a secure future if they didn't have time to enjoy it together?

"Come now, Sister," Peggy said, placing her hand in Eliza's and patting it soothingly. "You have seen Mama handle a houseful of guests in Papa's absence without breaking a sweat. And as I recall, you did a flawless job hosting that send-off for Alex and Papa a few years ago."

They gave Violetta a head start—no one wants to be upstaged by their maid, after all—then headed for the stairs.

Peggy led the way. At the door to the parlor, she paused in front of Eliza, blocking her from view.

"My lady; gentlemen," she said in a showman's voice, "I present, Mrs. Alexander Hamilton in her own home!"

Peggy stepped aside with a flourish, and Eliza had no choice but to walk into the room like a princess into court. Stephen and two other men stood up, while someone who must be Helena sat in the room's most comfortable chair, a large, broad wingback in a dark blue upholstery that swallowed her up a little. Even though she was sitting, it was obvious she wasn't much over five feet tall—a fact that was confirmed when she rose to her feet with a large, kind smile on her face.

"Oh, my dear Mrs. Hamilton! Peggy said you were lovely, but she didn't do you justice!" She walked across the room and clasped Eliza's hand in both of hers, beaming up at her. Eliza was immediately charmed. Though Helena was a few years younger than she, she possessed incredible— *enviable*—poise, somehow managing to put Eliza at ease in her own house.

"It is lovely to meet you, Mrs. Rutherfurd. I must thank you for extending such generous hospitality to my sister and brother-in-law, as well as for gracing my dinner table on such short notice."

"I think we do everything on short notice these days. New York is still so raw after its recent travails."

"No doubt, order will be restored soon enough."

"Indeed. But I suspect we will create some new traditions as well." Helena stepped back then. "Please, allow me to introduce my husband, Mr. John Rutherfurd, and my uncle, Mr. Gouverneur Morris."

Eliza shook John's hand first, then Gouverneur's. John was a genial-seeming fellow whose pronounced chin dimple rescued his face from plainness. Gouverneur, by contrast, as Peggy had mentioned, was quite young, maybe just a few years older than she, and with sharp eyes and a Gallic nose. His thick dark hair was swept back from his face and tied in a short ponytail, which only added to his rakish appearance. Eliza couldn't help but find him charming, and his presence only made Alex's absence at the dinner table clearer, which filled her with an empty ache.

"Goo-ver-*neer*," she said, sounding the name out slowly. "Is it French?"

Gouverneur smiled disarmingly. "It is, through my mother's line. It used to be pronounced 'Goo-vuh-*noor*,' but we Americans have added our own spin to it."

"Fascinating. And of course the Morris name is known far and wide. My husband and I were engaged in Morristown, New Jersey, which I believe was named after your . . . grandfather, yes?" she asked.

"Lewis Morris, yes. Not to be confused with Helena's father, also named Lewis, my older brother."

"Pardon me for saying, but you seem more like Mrs. Rutherfurd's brother than uncle," she said with a smile.

He returned it with a genial one of his own, and it was quite clear that their dinner guest was taken with their spirited hostess. "My father's first wife passed away, and he married my mother and began a second family only some time later. Helena's father, my half brother, is twenty-six years my senior."

"Ah, I see. I should also thank you on behalf of the Continental troops. My husband tells me that your reforms greatly ameliorated the conditions our boys served in during the war."

Gouverneur smiled modestly. "We all did our part. I have been told that your war drives clothed more men than all the tailors and dry goods purveyors in New York and New Jersey combined, so allow me to thank you as well," he said with a bow.

"And, Stephen," Eliza said, turning to her brother-in-law, "let me thank you for bringing Peggy down to the city. A familiar face is much welcome in this fascinating but still strange town."

At nineteen, Stephen was starting to come into his own. His body had thickened out of reedy adolescence and the whiskers on his chin and cheeks, though hardly constituting a beard, gave his lean face a bit more maturity. "I? Bring Peggy anywhere?" He scoffed. "I assure you that I merely follow along in the wake of your incredible sister, and endeavor to make the journey as comfortable as possible."

Nineteen or not, Stephen had always enjoyed talking like a forty-year-old. Perhaps it was the pressure of knowing he would be Patroon when he came of age. It was cute now, but Eliza wondered what it would be like when he was actually forty.

"I am told that we owe our aperitif to you," Eliza said now.

"Allow me," Stephen said, reaching for a decanter filled with golden liquid on the sideboard. Before he could grab it, however, a small figure darted out of the shadows and grabbed it first. Simon was back in his blue velvet footman's coat, with a matching pair of breeches having materialized to complement it.

"A cordial, Miss Eliza?" he said in a voice that was less formal than loud.

"You should refer to your mistress as Mrs. Hamilton," Violetta said from the dining room, where she was fussing with the table settings.

"A cordial, Mrs. Hamilton?" Simon boomed, already pouring some of Stephen's honey wine into a glass.

Eliza accepted the glass and sent him on his way, hoping no one would notice the youth or inexperience of their so-called footman.

The next two hours passed in pleasant conversation, although Eliza was hardly aware of it. As 7:00 p.m. gave way to 8:00, and 8:00 to 9:00, she kept glancing at the clock on the mantel, wondering when Alex was going to come home, wondering if he'd received Simon's note, wondering if he was caught at one of the wealthy estates north of the city with no safe method to make his way home in the darkness, or if perhaps he'd tried to make his way home and gotten lost, or fallen into a ditch and injured himself, or perhaps even been waylaid by the bandits who had returned to Manhattan Island with the settlers.

She tried to shake such morbid thoughts and reminded herself that Alex had not been home before 10:00 p.m. since he'd taken the Childress case, and most nights he came in well after she'd fallen asleep—and she usually stayed up sewing or reading past midnight. He might be late, but there was no call to start indulging in fantasies of his death.

But what if he'd never received the note? He could be sitting in his office right now, poring over old law books in search of legal precedents to use for the Childress defense, while his first real opportunity to mix in New York society passed him by. Should she send Simon out again?

While these thoughts were spinning around her head, the men were comparing the relative merits and drawbacks of farming in lower and upper New York and New Jersey, crop yields, the quality of milk the cows gave, how big were the eggs laid by hens, whether it was better to charge one's tenant farmers high rents and allow them to cheat you on the yields or go leniently on them and earn their friendship and loyalty but make less money. Eliza had never paid much attention when General Schuyler talked husbandry of the land and found it even harder to focus now, but Helena and Peggy's conversation was equally strange to her.

They were sharing the trials and tribulations of managing a large household—servants, siblings, in-laws, the number of parties to throw each month, how often to replace one's china, upholstery, wallpaper. These things seemed like pipe dreams to Eliza and, moreover, not a place she was eager to get to. Her life might be a bit drab when compared to Helena's or Peggy's, but right now all she wanted was to see Alex while the sun was shining. To share a cup of coffee with him in the morning and a meal with him in the evening, to have a conversation with him more substantial than "Will you be home for dinner tonight?" and "How was your day?" If this was adult life, it was for the birds.

If Alex was going to be so engrossed in his work that he had little time for anything else, then she should be just as busy, Eliza decided. Perhaps there was a charity or a cause she could lend her services to, like her earlier work with orphaned children—anything to be useful instead of just decorative. She would look into it soon, determined that she would spend no more days feeling sorry for herself.

Meanwhile, Violetta kept tromping between the parlor and the kitchen with an increasingly dour scowl on her face. She looked first to Eliza for direction, but as the party stretched into its second hour and the group made no move toward the table, she turned her attention to Peggy. Peggy waved her away, but by nine thirty, she, too, was looking at Eliza with a worried expression, and at one point, under the guise of pouring herself a bit more honey wine (as their "footman" had fallen asleep in a chair in the dining room), she leaned over to whisper:

"I fear that the honey wine will go to the men's heads if we do not get some food into their stomachs soon."

Eliza nodded and rang the bell. After two hours of shaking the pictures off the wall, Violetta appeared as if on felt slippers.

"Yes, Mrs. Hamilton?"

"Violetta, I wonder if we might bring up the first course, and—" Eliza's voice trailed off as she caught sight of the shiny silver pieces in the china cabinet in the other room. She suddenly realized that most of them would have to come down to serve the meal. At the Pastures, when they took the display plate down for a party, they always replaced it with other pieces, so the shelves wouldn't be empty. As empty as Alex's seat at the head of the table.

She was conscious of Violetta's eyes on her, and Peggy's, and the four other people's in the room.

"Mrs. Hamilton?" Violetta prompted again.

"Yes," Eliza said, speaking not to the maid but to the rest of the room. "I wonder if we might be a bit unconventional and serve the first course Roman style. In here." Alex was fond of spouting forth on ancient history, with Germanicus's campaigns a dinnertime favorite—that is, when he did make it home in time for dinner.

"In . . . here?" Violetta said hesitantly.

"Yes!" Eliza said, forcing the brightness into her voice. "I know it's unusual, but these are unusual times, no? They call for new traditions. We need not be hidebound and stuffy. It's just—" Her eyes turned again to the dining room.

"I think it sounds fun!" Peggy cut in. She grabbed Eliza's hand, and Eliza knew her sister understood how important it was that their *first* dinner not officially begin until Alex was there to take his seat.

Peggy turned to her husband. "You will forgive me, darling, if I say that after all those four-hour meals at Rensselaerswyck I am hungry—all puns intended—for something a little less formal."

Stephen, the youngest person in the room, was also, in many ways, the most conservative. In two years he would reach his majority and assume the Patroonship and control of his vast estates, and he studied tradition with the same diligence that Alex studied the law. He frowned now, as if pondering a difficult problem in mathematics or astronomy.

"Am I correct in understanding that you are proposing we eat . . . here?" He indicated the parlor as though it were a barn or the crow's nest of a whaling ship.

His wife raised an eyebrow, daring her husband to object. He did not. "How . . . how utterly fantastic!"

"Wonderful!" Peggy said, giving Stephen so a warm smile that he blushed.

"Are you certain?" asked Eliza.

"What? No? It will be exciting. Almost like camping!" he enthused.

"Camping?" a voice called from the hallway.

Eliza stood and whirled toward the door, where a moment later Alex appeared, still wrapped in his overcoat.

She had forgotten how handsome he was, and seeing him at the threshold, looking tired but happy to see her, all her frustration and worry disappeared at the sight of his crooked smile.

"Alex!" she exclaimed, rushing to him in joy and not embarrassed to show it to their guests, who looked on with amusement.

Her husband took her in his arms and kissed her on the lips in full view of their guests. "I'm so sorry I'm late," he whispered. "Work was tiresome."

"You're right on time," she said softly, and pulled him in for another kiss.

17

Don't Forget to Take Out the Trash

*W*ith the host's arrival, at last the party moved to the table and food began to appear from the basement kitchen in droves. Stephen's provisions were generous, and Rowena's culinary skills were even more remarkable than Alex and Eliza had heretofore realized. Each successive cut of beef and pork was succulently tender and juicy, some smoked, others cured, others fresh, with just the right amount of salt and pepper and dried herbs to set off their unique, savory flavors. A medley of winter vegetables complemented the meat—tubers like potatoes and rutabagas and parsnips, along with some of the more durable squashes from the fall, butternut and sugar pumpkin and acorn and dumpling, all accompanied by pungent herbs whose names Rowena (when she was summoned to the table by Helena, whose own cook was "hopeless" from October to May) refused to divulge, lest a competing cook track down her sources.

Honey wine had given way to Mrs. Childress's hearty ales, and the conversation flowed as freely as the spirits, by turns frivolous (which New York aldermen were attempting to pass off their wigs as their own powdered hair) to serious (the revolution being over, tea—delicate, pungent, refined tea—was at last returning to North America, and breakfast was no longer dominated by "Caribbean gunpowder," as Gouverneur referred to coffee, which "starts the day with all the subtlety of a jolt from one of Mr. Franklin's electric wires").

With a start, Eliza realized that even though Alex was home at last, she wasn't going to get to talk to him any more intimately. He took his place at one end of the table, and she, naturally sat at the other. There were a thousand little things she wanted to ask him about his day and his cases, but she had to content herself with being one more member of the conversational fray. And in such a brilliant, opinionated group, that was a chore in itself. A fun one, to be sure, but Eliza was filled with newfound respect for her mother and the deft way she had handled hundreds of such occasions.

Inevitably the talk turned to politics. Alex had visited City Hall during the day's errands, and the place was buzzing with rumors that State Chancellor Robert Livingston was working up a scheme to create a so-called land bank to facilitate investment in New York and boost the local economy. Chancellor Livingston was among the most respected figures in the state. Not only was he descended the Lords of Livingston Manor, but he had served on the "Committee of Five" that helped draft the Declaration of Independence, and now served as chief judicial officer of the state as well as the national government's Secretary of Foreign Affairs. In other words, it would not be easy to dismiss any proposition that came with his signature attached. Although a more direct problem to opposing the plan—or implementing it, for that matter—was the fact that no one was quite sure what a land bank *was*.

"A land bank?" Eliza said cautiously. "I confess I am not sure I understand the concept."

"That makes two of us!" Alex said.

"Am I to understand," Stephen said now, "that if I were to walk into my saddler and order a new seat for my charger—"

"Oh, to have such problems," Helena whispered to Peggy with a silly smile on her face.

"—or a side pommel for Peggy's palfrey—"

"Pommel," Peggy repeated. "Peggy. Palfrey."

"Touché," Helena whispered.

"—instead of paying him with shillings or Continentals, I would instead reach into my pocket and hand him, what, an acre of bottomland?" Stephen chuckled. "It seems rather—how shall I put this?—inconvenient."

Alex laughed with his brother-in-law. "Not the soil itself, of course, but a note that transfers ownership of the soil. At least as I understand it, that is the general idea. Though may I add that it sounds like a rather expensive saddle."

"Stephen likes a posh ride," Peggy said, popping the *p*. "Some of his saddles are made of leather softer than my silks. He doesn't mind a bit of detailing either—embossed patterns and silver tips and the like. I swear, he looks positively like Don Quixote sometimes."

Stephen blushed. "I believe Don Quixote was rather shabbily dressed. Didn't he use a chamber pot for a helmet?"

"But that's preposterous!" John said to Alex, except he didn't mean the helmet. "Before you know it the land will be broken up like so many stamps torn from a postal sheet. One's property would be scattered about like cards in the wind—like acorns fallen from an oak tree, or, or maple samaras!"

"Maple samaras," Gouverneur repeated. "My goodness, what a literary crew you have supping at your table, Mrs. Hamilton."

"They're the seeds, you know," Eliza explained, "that spin as they fall from the tree so they float farther away. Rather like Leonardo da Vinci's aerial screw." She felt proud of herself for pulling that one from the mists of long-ago schoolroom lessons.

"Da Vinci!" Gouverneur exclaimed. "Aerial screws! What a clever bunch you—"

"But-but-but," John cut in, knocking on the table, "*where* is the land for this plan to come from? The last I checked, New York was rather spoken for. Mostly by your family," he couldn't help adding with a wink at Stephen.

"No doubt much of it will be seized from loyalists," Alex answered with a frown. "But it is not clear to me that even if we cast every last supporter of the king into raw nature that we would have nearly enough capital for such a project. Land would likely be, ah, received from the great estates in New York," he said pointedly, looking around at his guests, each of whom was connected to one or another of those great estates.

"They'll take an acre of Rensselaerswyck over my dead body," Stephen declared hotly.

"That *would* be a travesty," Peggy said in a teasing voice. "Why, you'd only have nine hundred ninety-nine thousand, nine hundred ninety-nine left!"

"It is the principle that matters!" Stephen said. "Is Chancellor Livingston offering parts of Livingston Manor for this criminal enterprise?"

"With only five hundred thousand to his name," Eliza said with a smile, "he can afford to lose them even less than you!"

"He hasn't offered anything yet," Alex answered, "but to be fair to him, I doubt he will ever be called upon to do so, because his scheme is simply too far-fetched to catch on. Or at least I hope so," he added, in a voice that was only half facetious.

"It sounds like you have some ideas about this, Mr. Hamilton," Gouverneur said now. "Please, enlighten us."

"Now you're in for it, Mr. Morris," Eliza warned proudly. "Mr. Hamilton loves to talk finance."

Alex held up his glass to toast his wife. "To poor Mrs. Hamilton, who has heard me go on about this subject one too many times, I'm afraid. But the truth is, we need a bank. And not a state bank but a national one! A real bank, with deposits of gold and silver bullion in its vaults, and the ability to hand out minted coins and specie!"

("Specie?" Peggy faux-whispered to Eliza.

"Paper money," Eliza whispered back, as if everyone should know that.)

"A national bank implies a national government," Gouverneur said in a dubious tone of voice.

"Which we have," John said, though his tone was equally dubious.

Alex knew that both men were heavily connected with the powers that ran their respective states, and were likely to be skeptical of what he was about to say. Nevertheless, he was too carried away to stop.

"In a manner of speaking," Alex said. "But a government without the power to regulate the constituent bodies over which it has jurisdiction is a government in name only."

"A what now?" Peggy said.

"He means that the federal government cannot tell the states what to do," Eliza said.

"Or raise an army or regulate trade or collect taxes—"

"Now, see here," John cut in. "Didn't we just fight a war to rid ourselves of the scourge of taxes?"

"Taxation without representation," Alex clarified. "There is a difference."

"I for one do not miss paying taxes to one more body," Gouverneur said.

"No one likes to pay taxes, but we can all admit, however grudgingly, that they are necessary if a government is to do the work for which it is created in the first place. To maintain a militia and a navy, for one thing, so that it can to protect its citizenry, and to build roads and bridges and ports, and to assist in the education and well-being of its people," said Alex.

"But don't you think such issues are best handled locally?" John said. "Surely a governor or mayor knows what his constituents require better than a government located half a thousand miles away."

"Some of those projects are simply too large to be handled by local governments," Alex answered. "And what does local mean, anyway? The state? The city? The village? How long can you keep passing responsibility until we end up saying that each individual is responsible solely for himself—

"Or herself," Eliza threw in.

"—or herself, and can expect nothing from his—or her—government?"

"But why should a New Yorker, for example, come to the aid of a Virginian or a Georgian?" John said. "What does he—or she," he added, smiling at Eliza, "get out of it?"

"Why, he gets to buy Virginia tobacco without paying a customs duty, or Georgia peaches!"

"We can grow peaches right here in New York," Peggy said.

"They're not as good as Georgia peaches," Alex said. "And we cannot grow cotton and indigo and peanuts, nor can they produce wheat as we do."

"It's true about the peaches," Helena said. "It has something to do with the warmth of the summers and the rain and the soil as well. They're a class apart. John, we must go to Georgia at our first opportunity! I want a peach!"

"But can you not see," Alex said now, "that being divided into a patchwork of little states all jumbled on top of each other is precisely what is wrong with Europe? Why, not a day goes by when one of them is not declaring war on another, or these five are forming an alliance against those three, or some erstwhile bit of Spain is declaring itself 'the Netherlands' or bits and pieces of Italy are being auctioned off to the highest bidder."

"Yes, but Europe has the problem of all those different languages," Gouverneur said. "It would be next to impossible for them to create a single large country as we have here, or even two or three, if the citizens in the various provinces cannot understand each other. Here we have English to hold us together."

"Exactly!" Alex said. "And we must take advantage of the things that hold us together and build the kind of country that can rival Tsarist Russia or Cathay China in scope and power. But to do that, we must recognize that our common interests override our differences. That we can be united and be individuals at the same time. And for that, we *must* have a strong central government to provide the leadership such a vast project requires!"

John and Gouverneur laughed.

"You have a formidable husband, Mrs. Hamilton," John said. "Or at least a talkative one."

"Indeed," Gouverneur added. "I wonder that you ever manage to win an argument with him."

"Oh, trust me, the Schuyler sisters have resources of their own," Stephen answered. "It is Alex you should worry about on that front."

Eliza held her tongue, but exchanged a look with Peggy that said, *We'll deal with the boys later.*

"So, tell us," John said, turning back to Alex. "How is your law practice going? Do you find it much different in New York City as opposed to Albany?"

"Oh, certainly," Alex said. "In Albany I was able, if I may be so modest, to trade on the good name of my wife's family, which brought me more clients than I could represent. Here, though the Schuyler name is certainly respected, it is not personally known to many, and I have had to attract my own business, as it were."

"Attract business?" Stephen said. "You make it sound like so many flowers offering up their competing petals for a bee's attention."

"If I had to paint my face red or blue to feed my family, I would not hesitate," Alex said in a somewhat testy voice. He didn't like Stephen's insinuation that working for a living was somehow uncouth. "We can't all be born with the proverbial silver spoon in our mouths."

"In Stephen's case, it was more of a silver ladle, or maybe just a bucket," Peggy said, goosing her husband.

"Fortunately, things haven't come to that pass," Eliza said soothingly.

Stephen stared at Alex for a long moment, before taking a sip of his beer. "We are all born with different advantages. Most of us here were born with wealth, but I'm sure we would all trade a good portion of our fortunes to have a share of your intelligence."

"Oh, I don't know," John said. "I quite like being rich and stupid."

Helena rolled her eyes and pinched her husband's cheek. "You're so lucky you're cute," she said drily.

"Business is not so dire as Mr. Hamilton's words might suggest," Eliza said. "In the last week he has acquired nine, ten—" She looked at Alex for confirmation.

"Over a dozen now," Alex said.

"Over a dozen new clients," Eliza amended. "As these cases go to trial and Alex's name makes the rounds of official circles, he will no doubt have even more business."

"That sounds like quite a load," Gouverneur said. "Anything interesting?"

"Oh, all interesting, in their own way," Alex said. "And related to each other as well." He quickly outlined the details of Mrs. Childress's story and the loyalist conundrum.

"Oh, this vexing issue!" Helena said quickly. "It is so distressing to read all the nasty columns in the papers, but it is even sadder when you hear how it affects real people. A widow ought not to be disrespected so, no matter which side her husband fought on!"

"It is a topic that divides families as well as countries,"

Gouverneur agreed. "Why, my own mother gave our estate over to British forces willingly, to use as billet and depot."

Alex had known this, of course, but had chosen not to mention it.

"My great aunt!" Helena wailed. "And her husband's brother a signer of the Declaration, too!"

"And yet, now Mrs. Morris is as American as you or I," Gouverneur said in a calming tone.

"American, yes," Helena said. "As American as me? I am not so sure."

"But she *is*." Eliza felt she had to chime in. "Why, that is the very nature of our country, is it not? A place where people from all over the world gather to form one new country."

Alex looked admiringly at his wife, and Eliza flushed at his approval. She had missed him so, missed his quick wit and passionate conversation. Part of her wished their guests away so that they might be able to talk more intimately. She always had to share her husband with so many people, it seemed.

"That is a somewhat idealized version of the story," Gouverneur said. "We would do well to remember that this land was won from people who already lived here through the violence of war. And many of the people we call Americans were brought here unwillingly, either as indentured servants who sold themselves to pay their debts, or as slaves. And many of them have not been granted citizenship, and thus live without the rights we take for granted."

"Oh, we have our flaws, all right," Alex said. "We are creatures of flesh, after all. We make mistakes. But my wife articulates the truth of the American dream. We have our eyes fixed on an earthly ideal, and though we fall short of it, we should ever strive in that direction. Indenture has already been done away with, and though it may take some time, I have no doubt that slavery as an institution will eventually be banished from these shores."

"Yes, and women will be granted the right to vote, too," Peggy said. "One can only hope."

"It will happen," said Alex. "I don't know if woman's intelligence is different from man's, but the idea that it is somehow inferior is increasingly hard to maintain. Why, if King George had had half Queen Elizabeth's diplomatic skills, I dare say we would have never revolted in the first place, let alone won the war."

"I, for one, would like to vote," Eliza said, "but there are a few women—and a few men—who I wouldn't mind taking the vote from. I feel there should be some kind of test. People should demonstrate a basic understanding of the issues before they are allowed to cast a ballot."

"Oh, heaven forbid!" Helena said. "I am busy enough as it is! I cannot be learning how the world works."

Eliza did her best not to roll her eyes. And here she had thought Helena a woman of her own ideas. Perhaps John wasn't the only one in that marriage who was rich and stupid.

"Never you fear, darling," he said now. "My ignorance shall serve for both of us!"

"Thank you, dear. Sometimes oblivion is so much easier. Certainly," she said, raising her glass, "it's much more festive."

Alex could see that the Rutherfurds' jokes were upsetting Eliza, who disliked intellectual incuriosity under the best of circumstances, but positively despised it in her own sex, because she felt it contributed to their second-class status in society. Nevertheless, this was a party, and it was nearly midnight as well, and he had been up since 5:00 a.m. He caught Eliza's eye and winked at her. She winked back, and then he grabbed his glass and clinked it against Helena's.

"Let us let Mrs. Childress's ale do the talking for us," he said, and emptied his glass down his throat.

IT WAS NEARLY three in the morning by the time Alex and Eliza saw off the Rutherfurds and Van Rensselaers and exhaustedly climbed the stairs to bed. Eliza went straight to the fireplace to bank the coals. The activity had become part of her daily routine since moving to New York. For some reason, she had fallen in love with the task, and even after she'd removed the excess ash and added a log and narrowed the flue to a sliver, she knelt before the open grate, staring into the flickering coals.

Alex, who was about to change into his nightshirt, couldn't resist walking up behind her and wrapping his arms around Eliza's back. She reclined into them eagerly and accepted his kisses on her neck with gentle, contented sighs.

"I've missed you," she said, still staring into the coals.

"And I you," he answered. "I am sorry I was so late tonight. I picked up another new client today."

"Oh?" Eliza wrapped her hands over his where they sat on her waist. "Another loyalist looking to safeguard his property? You be careful, Alexander Hamilton, lest people think you *too* fair-minded and actually harbor monarchist views."

Alex chuckled softly. "A one-time loyalist, although he says that since he sipped from 'the cup of liberty,' he has renounced all other spirits. And fortunately or unfortunately for him, he has no property to worry about losing. Which is why he is in debtors' prison—he has long since lost the collateral meant to cover his liabilities."

"Oh, the poor man," Eliza said with genuine concern. She turned in Alex's embrace and slipped her arms around his shoulders. "But, dare I ask, if he is in debtor's prison, how will he *pay* you? We need to pay our mercer's bill before the interest becomes larger than the principal."

Alex winced slightly. The fact that his wife was now receiving bills pained him greatly.

"The Childress case will soon go to court. If I win, as I believe I will, the verdict will serve as a blanket judgment for all the other cases. The damages could amount thousands of pounds, of which I will receive between ten and fifty percent, depending on the case. We will be able to pay off the mercer, the butcher, and the cabinet maker and everyone else," he said.

"The mercer, the butcher, the cabinet maker," Eliza said. "It sounds like a children's rhyme." She kissed him on the nose. "I'm sorry, darling. I know you hate to talk about money. You were telling me about a new client."

"Yes. I am trying to help him raise funds."

"But you said he is in debtors' prison. How can a man possibly work in jail?"

"Well, he is a painter."

"A painter!" Eliza's eyes widened. "I confess I did not expect *that* word to come out of your mouth. It's so hard to imagine an artist languishing in a cell."

Alex felt a little smirk on his lips. "You might not have to imagine."

Eliza frowned with mock sternness. "Excuse me?"

"I have commissioned Mr. Earl to paint your portrait. Before his unfortunate incarceration, his paintings were worth dozens of pounds. It is part of his payment to me. But—" His voice trailed off.

It was Eliza's turn to smirk. "But I have to sit for it . . . in prison."

"Do you mind? You don't have to if you don't want to."

"Oh, it sounds like an adventure. And it will get me out of the house. But don't tell my father that you arranged for his daughter to visit a prison, no matter which side of the bars she is on. I dare say he'd skin you alive."

Alex kissed her the forehead. "I dare say you are the most remarkable woman alive, Elizabeth Schuyler Hamilton."

"Flattery will get you nowhere, Mr. Hamilton," Eliza said coquettishly.

"Not even into bed?"

Eliza pretended to be angry, then began to loosen the laces on her dress with a smile, and soon enough, her husband joined her in the task.

18

Prison Portrait

Debtors' Prison
New York, New York
January 1784

The debtors' prison in which Ralph Earl was incarcerated stood at the northern end of the Fields, the large park near the top of the city between Broadway and the Boston Post Road. It bore the unimaginative name, "Debtors' Prison." Before that, it had borne the equally unimaginative and even more inexpressive name, "New Gaol," but despite these failures of nomenclature, the building was a handsome three-story stone structure with a dormered attic floor, above which stood a large, graceful octagonal cupola. In a more bucolic setting, the building might have been mistaken for the country house of a member of the gentry, but the whipping post and pillory that stood just to the side of the entrance overshadowed any genteel feeling that might have been engendered by the stately architecture.

"Begging your pardon, m'lady," called the burly, Irish-accented man seated behind a desk at the far end of the lobby before Eliza had taken two steps inside, "but p'raps you're, well, lost?"

Eliza resisted the urge to shout her answer down the long, narrow anteroom, which smelled equally of smoke, cabbage, and a third element that Eliza didn't want to put a name to. (Suffice to say that it reminded her of the errand she'd made Alex perform before he came to bed last night.) She lifted the skirts of her overcoat and gown a little higher and strode toward the attendant across the not-particularly clean flagstone. Perhaps she had agreed too readily to Alex's request last night—that man and his kisses!

What was she doing here? Why had Alex sent her here? Was this even safe?

"Miss?" A tankard of dark liquid sat on the desk, which was strewn with what looked like a week's worth of news-papers—there had to be at least twenty pages—and the remnants of what might have been a mutton sandwich, or perhaps mutton stew.

"Good afternoon," Eliza said. "My name is Eliza Hamilton. I am here to see Mr. Ralph Earl."

"Oh!" the attendant said. "I should have guessed from the dress. Pretty color," he added, standing up. "What d'ye call it?"

"Um, pink?" Eliza said, wondering if this was a trick question. She looked down at the hem of her gown where it peeked out beneath her overcoat. Though the lobby was dark, the visible fabric was still, clearly, pale pink.

"Well, yes, o'course, pink. But champagne pink, y'think, or p'raps coral? Or, you'll pardon the impertinence, good old-fashioned sow's ear? No disrespect meant, o'course. The hue of a sow's ear is of unparalleled delicacy, if you ask me." While the attendant was making these bizarre pronouncements, he was leading Eliza down a hall and through an imposing if unlocked wooden door that looked to be at least four inches thick, with a small iron-barred window set in it at eye level. The hallway beyond retreated into darkness.

"Mr. Earl's been teaching me the names of colors," the attendant said as he led Eliza up a flight of stairs. "I always thought there was just five or six myself. Y'know, blue and green and red and the like. But there's hundreds. Thousands even. I think my favorite's peri*winkle*. The name, I mean, though the color's nice, too. Little cool for someone with your complexion, you don't mind my saying. The sow's ear warms your skin tone right up."

"I do think I prefer champagne or coral," Eliza said now. "No offense to you, or to pigs that matter, but they are not something I often think of wearing."

"Sure, sure," the attendant said good-naturedly. "Pig makes a fine leather, actually. Very durable. Good for boots. Also wine sacs, though I s'pose m'lady drinks from crystal, or at least pewter. Well, here we are," he said unexpectedly, pulling a good-size collection of large iron keys from a pocket and jangling one loose. He fitted it into the iron-framed keyhole, turned it forcefully, and pulled the door open.

"Here you are, m'lady," he said, flourishing a hand toward the open portal, through which Eliza could see naught but a stone wall.

She hesitated, then took a deep breath. *What on earth have I gotten myself into?* Before she could cross the threshold, however, the attendant's arm came down and blocked her way, nearly landing on her chest.

"Now, you wouldn't be carrying any weapons, would ye? Any knives or pocket-size pistols?"

"What? Of course not?"

"No files or rasps for sawing through bars?"

"I'm not sure I understand the question."

"No poison secreted in a vial of perfume so that the prisoner can take the easy way out?"

"Oh, for God's sake, O'Reilly," a voice called from within. "Let the poor girl in before she poisons *you*."

The attendant smiled sheepishly. "Just doing my duty, y'unnerstan'. No one would ever think a manifest lady like yoursel' would break the law." He stepped aside. "Regulations require me to lock the outer door. I'll be back in one hour to let you out."

"A-an hour?" Eliza said nervously, even as a pat of the attendant's hand was propelling her into the little room. The only answer she received was the sound of the door slamming behind her.

"Well, I guess it's just the two of us now."

Eliza whirled. She expected to see someone right behind her and was surprised to discover that the cell she was in was a room divided by a wall of iron bars. The voice came from a man who was standing on the far side of them, in a tiny nook that held nothing but a narrow cot, a small table with a four-tiered candelabra, and an easel. At the foot of the bed stood a dark vessel that, at first, she took for a chamber pot, but then realized was actually a small brazier, the only source of heat in the windowless room.

Oh, and the man of course.

He was tall and much younger than Eliza had expected — not yet thirty, and handsome, with rather long angular features made all the more rakish by the shadow of a beard that grazed his hollow cheeks. He was clothed in expensive-looking, if somewhat wrinkled and stained, white silk breeches with a matching silk shirt and a rather . . . pronounced chartreuse overcoat adorned with three of the eight gold buttons it should have had. In lieu of shoes, he was wearing socks — from the shapeless appearance of his feet, she guessed several pairs. Yet despite the silliness of his lumpy feet and missing buttons, he still struck a debonair, indeed flirtatious figure. She couldn't help but notice, despite her being a married woman. Said marriage and beloved husband being the reason she was here in the first place, of course.

Smiling crookedly, the man extended his arm through the bars.

"Ralph Earl, at your service, madam."

Eliza took a moment to calm herself, then, stepped forward and took his hand. "So nice to meet you, Mr. Earl. My name is—" .

"Your name could be none other than Eliza Hamilton," Earl said in a leading tone.

Eliza smiled nervously. "How did you know?"

"Your husband has been very complimentary about your appearance, although I dare say he did not quite do your beauty enough justice." He shrugged.

While Eliza was flattered, she was also a little taken aback by his aggressive flirting. Thankfully, the painter soon changed the subject.

"I wonder," he added in a somewhat keener tone of voice. "Did he happen to send anything with you?"

"Oh yes," she said then. She reached inside her coat and pulled out a small flask. "He said you would appreciate this."

Earl accepted the bottle with somewhat shaky fingers, pulled the cork from it, and took a long—quite a long—pull. His eyes closed, and a contented sigh passed from his mouth. Then he took a second, shorter nip and stowed the bottle inside his coat.

"It gets so chilly in here," he said, patting the bottle beneath his breast pocket. "This helps."

Eliza did not find the room too chilly, but she had just been outside, where the breeze was stiff and the ice hadn't melted on the streets for the past three days.

"You will forgive me if I seem rude, Mr. Earl, but you are not what I expected of a, of a—"

"A man in prison?" Earl said in a self-mocking tone. "I have done my best to pretend that I am in the salon of some elegant hostess in Philadelphia or Paris—or Albany," he added with a wink, "and, God willing, I will one day again, soon enough. Please," he said, beckoning toward a chair on Eliza's side of the bars. "Be seated. I feel as though I am conducting an interview."

Eliza unbuttoned her coat but, seeing no place to hang it, kept it on and sat in the chair, an elegant piece of carved oak covered in dark tufted damask that would have been at home in one of the salons Mr. Earl had just described. A heavy brocade curtain hung behind it, cleverly draped so as to reveal the gold fringe at its borders yet still hide the rough stone of the wall.

After taking another pull from his bottle, the artist sat down on the edge of his cot, his back ramrod straight. A stick of charcoal appeared in his hand, which only now did Eliza realize was stained with soot, as if he had been practicing his craft all day. His hand began to fly across the pad propped on the easel, which was turned in such a way that she was able to see his hand move yet could not see the results of its actions.

Several moments passed in silence. Eliza was afraid to speak lest she disrupt his concentration.

"You will forgive me for diving in immediately," Earl said at length. "Normally I would make some excuse about the light going quickly on winter afternoons, but of course we are all candles here. And thank heavens, too. The cells with windows may be filled with light, but they are unconscionably cold. All you can do is watch yourself freeze to death. No, here we are merely racing against Mr. O'Reilly's return."

"Of course," Eliza said. She felt somewhat out of sorts, even though this is what she had come here for.

"May I suggest that for your next couple of visits you wear something more comfortable? Though that gown is beautiful, and you are a vision in it, I will not be ready for oils for at least a few days. I must first learn how your face paints."

"My face paints?" Eliza laughed nervously. "Unless I were to take the brush between my teeth, I do not think it will paint at all."

Earl smiled at her quick wit.

"There are some faces, you see, that seem to lose their plasticity when they are drawn and become all rigid lines and a single dimension. Others lose precisely this definition and become nothing more than flesh-colored blobs, as lifeless as death mask. The painter has to discover the contours—the concavities, the convexities!—with good old-fashioned chiaroscuro, and fill them with the most quotidian shading before advancing to the tint of blush. The goal is to find the balance between the permanent, arresting shape that can fill a frame for centuries, and the breath of life that will ensure that no one forgets the subject was once a living, breathing beauty."

Eliza had been drawn and painted before, but mostly by Angelica and Peggy. But this was a different experience entirely. Earl's eyes roamed her body with a directness that would have been improper in any other situation (and in fact felt a little improper in this one). She had a sudden sense of her face as a thing apart from her, an intricate mask mounted before her cranium. But at the same time, she felt that mask growing hot with a blush.

"Do I—do I need to remain still, or is it permissible for me to speak?"

"From what Mr. Hamilton has told me, it would be a crime to silence you. He has told me that your beauty is only matched by your brain. Given that my sole conversational partner for the past eight months has been Mr. O'Reilly, I long for tones more dulcet."

"He's been learning his colors, though." Eliza smiled. "Coral and champagne pink and his favorite, peri*wink*le."

"It takes a true innocent to make a word like *periwinkle* sound scurrilous!" he said.

Eliza sat quietly, thinking that she had determined to do useful work instead of being merely decorative, and yet here she was sitting for a portrait. But she was helping somewhat, wasn't she? Giving this man a job of some sort? And doing what her husband bid her?

A few minutes later, in one quick motion Earl sat back from his easel and turned it toward her. The light from the four candles shone directly on the page, yet it still took a moment for Eliza to make sense of the wavering black lines that floated on the yellow parchment. It seemed impossible that anyone could have captured a likeness so quickly, and in so few strokes. Then she gasped.

For there she was. Her posture — the line of her back, the set of her shoulders, the demure press of her knees beneath her skirts, the drape of her silken gown and woolen overcoat. It was remarkable. With just a few hash marks and wavering strokes he had managed to capture the pattern in the lace covering her décolletage. And with seemingly imperceptible shadings, he had brought out the moiré luster in the dress itself. Yet even more incredible was the way in which he captured the flesh beneath the garments. Just looking at it deepened her blush.

The three eldest Schuyler sisters (well, not so much Peggy) were a fair hand at capturing what they called "outlines," which is to say the silhouettes of draped skirts, but when you looked at them you never got the sense that these garments were actually being worn by a human being. They could have been filled with air or straw. But Earl's drawing somehow captured the tenseness of Eliza's stilled legs and the constriction in her chest from trying not to breathe, or not to expand her rib cage when she did so.

She was so taken by the masterful way her body had been depicted that she almost didn't notice her face. Then she caught herself staring into her own eyes. Saw the curiosity there, and the amusement, and even the intelligence. It was as if she had caught a glimpse of herself in a mirror before she had time to compose an expression. She flushed to think of herself that way, but she hadn't drawn the picture after all.

She was suddenly conscious of eyes on her, and looked up to see Earl staring at her with a gesture that was both proud and questioning, as if he knew he had done a good job but was curious what sort of effect it had had on Eliza. It was almost as if he were wondering what sort of hold it might give him over her.

But Eliza was so taken with the sketch that all she said was, "Oh, Mr. Earl! It is remarkable."

"Bah!" Earl said, grabbing the bottom edge of the page and flipping it over roughly, exposing a fresh sheet. "It is all wrong. Your face looks as though you had just looked up from a psalter when it should be as if you had just read an account of a shipwreck or a great battle or the moment when Romeo holds a sleeping Juliet in his arms and mistakes her for dead. We start again! But first—"

He reached into his coat pocket and pulled out the flask Alex had sent. After a long drink, he sighed contentedly.

I'll have to bring a bigger flask next time, Eliza couldn't help thinking.

"It gets so chilly in here," he said, then wiped a few beads of sweat from his brow and started drawing again.

19

Out and About

*A*fter more than a month in virtual isolation, the
Hamiltons were suddenly discovered by society. Eliza
attributed their newfound popularity to Peggy—"she's in
town for *one night* and already knows more people than we
do"—though the truth is, Peggy was simply a conduit, and it
was Helena Rutherfurd who provided the real entrée.

The week after the impromptu dinner party at the
Hamiltons' Wall Street home, the Rutherfurds reciprocated
with an invitation to "a small supper" at their town house
on Hanover Square. The stone-fronted mansion was twice
as wide as the Hamiltons', much deeper, and a story taller,
with an interior as opulent as those grand proportions would
suggest. The floors in the entry were stone instead of wood,
while the parlors were laid with yellowy pine planks at least
a foot wide, and bordered by intricate marquetry work in

oak, walnut, and limewood. The ceiling coffers were more elaborately patterned than the mandalas of Hindustan. The wainscoting was a rich ebony as dark as tar, yet so naturally lustrous that Helena and John had made the daring choice simply to varnish it rather than paint it in one of the muted pastels that was all the rage—Wythe blue or tawny port or dusty rose.

The paneling's Spartan restraint, however, was more than made up for by the elaborately flocked wallpaper that covered each parlor in yards and yards of the deepest crimson and richest emerald, the most buttery of yellows or the surprising luster of burnished silver. Each chamber was its own jewel box, and Helena and John led the Hamiltons through them, one by one, with a pride that somehow managed to not be obnoxious.

Eliza whispered to Alex at one point, "If their taste had been one whit less perfect, this would all be too much." But the Rutherfurds had done a superb job and they knew it, and so instead of feeling as if their hosts were bragging, Alex and Eliza simply marveled at the beauty to which they were being treated.

The silk-lined chambers were the perfect setting for the dazzling pieces of furniture the couple had accumulated, with many examples by the three great English masters: Sheraton, Hepplewhite, and Chippendale, as well as a virtual museum of American practitioners: Gilbert Ash, James Gillingham, and dozens of others from Boston to Charleston and everywhere in between. The Rutherfurds talked about the individual pieces of furniture as though they were paintings, a Jonathan Gostelowe here, a Samuel McIntire there, and of course they *also* had a stunning collection of paintings, including the American portraitists Charles Willson Peale, John Singleton Copley, Gilbert Stuart, and even, Alex pointed out to Eliza, a Ralph Earl, all of which were hung in a stunning salon they called the galleria.

The silver. The china. Even the servants, in bespoke livery ("John has a *passion* for buttercup yellow," Helen confided to Alex). It was all too perfect. The mansion was everything he wanted in a home, and more.

Because it wasn't just the mansion he coveted, but the people who filled it. Despite Helena's remark about "a small supper," the Rutherfurds seemed to have invited a representative from all the major families of New York and the surrounding environs, starting with the Morrises (Gouverneur was there, along with two of his and Helena's cousins), and William Bayard and his fiancée, Elizabeth Cornell, and Lindley Murray, a lawyer like Alex, but also an aspiring writer. His mother, Mary, was revered throughout the Continental army for having invited General William Howe "to tea" at Inclenberg, the Murrays' estate north of the city, and entertaining General Howe so well and so long that George Washington and his soldiers were able to escape the advancing British army. ("Mama won't admit it," Murray joked, "but I'm pretty sure she spiked General Howe's tea with opium.") There were also Pierre Van Cortlandt, Jr., and his brother Philip, the former yet another aspiring lawyer, while the latter was the heir apparent to the vast Van Cortlandt Manor north and east of Morrisania, which was rivaled in New York State only by the Livingston and Van Rensselaer holdings.

Aaron and Theodosia Burr, the Hamiltons' one-time neighbors in Albany, and now their neighbors on Wall Street, were there, as were James and Jane Beekman, who turned out to be siblings rather than spouses. The Beekmans had grown up in a house called Mount Pleasant five miles up the coast of the East River, just across from the southern tip of Blackwell's Island. Mount Pleasant was known for its beautiful greenhouse—said to be the first in the New World—in which the Murrays grew the exotic delicacy known as the orange. Alex had loved them as a child in the Caribbean, but Eliza had never tasted one. Jane promised to bring her some the next time she called. Mount Pleasant was also famous (or infamous) for its role during the occupation: General Howe had commandeered the mansion as his headquarters (presumably after he recovered from Mrs. Murray's opium tea); it was there that the dashing Major John André, who had made such a profound impression on Eliza at the Pastures on the very same evening she met Alex, had stayed before sneaking off to meet the traitor Benedict Arnold, a liaison that eventually cost him his life.

There were Schermerhorns, Lawrences, Rhinelanders, and Wattses, and Abraham de Peyster, whose namesake ancestor had donated the land on which City Hall was built (not to mention the Hamiltons' own house), and of course a few inescapable Van Rensselaers and Livingstons, who were all related to each other in one way or another, and indeed to everyone else seated at the twenty-five-foot-long dining table the Rutherfurds had set up in the galleria. There was even Pieter Stuyvesant, great-great-great-grandson of the last Dutch governor of the colony of New Netherland, who was at least eighty years old. Like his namesake, he spelled his name with an *i*, spoke English with a Dutch accent, and in a truly eerie coincidence, sported a polished walnut peg leg that rattled the china in the cabinets as he clomped through the Rutherfurds' exquisite parlors. Though unfailingly polite, he still seemed to regard everyone as a step beneath his station. ("If the blood in this room were any bluer," Eliza whispered to Alex at another point in the dizzying tour, "we could have used it to dye the uniforms of the Continental soldiers!")

But of all the guests at the dinner, Alex's favorites were John and Sarah Jay—although to Alex she would always be Sarah Livingston, eldest daughter of William Livingston, the governor of New Jersey and the man who had sponsored Alex's passage from Nevis to the northern colonies. Alex had had a crush on her and her sister Kitty as a boy; but as the years passed and Eliza supplanted all others in his heart, he thought of the Livingston sisters as his own kin, the sisters he never had. He was thrilled that Sarah had made such an advantageous marriage. The Jays were perhaps not quite at the level of society as the Van Rensselaers and Schuylers—John's family were Huguenot merchants, having fled Catholic oppression in France a century ago—but in the

New World, one didn't have to have a title before one's name to be welcomed into high society.

Gold and silver earned in trade was every bit as shiny as inherited wealth, and spoke to a family's cleverness and industry besides, and not just the blind cosmic luck of being born into the aristocracy. John was a decade older than Alex, and also a lawyer—"one more and we could start a boxing club," he joked, which prompted Sarah to say, "Lawyers? *Boxing?*" and break out into laugher. John had studied with the renowned Benjamin Kissam, as had Lindley Murray, and, like Alex and Gouverneur Morris, was a graduate of King's College. Alex was pleased to learn from John that their alma mater, which had been closed during the British occupation, was slated to reopen in the spring, and under the non-royalist name of Columbia College.

But what really drew him to John was the older man's belief in the urgent need for a strong central government to unite the thirteen states, built around a code of laws—"a Constitution, if you will"—that would ensure that whether a citizen was in the Carolinas or New Hampshire or Virginia or Maine, the citizen would enjoy the same privileges and share the same responsibility as any American.

"Local pride is fine," John Jay said at one point. "Each state, each county even, has its specialty. But if we are New Yorkers first, or New Jerseyites—"

"Jerseyans," John Rutherfurd interjected.

"—if we are New Yorkers or New Jersayans first, we are Americans last and always. Virginia has its tobacco, Carolina its cotton, Maryland its crab, Massachusetts its miserable winters"—laughter all around at this observation—"but all of them have the American spirit, which is the spirit of freedom of industry and quiet but unshakeable piety. We judge a man not by his name or lineage, but by the accomplishments of his own hand and mind."

"And what, pray," Helena said, "do you judge a woman on? The cut of her dress, or of the figure beneath it?"

John reddened, as did several of the other men, while the women at the table all shared a knowing glance.

"Certainly, you would not say that beauty is a detriment for a woman to possess?" John said when he could speak again.

"I would say that it is a distraction," Helena replied, "and just as arbitrary a measure of her quality as a man's surname."

More laughter from the women and red faces from the men. Then, Alex was surprised to hear Eliza say, "I do not think any woman at this table would disagree with you, but I do think yours is a statement only a beautiful woman would dare make out loud."

It was the line of the evening, and it made the rounds of society parties in that mysterious way news travels, always arriving at whatever drawing room or dining table the Hamiltons found themselves at. For Alex, it was something of a relief not to have yet another gray-wigged, gray-shouldered matron or half-drunk dry goods merchant sporting a military-cut suit that had never seen combat say, "Are you the Alexander Hamilton who served with General Washington?" and then press him for story after story about the American savior. Now it was, "Oh, are *you* the Eliza Hamilton who stole the stage from Helena Morris at her own party? I've heard *so much* about you."

Eliza, confident but fundamentally shy, now found herself at the center of social groupings rather than on the fringes, and though she managed to hold on to her modesty, she also embraced her new role as a "woman of society," as she termed it, smirking a little as she said it, as though the term were somehow improper.

"People used to say that I married you for your name and money," Alex jokingly grumbled one night as they made their way wearily home after yet another late-night party. "Now they say that I married you for your beauty and charm. I can only wonder what on earth they think *I* bring to the union."

Eliza couldn't resist teasing him. "You are very good at holding doors and umbrellas, and in a pinch you can lace a corset, too. A girl could do worse."

Alex made her pay for that quip all night long.

20

⎯⎯◦◦⎯⎯

Weeping Widows

Ruston's Ale House
New York, New York
February 1784

*A*s busy as their social lives were, Alex wasn't on his way
to a party a few nights later. Instead he was en route to
his star client's home. Ruston's Ale House occupied the first
floor of a three-story building, rather like Samuel Fraunces's
Queen's Head Tavern just a few blocks away on the corner
of Pearl and Broad. The second floor was taken up by rooms
to let, some of which housed guests who stayed for months
at a time, while others were rented out on a night-by-night
basis. The third floor of the spacious building was given over
to an apartment for Mrs. Childress and her two children.
Alex passed through the bustling inn quickly. By now the
barmaids recognized him and, after requesting that a pint
of stout be sent upstairs—it was a cold evening after all, and
he needed something that would stick to his bones—Alex
quickly ascended the two flights. The staircase was quite

narrow and abutted the building's main chimney, so it was quite warm as well, and by the time Alex reached the closed door, he was rather flushed. He pulled the chain and heard the tinkle of a bell from within the apartment.

After some moments Mrs. Childress answered the door herself. She had long since let go of her domestic servants, and ran the ale house and inn on a skeleton staff. The inn itself was still quite busy, but the interest on the loan she had taken to purchase the Baxter Street building that had been seized from her, as well as the distillery equipment therein, ate up all her profits.

"Mr. Hamilton," she said, her pale face lighting up, "I did not expect you until tomorrow. Do please come in."

She stepped aside and Alex entered the spacious foyer. The Childresses' building occupied a corner lot, with rows of windows down two sides, and received as much light as the late February afternoon could offer.

Mrs. Childress led him into the parlor, a large room fronted by three tall windows framed by heavy draperies in a bronze-and-blue damask. She indicated a tufted sofa and took her place on an elegant, if well-used, Windsor chair to one side. She wasn't wearing one of her all-black mourning gowns today, but a midnight-blue dress with a black ribbon sewn so elegantly into the sleeve that it might have been mistaken for decoration.

"I am sorry to disturb you, Mrs. Childress," he said. "I did not realize you were having a private day."

"Oh, your visits are never a disturbance, Mr. Hamilton."

Alex wasn't sure, but he thought he saw a touch of color appear on Mrs. Childress's cheeks. He apologized for the time once again; it was after four and the sun was setting, and only one lamp was lit in the room.

A knock sounded at the door, which opened immediately, letting in a barmaid who carried a pitcher in one hand, two glasses in another. "Some stout for Mr. Hamilton," she said, setting it down on the table. "I took the liberty of bringing two glasses."

"Thank you, Sally. Would you like a bite to eat, Mr. Hamilton? The cook made a Yankee pudding today that will warm you through the coldest snowstorm."

"Well . . ." Alex meant to dine at home with Eliza, but Yankee pudding wasn't in Rowena's repertoire.

"Please bring a plate up for Mr. Hamilton," Caroline directed. "And some of those scones as well."

"Yes, ma'am." The maid hurried out.

"May I?" Alex indicated the pitcher of ale.

She nodded, her eyes shining with plaintive yearning. It was as if the only thing she had left to offer were her hospitality, and she were desperate that it be sufficient.

I suppose I must seem like her last chance, Alex thought to himself. *Then again, I suppose I am her last chance.*

"In fact, I have come here about court."

"Oh?" Mrs. Childress sipped at her stout as delicately as if it were a glass of tea. "Has there been *movement*?" She said the word tentatively. It was a term she had picked up from Alex.

"In a manner of speaking. A judge has been selected, and a date for the hearing to commence."

"Oh. Well, that is good news, isn't it?"

New York City's courts had been in chaos since the end of the occupation. Nearly two-thirds of the sitting judges, and an equal proportion of counsel, had been loyalists, and under Governor Clinton's new laws all of them were summarily fired. The positions were being filled quickly—too quickly, Alex thought. Lawyers who barely had a few more years' experience at the bar than he did were being named judges, the final authority in matters of law that they hardly understood.

"Mr. Hamilton?" A shadow clouded Caroline's fair skin. "If you don't mind me saying, you don't seem particularly happy."

Alex bit his lip. "It is not my intention to alarm you, Mrs. Childress. It's just that the judge, Lewis Smithson, who has been selected to oversee the case is a recent appointee of Governor Clinton's."

The mere mention of the name Clinton made Caroline frown.

"I see," she said, as if she already knew what Alex was going to say.

"Judge Smithson is not well-known in the city, but he is known to be . . . not exactly sympathetic to loyalist causes." Alex had considered using the word *hostile*, but thought it too pessimistic.

"I see," Caroline said again.

"I do not want you to give up hope," Alex said now, putting as much vigor into his voice as he could. "There is nothing to suggest that Judge Smithson's personal beliefs will bias him against either the rule of law or the evidence. He is inexperienced, yes, but the people who have met him say he is an honorable man. I am convinced that the soundest arguments, not to mention common sense, will carry the day."

"Inexperienced" didn't quite cover it: Though in his fifties, Smithson had been a member of the bar for less time than Alex had. It was Alex's understanding that he had been a farmer before.

Caroline was trying to remain calm, but there was a tremor in her hands as she took a long sip of her beer, and then another.

"So it essentially comes down to whether you are a better attorney than, what do you call it, opposing counsel?"

Alex couldn't keep a smile off his face. "You will forgive me for singing my own praises, but I have no doubts as to my own abilities as a rhetorician, either in print or orally."

"I am sure your opponent—my opponent, dare I say—must think the same things about himself."

Alex nodded, almost sheepishly.

"Opposing counsel does not lack for self-confidence."

"You speak as if you know him."

"Indeed, I have supped with him twice in the past week, once at the home of John and Sarah Jay, and once at his own home. He is an amiable fellow and quite charming, but strictly *entre nous*, he wins more cases on charm than on knowledge of the law."

"It seems to me not to matter if he wins by fair means or foul. It is still a loss for me."

"Why, Mrs. Childress!" Alex said, only half pretending to be affronted. "You speak as if you think there could possibly be a better lawyer in New York than I!"

Caroline didn't seem to realize that Alex was joking to try to set her at ease. Indeed, she looked aghast that he might think she doubted him.

"Oh, Mr. Hamilton, I could never doubt you! You are my last—my only hope! My life and the lives of my children are in your hands!" she said, nervous fingers kneading at the worn fabric of her dress.

To his surprise and consternation, Caroline suddenly leapt from her chair and knelt, prostate, at his feet. "I will do anything, anything you need!" she cried. "Anything you want, I am yours. Just ask!" She stopped her hysterics for a moment and turned to him with suddenly sly look. "Anything." It was more than clear what she meant by "anything."

Alex shifted uneasily in his seat. He had to make clear that such advances on her part were unwarranted and more important, unwelcome. While he had always been happy to flirt at parties with married and unmarried women, there was only one woman for him, forever, no matter what temptations might lie in his path now, or in the future, and should he ever fail Eliza, he would never betray her soul. With a stab of guilt, he realized he'd spent more time with Mrs. Childress than Mrs. Hamilton lately, and vowed to ameliorate the situation as soon as he could—as soon as this case was won, of course. A man had his responsibilities, not least among them securing his position and ensuring the household bills were paid.

"Mr. Hamilton?" Caroline asked, batting her eyelashes as she knelt at his feet.

"Please, there is no reason for such dramatics. I beg you, please get back in your seat, Mrs. Childress, there you go. Do not fear, and do not doubt me. I have nearly as much invested in winning this case as do you. I will not fail us."

His client resumed her place across from him and pretended nothing had happened, which Alex was happy to do as well. And he realized he should wrap this up and return to his patient wife, as soon as possible.

"But no one can predict the law," Caroline said. "And the mood is so poisoned against us! Can they not see that we are all Americans, no matter how we became so?"

"They will see it by the time I am finished," Alex replied. "I don't care if I have to talk for two hours, or four, or the entire day. You shall have justice. *I*," he added in a firmer voice, "shall have victory."

There was a knock at the door then, and Sally entered with a covered tray, which she set on the table beside the glasses of beer, then opened to reveal a large plate of Yorkshire pudding and roast smothered in gravy, along with a pair of scones glittering with sugar.

"Will there be anything else, Mrs. Childress?"

Caroline was still too overcome to speak in a normal voice, so Alex thanked the maid and sent her away. He insisted she eat some of his meal to calm herself, and took his leave.

"I hope you will forgive my outburst," Caroline said as she walked him to the door. "It has just been such a trying time this past half year."

"There is nothing to forgive," Alex said, putting on his hat. "Our court date is in four weeks, but you will see me many times before that, I'm sure, as we go over the facts of the case one last time, and review your testimony."

She crossed her arms. "You know, Mr. Hamilton, besides my children, seeing you is the only thing that brightens my day."

Alex ignored the comment. "Good night, Mrs. Childress," he said, in a professional tone. "I will see myself downstairs."

Caroline suddenly remembered something. "You never did tell me the name of opposing counsel."

"Didn't I?" Alex said. "He is a former colonel I knew slightly from my days in the army. His name is Aaron Burr."

21

A Change of Venue

Debtors' Prison
New York, New York
March 1784

*I*f the time Eliza spent at debtors' prison made her a little uncomfortable, there were other factors in its favor. The walk was not long, the weather was becoming increasingly fair, and the sitting itself only took an hour. Yet over time, Eliza came to realize that the preliminary sessions with the charcoal stick were not so Earl could "learn how her face painted," as he put it during that first meeting, but so that he could drink up half the contents of the flask she had brought him, which settled the tremors in his hands.

Although she and Peggy and Angelica had all had fun at parties, the Schuylers were by and large a temperate family, and Eliza had never encountered someone who didn't simply enjoy alcohol, but actually seemed to need it. She had always thought her mother a bit of a fuddy-duddy whenever she cautioned against "the vice of excessive drink," but she

could hear Mrs. Schuyler's warning voice in her head whenever she placed Alex's flask into Mr. Earl's trembling fingers.

His moist, slightly quivering lips, the slitted, almost accu-
sative eyes all made her nervous. Yet the sketches he turned
out one after another were exceedingly lovely, and when
he actually began to paint—it was remarkable! The way he
brought out the shine of the lace in her bodice, yet still managed to convey the contours of the skin beneath it. And the
pink in the ribbon at her waist, echoed by the light flush of
her cheeks. It was as if she had sat not in a small, windowless prison cell lit by a single candelabra, but in the finest of
drawing rooms with a chandelier blazing overhead. What
impressed her most were the eyes: dark and serious, inquisi-
tive even. They were the eyes Eliza saw when she looked in
the mirror; sometimes when she inspected the painting she
expected them to blink back at her. Any man who could
paint like that, and on a cup of whiskey, could not be said to
have a problem with alcohol. Could he?

During their sittings, Earl would grill Eliza for news of
the latest society gossip, which Eliza would answer as honestly as she could. In fact, everyone in their circle seemed
remarkably well-behaved, and Earl teased her that her stories offered little distraction for an incarcerated man. She
did notice, however, that whenever she brought up Alex, he
changed the subject. "Forgive me if it seems gauche, dear
Mrs. Hamilton, but no single man likes to discuss a beautiful
woman's husband. Can you not find me one rich widow I
can pine for, or, failing that, an unhappily married socialite

I can spirit away?" Eliza half imagined that he meant her, yet there was nothing insinuating in his tone as he spoke the words.

After a month of once- or twice-weekly visits, however, the portrait was nearly finished. In fact, the portrait had seemed done to Eliza for more than a week, and she was under the impression that Earl was drawing out the experience for the sake of the company, or the whiskey.

For her part, even as she disapproved of his excessive drinking, she enjoyed being around him, as he did endeavor to ask her about her childhood, her thoughts on the topics of the day, and her opinions on the changes happening in the city. Eliza greatly missed conversation—Alex was working so hard, he was hardly ever home, and it saddened her to think that Earl knew more—and was more interested—in her day-to-day life than her husband. While Alex had started to come home a little earlier a few weeks ago, and had been extra-attentive, almost as if he were courting her again for a spell, he was back to his old, late-night habits as the case drew nearer. Sometimes she anguished that they would never have time to start a family; for how could they, if they seldom had time together, and when they were in each other's company, one or both of them were asleep?

Earl was explaining "over-painting" and "varnishes," and she turned back her attention to the portrait. If she looked closely, it did seem to her that the picture acquired new degrees of luminescence and depth with each visit, but it could also be the power of suggestion.

IT WAS A clear blustery day in March when she headed to the prison for what she assumed would be the final sitting. The wet sea breeze was quite chilly, yet there was also a hint of freshness to it, a promise of a spring that, though still some weeks away, was definitely on the return. Eliza hurried through the Fields and in through the front entrance of the debtors' prison, where O'Reilly looked up with a surprised expression.

"Why, Mrs. Hamilton! Funny seeing you again!"

Eliza thought this was a strange thing to say, but let it pass without comment.

"Good afternoon, Mr. O'Reilly. Is Mr. Earl prepared for me?"

O'Reilly looked confused. "I shouldn't know, ma'am. He wasn't here when I arrived this morning."

"What? Did he"—Eliza had no idea why her mind went here—"escape?"

O'Reilly cracked a smile. "Depends what you think of lawyers' work, I suppose."

"Beg pardon?"

"Mr. Hamilton sent over papers yesterday directing that Mr. Earl be 'released on recognizance,' whatever that means."

"But—" Eliza's voice fell off. She had seen Alex for all of five minutes this morning, taking her tea in bed while he dressed, and had made a point of asking him to take down the mirror over the front parlor fireplace in preparation for

Mr. Earl's portrait, which she had told him she was picking up that day.

When she came downstairs, she had been a little hurt to discover that he had left without taking the mirror down, but now her ego was even more bruised. It seemed that not only did her husband not have any time for her these days, he didn't even have space in his mind for her.

But none of this was O'Reilly's concern.

"Oh, that's right!" she said with forced brightness. "How stupid of me. It completely slipped my mind." She had brought a basket of sandwiches and all but shoved them in O'Reilly's hands. "Please," she said. "For you and the less fortunate inmates." The debtors' prison didn't provide food to those incarcerated there, who were dependent upon the attentions of friends and family or the benevolent societies.

"Don't you want your basket?" O'Reilly called after her as she hurried from the building.

"Keep it," Eliza said, escaping into the cold sunshine.

HER MIND WAS awash with feelings as she walked home. Anger first, of course, at Alex's thoughtlessness, followed by guilt. Because surely her own husband couldn't be so careless of her time. Of her feelings. She racked her brain, trying to remember if he had said anything about Ralph's release, but nothing came. As much as she wanted this to be her fault so she could let Alex off the hook, it appeared that he had simply forgotten to tell her.

She let herself into her house in a daze, which is why she didn't hear the thrum of voices until after they stopped, leaving only the sound of a fussing baby.

Eliza stepped from her hallway into her parlor. Three figures sat there, each so unexpected that she almost didn't believe her eyes. The first two were Angelica and John Church, while the third was—

"Mr. Earl?"

Before Earl could reply, Angelica had leapt from her chair and thrown her arms around Eliza.

"Oh, we've surprised you! I hope our presence is not too unwelcome," said Angelica.

"No, no," Eliza said, returning her sister's embrace warmly. It was wonderful to see Angelica, but startling to see Ralph Earl in her home. "I mean, yes, I am surprised, but no, your presence is not unwelcome at all. And baby Philip," she said, at last stirring herself to notice her nephew, who was fussing on his father's lap.

"I presume that our letter didn't reach Mr. Hamilton?" John said.

"You wrote Alex?" Eliza turned to Angelica.

"John did. He had business to conclude with him stemming from the war."

John Church's secret relationship with the Continental army had been revealed following the cessation of hostilities. John had not sought the glory, but Governor Clinton had been on the verge of seizing his property as a loyalist, and the order to reveal his role had come directly from General Washington. Other presumed loyalists had similarly been revealed to be patriots, including Hercules Mulligan, whom Alex had brushed shoulders with in the lead-up to the war in the seventies.

"The Continental Congress still hasn't paid John what it promised."

"Oh, all the best people are welching on their debts these days," Earl said from his chair.

Eliza glanced at him, but she simply couldn't process his presence in her front parlor yet, and turned back to her sister. "They haven't paid Alex either. He says it's because they lack the power to levy taxes—" Eliza shook her head. "But this is hardly the time to discuss fiscal policy. You say John wrote Alex?"

Angelica nodded.

"Perhaps he just neglected to pass along the news," Ralph Earl said. "Judging from the look on Mrs. Hamilton's face, I would say that my presence here is as much of a surprise as is yours."

Earl's words were slightly slurred, and Eliza noted the glass on the table beside him, as well as the nearly empty decanter of honey wine Stephen had brought down from Albany. It had been full when she left a little over an hour ago. Perhaps Angelica and John had had some. But glancing at their chairs, she saw no glasses.

Eliza did her best to cover for Alex. "He mentioned that you were being released on, released on recognizance," she said, pulling the word out and hoping she was pronouncing it correctly. "I assume the, ah, recognizance is ours."

"Thanks to your husband tirelessly providing me with commissions, and to his keen negotiating skills, I have been able to reduce and pay off my debts. But I am still without ready income, not to mention a place to stay. Your husband was gracious enough to offer me the use of your guest room for lodging, as well as your parlor for painting a few outstanding commissions—first of which will be his own portrait." He smiled messily at John. "What about you, sir? A family portrait? Or perhaps just one of the little namesake?"

"My name is John Church," John said testily. Clearly, he had been dealing with Earl's drunkenness for some time. "Our son is named after my wife and sister-in-law's illustrious father, General Philip Schuyler."

"I'm a man of peace myself," Ralph Earl said, refilling his glass and taking a healthy swig. "Are you sure don't want some of this decoction? I don't know what it is, but it is *quite* satisfying."

"No, thank you," Angelica said firmly. "I don't usually drink before lunch."

Eliza seized on the last word. "Lunch! I'll have Rowena prepare you something!"

"Is that your maid?" Angelica said. "She let us in but then promptly ran off to market. She said her larder was nearly empty. We have been attended to by a very cheery lad, although I fear Mr. Earl has been giving him tipples of drink. I think he may have fallen asleep belowstairs."

"Mr. Earl!" Eliza said, her indignation only half feigned. "Please tell me you have not been giving Simon honey wine to drink? He is but nine years old!"

"The lad said he wanted to be a footman. How on earth can he serve drink if he doesn't know what he's offering up?"

Eliza shook her head in exasperation and turned back to her sister. "At any rate, I gather that you have met our house-guest. And where are you and John staying?"

Angelica frowned. "Well, we had written Mr. Hamilton to see if we could perhaps stay here, but I gather from Rowena that you have just the one guest room?"

"Oh! Of course!" Eliza said. "To sleep under the same roof again! It would be so fun! But . . ." She turned and glanced at Earl, who was making goo-goo eyes at the baby, or perhaps at John—his focus was rather glazed. "It's true, we have just one spare bedroom. There is Alex's study, though. I'm sure we could procure a bedstead and mattress. But by tonight?" She shook her head in consternation. "When did you write Alex to say that you were coming?"

"It must be three weeks ago now."

"Three weeks? The mail was spotty when the city was first liberated, but service has been reliable for the past month. How could he not have received it? You wrote to the Stone Street address? He has been so busy. Perhaps it escaped his attention."

Angelica shrugged in confusion. "It sounds like his practice is going well then?"

"In a manner of speaking," Eliza said to her sister. "He has more clients than he can handle, but he has yet to take a case to trial, and thus to secure a judgment. And until there are judgments, the payments are"—she waved a hand at Earl—"nominal."

"A journeyman's days are never easy," John said from his chair. "But we all have faith in Alex's ability. Be patient, Eliza," he added more pointedly. "Angelica and I barely saw each other for the first three years of our marriage either. And now we return to London, where I aim to stand as a member of Parliament. With the war is over, it is imperative that America and Britain restore normal diplomatic and trade relations. We have too much in common to remain enemies."

But Eliza barely heard the second half of John's speech.

"Return to London?" She whirled to Angelica. "Is this true?"

Her sister nodded her head, a curious mixture of sadness and excitement on her face. "It was in John's letter to Mr. Hamilton. We sail on the tenth."

"The tenth? Of April? But that is less than a fortnight away! Two weeks, and then I may never—"

"Hush," Angelica said. "You *will* see us again, on this side of the ocean and, if you are feeling intrepid, in the Old World as well. My husband may be British, but our son is American, and I mean for him to know the country of his birth."

Eliza felt like she couldn't stop shaking her head. The slouching form of Ralph Earl melted into his chair in one corner of the room, while in the other, her brother-in-law dandled her nephew on his knee.

"You must stay here then," Eliza said. "I have to have as much time as possible with you. If only Peggy could be here as well!"

"We saw her before we left the Pastures, and we have had ample time with her these past few years. And Stephen promises to take her on a European tour sooner rather than later."

Eliza glanced around the room in desperation, as if a door might suddenly appear, leading to a fully kitted-out extra bedroom.

"If only I'd known you were coming. I would have made arrangements!"

"Do not worry about it, Eliza. John and I can find an inn at which to stay."

"An inn?" Eliza said, as if Angelica had just announced that she would sleep under a bridge. "This is not how our parents raised us. To turn guests over to strangers. I would sooner sleep in an inn myself than send my eldest sister to one."

She continued pacing, then pulled up short and turned for the door.

"Eliza?" Angelica said. "Where are you going?"

Eliza barely slowed, feeling that if she stopped to explain herself she wouldn't be able to go through with her plan. "I will be back shortly. I have an idea!" she announced with more sureness than she felt. She shook her head at Ralph, who appeared to have fallen asleep in his chair. "And please, keep him out of the honey wine. One drooler is enough," she said, pointing at baby Philip. "Oh, the baby! I never kissed the baby!" And she ran over and planted a wet one on each of his cheeks, put on a wrap, then hurried out the door.

It was but a few minutes' walk to 3 Wall Street, an elegant town house that stood almost in the shade of City Hall on the corner of Broad Street. Eliza mounted the stone steps and, after catching a breath, rapped the brass knocker firmly. A servant opened the door and showed her into the parlor, where a moment later a handsome man about Alex's age joined her.

"Why, Mrs. Hamilton, what a pleasant surprise."

Eliza shook his hand cordially.

"Good afternoon, Mr. Burr. I've come to ask a favor."

22

Burning the Candle at Both Ends

Hamilton Law Office
New York, New York
March 1784

*A*lex didn't realize how late it was until his lamp sput-
tered out and he was plunged into darkness. One minute his pen was scratching across a sheet of paper, the next
he was engulfed in inky blackness, with only the faint smell
of smoke letting him know that he hadn't been whisked out
of this world completely. Still, he was so disoriented that he
found himself frozen in his chair, half afraid to move, as if
a gap might have opened up in the floor, ready to swallow
him up.

I have been working too hard, he said to himself. *I need
a good night's sleep.*

At length, he reached for his desk drawer, pulled it open,
and rooted around inside until his fingers brushed against
a box of spills. He was lucky to light it from the fireplace,
then used its light to find the candlestick that sat on one of

his bookshelves. He lit it, and a thin glow filled the center of the room, though the corners of the small room remained steeped in darkness. He opened another drawer reflexively and pulled out a bottle of lamp oil, reached for the empty lamp, then paused. He retrieved his watch from his pocket and squinted at the tiny hands.

Could it really be 11:08 p.m.? The last time he remembered looking at his watch it was just after 6:00. He thought of Eliza, all alone at home. She would be asleep by the time he got there. She never said anything, of course, his stalwart angel, but he knew she missed him, and he did miss her. So much.

A survey of his desktop told him his watch wasn't lying. Stacks of paper were everywhere, inches high. He must have answered a hundred letters today. One prince, three ambassadors, two governors, five lieutenant governors, and fourteen congressmen numbered among his correspondents, along with dozens of current and former servicemen and twice their number of bankers and lawyers. Some of the notes were only a few lines long, but others ran to three or four tightly scrawled pages. Everything from condolence letters to tariff negotiations to banking proposals, the bulk of it ancillary to his legal work, but necessary if he was to secure the kind of well-connected, well-heeled clients he wanted in the long term. Necessary, too, if his point of view was to be heard in the formation of the new government, and the new country.

But the workload was taking its toll. This morning as he combed his hair he noticed his brush was littered with broken strands, and the dark circles under his eyes looked as if Ralph Earl had painted them on. But most unnerving were the effects on memory. He would get so focused on whatever was in front of him that he would forget about everything else. Even now, as he packed up his office, he found himself nagged by the feeling that he was neglecting something important. Something to do with Eliza, which made it even worse.

Eliza . . .

As he stepped out into the chilly evening, his mind filled with a picture of his wife. After a frenetic winter season of party after party, in which the young couple had found themselves embraced by both the best families and the most powerful politicians and businessmen in New York, life had quieted down, at least on the social front. But even as their party calendar emptied, Alex's workload grew. His first court dates for the Childress case came and went, largely procedural affairs, although Aaron Burr made it clear that the state would show no quarter. Given Caroline's precarious financial state, Alex had thought it might be best, for her sake, to try for a settlement. If he were to push the case to trial, he could set a legal precedent that would score a victory for all of his former loyalist clients—sixteen now and counting—in one fell swoop. But a trial could take months, even years to secure, given the backed-up state of Governor Clinton's courts. Indeed, Burr, sensing the plaintiff's desperation, had already begun filing delays in an attempt to bleed her dry.

It was a clear stalling tactic, but just because it was obvious didn't mean it wouldn't work. The law was very open-minded that way. It didn't care if your strategy was sophisticated or sloppy. It only cared about results.

Alex shook his head. Here he had meant to focus on his wife, and once again his work had taken over. Caroline's demands on his attention had grown as the weeks passed. At the beginning, her talk was of her dead husband and her dire financial situation, but as time went by, she spoke about her loneliness, about her future and children's. Though she had never said or done anything improper after he had made it clear her advances were unwelcome, she found excuses to clasp his hand or arm or knee, to confess her absolute, utter dependence upon him, not just for her family's security, but for her future happiness.

Alex wasn't sure what she wanted from him. Which is to say, he was pretty sure he knew exactly what she wanted from him, she had made it all too clear during their meetings. The sooner the case was settled, the better. He was a married man, with a beloved and much-missed wife at home, and he made it clear to his client that, while he was sensitive to her plight and her children's, his heart was loyal to his own, and what she was intimating was impossible.

But enough of business. Alex was going home to said darling wife, and though he may have (once again) missed the chance to dine with her at a civilized hour, they could hopefully spend a pleasant hour or two together before bedtime.

Then there would be a quiet weekend, just the two of them. He would lose the keys to his office and devote all his attention to Eliza.

But even before he entered his house, he sensed that his plans were not going to come to fruition. As he walked up Wall Street, he saw that the windows of the front parlor were blazing with light, as if a dozen lamps were burning within. So bright was the glow that for a moment Alex was afraid the house was on fire, but the gleam was steady rather than wavering, and the only smoke he smelled was the regular tang of the neighborhood chimneys. The lower shutters were drawn, though, so he couldn't see in to find out why all the lights had been lit.

As he pushed the door open, a din of voices greeted his ears.

"No, no, closer together. Mrs. Hamilton, do please try to look as if your brother-in-law had not had an unfortunate encounter with a skunk. That's better!"

Brother-in-law? Had Stephen and Peggy returned to the city? Funny that they hadn't written to announce their arrival.

Alex poked his head around the corner. Clustered on the sofa sat Eliza and Angelica, with John Church sitting between them. The sisters were attired in elegant if loosely fastened gowns, uncorsetted and unlaced, and bedecked haphazardly with gaudy costume jewelry and wigs that sat on their heads as if they had fallen there off a tree branch. John was wearing a jacket that, besides being a rather shocking shade of gold, was also far too large for him. It was as though they had gotten dressed in the dark, or after they'd had several drinks.

Well, it certainly wasn't dark.

"Alex!" Eliza called out gaily. "Look who's home!" She lurched off the sofa unsteadily, and her wig fell in John's lap.

"Alex!" another voice sang out. "Just in time!"

Alex turned, and suddenly everything fell into place. Ralph Earl stood at an easel. He was jacketless, his white shirt stained with sweat and his face flushed with drink. There was a paintbrush in one hand. With the other he snatched up a bright heap of gold fabric and came toward Alex with it.

"Here, here, put this on! You must join the picture!"

"Mr. Earl, I—"

"No, no," Eliza said, coming up behind him. "Mr. Earl wants you in the picture, so into the picture you go!" She took what turned out to be a twin to the jacket John was wearing and, pulling at the buttons of his overcoat, began simultaneously trying to slip the new garment on him before the first was even off. Alex could smell the sweet scent of honey wine on her breath, and her uncovered locks were in a state of shocking, if humorous, disarray.

"Eliza, darling, please, I haven't even—"

But Eliza continued to pull on his overcoat. She had it open now, and was sliding it off him, but since she'd also slipped the gold jacket over it, the latter garment now fell to the floor.

"Hello?" she said in confusion. "How did that happen?"

On the sofa John Church was stroking Eliza's fallen wig as though it were a sleeping cat. Angelica, on the other hand, seemed to *be* asleep, her head resting on her husband's shoulder, her wig threatening to join her sister's in John's lap.

Eliza retrieved the fallen gold jacket, meanwhile, and was once again attempting to slip it on Alex, who was still wearing the gray jacket he'd gone to work in.

"Darling, please." Alex caught the jacket and took a step back. "What in the world is going on?"

Eliza smiled at him a little crookedly. "Why, whatever do you mean, *darling?*" There was just the slightest stress on the word *darling*, but Alex didn't heed the warning.

"I mean all this." He waved a hand at the chaotic parlor. "Houseguests and pantomime and what seems to have been a significant consumption of alcohol."

"But, *darling*," Eliza said, laying still more stress on the word, "surely you know all about it, since you arranged for Mr. Earl to come stay with us after his release from prison, and you received John's letter announcing his and Angelica's arrival. As for the rest, well." Eliza shrugged. "Since we have a houseful of guests, we might as well have some fun."

Alex shook his head in confusion. "In the first place, I never received any such communication from John, or I would have told you about it. And in the second, it seems to me that it is you who forgot that Mr. Earl was coming to stay with us."

"Forgot!" Eliza said, real heat coming into her voice. "How could I forget something I was never told?"

Alex racked his brain. He was sure he had told Eliza about Earl's stay. He had arranged for it nearly two weeks ago. But he couldn't remember a specific conversation.

"But I mean, surely, I must have—"

"And as for Angelica and John, I know you received the letter, because I found it open on your desk in your study."

"In my study? Were you snooping on me?"

"No, Alex, I wasn't *snooping*. I was preparing the room to sleep my sister and her husband, since you had promised the other to Mr. Earl."

"But there isn't even a couch in there. Surely you're not going to put them on the floor."

"Of course I'm not going to put them on the floor. I borrowed a bedstead and mattress from our neighbors."

"Borrowed a—from who? Whom?"

"Theodosia."

"Theo—you mean Theodosia *Burr*?"

"Is there another on this block?"

Alex could barely believe his ears. "I'm not sure I appreciate your tone, Mrs. Hamilton."

"Oh, really, Mr. Hamilton? Well, I'm not sure I appreciate being saddled with a houseful of guests with no advance warning. But guess what? We're going to make the best of it. You're going to put this gold jacket on and join us on the sofa, and Mr. Earl's going to paint a *fabulous* picture of us."

"You're going to have to wake him up first," John said from the sofa.

Alex glanced over and saw that Earl had wandered to the dining room, where he pulled three chairs out from the table and laid himself across them. Wet snores bubbled out of his mouth, which was slick with spittle.

"Nope!" Eliza called. "Mr. Earl! Up!"

Earl ignored her, turning onto his stomach and burying his face in his hands.

Suddenly a faint crying came from up the stairs.

Angelica sat up as if a shot had gone off. Her wig went flying over the back of the sofa.

"The baby!" she said, her voice less panicked than automatic. She lurched up and headed for the stairs, her half-tied dress sagging around her waist, revealing the lace of her chemise.

John smiled at them wanly. "It looks like our party is over. I'll, uh, just give Angie a hand." And setting Eliza's wig delicately on the sofa, he set off after his wife.

Alex waited till his brother-in-law was gone before turning back to Eliza. "My darling, I—"

"Don't you 'darling' me, Alexander Hamilton." Eliza's tone was quiet but firm. The alcohol was gone from her voice, and Alex now wondered if it had been there in the first place.

"Eliza, please. I'm so sorry. I've been running in so many different directions lately. I—I must have lost track of things."

"Well, I know one direction you haven't been running in. To me." And now a little hurt crept into her voice.

Alex felt his knees quiver. "It's true. I'm so, so sorry." He put his arms around her. "Let me make it up to you?" he said, kissing her forehead, her nose, her lips.

Eliza let her lips linger on his. "Don't think you can kiss your way out of this, Mr. Hamilton."

"I wouldn't dream of it," Alex said, kissing her again. "Mrs. Hamilton."

Another kiss, and then he took her hand and turned for the stairs.

"What say we continue our fight in the morning?"

Eliza just shook her head at him. "I might find you irresistible, Mr. Hamilton," she said. "But I believe you are overestimating your powers of persuasion."

She headed up the stairs alone, leaving Alex's jaw hanging open. From the dining room came the throaty rumble of Ralph Earl's snores.

23

Salad Days

The Hamilton Town House
New York, New York
March 1784

"Tell me again," Eliza said.

"Lettuce," Helena Morris said.

"Let us . . . ?" Angelica parroted in disbelief.

"Let us . . . eat lettuce," Helen answered with a laugh.

Ralph Earl reached a hand forward and fingered the green leaves. "It certainly *feels* like lettuce," he pronounced, to the obvious disbelief of the Schuyler sisters.

"That's because it *is*," Helena said. "Lettuce. L-E-T-T-U-C-E."

"But it's the twenty-seventh of March," Eliza said. "How on earth can one have lettuce on March twenty-seventh? It's like . . . it's like a mule having babies."

"Mules can't have babies?" Ralph said. "Then how on earth do you get more mules?"

"A mule is a cross between a donkey and a horse," Angelica said, fingering the lettuce nervously. "It does feel . . . like lettuce."

"You're making that up!" Earl scoffed. "Donkeys and horses—preposterous!"

"People!" Eliza clapped her hands. "Focus! We are trying to decide what this very lettuce-looking substance is that Helena has placed before us. My guess is that she wrinkled some paper up and then had Mr. Earl paint it green."

"Oh, for heaven's sake!" Helena snatched a leaf and popped it into her mouth. She chewed, swallowed. "See? Not paper. Lettuce. I told you. It's a gift from Jane Beekman. Her parents' greenhouse is apparently as balmy as the tropics. They grow green vegetables all the year round. Try it," she insisted, pushing a head toward them.

Eliza looked at Angelica and Mr. Earl to see if either of them would volunteer. Both shrank from the table. Well, Eliza supposed, it was up to her. "I got a taste of an orange from Jane's greenhouse the other day," she said.

Nervously, she reached out and pulled a small piece from a leaf. It certainly felt real. Tender, slightly damp, with a bit of a crunch as it ripped free. She took a breath, then tossed it in her mouth. She expected some kind of rancid taste, as when, as a little girl, she had licked a painting of cake, thinking it would taste like frosting, only to have it taste like paint smells. But this tasted like . . . lettuce.

"Remarkable!" she after a moment. "It really is lettuce."

She tore off another piece. She turned to her sister and the artist. "You must try it!"

"Delectable!" the artist crooned.

"Oh!" Angelica said. "I don't think I've had a green vegetable since September. Just soft potatoes and mealy apples and squash. This is divine! I feel my complexion brightening and my bones growing straighter! What a miracle!"

"Helena," Eliza said, stuffing her mouth with the green goodness. "I would marry you if I weren't already married."

"And if she weren't a woman," Angelica said with a laugh.

"A technicality. I would find a way around it. This really is wonderful. It makes me long for spring's full arrival."

"Now, now, don't eat it at all," Helena said, laughing, as they reached for a second head. "Save some for Mr. Hamilton."

"Mr. Hamilton can fend for himself," Eliza said, but she stopped herself from digging into the second head, and swatted Mr. Earl's hand away when he reached for it.

"Mmmm, how did that go last night?" Angelica said. "You seemed rather upset with him."

"Oh, he was suitably apologetic, after I finally got him to admit that he had forgotten to inform me that Mr. Earl was coming to stay with us, and that your and John's arrival was imminent. It behooves me to remember that he is doing the jobs of five different men at present, and I need to be understanding."

"And what are you, a hat tree in the foyer?" Helena laughed. "There when he needs you, forgotten when he doesn't? I told John when he proposed to me: I would rather spend my life with a cabbage farmer in some godforsaken place like Easthampton or, or *Ohio* than with a man who neglects me."

"But, Helena," Eliza said. "It falls to the men to work outside of the home and to provide for their womenfolk."

"And whose fault is that?" Helena retorted. "No one's but their own. Why, would you feel sympathy when your jailor complained about the long hours he spent guarding you? Of course not. You would tell him to release you, and then you could both get a good night's sleep."

"Hear, hear!" Earl said, once again reaching for the lettuce. Eliza snatched the basket away and folded the cloth covering over it.

"Surely you are not suggesting that women could do the same work as men?"

"Suggesting it?" Helena said. "Of course not. I am stating it as absolute fact. Why, many's the time I've looked over John's account books and spotted some error or other he missed."

"Well, I've looked over Alex's court papers on a few occasions but I'm afraid I'm not much help in that department."

"But did you train as lawyer?" Helena asked. "Did you clerk at court? Did you go to college even? I'm betting you did not. I'm guessing that you and Angelica and Peggy were educated just like me and my sisters: at our mother's knee, in the schoolroom at home. And after everyone had learned the basics of reading and writing and sums, the boys went on to science and history and philosophy while you had a needle and thread stuck in your hand, or a bow and arrow—but a dainty one, not one that you could use on the field of war—or perhaps a pianoforte."

"What on earth is wrong with playing the pianoforte?" Eliza asked.

"Nothing," Helena said. "But it won't exactly help you solve the problem of paying for a standing militia without a federal tax program, or correcting our trade imbalance with France."

"Well!" Angelica exclaimed with a laugh. "Our little Helena is one of Mr. Locke's rationalist empiricists, or whatever they're called."

"I don't even know who Mr. Locke is, let alone a rational whatchamacallit. My observations are based on what I see with my own two eyes. Speaking of which," Helena interrupted herself. "Angelica and I really should be off. I've promised to take her to my tailor to get some dresses made for her journey. Angelica's garments are far too American to wear in Europe."

"Imagine if a man had to spend half as much time on his appearance as we do," Angelica said as she followed Helena to the wardrobe in the hall, where she retrieved her coat.

"They would not start half the wars they do," Eliza joked.

"No, no," Helena said with a laugh. "They would start them, but they would never show up to the field of battle because they'd be forever getting dressed."

"And with that, my beautiful sister, I bid you au revoir," Angelica said. "John said it was unlikely that he would be back in time for dinner, but I will do my best."

"And if we do run late, then I will make sure she's fed and watered somewhere," Helena said.

Angelica waited for the maid to retrieve Philip from his crib upstairs. Eliza had offered to watch him but Angelica said that unless she was hiding a wet nurse somewhere, the baby had best stay with her. Kissing Eliza good-bye, she and Helena headed out into the bright March day.

"Well, Mr. Earl," Eliza said, turning from the closed door, "it seems like it's just you and me."

And the decanter, she added mentally, for when she returned from the hall she saw that Earl had made his way to the drinks table and poured himself a double helping. Eliza had made Alex hide the honey wine before he left, leaving out only the heavy red wine her father brewed at the Pastures. Her father was, by his own estimation, "an unaccomplished oenologist," but had taken the precaution of fortifying his liquor with strong Portuguese brandy. The resulting beverage was not particularly tasty and the dregs turned your tongue as black as a berry, but it got the job done.

"Hmmm," Earl said after his first sip, which drained half his glass. "The honey wine seems to have lost a bit of its sweetness."

"Alas, we seem to have drunk all the honey wine last night," Eliza said. She told herself that technically it wasn't a lie, since last night's party had indeed drained the opened cask, and the remaining ones were stored below in the kitchen. "Well, Mr. Earl, you are a free man. How do you wish to spend your first day out of a cell?"

Ralph had already refilled his glass, and now he sprawled across a sofa. Eliza winced, fearful that he should spill the dark purple liquid across the delicate yellow silk upholstery, but Earl handled his glass with the same delicacy he handled his brushes and spilled not a drop on the sofa or himself.

"In the company of a beautiful woman," he said now, so roguishly that Eliza found herself blushing.

"Mr. Earl! Have you a paramour that you've failed to mention?" But even as the words left her mouth, she realized that he was referring to her.

"You are too modest, Mrs. Hamilton. And too formal with me lately. It seemed that we were closer when there were bars between us."

Eliza stiffened. She was suddenly aware of their intimacy and isolation. She had not been alone with a man other than Alex since she left Albany. "I do not at all want you to feel unwelcome, but I must confess to being very startled by both your and my sister's presence here yesterday."

"I hope I will not inconvenience you for any longer than is necessary, Mrs. Hamilton." Eliza also couldn't help but notice that he didn't specify any kind of time frame for finding a place of his own.

"Your and Mr. Hamilton's immense generosity in my hour of need has meant more to me than I can possibly convey," Earl continued, "or repay for that matter. I painted no fewer than seventeen portraits during my time in prison, and all but two of the commissions were sent to me by your husband. It is thanks to him that I was able to pay my creditors and earn my freedom—or should I say"—waving a hand at the parlor—"release to a far more luxurious cell."

Eliza took a moment to look around the parlor. She had to admit that after four months in New York, she and Alex had created a beautiful home. The walls, which had been a handsome but somber cerulean shade when they first moved in, was now covered with mint-green wallpaper with a toile pattern in a color that both Alex and Eliza had delighted to learn was called Hooker green. The darker of the two greens depicted a seven-bayed brick house in a pastoral setting that bore more than a passing resemblance to the Schuylers' Albany mansion.

The heavily carved walnut sofa was long enough to seat three, and covered in beautiful yellow silk jacquard. It was flanked by a pair of wing chairs, which, though not a set, had also been covered in yellow silk and thus complemented the sofa without being too much of a piece. A low oval table with a pale gold lacquer finish held table and chairs together, while a second, smaller sofa in matching yellow silk, flanked by pair of delicate cane chairs and one well-worn Windsor chair, rounded out the room. The Windsor had the look of a family heirloom (it was), along with a couple of tiny wooden tables with painted tops, and added just the right note of hominess to the room, which otherwise might have looked too impersonal in its newness. The clock on the mantel was marble and silver, flanked by the Revere candelabra that had formerly been in the dining room.

It was indeed "luxurious," as Mr. Earl said. She and Alex had chosen each piece with care, and at the time Eliza had thought they were creating a room—a home—that they would share together and start their family in. Yet it seemed the only time they ever shared the room was when it was filled with a half-dozen guests besides. The rest of the time it was just Eliza's prettily decorated cell.

She chose to keep this feeling to herself, instead saying:

"Seventeen paintings. And how long were you incarcerated?"

"For just over eight months." Ralph said it almost longingly, as if he had visited one of the southern states during winter, and enjoyed the balmy winter. And indeed he continued. "I must admit, though, that prison agreed with me in some way. I have never been a particularly gregarious man, preferring the company of just one or two quality people to that of the mob. And I have never had such a sustained period of productivity in my life."

"Yes, I was trying to sort that out in my head. You worked on the portrait of me for nearly a month, and it was still 'not quite finished' when you were released yesterday. So how on earth did you manage to paint—sixteen, is it?—in the seven months prior?"

Earl tried to stone-face her, but failed. A smirk cracked his face, quickly widening to a grin, and a moment later he broke out into peals of laughter. So violent were his paroxysms that he actually relinquished his wineglass, setting it down on the lacquered table (mercifully without spilling atop it). Eliza did her best to laugh with him, though she had no idea what he was laughing at.

"I'm afraid you have found me out," he said when at last he could speak again, which is to say, after he'd cleared his throat with a hearty swig of wine, and refilled his glass. "I was stalling."

"Stalling? You mean, deliberately prolonging my visits?"

"Prolonging the pleasure of one whose charming visage is only matched by her charm of temperament. I confess that toward the end I would prepare my palette with paints the night before, so they would be dry by the time you arrived. Then I'd daub a dry brush into them and across your portrait."

"Why, Mr. Earl, you scoundrel!" Eliza said, only half joking. "Had you no qualms about continuing to invite a lady into such an environment? Were you not afraid that my virtue might be compromised?"

Ralph shrugged. "It was not I who initiated the visits, but your husband. If he believed no ill would befall you, then I saw no reason to assume contrariwise. After all, I am a gentleman, and I lived there day in, day out. I know ladies are more delicate—"

"Be wary of what you say, Mr. Earl," Eliza warned with a twinkle in her eye, "lest Mrs. Rutherfurd get wind of your retrogressive ways, and return to school you in women's equality."

"Well then, Mrs. Rutherfurd will surely take my side. If a man can stand such conditions, surely a woman can, too."

Eliza had to admit to herself that she had suffered no harm during her month of visits, and, in fact, had found the experience interesting, illuminating even. She had been shocked to learn, for example, that the inhabitants of debtors' prison were not, like regular criminals, wards of the state, and as such, the state did not provide for them. It struck Eliza as an absurd, not to mention cruel, system. A man is unable to pay his debt so he is locked away from gainful employment, and forced to go still deeper in debt just to pay his upkeep? There was no way for a creditor to recoup his losses in such a scenario. It was purely punitive. It was yet another holdover from the Old World that she hoped her country would do away with sooner rather than later.

"Well then," she said now. "I suppose it behooves me to ask if my portrait is actually finished, and can be hung in some place of prominence." As she spoke she was glancing above the mantel, only now noticing that the silver-framed mirror that normally hung there had been taken away.

Why, Alex! she said to herself. *You remembered!*

"In fact, it does require a touch more shading. Your gown was of such subtle luminescence. I want to do it, and of course your exquisite complexion, justice."

She felt a blush add itself to her "exquisite complexion," then nodded and went upstairs to change quickly from her everyday frock into the silver-pink gown. It fastened in front so she didn't need Rowena's help to put it on, and she decided to forego the wig unless Mr. Earl insisted on it. Twenty minutes after she went upstairs she was back down. Earl had set up his easel and paints, thoughtfully pulling over one of the cane chairs that had no fabric to stain, should he drip.

And there was the painting. She had caught sidelong glimpses of it before, but Mr. Earl hadn't let her have a good look in some time—no doubt because he was hiding how close to completion it was. If his sketches had somehow managed to capture the heart of her being, this painting, in its exquisite lifelike detail, gave that heart flesh that seemed to pulse and perspire.

"Oh, Mr. Earl! It is so beautiful!" She blushed anew. "That makes me sound vain. I mean the painting is beautiful, not its subject."

"Do not apologize for what God has graced you with, Mrs. Hamilton," Earl said, but he was frowning, and looking back and forth between her and the picture. "There is something missing. Something—here." And he waved a dry brush in front of the long, bare, pale column of her throat and décolletage. "There is too much white. It lacks an edge. I know!" He reached into the valise in which he stored his oils and retrieved a simple black grosgrain ribbon. "If you would allow me," he said, stepping toward her.

Eliza was not sure what he was doing until he reached up to her neck and looped the ribbon lightly around it, tying it in a simple bow that draped down to her chest. His touch was as deft as a lady's maid's, yet Eliza was acutely conscious of his eyes on her, which gleamed with an adoration that no maid had ever bestowed.

She thought about pointing out that Mr. Earl could have just painted the bow into the picture without adding it to her ensemble, but she kept that to herself, feeling awkward and uncomfortable.

He stepped back, and gazed at her with revering eyes.

"I was going to say that the light in this room was beautiful, but as I look at you I realize the light is superfluous. My brush is honored to preserve even the tenth part of such radiance."

He lingered then, staring at her, and for a moment Eliza thought he might even kiss her. She even imagined him leaning in, their lips meeting, his arms around her waist . . .

And then, with a thoroughly unromantic cackle, Earl whirled toward his canvas, grabbed a brush and stabbed it against his pallet, and Eliza realized with a mixture of relief that in the end, like all men, his first love was his work.

She didn't know whether she was relieved or disappointed, but her mind filled with a picture of Alex's face and she was overcome with tenderness. *Such fragile creatures, men,* she thought. *What on earth would they do without us?*

24

If It Please the Court

New York State Supreme Court
New York, New York
March 1784

Suddenly, after ages of interminable back-and-forthing, the day of the trial was upon him.

Alex had been preparing for months. He knew the legal issues inside and out. He could cite English and Colonial precedents as well as the dozens of different—and conflicting—statutes the various new states had passed to handle the loyalist issue. He knew Caroline and Jonathan Childress's story backward and forward. Yet he still felt like he did on that long-ago day when he walked into a King's College classroom as a newly arrived immigrant, deeply conscious of his Caribbean accent and hand-me-down clothes. He had practiced law in Albany for a year and argued before the bench numerous times, but he couldn't shake the worry that he was about to be judged based not on his research or his arguments but on who he was. A Johnny-come-lately in a world of silver spooners and blue bloods. A striver.

However, the courtroom itself was oddly soothing. Alex reveled in the sober probity of its lines: the beamed ceiling and the paneled walls, both lacquered in a cool blue-gray, gave the room an elegance that recalled a Greek temple, without the ostentation of friezes and scrolls and naked statues. The benches were as solid as pews, and simple arched windows allowed the wet March sun through in angled rays. Even the floors were of well-trod planks, their varnish worn away to a smooth paleness, attesting to the steady passage of justice through these halls.

And if nothing else, it was convenient. The case was being tried in City Hall, just a few steps from his front door.

He arrived early and waited for Caroline on the front steps, wanting to escort her into the building and to the courtroom. The case had not received any press, yet he had heard whisperings here and there. *The war hero Alexander Hamilton was defending a loyalist! Was he one of those secret monarchists, who had fought to toss out one king so that he could enthrone one of his own choice?* The federalists outnumbered the loyalists two to one, but their leaders were numerous and fractious, preventing any one person from amassing too much power. But the loyalists were rudderless and adrift. If someone were to step up to defend their interests, that person could find himself with a full third of the country at his back. The potential for power—for income and, should the tide turn that way, votes—was enormous. And all this speculation about Alex was being focused through the slim, delicate form of Caroline Childress, who was less a lens than a funnel through which a raging torrent was about to pour. Alex wanted to make sure she had all the support she needed, lest she be washed away in the flood.

On Alex's advice, Caroline arrived at City Hall on foot rather than in a carriage. It was important that she not appear too prosperous, as though she had grown rich off British silver during the occupation. He had also purchased a black coat for her. It was crucial that everyone, even spectators, be reminded that she was, after all, a war widow, no matter which side her husband had died fighting for.

"Good morning, Mrs. Childress."

Mrs. Childress started, before accepting his hand gravely.

"Mr. Hamilton! I did not recognize you in robes and wig!"

Alex smiled uncomfortably, and resisted the urge to scratch beneath the stiff hairpiece screwed on over his own perfectly ample head of hair. He found the custom of judicial dress to be ridiculously formal and archaic — one of the many lingering Briticisms he, like Eliza, hoped would soon be abolished from American life. But for now it was the custom, if not the law, and so he had let Eliza pin the dusty-smelling wig to head and sprinkle it with powder, then donned the long black wool robe.

"We make a fine pair of shades," he joked. "Though put a hat on me and I fear I would look like a country parson."

If Caroline heard, she didn't answer, but only wrung her hands, staring at the people passing by on the street.

"I suppose it is the very purpose of the costume," he continued. "To submerge the individual, as it were, behind the anonymous veil of the law."

Caroline let this statement, too, pass without answer. She was clearly nervous, and at length she glanced at the low, cloudy sky.

"I fear we will have rain before lunch."

Alex offered her his winningest smile. Her anxiety was perfectly understandable, but a nervous client looked like a guilty one. He needed her calm, and perhaps slightly sad, the aggrieved widow rather than the greedy schemer.

"Then let us hie inside, where we will be protected by the sturdy joists and pillars of justice."

Together they headed through the foyer and up the stairs. They found the courtroom perhaps three-quarters filled with spectators. A few were witnesses for one side or the other, a few had the look of reporters, with their tattered notebooks and knife-sharpened pencils, but most were clearly there out of curiosity. The courts have always attracted gawkers, just as the church has. People are fascinated by the collision of the individual with a force that has the power to convey life or death, liberty or bondage, riches or poverty. Sometimes they had a vested interest in one side or the other, but often it was just the process itself that drew them.

Judging from the harsh stares, however, Alex sensed that today's audience was far from impartial. Well, it was New York, after all. The city had suffered under military occupation for seven years, and seen the bodies of its native sons wash up on shore every morning, tossed from the prison boats during the night. You wouldn't expect to find a lot of warmth among the populace for a British sympathizer. And if they did feel it, they'd probably keep it to themselves.

But this wasn't a jury trial. Alex ultimately need worry about only one man's opinion: that of Judge Smithson, who had yet to enter the room. Opposing counsel was also still absent. Alex had seen Burr socially two or three times over the last month, but had avoided a tête-à-tête. He'd overheard Burr making jokes about Alex's "poor loyalist widow" and had to bite his tongue to keep from being drawn out. Burr's comments weren't particularly barbed, and he was at least gentlemanly enough not to slander Caroline's reputation. In a way, that made it worse, because Alex could tell that Burr regarded the upcoming trial as a kind of game, and a low-stakes one at that, like an after-dinner hand of whist or quadrille. If he won, he would gloat for a moment, then forget about it. If he lost, he would be theatrically concilia-tory, and forget about that, too. Which is to say, win or lose, in a few weeks' time the name "Caroline Childress" would probably mean nothing to him, whether she was once again running a thriving business that would see her and her chil-dren through life, or was turned out of her home by fiendish creditors. Burr's opponent in this trial was not the defendant but Alex.

As if on cue, Burr swept into the courtroom. He was look-ing exceptionally rosy-cheeked this morning, as if he had walked around the block rather than from his house two doors down. The color in his complexion was heightened by his wig, which also did a good job of hiding his thinning hair. His jabot was tied with a flourish befitting a serenading swain, and unlike Alex's, Burr's had the sheen of silk rather than wool.

"Does he think he's playing dress-up?"

Alex didn't realize he'd spoken aloud until Caroline said, "Beg pardon, Mr. Hamilton?"

"Oh, nothing, nothing."

Burr worked his way up the aisle, greeting several people by name, with handshakes all around. Had he packed the courtroom with anti-loyalist agitators?

Stop indulging in paranoia, Alex chided himself. *The man is a gadfly. No doubt he knows them the same way a good bar mistress knows the names of the local sots—because they're always here, clambering for more spirits.*

Burr swept up to his own table, at the last moment turning to greet Alex.

"Oh, Hamilton. I didn't realize it was you. I thought it was the chaplain come to swear the oaths." He winked mischievously at Alex's client. "Do not judge your attorney by the quality of his robes, Mrs. Childress. His mind is much sharper than the scissors with which that rather shapeless garment was cut."

"Good morning, Mr. Burr," Alex said in his most formal voice.

"Brrr," Burr said, pretending to shiver. "Is it cold in here? Well," he added, licking his lips. "I guess the duel is on."

He turned to his table just as the rear door of the court opened and a bailiff entered.

"All rise!"

Burr was already standing, so that it seemed as if everyone else was following his lead. Alex couldn't help but wonder if he'd planned it this way. Again, he chastised himself to stop being paranoid. There was no way he could have known the judge would enter now. Was there?

The door behind the bailiff filled with a huge shadow. For a moment, it seemed like whatever was beyond wouldn't be able to pass through the narrow aperture. Then came a chafing noise as heavy fabric scraped against the wooden frame, and Judge Lewis Smithson was in the room.

The judge was an imposing man in his early fifties. He was at least as tall as General Washington, which is to say six four, and his tightly curled white wig added two or three more inches to his frame. But he was big in a way that Washington was not, as thick around the waist as a vat of whale oil, with legs like sooty Roman columns. Alex had seen the man once or twice outside of chambers, so he knew the man's bulk was all blubber, but in his black robe and extra-wide jabot he had the appearance of a lichen-covered boulder rising out of turbulent seas, ready to rip a jagged hole in the hull of an unsuspecting vessel.

Beside him, Caroline caught her breath. Alex hoped she would keep her composure throughout the trial.

Judge Smithson mounted the steps to his dais, which creaked and shifted beneath his weight. The dark oiled walnut of the bench only added to his imposing form. He was a snow-capped mountain now, daring Sisyphus to try to scale him one more time.

The judge took his seat and motioned for the rest of the courtroom to follow.

"We are here today to hear the case of *Mrs. Jonathan Childress v. State of New York*, concerning a property located at Seventeen Baxter Street which the state believes was illegally acquired by the plaintiff during the occupation of New York City by British forces."

"With all due respect, Your Honor," Alex said, standing up. "The state seized the property some four months ago, and now merely wishes to codify the transfer of property with an ex post facto legal action."

"Your Honor!" Burr rose to his feet. "Such an accusation veers on disrespectful to the institution of our government, which many people in this room risked their lives to bring into existence!"

Cries of "Hear, hear!" were heard in the gallery. The judge, who was known to be a man of strict order, did not gavel them to silence. Alex took that as a bad sign.

Alex took a calming breath. "Does opposing counsel dispute the fact that the building located at Seventeen Baxter Street has not been in Mrs. Childress's possession since November? Let me save you the trouble of answering," he continued, waving a startled Burr silent. He pulled a piece of paper from his satchel. "I have here a copy of a bill of sale for Seventeen Baxter Street dated November nineteenth, 1783, transferring ownership from the state of New York to one Elihu Springer. So, as I said, Your Honor, the state has already taken the building, and sold it at a handsome profit. This proceeding, then, can have no other purpose but to determine the legality of that action."

Judge Smithson seemed to be fighting to keep a grin off his face. He turned to Burr.

"He's got you there, counsel."

A chagrined Burr sat down without looking at Alex. Alex took his seat as regally as he could, hoping his face didn't look smug.

"Well then," Judge Smithson said. "It sounds like we are in for an entertaining couple of days. What say we—"

The door at the back of the courtroom opened. The judge looked annoyed at first, then startled. At his expression, Alex turned, along with everyone else in the room.

The figure entering the courtroom wasn't as tall as Judge Smithson, or as big around, but he was that curious kind of fat that is almost entirely centered on the stomach, a sagging sack over a pair of comparatively spindly legs.

It was Governor George Clinton.

A wave of recognition went around the room in a series of whispers and gasps. Governor Clinton didn't acknowledge anyone save Judge Smithson, whom he nodded at formally, but with a gleam in his eye, then took a seat in the very last pew.

Judge Smithson waited a moment, then picked up his gavel and struck it once.

"Let us begin!"

25

The Bonds of Sisterhood, Part Two

Broad and Nassau Streets
New York, New York
March 1784

In a stroke of bad luck, Angelica and John's passage over the Atlantic was pushed up by a full week. Eliza had made plans to throw her sister a fabulous send-off, and now found herself with but three days to pull it together—and all while Alex was trying the most important case of his life!

But she was determined to make it a success. For Angelica's sake, of course, but also for her own. This was her moment to prove that she more than just an accessory to a handsome, well-regarded man, be it husband or father. She threw herself into the party preparations with a vengeance. She would avail herself of Jane Beekman's greenhouse salad vegetables and Stephen's honey wine, but everything else she would procure on her own, with her own hands and, more important, her own money. Or at any rate her own line of credit, as the Hamiltons' coin was all but depleted at this point, and would be until Alex completed his case. Assuming he won, of course. If he didn't, Eliza really had no idea *what* they were going to do.

"I can't believe how much the city has changed since before the war," Angelica said as they strolled up Broad Street toward Nassau. She had visited once in 1775, on her way to visit the Livingstons in New Jersey.

"It is a positive boom town," Eliza answered. "When the British invaded, people fled by the thousands. They say the population of the city dropped by half that first year." She gestured to the shuttered shops that still dotted the bustling street. TO LET. AVAILABLE. FOR SALE. PLEASE TAKE. "At first, it looked as though everything would return to normal overnight, but as you see, there are still so many empty buildings and storefronts."

"But why aren't people moving back in?"

They paused at a shop that *was* occupied, where Eliza signed a note for no less than a gross of white tapers and directed the shopkeeper to send them to 57 Wall Street.

"They're empty," she said when they were back outside, "but they're not actually available. They say speculators have swooped in and snapped them up for a song, and are sitting on them until prices go up." She paused a bit. "Have you met Sarah Livingston's husband, Mr. Jay?"

"I have not. I was going to say that I hope they'll be at the party, but the tone of your voice seems less . . . receptive."

"Oh, I don't mean to speak ill of them. I was just going to say that I have heard that John is one of the people purchasing properties for pennies on the dollar. I would say that he is going to make his fortune, but he already has one, so he will be merely adding to it."

"Still, Sister, it sounds as if you disapprove. After all, surely it is good business sense to buy low and sell high?"

Another errand interrupted the conversation, this one at a bakery. "Rowena is a wizard, but she will not be able to provide for a houseful of revelers," Eliza said as she ordered dozens of loaves and rolls, as well as half a dozen sweet and savory pies, again signing a note rather than paying in coin.

When they had completed their errand, though, she took up Angelica's question immediately. It was something that had been on her mind. She had come to love New York City, or, if not to love it, then to think of it as home, and she did not like to see it ill-treated.

"From a business point of view, of course, it makes sense to maximize one's profits. But from the point of view of society, it seems rather . . . limited, I'll say. There is an opportunity for thousands of people to gain a toehold in New York. To buy a house or a shop that they can pass on to their descendants just as Papa built the Pastures for us. Instead a handful of men have snatched up nearly all the properties, and the poor people locked out of the deal are forced to rent rather than buy."

"Locked out of the deal?" Angelica seemed both shocked and dubious. "Do you think there has been collusion on the part of Mr. Jay or the other investors?"

"Collusion is a serious word. I would say that it is simply a case of opportunity. The men who make the decisions and do the deals all come from a very slim section of society — perhaps one percent of the whole population. They live and work near each other, attend the same clubs, have each other over to parties."

"Like the one you're about to throw," Angelica couldn't resist interjecting.

"Oh, indeed. We are as blessed as they come. But by the time a poor man gets wind of an available property, it will have long since been snatched up."

"Pardon me, Sister," Angelica said in a curious tone. "But since you and Alex move in that same circle of the 'one percent,' as you call it, how is it that you have not managed to purchase a house if they are so cheap? Not that the house you rent isn't quite lovely, but it seems that the time to strike is while the iron is hot."

In answer, Eliza turned into another shop, where she purchased a crystal punch bowl and a set of embroidered, lace-edged napkins, again paying with a promissory note. Back outside, she shrugged. "A house that once cost a thousand pounds and now costs a hundred still costs a hundred pounds. Five pounds of credit here and there is easy to come by," she said, waving a hand at the shop they had just come out of, "but for that kind of purchase one needs cash to hand, and we have almost none."

"But surely Papa—"

"Alex refuses. Papa and Mama were generous with furniture and moving expenses, and of course they put us up, off and on, for over three years. Alex is determined to make it in New York on his own terms. My husband is a very proud man, and I have to support him in that decision. And I would rather be married to a man who cares more about what he does than what he has."

"I suppose I agree with you," Angelica said doubtfully, "but I must say I'm happy to have found a man who has moral convictions that are financially lucrative."

Eliza laughed. "Between you and Peggy, I suppose I will always be known as the poor Schuyler sister. But I have no doubt that Alex will do well by us. Besides his law practice, his fingers are in virtually every pot. In finance, and trade relations, and alliances with European powers, and the military, and something that for want of a better word I would call general political theory."

Angelica frowned, unsure if she wanted to open this topic. "What do you mean?" she asked cautiously.

"He thinks we need a document, a charter similar to the Articles of Confederation, but more extensive and more binding. Something that will finally make a genuinely united nation of us, rather than a motley collection of states."

"Those sound like the words of man with political ambitions."

"No doubt, just like Papa, and Peggy's Stephen, and your John. I expect he will make senator at the very least."

"At the least? What is higher than a senator?"

"Alex thinks the United States needs an executive vested in a single person."

"A king?" Angelica almost gasped.

"No, more like a prime minister. But not of the British variety—a toady who has to report to his monarch. More like the head of a corporation, whose only responsibility is to his shareholders."

"So much power granted to a single person can be dangerous."

"Alex agrees, which is why he thinks it needs to be balanced by other branches of government. A strong congress and an equally strong judiciary. Each branch can keep the other from crossing the line to tyranny."

"My word!" Angelica laughed. "Listen to you! The last time I saw you, you were helping to change Kitty's diapers. Now you're outlining plans for a whole new government!"

Eliza laughed modestly. "Oh, it is mostly dinner party gossip," she said, though the truth is, she was proud of herself. This was her future, after all, not just Alex's. "It's all anyone ever talks about in society. I look forward to the day when all we have to worry about is catching the fashionable play or opera and securing the best dress fabric."

"You liar," Angelica teased. "You love it. But still . . . ?"

"Yes?" Eliza prompted when Angelica's voice trailed off.

"All of this is man's world, to which woman can only be spectator. Does it do to take too much interest in politics, rather than in, say, culture—music and painting and plays— over which we can have more sway."

"I suppose they are men's things, in the sense that men make the decisions that keep things this way. But as Helena said, women don't take a hand in politics, not because they can't, but because they are shut out of it. When circumstances allow them in, they can do great things. Look at Queen Elizabeth—it was she more than any of her male predecessors or successors who made England the great power it is. Or Catherine of Russia. They say she is the most powerful woman on the planet, ruler of the largest empire the world has ever known. Why, under her reign, Russia has replenished its treasury and won a war against Turkey. Why should we not have a similarly powerful woman here in America?"

"Let's hear it for sisterhood!" Angelica said, making a fist. "But is it what you want to do, Eliza?" This last question came after yet another stop, at a distillery to procure some stout whiskey. Mrs. Childress had given them all the ale they could drink, but you couldn't have a party with just beer and honey wine. "Don't you want to start a family?"

"I would love it but we have not yet been blessed," said Eliza. "When we moved here, I thought it would happen immediately, yet with everything else that's has been going on—finding new friends and work and just learning how to live on our own—I have to say that I am a little relieved that we have not had a child added to the mix. It might be too much. But still . . . ," she added, her voice fading off wistfully.

"It will happen," said Angelica with a sympathetic squeeze. "Families are like rain showers. They always come in time, but they are not exactly a goal, if you see what I mean, any more than eating and sleeping are. They are just a part of life."

Eliza nodded, trying to stop the full feeling in her throat. She was glad to have her sister by her side to understand her pain so acutely. She took a moment to recover, then pulled up in front of a window through which could be seen an exquisite bolt of lace.

"For now, all I want to do is buy that tablecloth," she said, pushing open the door. "So I can throw my sister the best bon voyage party New York has ever seen!"

26

---◆◆◆---

Closing Arguments

Burr's strategy over the next three days seemed to be to wear everyone down. He did so by calling a veritable parade of witnesses, all of whom said more or less the same thing: that Caroline Childress had operated a bustling alehouse on Water Street all through the occupation, serving any British soldier or sympathizer who came in. Alex didn't know why this should be any more damning than the simple fact that Mrs. Childress, like her deceased husband, had herself been a loyalist, until he heard the increasing murmurs from the gallery. Burr's witnesses made Ruston's Ale House sound like a raucous establishment. Not improper, per se, but it seemed as if Mrs. Childress had partied through the war. Alex was able to counter the latter claim by getting Burr's witnesses to admit that Mrs. Childress was in fact rarely if ever in the bar room, being usually occupied with managing inventory and production and staff, and when she did appear, she was dressed soberly in honor of her fallen husband. Still, the impression was that she was creating a festive space for the redcoats who had seized Manhattan. With each successive witness, the murmurings grew louder, till eventually they approached outright jeers. But even worse than this was the fact that Judge Smithson did not silence them, but only shook his head in tight-lipped anger at the account of the festivities.

Alex knew he had to go on the counteroffensive. After Burr's twelfth witness, a scruffy-looking man of about thirty named Robert Frye, had delivered his clearly rehearsed account, Alex was awarded cross-examination. He had eschewed any questions for Burr's previous witnesses, but this time he all but leapt from his chair.

"Mr. Frye," he said as he strode across the room. "You seem to be very well acquainted with the goings-on in Mrs. Childress's alehouse. Is that because you are a neighbor of hers?"

"Why no, sir," Frye said. "I live on a small farm just north of the city."

"Ah. So your accounts are hearsay then?"

Alex knew this wasn't the case, but he had an idea how Frye would respond. The farmer struck him as a proud man, and he didn't disappoint Alex.

"What I said I seen with my own eyes!" he said huffily, turning to the judge and nodding at him. "I don't make up stories, and I don't pass on gossip, Your Honor!"

Alex dug the knife in deeper.

"So I take it you are a loyalist then?"

"Your Honor, please," Burr said, standing up. "Mr. Hamilton's question would seem to have no point other than to insult the good name of Mr. Frye."

"If it please, Your Honor, I do have a point in mind," Alex rejoindered.

Judge Smithson frowned at him. "Get there quickly, counsel." He turned to Frye. "You may answer Mr. Hamilton's question."

Frye had been squirming in his seat with his desire to speak.

"I am absolutely one hundred percent not a loyalist, sir, and I resent the implication! I am a patriot through and through."

"Very good, sir," Alex responded with feigned deference. "I myself served in the Continental army with General Washington, as did my estimable colleague Mr. Burr. Well, he did not work with General Washington, but he did serve *somewhere*." Alex paused as a few snickers ran through the room. "But may I ask, Mr. Frye, why you as a patriot drank in a loyalist bar?"

"I never said Ruston's was a loyalist bar. Why, there were lots of us patriots who drank there!"

"More patriots than loyalists, would you say?" Alex asked in an innocent voice.

"I should say so. I don't suppose we'd have felt comfortable otherwise." Frye's voice had lost some of its certainty, and he turned to Burr's desk. Alex moved quickly to interpose himself between the witness and his lawyer. At last, his robes proved good for something. He was as wide as jib sail, and completely concealed the squirming lawyer from his nervous witness.

"I just want to make sure that I understand you fully. You're telling me that Mrs. Childress ran Ruston's as an establishment for anyone who chose to enter, loyalist or patriot, but generally speaking more of her clientele were American patriots rather than redcoats."

For the first time, Frye seemed to realize what he'd done. His face fell, and he craned his neck to find Burr's eyes.

"Mr. Frye?" Alex prompted. "Did you understand the question, or do I need to repeat it?"

"I, um, I believe you have described the place accurately," Frye said, trying to sound formal, as if that would undo the damage of his testimony.

"Oh no, sir," Alex said. "I believe *you* have described Ruston's Ale House accurately." He turned to Burr. "No further questions."

As he returned to his seat, his eyes found Governor Clinton's where he sat in the back row. The governor's eyes were two tiny seething slits, all but lost inside his plump cheeks, but you could still see the bile from fifty feet away.

ALEX'S CROSS-EXAMINATION MARKED a turning point in the trial. After two and a half days of hammering, Burr's spirits seemed to sag. He was barely halfway through his list of witnesses, but he called subsequent ones with less obvious glee. He put them through their paces quickly, even cutting them off when they waxed on about the loyalist crowds swilling Ruston's ale, knowing that Alex was just going to get the witness to confess that he had rubbed shoulders with all the loyalists he had just been maligning. Peter Goldman, a cooper, admitted he had sold barrels and baskets to redcoats. Matthew Landesmaan, a smith, had shod their horses and sharpened their swords. Frederick Karst, a fisherman, had sold them cod and clams, and so on down the line. After running through five more witnesses in the time he had previously spent on one, Burr rose from his seat.

"If it please, Your Honor, I would like to skip witnesses eighteen through thirty-one and proceed directly to witness number thirty-two."

Alex glanced at the list of witnesses. Thirty-two was the last witness. He kept his face as still as possible, but inside he was crowing.

Judge Smithson, however, didn't try to hide his relief. "By all means, Mr. Burr. It grows tiring watching your witnesses make your opponent's case for him."

Burr visibly paled. He took a moment to compose himself.

"Thank you, Your Honor. The State calls Antoinette Le Beau."

Caroline sat up. "Mr. Hamilton!" she hissed.

Alex tried to reassure her as best as he could. He had told her Miss Le Beau was going to be testifying, but she was still trembling.

"Take strength, Mrs. Childress," he said. "Remember, the Le Beaus are not your enemy."

The doors opened and a girl of no more than seventeen entered the courtroom. She was dressed in smart but shabby clothing, as if, like Caroline herself, she had once enjoyed prosperity, but those days were even longer past than were Caroline's. She walked down the aisle without looking to the left and took her seat in the stand. Her hand on the Bible was unshaking as she took her oath. Even Alex started to feel a little nervous.

Burr rose from his seat.

"I want to thank you, Miss Le Beau, for joining us here today. I know the court is not convenient for you."

"Indeed, it is not," Miss Le Beau answered. "I live in Harrisburg, Pennsylvania. Passage by mail carriage and ferry is quite dear, and the cost of an inn is a burdensome expense to one such as myself."

As if she paid for her own trip. Alex had no doubt Burr had brought her over himself and paid for her room and board out of his own pocket.

"Have you always lived in Harrisburg, Miss Le Beau?"

"Oh, good heavens, no. I'm a New York lass through and through."

"Ah, so you lived in the city then?"

"Yes, sir."

"May I ask where?"

"At Seventeen Baxter Street."

A murmur in the courtroom. Burr had set the stage perfectly.

Burr retrieved a piece of paper from his table.

"Your Honor, here is a copy of the property deed for Seventeen Baxter Street dated April eighteenth, 1769. It shows the property belonging to one Jacques Le Beau, having been paid for in full over the course of the previous ten years."

The judge glanced at the document and set it aside.

"Miss Le Beau," Burr continued. "Would you please tell the court your relationship to Jacques Le Beau."

"He was my father, Your Honor."

Burr grinned in feigned modesty. "I'm just Mr. Burr. Judge Smithson is the honorable one."

Antoinette turned to Judge Smithson. "Jacques Le Beau was my father, Your Honor. He died at the Battle of Monmouth."

Alex twitched. He had already known Le Beau had died during the war, but he didn't realize it was at Monmouth, where he himself had nearly been killed.

I may very well have been the person who wrote her informing her of her father's death, he thought.

"I'm very sorry to hear that, Miss Le Beau," Burr said. "And just so we're absolutely clear, your father died fighting in the Continental army, yes?"

Antoinette nodded. "Yes, sir. He was a corporal in the Fourth New York."

"His sacrifice will not be forgotten," Burr said solemnly. "Now, Miss Le Beau, may I ask you why you left Seventeen Baxter Street, where you had lived since you were born?"

"Are you jesting, Mr. Burr? My sisters and I left because the British captured Manhattan. With a father and three brothers in the Continental army, my mother and sisters and I feared for our safety, and fled across the river."

"Your brothers also served in the army?" Burr said, as if he didn't know.

"Yes, sir. Pierre died defending Manhattan from the British invasion, and Louis died at Monmouth with my father. Only Jean made it back, though he left one of his legs at Yorktown."

Another wince from Alex. The ties between himself and the witness were too close for comfort.

She turned to Judge Smithson. "He'd have been here, Your Honor, but he has yet to learn to get around well on his crutches. And the expense, well, was something we couldn't spare."

Judge Smithson nodded sympathetically. After his earlier boredom, he now seemed rapt by Antoinette's story.

"Did the British offer you any compensation for your property?"

"Compensation? They told us we were lucky we were not imprisoned for aiding the enemy! My sisters and I feared for our virtue on more than one occasion. That we escaped unstained is the only silver lining in this whole sad affair."

"And how have you lived since you left New York?"

"Hand to mouth, as my dress probably indicates. Our entire livelihood was tied up with the Baxter Street building. My father ran a very successful dry goods shop out of the first floor. Virtually all our stores were seized with the building, as well as most of the furniture, too. And with our menfolk away, there has been little besides cutwork and service for us girls. I once had dreams of marrying well and living in a fine house close to my parents. Now I hope to find work as a lady's maid, so that at least I will live in a warm house, even if it's not mine. Unless that is"—she looked at Mrs. Childress for the first time since she had entered the courtroom—"I can get back what is rightly my family's."

Again Caroline startled.

Again Alex tried to reassure her. "Remember," he whispered. "You did not take her property, nor do you have it now. You have not transgressed against this girl."

Yet all eyes in the courtroom were on Caroline, as if she had turned the girl out with a broom.

"No further questions, Your Honor," Burr said.

"Mr. Hamilton?" Judge Smithson prompted.

"Your Honor, the defense would like to thank Miss Le Beau for traveling to the court today. We have no questions for her at this time."

Miss Le Beau was dismissed and led from the courtroom. Burr waited until she was gone. Then, looking at Alex smugly, he said,

"The State rests, Your Honor."

Judge Smithson turned to Alex again. "Would you like to call your first witness, Mr. Hamilton?"

Alex looked down at the witness list in front of him, a litany of names of people who would speak as glowingly of Caroline Childress as Burr's witnesses had been scathing. But they would tell Judge Smithson nothing he didn't already know: that Caroline had survived the occupation like thousands of other New Yorkers, anyway she could. On top of that, he couldn't stop thinking of Angelica's party, which was, of course, really Eliza's party. Tonight was the night. Guests would be arriving in a matter of hours. He could not show up in his lawyer's black robes, looking like a mourner at a medieval funeral.

"Mr. Hamilton," Judge Smithson said again.

Alex looked at the judge. "Your Honor, the plaintiff rests."

Judge Smithson looked confused. He blinked once, twice, a third time, so vigorously that his chin fat wiggled above his jabot. Finally, he nodded.

"Very well then. The court will take a half-hour recess for tea, and then reconvene at five o'clock for closing arguments."

"But, Your Honor," Alex said, taken aback. "Given the hour, oughtn't we to wait until morning?"

"Oh no, young man. You seem to want to get this over with in a hurry. Well, let's get it over with."

Without another word, the judge gaveled once, then squeezed himself out of the courtroom by the rear door.

As Alex filed out of the main entrance, he saw that Governor Clinton was still sitting in his bench while the court cleared. The governor's face was calmer than it had been earlier, which is to say that anger had given way to mere contempt.

"I do not know what your ploy is, Mr. Hamilton, but I assure you that you won't take in a judge as perspicacious as Lewis Smithson."

"Perspicacious?" Alex said. "I didn't notice him sweating at all."

With those parting words, he marched out of the room.

27

---◦◦◦---

Queen of Manhattan

Hamilton Town House
New York, New York
April 1784

*E*verything was perfect.

The silver was polished to a reflective sheen, bouncing the lights of a score of candles around the softly papered walls and giving the front and middle parlors the feeling of underwater caverns. The table linens and napkins were crisply laundered and bright as snow. Beautiful silk tulips, lilies, and roses, as delicate as the real thing but ten times more vibrant, were set out in six Delft vases that competed with their bouquets for vividness of color. The crowning touch, though, was Ralph Earl's completed portrait of Eliza, which hung over the fireplace in the front parlor, and elicited gasps from each arriving guest.

Eliza had stationed Angelica in the front room so that it did not seem as if she were fishing for compliments, but even in the middle parlor and dining room she could hear the oohs and aahs. Fortunately, she had gone for a formal maquillage, her face regally serene with its dusting of silvery-white powder, complemented by the simplest red lip and dark mascara. Beneath it, though, she was blushing like mad.

No one comes to party for the decorations, however. They come for the food. And Rowena hadn't let Eliza down. She'd worked every last one of her connections to track down the most succulent cuts of beef, pork, lamb, turkey, and duck. The table was as laden with meat as a Parisian charcuterie, sausages and schnitzels, racks and rib eyes, stews and aspics, and, presiding over them all, a massive joint of smoked bear—yes, bear!—mounted on a spit, from which a footman carved wafer-thin slices with a knife the size of a small sword. The meat itself was a little bland in Rowena's opinion (Eliza herself refused to try it), but the wow factor was off the charts. A half-dozen sauces and jellies accompanied the meats, from a brown onion gravy so rich that you wanted to eat it like soup to a horseradish sour cream so spicy it made your eyes water. Last year's gourds and tubers were still the only vegetables to be had—roasted squashes in colors ranging from pale yellow to intense orange, along with roasted and riced potatoes and a tart applesauce redolent of cinnamon and nutmeg. If Eliza was being honest with herself, though, she had to admit that the star of the banquet table was Jane Beekman's lettuce. At one point, she actually saw eighty-four-year-old John Van Schaick elbow Ralph Earl out of the way to snatch up the last few leaves in the bowl.

"I'm old, young man," he said, only half joking. "If I don't eat this, I may die."

"Never fear," Eliza said. "There are a dozen more heads downstairs. Of lettuce," she said, when Van Schaick looked at her blankly. "Heads. Of. *Lettuce.*"

The presence of an éminence grise like John Van Schaick—a man whose house on Cohoes Island had once served as the capital of New York State—along with at least four dozen other guests, was a testament to Simon's wherewithal as much as to the growing appeal of the host and hostess. Rowena's son had (happily) shucked his footman's uniform for rougher garb, hopped atop a hired horse, and ridden a good two hundred miles over the last week, delivering invitations from one end of Manhattan Island to the other, and beyond. He had been as far north as Morrisania and Van Cortlandt Manor, stopping at Inclenberg to call on the Murrays and Mount Pleasant to invite the Beekmans.

Thank heavens, the Rutherfurds were still in town—a journey across the Hudson to the western border of New Jersey would have taken at least another three days. But everyone who was anyone had accepted, and they'd all shown up as well. From John and Helena Rutherfurd to James and Jane Beekman, from Lindley Murray and Gouverneur Morris to John and Sarah Jay, from William and Elizabeth Bayard to Philip and Pierre Van Cortlandt, along with more Duanes, Reades, Veseys, Brevoorts, Pecks, Wyckoffs, Van Dusens, and of course Van Rensselaers and Livingstons than you could shake a stick at.

Even old Pieter Stuyvesant had deigned to come. He had used his cane to beat himself a path to the big yellow sofa, his heavy wooden leg threatening to crack the floorboards, and seated himself squarely in the middle of the cushions, telling one of the two hired footmen serving drinks that he was to attend to him and him alone. For the first hour, everyone was too intimidated to sit beside him, until at last, Angelica dropped down next to him, nearly smothering the old man with her skirts, and then, to Eliza's horror (and delight), plopping baby Philip in his lap—and leaving him there.

"You! Are! Terrible!" Eliza whispered as Angelica swept over to her.

"Just you watch," Angelica said. "Philly can soften the heart of the meanest, most miserly Dutchman in Old or New Netherland. Within five minutes, ol' Peg Leg Pete will be bouncing him on his knee."

"On the good knee, I hope," Eliza said. "Else poor Philly is going to have bruises on his bum!"

Yes, everything was perfect. Except Alex wasn't here.

It was a cruel twist of fate that Mrs. Childress's trial had been moved up, but even so, the court almost always adjourned by five, and never stayed in session past six. And yet, it was half seven and still no sign of him. Eliza had even sent Simon to the court at seven to see what was going on, but he returned to report that the building was all locked up, and he had seen no sign of Alex anywhere.

"Was there any news of the trial itself? Surely there must have been a guard around to ask."

Could it be over already? she asked herself. Alex had told her of his litany of witnesses. He couldn't possibly have run through them so quickly, could he? And if the trial was over, did Alex win or lose? She prayed that he won something, because the party had used up every last penny of credit the Hamilton and Schuyler names could fetch. Once the leftovers were gone, they would be existing on air until some cash came in.

"I did ask one man in uniform for news of Mrs. Childress's trial, but he just said I was a little young to be chasing after widows and laughed me away. I even stopped in at the Burrs' house, pretending to be looking for work, but the servant told me the master hadn't returned and the missus didn't hire boys under eighteen."

Eliza shook her head in consternation—then quickly stilled it to keep her towering wig from shaking too much. Here they were with yet another dinner party, and Alex late again! It was clear she was but a low priority on his busy schedule. But if she gave in to her consternation, she would start screaming. In as calm a voice as she could muster, she said:

"Thank you, Simon. Now, head downstairs and wash up. We may need you to play footman if Mr. Stuyvesant refuses to release Andrew from his side. And make sure your mother feeds you. You look like you burned off ten pounds this week, and you were a skinny lad to start with."

Simon ran off, quickly replaced by a figure in yellow and pink. It took Eliza a moment to recognize Ralph Earl, whose wig looked like something from the court of Louis XIV and whose coating of powder was if anything thicker than her own. But even more startling than his European visage was his suit. Eliza remembered Alex's stories of Baron von Steuben, the German general who constantly surrounded himself with a bevy of handsome young men and dressed in suits made from jacquards and toiles more suited to upholster the furniture in a courtesan's receiving room than a gentleman's torso. The yellow of Earl's suit was not quite as gaudy as Alex had described Baron von Steuben's attire, but only just. It outshone the buttery wallpaper they had chosen for the middle room, and was made rather more garish by the pink embroidery. Well, not garish really, but decidedly feminine. With her raven tresses, Peggy would have looked fabulous in a gown made of such material, but Earl looked a little like a French count who had run out of money, and was now having suits made from the remnants of his wife's curtains. She wondered that she had ever found him attractive.

"A brilliant party, Eliza. You have gone from being the most sought-after guest in New York society to the most celebrated hostess in a single evening. Brava!"

Eliza immediately felt guilty for making fun of Mr. Earl's appearance in her head. He even sounded more sober than usual, though a wineglass was, as always, clutched in his hand.

"Why, thank you, Mr. Earl. I cannot take all the credit. Helena Morris really did introduce us to the right people, and of course everyone wants to say they're friends with Mr. Hamilton, General Washington's right-hand man."

"Where *is* the hero of Yorktown?" Ralph asked, his voice so smooth that Eliza couldn't tell if he were joking or not.

"I assume his duties kept him late at the—" She was going to say "at the courthouse," but could not bring herself to lie. "At the office," she said, a little lamely.

"A brilliant man's work is never done," Earl answered, his voice once again so supercilious that it was impossible to guess his intent. "You should rejoice in his success, but resign yourself to evenings such as this. Neither commerce nor politics cares for the plight of the lonely wife, but you still control his social life."

"Oh, I should hope not. Mine is more than I can handle. But speaking of brilliant men. I do hope it's okay that I've pointed you out as the painter of my portrait. Everyone is asking, and I should think you will leave tonight with rather a few commissions."

And pay your legal bills, she couldn't resist adding mentally. *Or at least find a home of your own.*

"Indeed." He lifted the flap on a bulging pocket, which was full of calling cards. "I have gone from debtors' prison to portraitist of the rich and famous in the space of a week. I will be busy from now through the turn of the century."

"Well then, bravo to you, too." Eliza clinked her glass with his and took a sip even as Earl drained his in one gulp. "If you'll excuse me, I need to find Angelica and make sure Philly—er, baby Philip—is taken to bed."

She found her sister in the middle parlor.

"Do you need me to summon the maid to put the baby to bed?" she asked.

Angelica pointed. "I think you will have a hard time tearing him away from his new best friend."

Eliza turned to see that, true to Angelica's prediction, Pieter Stuyvesant was bouncing the laughing boy on his (fleshy) knee while a group of onlookers cheered them on.

"Oh, dear. We should commission Mr. Earl to do a sketch. No one will ever believe us without proof."

"This sight alone would have made for a memorable party. But truly, Sister, you have thrown John and me a remarkable sending-off. I only wish—"

She broke off.

"What is it, Angie? What can I get you?"

"Oh, it's nothing. I was just going to say that I only wish the family was complete. For your sake," she said meaningfully, letting Eliza know that she had noticed Alex's absence and felt for her.

"I am learning," Eliza said now, "that much of marriage is time spent apart. I think of all those times Papa was away, at war, or at Saratoga on the farm. It is the norm."

Angelica took her sister's arm tenderly. "But, my darling, I hope you are not *too* lonely."

"What? No!" Eliza said, feeling disloyal. "Alex and I do have our social life. I suppose I had assumed once we were married we would have more time for just the two of us. I did not realize marriage was actually so inconvenient for . . . intimacy."

"I do not think it is marriage as much as it is adulthood."
Angelica laughed ruefully. "I must say, there are days when
I do miss being sixteen without a care in the world. Not that
I'd go back."

"Oh, heavens no. The spots, for one thing."

"As if *you* ever had spots," Angelica teased. "You have
always had a flawless complexion, whereas once a month I
gain half a stone and have to cover myself with a veil!"

"Ha! You are misremembering my experience as your
own," Eliza said, laughing. "I was such a homely girl. All
elbows and frayed ends. But I think we can both agree that
Peggy sailed through adolescence unscathed."

"And landed the richest husband, too!"

The two sisters enjoyed a hearty laugh.

"Oh, Angie, I can't believe it. You're moving to London!
With your husband and son!"

"And you live in a Wall Street town house with the most
sought-after lawyer in New York City. A future, what did you
call him, president? How did we become so grown-up?"

Another shared laugh, though this one was tinged with
melancholy.

"I'll miss you terribly, you know," Angelica said at length.

"I'll miss you more. You will have all of London—all of
England, of Europe!—to discover, while I'll be stuck here in
plain old New York."

Angelica beckoned at the rich and powerful guests
thronging the two parlors and the dining room, nibbling at

succulent cuts of meat and sipping strong ale or wine or whiskey.

"As if this could ever be boring! Listen to them, Eliza. They are literally planning the future of this brand-new country. Whether the United States be a democracy or a monarchy, a single country or a loose-knit confederation, whether slavery be abolished or women be granted the vote—the stage for all of it is being set right here, right now. History is happening in your house, Eliza, and *you* are its hostess." She shrugged, as if embarrassed by her flight of fancy. "And you will have Mama and Papa and Peggy and John and Philip and Ren and Cornelia and little Kitty all close to hand, while I shall only have acquaintances."

"You will have your husband's family."

"He has few relations, and what little he has, he doesn't get on with. No, I will have to make some dazzling friends, or we shall have to make our own private world," said Angelica with a smile. "Even as you and Hamilton make the larger one."

"If he ever gets home!" Eliza said, finally giving vent to her frustration. "It's nearly ten! I fear people will start to leave soon if their host doesn't bother to put in an appearance."

As if on cue, there came the sound of the front door opening. Eliza turned with a smile, only to hear a rough voice say:

"That's all right, son, I'll announce myself."

The voice sounded familiar, but Eliza couldn't quite place it. She prepared her most welcoming hostess smile, only to have it freeze on her face as a corpulent man walked into view, unbuttoning a well-made but somewhat dirty overcoat to reveal a gaudy but even more disheveled gold jacket beneath.

"Well, hello there, Lizzy," Governor George Clinton said with a self-satisfied smack of his greasy lips, which looked as if he'd once again been snacking on a chicken leg in his carriage. "Bet you're surprised to see me and not that lout of a husband of yours. After the furor he caused in court today, I'd be surprised if he ever shows his face in public again."

28

Mr. and Mrs. Alexander Hamilton

Hamilton Town House
New York, New York
April 1784

*A*lex raced down Wall Street, his black robes flapping behind him.

When Judge Smithson had announced his verdict, the courtroom erupted in pandemonium. The closing speeches by Alex and Burr seemed to have left the audience divided evenly between jeers and hisses and hurrahs and cheers.

Alex had turned to Caroline to see how she took the news. She was visibly trembling, with tears running down her face. Her hands clutched at his robe, as if to hold on for dear life. "I don't believe it."

He exhaled. "I did my best."

She nodded, but clearly didn't trust herself to speak again. And then she fainted clean away.

It took nearly half an hour to clear the room, by which time Caroline had revived but was still too woozy to be left unattended. Alex wasn't sure what to do. Her house was nearly half a mile away. Was he to carry her through the streets?

The front door of the courtroom opened, and Aaron Burr entered. Alex stood up quickly and hurried down the aisle to keep him from getting too close to Caroline.

"Mr. Burr," he said in a short voice, "the trial is over, and as you can see, it has been a taxing process on my client. I would ask you not to inflict any more damage upon her psyche than you already have."

Burr waited all this out in silence. Then:

"I merely wished to inform you that I have given instructions to my driver to take you and Mrs. Childress wherever you need to go. She is obviously far too fragile to walk home."

Alex's jaw dropped. "Oh, I see. I, ah, feel terrible now."

Burr offered him half a smile. "If it makes you feel any better, so do I." He nodded at Caroline beyond them. "The law is a rather blunt instrument sometimes, and your client was lucky she had you to protect her from the worst of its blows." He stuck out his hand. "Good evening, Mr. Hamilton. I have no doubt we will find ourselves on opposite sides again in the near future, but there is no need for the animus to become personal."

Alex shook Burr's hand.

"That is perhaps the first statement you've said in three days that I can agree with."

Burr threw back his head and laughed. "Touché," he said, and nodding at Caroline, who had turned to stare at the two men with a bewildered expression, he took himself out of the room.

Alex helped Caroline out of the court, down the stairs, and into the cozy confines of Burr's carriage. The teeming, rowdy crowd Burr had summoned had dispersed now that the show was over, and Alex was thankful none of the rougher types had stuck around to rub salt in Caroline's wounds.

The vibrations of the carriage over Wall Street's rough cobblestones seemed to pain Caroline's head, and she took the journey in silence, with her eyes pressed tightly closed and one hand across her forehead. At her inn, she stirred herself enough to walk through the first-floor ale room unaided, but the effort was almost too much for her, and Alex had to help her up the stairs. He installed her in a chair and tucked a blanket over her lap, then turned to the fire and built it up into a blaze. As he added one last log, he heard her voice behind him.

"Oh, but wood is so dear."

He put the log on anyway. "It's okay, Caroline. You've earned it."

A faint laugh burbled from her. "I suppose I have." She sighed. "I am embarrassed that I am reacting this way. It seems so, so weak of me."

"There is nothing to be embarrassed about," Alex said. "You have been dragging a heavy burden for so long that its weight seems a part of you. It is gone now, but it is only natural for it to take a while for you to feel normal again."

"I do not know that I shall ever feel normal again. This trial—the vitriol! I wonder how a country so divided can stand?"

"We will only stand if we learn to accept and even embrace each other's differences rather than allow them to divide us. It is a childish fantasy to expect everyone to agree all the time, but how much better to live in a country where one is free to think differently from one's neighbors, and even one's government, without risking life and limb."

She looked at him dubiously. "You sound as if you are still in court."

He placed his hand on hers. "Just think of me. I fought on the opposite side of the war as your husband. I lost men, friends"—an image of Laurens filled his head, and he pushed it away—"to British bullets. But I still fought for you, because I believe the idea of America is bigger than sides. If I can come to that conclusion, other people can, too. Other people *have* come to that conclusion."

She nodded her head and closed her eyes. Soon her breathing evened out, and he assumed she was sleeping. He stayed with her for another half hour, though, his conscience was racked by thoughts of Eliza playing hostess all by herself, but still unsure if Caroline could be safely left on her own. At length, there came a knock at the door. Sally, the barmaid, entered, with a stein in her hand.

"I saw you and Mrs. Childress come in and thought you might like some ale," she said, peering anxiously at her mistress.

Alex stood up. "Thank you, Sally, but I really must be going. Mrs. Hamilton is having a party for her sister tonight, and I am already hours late. I hope she will still let me in the house, honestly."

Sally nodded, though her eyes never left Caroline. "Is she all right?"

"I'm afraid the trial was a bit hard on her nerves, but she will be fine after some rest. Perhaps some bone broth would do her well."

"Of course. Mr. Hamilton," Sally said as Alex turned for the door. "How did . . . I mean, did she . . . ?" The barmaid couldn't finish her question.

"It's not my place to divulge that information. I will let Mrs. Childress explain everything to you when she awakens."

"But I mean, we're okay, aren't we? Mrs. Childress won't be turned out, will she?"

Alex glanced back at the sleeping figure. In sleep, her cares had melted from her face, and though her skin seemed all the more pale in its black silk frame, she still looked more like a child than a mother, let alone a widow.

"Not according to the verdict in any event," he said with a smile, then took his leave.

HE RACED THE last few steps to his house, chastising himself for sending Burr's carriage home earlier. He should have ordered the man to wait. He wanted to glance at his watch to see what time it was, but it was too dark to see. That in itself was a terrible sign. It had been half nine when he left Caroline's.

As he ran past his neighbors' house, he happened to glance over at their darkened windows. There was just enough light for him to catch his reflection. Although, really, there wasn't much to see, because he was shrouded in black. Only the glowing white wig made any real impression.

He was still wearing his lawyer's robes! He couldn't enter the house like that. Eliza would have a fit.

He glanced at his own windows next door. They were blazing with light and shadows danced about on the ceiling, but the lower shutters had been drawn, so he couldn't see how crowded or empty the room was. There could be fifty people in there, or just five. Everyone could have gone home.

He ran past the steps to his doors then, and ducked around behind them. On the far side, a short, narrow door under the porch led into a dank corridor, and thence into the kitchen.

"Oh!" A startled Rowena looked up from a pot she was stirring in the fireplace. "Mr. Hamilton! I thought it was death himself come to take me!"

"Sorry to scare you, Rowena," he said, ripping at the buttons of his robe. "I just need to freshen up before I go upstairs."

"You had better look fresh," Rowena said. "The missus is sorely aggrieved at your tardiness." She fixed him in the eye. "I do hope you have good news for her."

"What, is my presence not good news enough?" Alex said slyly, using a pewter tray as a mirror as he styled his somewhat damp hair, which had been buried beneath a wig for more than fifteen hours. Fortunately, anticipating a potentially late day, he had thought to wear his finest suit under his robes.

"How do I look?"

Rowena shrugged. "A little scrawny for my taste, but not much to do about that now."

"Never change, Rowena," Alex said with a grin, flicking a little flour on her moist cheeks. "Never change."

He ran past Simon, who was curled up in a chair like an eel in a barrel, sound asleep, and dashed up the stairs. Just before he reached the door he paused and composed himself, then pushed it open.

A swarm of noise assailed his ears.

"I heard Mr. Burr's closing oratory went on for more than an hour!"

"That's nothing! Mr. Hamilton spoke for nearly two!"

"Mr. Burr may be the finest lawyer of his generation. His arguments cut through the sterile logic of the law and went straight to the heart!"

"Hamilton was magnificent! Thrice he was interrupted by standing ovations! People were weeping in their chairs! The judge himself clapped at the end!"

Apparently, word of the trial had reached the party.

Alex squinted against the bright lights. A swarm of odors assaulted his nose, from the delectable smells of Rowena's cooking (now sadly decimated, to the consternation of his empty stomach) to the cloying perfumes of dozens of ladies and gentlemen bedecked in the finest brocades and jacquards. He did not realize his house could hold this many people. He wondered that the floor didn't collapse beneath their weight. But his eyes ignored the throng as he searched for one face in particular. The only face that mattered.

"He's here!" a voice called then. "It's the man of the hour!"

The voice turned out to be John Church, who grabbed him in a bear hug. "Well done, Alex! You did it!"

Suddenly, other hands were grabbing him. John Rutherford. Gouverneur Morris. Even the painter Ralph Earl. Before he knew it, he was being hoisted in the air on their shoulders.

"Hip hip hooray! Hip hip hooray!"

Alex rocked back and forth on the shoulders, tilting his head slightly to keep from knocking against the ceiling. So intense was the bouncing that he could not make out the faces in the room, which seemed like so many glazed masks beneath their powder and rouge and wigs. But then—at last!—he spied a single face in the front parlor, seeming to float in the air.

It was Eliza.

Her hair was a silver halo above her head, made all the more ethereal by a gauzy veil draped over it. Her skin was smooth as the flesh of a peach, with just a spot of color at cheeks and lips. Her eyes were two dark coals gleaming out at the world with untold depths of intelligence and strength, her mouth set in the very tiniest of smiles, as if she reserved judgment on all who passed beneath her gaze. She was not just the most beautiful woman Alex had ever seen. She was the most regal.

"My darling," he said, as if she could hear him across two rooms.

"Yes?" a voice said at his feet. "Alex?"

He looked down, and there she was again: Eliza, only this time she was in a pale green gown and tighter, unveiled wig. Her face was decidedly pinker, too, as if she had been dancing for hours.

He looked back up. Only now did he realize that the first image had been Ralph Earl's painting.

I get to live with her for the rest of my life, he said to himself in astonishment. He had never realized life could be so fulfilling. And then, looking down at his flesh-and-blood wife, he thought: *This beautiful creature is who I get to live with for the rest of my days.* No painting could ever compare.

His wife threw her arms around him and he returned the embrace. *I get to live with the real woman* and *the portrait,* he said to himself. *A more fortunate man has never lived.*

"My darling," he said, looking right into her beautiful brown eyes, the eyes that had so bewitched him from the beginning. "It is perfection. And I am sorry . . ."

"Shush," said Eliza. "It is enough to have you home for dinner for once."

Vaguely, he knew there were many people in the room, guests, dignitaries, the most important people in New York, but to Alex, there was only one face, one person, who was the most important. He ushered her into a private corner.

"I want to focus on our family," he said, leaning to whisper in her ear. "I believe it is about time we were serious about that endeavor."

Eliza colored prettily. "It is my dearest wish as well," she replied, melting into his arms.

He kissed her then, because he had to have her right then, wanted nothing more than for the two of them to be alone and putting every effort into this new and exciting project.

They were still kissing when a voice interrupted, rising above the din. The Hamiltons reluctantly pulled away from each other.

"Well, there he is now. The man of the hour. Or should I say, the traitor of the hour?"

Alex turned as the crowd parted like the Red Sea to reveal not Moses but Pharaoh, which is to say, the corpulent, gold-clothed figure of Governor Clinton.

"Well, I hope you're proud of yourself, young man," the governor said, or spat. "You, who served as the right hand of General Washington himself! Providing aid and comfort to the enemy! You are lucky that I don't have you strung up. But I'll see you disbarred from ever practicing law in New York State if it's the last thing I do."

Alex stood there, tongue-tied. After the exertions of the day, taking care of Caroline in her weakened condition, the run home, the cheers and smells and jostling, and Eliza's painting. Eliza . . .

He turned to his wife, and grabbed her hand.

"Always hiding behind a woman's skirts," Clinton jeered. "That's what they'll say about Alexander Hamilton in the history books, if they bother to record him at all. First, he uses the plight of a silly barmaid to advance his own loyalist cause, and then, he runs home to hide behind his wife, whose family name is far more distinguished than his own will ever be. I expect Philip Schuyler will be none too pleased when he learns what kind of man you've hitched yourself, too," he said to Eliza directly.

Alex tried to open his mouth but still his jaw refused to move. Governor Clinton glowed and shook like a torch in the breeze threatening to set his house on fire, yet after a full day of brilliant debate in court, capped by a scintillating final argument that had, as someone said, moved people to tears and applause, Alex found himself unable to think of a single word to shut up this ugly boor.

Fortunately, he didn't have to.

"Why, George Clinton!" Eliza said in a voice that was less angry than amused and belittling. "My father has counted you as a friend, or at any rate a colleague, for more than thirty years. If he knew you were speaking to his daughter in this way, he would call you out!"

Governor Clinton smirked. "I do beg your pardon, Mrs. Hamilton," he said in the least sincere voice Alex had ever heard.

"Oh, shut up, you horrible toad," Eliza said, her voice less agitated than nonchalant, as if Clinton were not worth the trouble. "I care not a whit what you think of me, and neither does my husband. Now, you listen to me. This man whose hand I hold and whose ring I share put his life on the line for this country over and over, and for anyone to call him a traitor is not only laughable but traitorous in itself. The United States of America is not what you would have it be, sir," she continued. "Nor is it what I would have it be, or Alex, or anyone in this room. It is a shared space and a shared vision, and only when we learn that our different points of view give us a special strength will we tap into the full potential of our unique, *united* sensibilities. Only then will we make good on the debt we owe to the brave men—yes, and women—who fought for our freedom. And until you can get that through that unruly head of hair, I invite you to shut your mouth—or go stuff it with food, since you are obviously far better at eating than speaking."

Stunned silence filled the room. Then from the front parlor came the sound of a titter. The crowd turned to see old Pieter Stuyvesant laughing so hard his wooden leg pounded the floor.

"Oh my stars! That is the best show I've seen in ages!" And he broke into peals of glee.

Within seconds, the whole house was shaking with laughter. A dejected George Clinton slunk off with his tail between his legs, but somehow managed to end up at the buffet table, where he did indeed begin stuffing his mouth with food.

Alex turned to his wife. "And they say I am the orator."

"They will say it for the next hundred years, and even more, if I have anything to do with it," Eliza said. Her face was shining with love and pride. "You won, Alex! You won!"

"Well, it was a split decision, really," Alex answered honestly. "The Baxter Street building was returned to the Le Beau family, but Judge Smithson ordered the state to pay Mrs. Childress damages in the amount of fifteen hundred for lost investment and—"

Eliza put a finger on his lips. "A victory! You won."

Alex kissed her on the lips. "*We* won, my darling. And we always will, as long we stay by each other's side."

"Always," she said with a smile. "Come now, let's take our bows." Eliza waved a hand at the dancing, drinking, swirling mass before them. "We're a hit!" Then she turned to him, and this time it was her voice that was soft in his ear. "But all I ever needed was you."

In answer, he kissed her again with all his heart and soul, his passion for his wife as keen as on the first day they'd met, and whatever flaws and transgressions lay on the rocky road ahead of them, he knew that she was right: They could meet every obstacle and temptation in their path as long as they were by each other's side, in love and war, failure and victory, poverty and prosperity, until the curtain closed on their story.

AUTHOR'S NOTE

*W*hile this story is inspired by and mostly based on historical fact, the biggest departure of course that anyone can easily discover and point out to the author (but please don't!) is that Alex and Eliza had children almost immediately after their marriage. So please forgive this young-adult author for wanting to keep them newlyweds for a little while longer and not deal with the reality of children just yet.

Aside from that, Part One hews closely to historical record. Alex and Eliza did move around a lot during the first three years of their marriage and lived at the Pastures after their wedding.

Alex famously strong-armed Washington into giving him a command at Yorktown, and Laurens did serve under him, as did the other officers. Fort descriptions and such are also fairly accurate.

Eliza was at the Pastures when her mother had Kitty, her last baby.

The story about the British raid on the Schuyler house is widely reported, but no one knows if it is true or not.

Supposedly, it was Peggy who confronted the invaders, as Eliza retreated upstairs with her infant son, Philip. Aaron Burr was not the officer who checked on them afterward, although he did move to Albany around that time and I thought it would be fun to place him in the scene.

Part Two is much more fictional, however the names of all the society people, as well as their marriages, houses, and anecdotes attributed to them (like the Beekmans' greenhouse and Mrs. Murray's invitation to General Howe for tea so George Washington could escape) are real.

Alex and Eliza lived at 57 Wall Street. Aaron and Theodosia Burr lived down the street at 3 Wall. They were neighbors!

Eliza did sit for her well-known portrait by Ralph Earl in debtors' prison. And Mr. Earl did stay with the Hamiltons after he got out jail.

Alex was known for defending former loyalists from prosecution by the government of Governor George Clinton, and he frequently faced off against Aaron Burr. However, Caroline Childress and her trial are completely fictional.

What is true is that Alex and Governor Clinton were decidedly not fans of each other. And I imagine our strong-willed Eliza would have come to her husband's defense in all and any social and political skirmishes.

They were a good team, and their story—at least my part in telling it—does not end here.

ACKNOWLEDGMENTS

This book would not exist without the love of my family, my family of friends, and my Penguin family. Thank you especially to my editors, Jennifer Besser and Kate Meltzer, President Jen Loja, Vice President Jocelyn Schmidt, PR maven Elyse Marshall, marketing stars Emily Romero and Erin Berger, and copy editor extraordinaire Anne Heausler. Thank you to my 3Arts family, Richard Abate and Rachel Kim. Thank you to my family-family, the DLCs (Mom, Chit, Christina, Steve, Aina, Nicholas, Josey, Seba, and Marie), Friday Night Taco Club & Hollywood Beach division (Jill, Cole, Tiff, Heidi, Andy, Tony, Carol and all the taco and basketball kids!), the Terrible Trio (Raf & Marg & um, me), and my YALLs of Fest and West. Thank you to my dear readers, loyal and new. Mike and Mattie are thanked at the beginning of this book and at the end, for I begin and end with them.

Turn the page

for a sneak peek of

1

Her Brother's Keeper

New York Harbor
New York, New York
June 1785

To passersby, they must have looked like any other young couple enjoying the bright sun and cool breezes of a June day in New York City. Broadway was crowded with similarly affectionate pairs, arm in arm, or holding hands, or even giving in to the urge to steal a kiss, regardless of who was watching. City Hall Park was in full bloom, and the only odor that could push through the heavenly fragrance of lilac was the salt of New York Harbor, less than a quarter mile away. But unbeknownst to their fellow *flâneurs*, Alexander and Eliza Hamilton were engaged in that most high-stakes of marital negotiations: their social calendar.

"No, no," Eliza admonished Alex as gently she could. "We dine with the Van *Cortlandts* on the morrow. They are in town for just four days. We are seeing the Van *Wycks* on Thursday."

From the corner of her eye, Eliza saw Alex's brow furrow beneath his hat, a narrow-brimmed midnight-blue tricorne that brought out the red in his hair and the twinkle in his pale blue eyes. "But I thought we were dining with John and Sarah on Thursday."

"No, the Jays are Friday," Eliza said as soothingly as possible, regarding him from beneath the brim of her own bonnet, which was a handsome chocolate brown trimmed with pink ribbon that accentuated the apples in her cheeks. She patted her husband's arm as though he were a little boy. For a man who had supervised the schedule of the commander in chief of the Continental army for five years, he had a notoriously hard time remembering whom he was going to have dinner with three days out.

"Friday?" Alex repeated, as though she'd just told him Congress had voted to return the United States to British rule. "Then when are we seeing the Morrises?"

"Do you mean Gouverneur, or Helena Morris that is now Rutherford?" Eliza responded. "We're having Gouverneur and his latest *belle du jour*, Miss Du Pont, to tea a week Saturday," she continued without waiting for her husband to answer, "and taking luncheon with John and Helena at their city residence after services on the Sabbath. Or, no," she corrected herself. "We are joining James Beekman at Mount Pleasant after church. The Rutherfords have had to push back their arrival until Monday, but we have tentative plans to join them for supper."

" 'Tentative plans'?" Alex laughed. "How on earth can

such a schedule accommodate a tentative plan? My good wife, you manage our social calendar with more precision than General Washington arranged his parlays! If you were foreign minister to King George or King Louis, there would never be another war in Europe again!"

"As I recall," Eliza said, chuckling, "it was *you* who arranged General Washington's social calendar, which makes it that much more surprising that you cannot keep track of your own." She held up a string purse whose pink ribbon matched her bonnet. "If it makes you feel better, I have everything written down in a little diary I keep with me at all times."

"When I was General Washington's aide, I didn't *have* a social calendar," Alex said, laughing. "All my time was spent racing after him. It is your own fault, my darling," he continued, squeezing Eliza's silk-clad arm with a kid-gloved hand. "You are as impressive a hostess as you are a guest. Everyone wants you in their salon, and if they're not soliciting your presence at their table, then they're begging for a spot at ours."

Eliza blushed prettily at the compliment and allowed a few steps to pass before she answered. Catching a glimpse of herself in a shop window, however, she couldn't help but think that Alex might be right. He in Prussian-blue wool, she in dark rose silk with pink and chocolate accents—they were the picture of urbane, young New York society, and she noticed more than one set of eyes glancing at them both approvingly and enviously.

"Oh, pshaw!" she said at length. "I am naught but the wife of a war hero, who just happens to be the most capable attorney in New York City. If people court my presence, it is only so they can be closer to you." At that, she squeezed his arm to let him know that none could come closer than her.

"Did you just 'pshaw' me, Mrs. Hamilton?"

"I believe I did, Mr. Hamilton."

"That's Colonel Hamilton to you."

Eliza pretended to be shocked. "Of all the cheek—"

Alex soothed her with a kiss. "The only cheek that I'm interested in is the one my lips are pressed against," he murmured.

"Just be sure you don't neglect the other one," Eliza said, touching the opposite side of her face. "It will get jealous."

Alex dutifully leaned across his wife to give her a second kiss, then threw in one on the lips for good measure, and they continued on their way down Broadway. Eliza went on informing him of their social schedule, as Alex shook his head in disbelief at the number of bowls of creamed spinach he would be expected to consume in the next three weeks.

Such was the price of being the most popular couple in town.

Since the smashing going-away party Eliza had thrown for Angelica and John Church last winter, where everyone who was anyone in New York and New Jersey society had been present, the Hamiltons' hall table had been littered with calling cards. To accommodate all the requests, Eliza began hosting Thursday night dinners and Friday night salons, which quickly became the most coveted invitation in town. She was adept at mixing lawyers with painters, businessmen with artists, so the conversation was always knowledgeable and varied, and everyone left feeling like they'd learned a little bit more about how the world functioned, from the workaday business of brewing one's own ale to the exalted labor of forming a new country from the ground up.

For if Eliza provided the culture, Alex provided the politics. His brilliant and compassionate legal defense of Caroline Childress, the widow of a British soldier who'd fought against Continental troops in the War for Independence, not only had made him the most sought-after lawyer in town—the man who could win the unwinnable case—but also led to repeated calls for him to enter politics at the highest level. Several people approached him to run against New York's corpulent, corrupt governor, George Clinton, while others suggested something at the national level—senator, or perhaps foreign minister, should Congress decide to create an executive office. He might even be prime minister or president or whatever title they would bestow on the new leader of the country.

The Hamiltons' combined success had made them the It Couple in New York City. With Eliza's family relations to the Van Rensselaers, Livingstons, Schuylers, and the rest of the New World gentry, and Alex's military and legal connections to General Washington and other heroes of the revolution, there wasn't a soul in New York who didn't want to meet them, whether to bask in their glory or ride on their coattails. But right now the Hamiltons were on their way to meet someone who meant more to them then all the tow-headed Dutchmen and high-collared Anglicans you could stuff in a parlor.

As THEY TURNED a corner, the vista opened before them, revealing the clear southern sky over New York Harbor, whose sparkling waters were dotted with masts and brightly colored flags waving in the soft breeze.

"Papa's letter said that Johnny was nervous about the journey down," Eliza said, sounding a bit anxious herself. "It's been such a stormy spring, and apparently he gets sea-sick, even on a riverboat. Although," she continued, "I must say, *my* stomach feels rather restless this morning. I think Rowena's eggs were a bit underdone at breakfast."

"I found them delicious as always. I think you are just missing your Jenny or Martha, or whatever you called her."

"We just called her Cook," Eliza said.

"No doubt. To a child, she must have seemed the source of all food, and no eggs, regardless of how well they are scrambled, can possibly taste as good as the ones your Cook made you for the first eighteen years of your life."

Eliza knew Alex had a point, but still, Rowena's omelet had seemed a little runny to her. Rather than linger on break-fast, she tried to focus on her excitement at being reunited with her brother, who was to start at Columbia in a few weeks. Everyone in her family was proud of the university's new name, no longer saddled with the British monarch's title as King's College. Since he was the eldest son, great things were expected of Johnny, and as her parents' representatives here in New York, Eliza understood it was her job to see that he was kept in line. Johnny was also the first child after the sisterly triumvirate of Angelica, Eliza, and Peggy—the first to survive, at any rate—some nine years her junior. Though she was grown now, and he nearly so, she still couldn't help but think of him as the baby she and Angelica and Peggy had fussed over for the first three years of his life, until Philip Jr. came along. They had coddled their brother and made a pet of him, and she knew that he wouldn't stand for runny eggs.

"You will admit that Rowena has been very distracted since Simon went away," she said now. "I do wonder if it was the right decision."

Rowena's son, Simon, had been in training as their footman, but from the start the energetic eleven-year-old showed no aptitude for it. He was an outdoorsy child, preferring bare feet to shod and loose cotton or linen to fitted wool. When, on an errand to the Beekman estate, Mount Pleasant, five miles north of the city, he had gamely assisted the chauffeur in delivering a mare whose foal was breach, Jonas Beekman was so impressed with his performance—both mare and foal pulled through swimmingly—that he offered Simon a job as a groom at a grown man's wages. Rowena had reluctantly agreed to let him go, but took it hard. Simon would have to go live at Mount Pleasant, and, since the death of her husband in the war, she would be all alone.

"The right decision for Rowena?" Alex now asked pointedly. "Or for you?"

"Oh, don't tease me when my stomach is upset," Eliza said, but she had to admit that, like her mother, she firmly believed that happy servants made for a happy house, or, at any rate, that a house in which the staff was miserable would share in their pain. Fires would go out, dust would accumulate, the eggs would separate on the plate. And as the thought of them returned, her insides churned anew.

"Well, the nephew should be here next week," Alex said. "What's his name again?"

"Drayton," Eliza said. Drayton Pennington was the eldest child of one of Rowena's sisters. He was said to be a hale lad of seventeen, though Rowena had not seen him in nearly a decade: The Penningtons had moved to the Ohio Territory to avoid the war. They transformed a considerable bit of land into a farmstead, but it was still essentially wilderness, and Nigella, Rowena's sister, had written that Drayton seemed somehow "cut of an urban cloth." He knew his letters and read every book he could get his hands on, was even better at math, and, owing to a dearth of sisters, was remarkably spry with needle and thread.

"Drayton and Johnny, both arriving within a week. Our household will be incredibly full."

"Not *too* full," Eliza said, patting her all too flat stomach.

"There, there, my dear," Alex said, squeezing his wife's arm tenderly. "It will come."

After Alex's momentous victory in court last year—and the settlement fee—the Hamiltons had at last felt ready to start a family of their own. But eight months of "carefully coordinated activity," as Eliza had referred to it in a recent letter to her mother, produced nothing in the way of nascent Hamiltons. In an earlier letter, Mrs. Schuyler asked why Eliza had not joined her two sisters in giving her a grandchild to spoil, and, in a rare moment of candor, pointed out that the activity in question was not without its own charms: "You and Alex should persevere, and take pleasure in the perseverance," she concluded. Eliza had thought the page in her hands would spontaneously combust when she read those words, but it was just her cheeks burning. And yet, her mother's disappointment did not compare to Eliza's greater one. Her wish for a child was much too painful at this point.

"Having Johnny here will be almost like having a child I suppose. Though he is nearly grown, Mama says that he is as headstrong as Cornelia, who is not even five," she told her husband.

Alex stifled a groan. "I hope he is ready for school. Columbia is fast becoming one of the best universities in the country—I heard enrollment will reach nearly twenty students this year, and they have brought on a fifth professor! It will be big change for a boy used to studying with his brothers and a tutor in the schoolroom."

"How hard can it be? They let *you* in," Eliza teased. "Although as I recall, you didn't stay around to graduate."

"Hmmm," Alex mused. "*I* seem to recall a little revolution getting in the way."

"Excuses, excuses."

Alex chuckled. "At any rate, I'm less concerned about Johnny's ability to handle the classwork than the distractions of the city. New York is a far cry from Albany. There are theaters and parties and museums and visitors from a score of countries all vying for a young man's attention."

"And girls," Eliza said. "Don't forget the girls."

"And girls," Alex agreed. "But I trust the formidable Mrs. Schuyler will have imbued her eldest son with a firm sense of decorum and probity."

"Well, let's see," Eliza said. "Of her three eldest daughters, the first eloped with a man rumored to have fled debtor's prison—and possibly a wife—in England, the third was engaged for nearly a decade before she *finally* got her intended to commit to a wedding, and the second, ahem"— Eliza goosed her husband's arm—"ran away from her fiancé at the altar to marry a boy from the Indies with no name."

"I take exception to that statement," Alex pretended to protest. "The name Hamilton is one of great distinction. My grandfather is an earl or duke or laird or something in the old country."

"Well then, yours is the worst Scottish accent I have ever heard in my life," Eliza said with a giggle. "It's not even a good Caribbean accent, for that matter. And the very fact that you don't even know your grandfather's title calls into question your claims of aristocratic lineage. Correct me if I'm wrong, but you never even met your *father*, let alone your grandfather."

Eliza suddenly caught herself, worried that she'd gone too far, as she knew her husband was sensitive about his background. But Alex only laughed, if a bit cynically.

"And a good thing, too, lest I ended up following in that incorrigible man's footsteps." Shortly after Alex was born, his father had abandoned his mother and never reappeared in his young sons' lives, even after Rachel, Alex's mother, succumbed to yellow fever when he was eleven.

"Well," Eliza said soothingly. "You seem to have done pretty well on your own."

"On my own? No, my darling. Whatever I have and whatever I've accomplished, I owe half of it to you. Without your constancy and steadiness, I would be nowhere."

"Goodness," Eliza said, though she blushed with pride. "I'm not sure if you're describing a wife or a saddle pony upon which one might teach a child of five to canter. Oof!" she added as Alex pulled her into a bear hug and covered her face in butterfly kisses. "The corset's bad enough after Rowena's eggs. Don't squeeze so hard!"

THE TWO CONTINUED their banter for the next hour as they made their roundabout way to the docks on the Hudson River. It was a glorious day at the beginning of summer, the sky as blue as Delft tiles and the mercury hovering in the mid-seventies. Horses' hooves and wagon wheels clattered over the rutted roads with the insistent jangle of commerce — it hadn't rained in nearly a week and the dirt was baked hard as bricks. The streets and sidewalks were alive with tradesmen and women hawking their wares, and servants and messengers hurrying about their masters' business. Wheat and corn from the fields of upper New York State, tin and pewter from Pennsylvania, cotton from the southern states, fragrant spices and sugar from the Caribbean and farther afield: With a population of thirty thousand, New York had surged past Boston and Philadelphia to become the young nation's largest city, and virtually anything you desired could be had there, and at any price, from the cheapest bits of dented, tarnished flatware to the most exquisite silks and china (these safely ensconced behind store windows, but still easily visible from the broad wooden sidewalks of lower Manhattan).

The sun had just passed its zenith when they emerged on the river just above New York Harbor. The Hudson was more than a mile wide here, an impressive, flat, gray highway upon which ran hundreds of boats, from the tiniest oared dinghies to ships of the line measuring nearly two hundred feet. The mail ship from Albany was a single-masted, heavy-bellied vessel that sat low in the water, and it took a few minutes before the Hamiltons were able to make it out amid the larger merchantmen at dock.

When they spied it, Eliza hurried forward. After dawdling and window-shopping through the city, she was suddenly impatient to see her brother. It had been a year since she'd seen anyone in the family, and two since she'd seen Johnny. Loosing her arm from Alex's elbow and taking his hand instead, she pulled him through the crowd, equally divided between stevedores and porters and other dockworkers, and people like her and Alex, there to greet an arriving loved one or see someone off.

"I can't believe he's really here!" she said excitedly. "I cannot wait to show him the sights! Bayard's Mount and Collect Pond and Federal Hall and Fraunces Tavern. Oh, I do hope he loves the city as much as I do and doesn't miss the country too much!"

"He need only hop on a horse and ride a half mile north of Chambers Street and he'll have all the country he wants. But I suspect he will take to the big city like a fish to water. Johnny has always been a worldly boy," Alex replied.

"You speak as if you know my brother better than I do!" Eliza said. "He is a delicate child! The noise and bustle may be too much for him!"

"A delicate child! As I recall, he took a shot at the British raiding party that came to kidnap your father in the last year of the war. I say New York should look out for *him*, and not the other way around."

"Well, I say *we* should look out for him right now. The pier is so crowded today, I don't know how we'll ever find him."

Alex took a moment to glance around. "I think I have an idea where he might be," he said then, and, taking Eliza's elbow, steered her off to the right.

Eliza peered ahead, but all she saw besides the dockworkers

was a group of women crowded in on one another as closely as their bustled skirts and parasols would allow. The way they were huddled together, Eliza assumed they must be inspecting some exotic goods just off a merchantman from the Indies or Europe. *Maybe there'll be oranges!* she thought. Since Jane Beekman had introduced her to the unusual fruit last year, she couldn't get enough of them. Alex recalled them fondly from his youth in the Caribbean, although he said he preferred something he called a "banana." The way he described it made her think he was pulling her leg, but apparently they were quite delicious.

As it happened she was half right. The women, who ranged in age from sixteen to thirty and change, were indeed inspecting a new arrival fresh off the boat. But the merchandise they were haggling over turned out to be—

"John Bradstreet Schuyler!" she cried. Eliza's upset stomach fluttered again as the covey of women whirled around in unison, revealing the slim figure of Eliza's eldest brother, seated on an upended steamer trunk. His cheeks were so red that at first glance Eliza thought they were covered with lip rouge from multiple kisses, but it was just a blush. He sprang to his feet with a sheepish smile even as one of the girls said in an accusatory voice: "John? Why is this *woman* speaking to you?"

Eliza didn't like the way the girl said "this woman." It made her feel as though she were forty years old.

"Johnny," she said in her most commanding older-sister voice, "why is this *girl* speaking to *you?*"

Johnny stepped in, his arms out wide for a hug, but Eliza's look held him back.

Several of the women, sensing a familial authority in Eliza's demeanor, lowered their hackles slightly, though they were still clustered around Johnny as if he were a skittish kid goat and might bolt if they let down their guard. But the boldest one of the pack did not back down and turned to Eliza with her fists on her waist and her chin jutting.

Eliza summoned all the dignity her mother had instilled in her. "He's seventeen," she said serenely. "Maybe you should hunt for something a little closer to your own age."

The woman's jaw dropped open.

"And as for the rest of you, you are free to call on *John* in the proper time and place—which is not a busy dock on a weekday afternoon."

"And what is the 'proper time and place'?" said one of the girls, a rather pretty little thing, Eliza had to admit, though her hair looked a tad dirty beneath its powder, and her dress, which had never been fine, and might even be considered gaudy, was in need of patching.

"I'll leave that up to *John*," Eliza said. "If you don't mind now, we need to get my brother home."

The girl was ready to ask for her address, but the look on Eliza's face stopped her.

"Come along, ladies," the girl said. "I'm sure the son of General Philip Schuyler won't be that hard to track down. Bye, *John*," she said, all but throwing him a kiss, and then she and her companions tittered away.

"Check your pockets," Eliza told her brother when they were out of earshot. "Make sure you still have your coin purse."

"Oh, Eliza, please!" Johnny said. "I know they weren't exactly our set, but they were perfectly respectable. Don't be such a snob."

Alex chuckled. "Your sister is the farthest thing from a snob, as you well know. She married a poor man, as she reminded me not twenty minutes ago, and I'm sure would back you if you chose to give your heart to a penniless girl. Nevertheless, those delectable beauties, who just, ah, paid their respects to you, were not doing so merely because they found you a strapping specimen of young manhood."

Johnny looked a bit hurt, and Eliza softened toward her younger brother, of whom she had always been very fond. She was struck by the fact that little Johnny had had quite the growth spurt since the last time the Hamiltons saw him, and stood nearly six feet tall, lean and lanky. His wrists and ankles protruded slightly from his sleeves and pants, which only added to the perception that he was a boy who was not yet a man.

"What do you mean about those ladies?" John said at last, self-consciously pulling at his cuffs to cover the exposed bones of his wrists.

"Let's just say that their time is not exactly free," Eliza said.

John's brow furrowed. "I don't understand."

"Your sister means that if you wanted to continue your,

ah, intercourse with them, a certain quid pro quo would have been expected."

"Quid pro quo? You mean . . . payment?" John seemed even more confused. "But payment for what?"

Alex turned to Eliza helplessly, but she only covered her smile with her gloved hand.

Then John's eyes went wide. He whirled toward the crowd of women, who were now descending on their next target in a flurry of silks and laces and titters. Their gloved fingers danced nimbly over the shoulders and arms of their new mark, as they had done on John's just a moment before.

"No! You mean they're—"

"Now, Johnny," Eliza cut him off. "There is no need to name names. Their situation is unfortunate, but we do not have to add indignity by saying it aloud."

"Wow!" John said, even as Alex flagged down a porter and directed him to have John's luggage sent to the Hamiltons' Wall Street home. "My first hour in the city and I've already been solicited! How exciting!"

"Welcome to New York," Eliza said, finally giving her brother that hug. "And I was serious before. Check your pockets and make sure they didn't steal your purse."

Turn the page

for a sneak peek of

Melissa de la Cruz's new series!

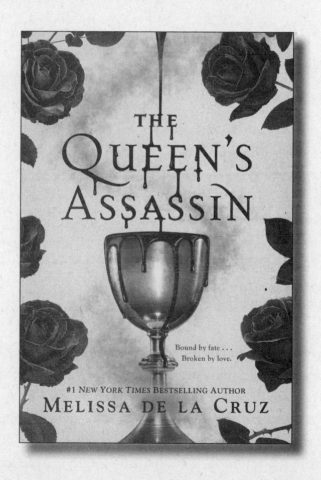

CHAPTER ONE

Shadow

SOMETHING OR SOMEONE IS FOLLOWING me. I've been wandering the woods for quite a while, but now it feels as if something—or someone—is watching. I thought it was one of my aunts at first—it was odd they didn't chase after me this time. Maybe they didn't expect me to go very far. But it's not them.

I stop and pull my hood back to listen to the forest around me. There is only the wind whistling through the branches and the sound of my own breathing.

Whoever is following me is very good at hiding. But I am not afraid.

Slivers of light penetrate the dense foliage in spots, shining streaks onto the blanket of decaying leaves and mud under my boots. As I slice through thick vines and clamber over rotting logs, speckled thrushes take flight from the forest floor before disappearing overhead. I pause to listen to them sing to one another, chirping elegant messages back and forth, a beautiful song carrying warnings, no doubt, about the stranger stomping through their home.

Being out here helps me clear my head. I feel more peaceful

here among the wild creatures, closer to my true self. After this morning's argument at home, it's precisely what I need—some peace. Some space. Time to myself.

My aunts taught me that sometimes when the world is too much, when life starts to feel overwhelming, we must strip away what's unnecessary, seek out the quiet, and listen to the dirt and trees. "All the answers you seek are there, but only if you are willing to hear them," Aunt Moriah always says.

That's all I'm doing, I tell myself. Following their advice. Perhaps that's why they allowed me to run off into the woods. Except they're probably hoping I'll find *their* answers here, not my own. That I'll finally come to my senses.

Anger bubbles up inside me. All I have ever wanted is to follow in their footsteps and join the ranks of the Hearthstone Guild. It's the one thing I've wanted more than anything. We don't just sell honey in the market. They've practically been training me for the Guild all my life—how can they deny me? I kick the nearest tree as hard as I can, slamming the sole of my boot into its solid trunk. That doesn't make me feel much better, though, and I freeze, wondering if whatever or whoever is following me has heard.

I know it is a dangerous path, but what nobler task is there than to continue the Guild's quest? To recover the Deian Scrolls and exact revenge upon our enemies. They can't expect me to sit by and watch as others take on the challenge.

All the women I look up to—Ma, my aunt Moriah, and Moriah's wife, my aunt Mesha—belong to the Guild; they are trained combatants and wise women. They are devotees of Deia, the One Mother, source of everything in the world of Avantine, from the clouds overhead to the dirt underfoot. Deia worship was common once but not anymore, and those who keep to its beliefs have the Guild to thank for preserving the old ways. Otherwise that knowledge would have disappeared long ago when the Aphrasians confiscated it from the people. The other kingdoms no longer keep to the old ways, even as they conspire to learn our magic.

As wise women they know how to tap into the world around us, to harness the energy that people have long forgotten but other creatures have not. My mother and aunts taught me how to access the deepest levels of my instincts, the way that animals do, to sense danger and smell fear. To become deeply in tune with the universal language of nature that exists just below the surface of human perception, the parts we have been conditioned not to hear anymore.

While I call them my aunts, they are not truly related to me, even if Aunt Moriah and my mother grew up as close as sisters. I was fostered here because my mother's work at the palace is so important that it leaves little time for raising a child.

A gray squirrel runs across my path and halfway up a nearby tree. It stops and looks at me quizzically. "It's all right," I say. "I'm not going to hurt you." It waits until I start moving again and scampers the rest of the way up the trunk.

The last time I saw my mother, I told her of my plans to join the Guild. I thought she'd be proud of me. But she'd stiffened and paused before saying, "There are other ways to serve the crown."

Naturally, I'd have preferred her to be with me, every day, like other mothers, but I've never lacked for love or affection. My aunts had been there for every bedtime tale and scraped knee, and Ma served as a glamorous and heroic figure for a young woman to look up to. She would swoop into my life, almost always under the cover of darkness, cloaked and carrying gifts, like the lovely pair of brocade satin dance slippers I'll never forget. They were as ill-suited for rural life as a pair of shoes could possibly be, and I treasured them for it. "The best cobbler in Argonia's capital made these," she told me. I marveled at that, how far they'd traveled before landing on my feet.

Yes, I liked the presents well enough. But what made me even happier were the times she stayed long enough to tell me stories. She would sit on the edge of my bed, tuck my worn quilt snugly around me, and tell me tales of Avantine, of the old kingdom.

Our people are fighters, she'd say. *Always were.* I took that to mean I would be one too.

I think about these stories as I whack my way through the brush. Why would my mother tell me tales of heroism, adventure, bravery, and sacrifice, unless I was to train with the Guild as well? As a child, I was taught all the basics—survival and tracking skills, and then as I grew, I began combat training and archery.

I do know more of the old ways than most, and I'm grateful for that, but it isn't enough. I want to know as much as they do, or even more. I need to belong to the Guild.

Now I fear I never will have that chance.

"Ouch!" I flinch and pull my hand back from the leaves surrounding me. There's a thin sliver of blood seeping out of my skin. I was so lost in my thoughts that I accidentally cut my hand while hacking through shrubbery. The woods are unfamiliar here, wilder and denser. I've never gone out this far. The path ahead is so overgrown it's hard to believe there was ever anyone here before me, let alone a procession of messengers and traders and visitors traveling between Renovia and the other kingdoms of Avantine. But that was before. Any remnants of its prior purpose are disappearing quickly. Even my blade, crafted from Argonian steel—another present from Ma—struggles to sever some of the more stubborn branches that have reclaimed the road for the wilderness.

I try to quiet my mind and concentrate on my surroundings. Am I lost? Is something following me? "What do I do now?" I say out loud. Then I remember Aunt Mesha's advice: *Be willing to hear.*

I breathe, focus. Re-center. *Should I turn back?* The answer is so strong, it's practically a physical shove: *No. Continue.* I suppose I'll push through, then. Maybe I'll discover a forgotten treasure along this path.

Woodland creatures watch me, silently, from afar. They're perched in branches and nestled safely in burrows. Sometimes I catch a whiff of newborn fur, of milk; I smell the fear of anxious mothers protecting litters; I feel their heartbeats, their quickened breaths when I pass. I do my best to calm them by closing my eyes and sending them benevolent energy. *Just passing through. I'm no threat to you.*

After about an hour of bushwhacking, I realize that I don't know where I am anymore. The trees look different, older. I hear the trickling of water. Unlike before, there are signs that something, or rather someone, was here not long before me. Cracked sticks have been stepped on—by whom or what, I'm not sure—and branches are too neatly chopped to have been broken naturally. I want to investigate, see if I can feel how long ago they were cut. Maybe days; maybe weeks. Difficult to tell.

I stop to examine the trampled foliage just as I feel an abrupt change in the air.